PHILIP HENSHER

A SMALL
REVOLUTION
IN GERMANY

4th ESTATE • London

4th Estate
An imprint of HarperCollins*Publishers*
1 London Bridge Street
London SE1 9GF

www.4thEstate.co.uk

HarperCollins*Publishers*
1st Floor, Watermarque Building, Ringsend Road
Dublin 4, Ireland

First published in Great Britain in 2020 by 4th Estate
This 4th Estate paperback edition published in 2021

1

A catalogue record for this book is
available from the British Library

ISBN 978-0-00-832310-3

Set in Adobe Garamond Pro
Printed and bound in Great Britain by
CPI Group (UK) Ltd, Croydon

For Herbert Grieshop

History has taught you a lesson, it has shattered this illusion. Yes, the German revolution is growing, but not in the way we should like it.

v. i. LENIN, Political Report of the Central Committee, Extraordinary Seventh Congress of the RCP(B), 6–8 March 1918

To be jealous of what only appears to exist is a waste of effort. My wisdom secretly tells me that everything only appears to exist, nothing actually exists, we must be satisfied with that. Good night, prophet. Pleasant dreams, comrade.

JOSÉ SARAMAGO, *The Stone Raft*

Part one

When I was a boy, I liked to watch men at work. I still do, in fact. What I like is both the confident display of expertise, and moments when disaster intervenes. A workman is there to carve a block of stone into slabs, say. He wears yellow goggles. His stiff gloves are too big for human hands. He might take his circular saw. In retrospect his magisterial confidence is quite funny. (I mean no disrespect to the working man.) Small boys stand around in a circle, fascinated and patient. The saw starts its high electric whine. The worker lowers it to a slab of white marble glistening under a jet of water. His gesture suggests the showman. Wet, the marble slices as easily as soap. The whine of the saw lowers to a growl. There is a sudden sound out of nowhere, like a shriek of despair. Before you know *what* has happened, *it* has happened. The blade of the saw lies in five pieces on and around the marble. The centre of the blade is spinning uselessly to a halt. Nobody has been hurt, but the blade is shattered. Somewhere inside the block of marble, apparently as soft as soap underneath the saw, there was a vein of quite different stuff, of hard metal or of granite. The workman expected the blade to cut without effort. But sometimes a blade meets a streak of stuff that won't be cut through. The blade lies in pieces on the floor. Calm command stands aghast, hands spread in dismay.

The school I went to had been going for years. It's had a sourly drilled series of centenary celebrations by now. We thought it was a terrible school – the capacity for loyalty was not highly cultivated in us. It was terrible in traditional ways, top down, mortar-boarded. The masters leant over us sarcastically, demanding the subjunctive form of the verb *avoir* as if it had been stolen from them. They called each of us 'boy'. Twenty years before, the school had been fundamentally altered by the whims of politicians. For two decades it had been a comprehensive, obliged to take in any child it was told. It was just like every other school in the city, no better, no worse.

But, of course, it is not the fundamental nature of things that matters. It is the superficial things of the world that we notice, and that shape our lives. I would be a different person if I had not gone to a school where the front consisted of a massive Corinthian portico with two pillars too many. The Edwardians thought the task of education deserved a statement of grandeur. Some of us dealt with these pretensions briskly. On Friday nights the kids used to break in and gather under the portico in the dark. Every Monday morning the caretaker would have to scrub the new felt-tip obscenities off the wall, would have to shovel up the day-old mounds of human shit left in corners, cursing the filth that had done this. It was done by a tough girl called Beverley – you didn't call her Bev unless you were prepared to prove yourself as tough as her. Bev could shit on cue. She was quite well known for her party trick.

One of the elements of the school's superficial substance, along with the orienteering club, Latin, calling homework *prep* and the indulged paedophilia in the masters' common room, was the occasional presence of the armed forces. I don't understand, now, what the connection between our education and the military was. But twice a year or so an officer from the army or the navy would turn up to talk about duty and discipline and the opportunities awaiting anyone who went in for a career holding, or more likely counting, guns. They came with recruiting films suggesting that much of your duty in the army would be spent on tropical beaches lounging beneath palm trees.

In recent years I often thought of those recruiting films when the news came back from Iraq or Afghanistan. I imagined boys who had died where politicians had decided they would die. I think that now largely because of Percy Ogden. The only kids who went into the army were the poor sods in the remedial classes. I don't suppose they're all dead, of course.

I spoke to one of these visiting officers only once. At sixteen, I was obsessed with the poetry of the Sitwells and of Mallarmé; I once spent an entire week with my face wrapped in a gauze scarf, the better to appreciate the world's colours. (I had been reading Baudelaire, I expect.) The armed forces would bring one major piece of kit to the school, where it sat with morose insistence in the playground. That day the army brought a tank. The officer stood aside with the headmaster. He smiled as the boys clambered over it. I was a boy who had no intention of clambering. I had a horror of motor oil. I found myself next to the major. He looked at me, expectantly.

I had no idea what to say. My father's injunction always to make an effort in conversation rose up in me. I found a question to ask. 'Do you,' I said, 'paint it that lovely shade of dull green yourselves? Or does the manufacturer deliver it up like that?' He was immensely disappointed. I had looked keen as mustard. But my aestheticism was of the sort that emerges in cropped hair and parodically precise, even exquisite, adherence to the structures of school uniform. 'They do it,' he said eventually.

The headmaster rocked back and forth on the balls of his feet, his avuncular smile tested for the moment. 'You stupid boy,' he said the next day, passing me in the corridor.

Stupidity was the worst they expected, not open revolt and insult. After the presentation of the tank we were summoned into the assembly hall, a space with a glistening orange parquet floor, smelling strongly of shepherd's pie from the school kitchens next door, and overlapping that, an inexplicable odour of wet nappies from the huge blackout curtains. The film was shown. The major had the spirit to mutter and grumble at its minor inaccuracies. We listened in silence. At the end, six favourites of the headmaster had been primed with questions. What sports could you play in your spare time? What were the opportunities to do an engineering qualification? When did the regiment's uniform start to include – oh, I forget what the uniform included, but could it have been buttresses? – and (an indulgently drafted one) did the regiment have a mascot, and if so, what was it?

A goat.

The headmaster had had experience. He hardly expected an assembly of pubescents to raise a question without being primed. The six questions came to an end. He was about to call the event to a successfully controlled close. The major had not been briefed. 'There's another question,' he said. 'The boy there, at the back.'

The headmaster demurred. He liked to know what was going to happen and what would be permitted to be said at these events. But there were ten minutes left. 'Boy at the back,' he said.

The boy at the back was Percy Ogden. He stood up to ask his question.

I suppose it always begins like this – with a boy standing in an audience, denouncing, jabbing his finger at a figure on stage. His voice raised and cracking with the strain, or the joy of speech. All around him – always, always – a small group of supporters, nodding in their phalanx. Beyond that, varied responses, a mind not made up, amazement, open tutting disapproval, here and there a sycophantic performance of amusement for the sake of the official speaker. But political lives always start like this. A boy rises from his seat. His finger is already pointing in rage.

'Can I ask a question?

'How much does it cost to educate someone to the age of sixteen, or eighteen?

'Take a guess. I would say it costs the state about twelve thousand pounds a year per pupil. So we're delivering up to you a resource where the investment has been between £144,000 and £170,000, from the point of view of education alone.

'I'm putting it like that – I'm serious, don't shake your head – because I guess you understand financial investment and return and amortization and things like that. There are other ways of looking at it.'

'Can you ask a question?' the headmaster said. 'We haven't got all day.'

He was held back from cutting Percy Ogden off. He must have been thrown by the word *amortization* – an A-level word. Whether he did not know what it meant himself, or was impressed by the display of intelligence – or, rather, the display of a word not much used by most people, not much understood, which can be the same thing – in either case he let Percy Ogden continue.

'I'm coming to my point,' Ogden went on. 'Is it really a responsible use of public resources? I'm putting it like this because I don't think you understand anything else, not the human waste and cruelty and sheer wrongness of the whole thing. Are you managing public money sensibly? When you take a unit of public investment into which a quarter of a million or more has gone, once you've factored in healthcare and your training programme, and sent him – I'm sorry, I mean *it*, or do you say *him* of these units, like you say *she* about ships – sent him off to some remote imperial war on the other side of the world, I say, some *imperialist* war over *territory*, a few *islands* where this valuable piece of kit, this human being, called Joe or Jim or Steve is going to have a bullet in his head on the third day, be killed in any number of horrible ways – I'm coming to my point – that's an incredible waste of investment, isn't it? Are you proud of your responsible stewardship of public money, not to say of the human beings called Joe or Jim or Steve who are now going to have to be shipped back expensively, at public expense, in *pieces*, in a *box*—'

The headmaster had been talking over Percy Ogden for some time now in disgust and command. Although he had the advantage of amplification, and Percy Ogden only had his voice and his jabbing finger, it was Ogden's voice I heard. Ogden's words: his ideas. The reactions to Ogden in the assembly were quite various. He was surrounded by his usual supporters – Mohammed Ahmed, Tracy Cartwright, James Frinton, Eric Milne, that lot. They were nodding. Eric Milne was pounding demands into the air between his widespread thighs. He had been told by a master that he should take up sprinting, for no other reason than that he was black. Injustice was strong in him. He was a skinny flexible boy, like a model of a boy made out of things, but he only stretched for a book on the top shelf. They had known this was coming, and were enjoying it with fervent assent. More obvious, I guess, was the weary or cynical response in much of the hall – once they realized that Percy Ogden was making some kind of political argument. They turned to each other. They sniggered and tittered. They started their own conversations, they pulled faces, they yawned in a performance of boredom, they cast sympathetic looks towards the platform. I expect they wanted to be noticed. They wanted to gain credit by their attitudes. Percy Ogden was not, in fact, very popular.

Here and there were people to whom Percy Ogden's long question meant something quite different. Those were the ones who listened to his words. He went on probably too long. But it now seemed to me that I had been wrong in the past in groaning and trying to catch the teacher's eye whenever dissent surfaced. Now I understand that what Percy Ogden was doing that day was conducting a thought experiment, but I entered into that one, considering what existence would look like if it were weighed against money. I thought about an act of destruction in terms of resources. A warship went up in flames. How much had the ship and all its weaponry cost? How much investment of funds had gone into each of those men, how much trained expertise? I threw myself into the exercise while Ogden was speaking. I felt with revulsion that I was momentarily transforming myself into a quite different person. All the time, the transformation, a permanent one, was taking place in another direction.

It seems to me now, as I have read, that if most people found themselves in a world where every other human had become blind, they would pretend that they were blind too. They might come to believe that they truly were blind. Only a few people would look about them at the halls filled with the blind and place a value on their ability to see.

I looked around me that afternoon.

The questioner was silenced. The headmaster turned to the soldier. 'I don't know if you want to say anything in response to that,' he said. 'It seemed to me that Ogden was making a point all his own. It wasn't really a question, was it?'

The soldier had been keeping an upright bearing until this point. His buttons were polished. His stance was vertical. But now he did something unexpected: he giggled.

'Yes, maybe,' he said. 'I know I'm not going to – I mean – that's always—'

'I think,' the headmaster said, 'we'd all like to thank Major Urch for his valuable time and a fascinating talk. Let's thank—'

Where this came from, I don't know and can't guess, but Major Urch had something else to say. 'I mean,' he said, to nobody in particular, 'I mean, Trotskyites!'

That must have been the moment when I understood what had happened. Sometimes a saw, passing through soft marble, hits a vein of iron, and shatters. It would not have been hard for someone in the major's position to answer convincingly. But he did not and could not. His purpose had been to demonstrate power. Our role within his purpose was to sit and listen and ask what we were told to ask. That afternoon, I understood that never again would my resistance to the exertion of power be limited to asking insultingly gracious questions about the colour of paint, like the Queen Mother in an abattoir. Most people are good and docile and blind, and the world could not do without the obedient, who are led from place to place. I had never been obedient, but from now on they would know about it. The saw had met a vein of iron within. It lay in pieces all around.

What Ogden had done had not, as I thought, only been done to me and perhaps a very few others. We very few had done that thing that humans hardly ever do, and generally with much pain and shame, or so I thought: we had changed our minds. About a week later, however, I found that I was wrong. The school was summoned to a Monday-morning assembly. The caretaker had started work that morning to discover, yet again, a mound of human shit beneath the portico of the school. It was Beverley, of course. Everyone knew that. But there was no means of extracting the information from any one of us. The threat Beverley represented, in playground, bus and street, was much more immediate than

anything the headmaster could summon. Of course, these
days, surveillance cameras would have long put a stop to the
nuisance. DNA testing would have identified the culprit. The
headmaster, then, worked himself up into a rage, having no
alternative. He made a promise.

'You needn't think you're safe,' he shouted, 'just because you
haven't been informed on by your fellow pupils. Our investi-
gations start here. And they're serious. And we never fail.
You've heard of MI5. And MI6. Well, we're not MI6. We're not
MI5. We're MI10. We get ten out of ten every time. Come up
against MI10 and see what happens. I promise you …'

But a tremor of doubt had crept into the headmaster's
voice, because an unaccustomed sound was in the hall. All
through the room, people were turning to their neighbours
and saying, 'MI10,' before shaking their heads. They were
laughing. The headmaster was ridiculous. We had discovered
that. Percy Ogden's question, a week before, had not been
forgotten.

'I promise you—' the headmaster said.

'Trotskyite!' a boy somewhere in the middle of the hall
called. The word had never had any meaning, but in the week
since Major Urch's visit, it had been taken up in the yard. You
heard it everywhere.

'Who was that?' the headmaster said. 'Who shouted out?
Mrs Macdonald, did you see who called out?'

'I did not, Headmaster,' Mrs Macdonald said, from the
side of the hall where she sat. She was an English teacher, deep
in Keats and Yeats. I think now she must have seen, as I did,
the importance that investigative powers attach to insubordi-
nation. *Trotskyite*. The headmaster's powers were gone.

Once the event with the major had dissolved into a series of embarrassed thanks and calls for acclaim, Percy Ogden had left the hall. He stood with his supporters outside. People leaving were treating him as some kind of host, as if he were saying thank you for coming, or perhaps welcoming them in at the beginning of festivities. They said, 'You twerp,' or 'Fuck off, Ogden,' or, now and then, they chortled and offered congratulations. Ogden hardly seemed to register any of this. I hesitated and watched him accept or deflect the comments of passing children. I knew who he was. I had no idea whether he would recognize someone as insignificant as I was. He stood with his phalanx. They were not like him. If there was a common style to them, as there was to most groupings in school, it was in their dissimilarity. A couple of years back, they were the failed and disorganized dregs of the school, the ones who were friends with each other in a dissatisfied way only because nobody else would pick them up. The black boy, the one whose parents wore clothes from India and could not speak English, the girl constantly being excluded for fighting. They had nothing in common, as far as anyone cared to see, but they all had to talk to someone. That someone had, strangely enough, been Percy Ogden. He had always been, by contrast, a sort of heroic figure, changing at ten from a bright boy with interests – trains, cactuses, dinosaurs, historical buildings – into someone marked by the curled lip and the smart comeback. He had elevated each of them by his interest. It had never occurred to anyone but Percy Ogden that there might be a dignity in the girl who even eleven-year-olds shouted 'Slag' at, the boy whom the French teacher called Mustafa, eliciting a laugh every time.

(His name was not Mustafa. It was Mohammed. He was named after the Prophet, peace be upon him. That was what Ogden had said once, on Mohammed's behalf.) The oppressed outcast (I am talking in Ogden's terms now, the terms I would soon be repeating) joined up with another, and gazed at the powerful levelly, with patience. They imitated Percy Ogden, of course they did. Just now James Frinton, the boy no one would sit with because of his dirt, his soiled socks and his smell of old boiled peas, was rubbing his nose with the heel of his palm in just Ogden's way. Soon he would lower his hand and honk as they all did, use the words *amortize* and *hegemony* and *cunt*. What Ogden was imitating and learning from, I don't know.

I approached the group of them. I knew that soon I would be laughing like Ogden and repeating his words. I was not an outcast. I would make myself one.

'You don't think that,' I said to Ogden.

'Who's this?' said Tracy Cartwright.

'You don't think that,' I said. 'About measuring how much it costs the state when someone's killed.'

'I meant what I said,' Percy Ogden said, but genially.

'There's other ways of looking at it,' I said. 'It's not just because it's wasted, all that money.'

'If you're merely going to kill them,' James Frinton said, 'then why bother educating them at all? Feed them and exercise them and then send them out to be shot. Or burnt to death. Or dropped from a great height. From a plane. With a malfunctioning parachute.'

'Splat,' Mohammed Ahmed said. They all laughed – that Ogden honk. It was famous in the school. Ogden was looking at me. He wasn't laughing. If he had been forty years older, I would have said he had a twinkle in his eye.

'What's your name?' he said. 'We've seen you around.'

'In geography. And history,' Eric Milne put in. 'What do you think of Dick?'

I had no idea what he was talking about. The group was so resilient and enclosed that it not only had nicknames of its own for school figures, it assumed that the world in which these nicknames were understood was the entirety of the world.

'Dick and the capitalist miracle,' Ogden said. 'I wouldn't waste my breath on him. Do you know who his hero is? Take a guess.'

'Cecil Rhodes,' Tracy Cartwright said, performing a kind of dance, three steps up towards the physics lab, three steps down, her arms in the air. 'Harold Wilson. Nixon. Clive of India.'

'We love Clive of India,' Eric Milne said. 'He wrote a little book to show men what they were shooting at. Go on, ask me anything. Who caused the French Revolution, Mary Queen of Scots and her haemophilia, that's who. Ask me another.'

'Russian,' Ogden said. 'So what's wrong with totting up the value of the lives you're disposing of – the public resources you're spending?'

'Because the army, when it acquires the *property*,' I said – I tried to do the sarcastic fall of the voice – 'doesn't buy it. It leases it. I mean, you sign up for five years, don't you? It doesn't pay anything like the value of the investment. If it had to pay a quarter of a million upfront, then it would value the acquisition. The cost of the purchase would be commensurate with the investment.'

It was that word *commensurate* that did it – that word so remote from speech, which I had spoken. The Ogden clan relished grand, empty, abstract words, the noise they made, like thunder, though they were only peas rattling around a drum. By now almost everyone who had been in the hall had gone. We were in the school's atrium by the two half-dead Swiss cheese plants and a whiteboard advertising the music teacher's production of *The Mikado* with a willow tree and slant-eyed masks. The world could have gone in so many other directions, and stopped me meeting Percy Ogden and the others at this, the exact right moment. If the headmaster and his guest, Major Urch, had come out the same way as the pupils, Ogden would have been engaged in some way, in reprimand or continued disagreement. All the others must once have gone in either direction, towards Ogden or away. Each of them had had the experience of what followed, which was Percy Ogden saying, 'What are you up to? We're going to Carole's. That café. We need to talk.'

'Okay,' I said.

I walked through the hall with faint dizziness. I was in the Ogden group. I had joined it not through a lack of options but through my own choice. But that reading of the group, as a miscellaneous bunch of losers, was fading quickly. We didn't use the word *loser* then, but we certainly had the concept. They had no reason to see themselves like that. There was no one left to watch me take a first step into this world of the commensurate, of amortization, of a shared purpose and commitment except two fourth-formers who were sitting on a bench, kissing furiously, as if inspired by this talk of death. They weren't watching.

'What are you, then?' James Frinton said, once we were outside. He had a mellifluous, mild voice, a television announcer's way.

'He doesn't know what you mean,' Tracy Cartwright said. 'He thinks you mean is he a boy or a girl.'

'What does he mean?' Eric said. 'The question is inadequately defined. It could mean anything. He could answer, "A multi-cellular organism," or "The product of historical forces latent towards the end of late capitalism," or, as you say, "A boy." Define your question and get an answer.'

Tracy Cartwright had joined in with the last three words, making me think this was a maxim among them.

'You know what I mean,' James Frinton said. 'What are you, Eric?'

'I'm a classical Marxist,' Eric said.

'He believes in perpetual revolution,' James said, 'and Tracy's an anarcho-syndicalist.'

'And James invests too much in single-issue causes,' Tracy said. 'Bourgeois diversions. Animal rights. CND ...'

We had reached the bottom of the steps that led down from the school's main entrance – an entrance we were not, as pupils, allowed to use. If the portico at the front had ever been used as a grand entrance, it was not within our memory. The main entrance now was at what might be assumed to be the side of the building. At the mention of CND, Eric dramatically collapsed, spinning around gracefully, a finger in his mouth to fake puking.

'It wasn't CND,' James said. 'Or only for five minutes.'

'What's—' I was about to ask what was wrong with CND. For me, the Campaign for Nuclear Disarmament, with its clear and surely indisputable proposal that mankind should not be wiped out and, even more, its simple and elegant logo, was exactly the sort of thing that thinking people would support. I held off while Eric got up off the dusty driveway, brushing himself down. In time I would learn why CND was beyond consideration. In the last hour, I had had my definition of *thinking people* changed quite sharply. I had a CND badge at home – I had worn it in public, putting it on my winter coat once I was safely far from home and not likely to be glimpsed by my father. Whatever the Ogden lot's objections to nuclear disarmament were, they were not the same as my father's.

The writer I have come to love best has told us that 'We would know far more about life's complexities if we applied ourselves to the close study of its contradictions instead of wasting so much time on similarities and connections, which should, anyway, be self-explanatory.' The different and contradictory attitudes I took now, on that short walk down the hill to the Café Carole, towards my father's and Ogden's shared scorn for the disarmament movement, had nothing to do with their reasons, which no doubt were different. I had never bothered to listen to one. I hadn't yet heard the surprising other. The complexities and irreconcilable differences coming down on me were many, though at that moment it felt, falsely, as if a huge and single truth was opening up, a solid shining object for my embrace, or my worship.

I had walked past Carole's a thousand times. I had never thought of going in there. It was a business that, like bookmakers or city pubs, I just did not see. It had nothing to do with the purposes of my life. I don't know that Café Carole had anything to do with anyone else's purposes but her own. In the weeks and months afterwards, we went in there many times as a group. We were almost always the only people in it. It was a little girl's suburban dream of the café she might run when she grew up. The interior was pale pink and blue and white, like Edinburgh rock. The cakes grew stale under large glass bell domes. There were frilly lace curtains, which went halfway up the window, hanging from a brass rod. The sign of the café was in pink on green, *Le Café Carole* in cursive handwriting, curlicues heading off fancifully. Carole herself was sitting behind the counter, smoking a weary cigarette and reading with flaccid inattention about the doings of tiny Prince William. The business had not gone far. Carole was a divorcee of fifty-seven. She still made the tea in the café she had named after herself. She still looked, without surprise or interest, at who was coming into her scuffed pastel café at three forty-five on a Tuesday afternoon.

We took a table in the window. James got a packet of menthol cigarettes out. He offered them round. Only Tracy took one.

'I was in a plane, a jet plane,' Mohammed was saying, in a meditative way. He was continuing a conversation he had been having with Tracy and James, walking down the hill from school. 'It was flying quite low over the landscape – I could see the countryside very clearly, it was all English, wooded and hilly and green.'

Tracy had not been looking at him. She had taken the cigarette from James without looking at him either, but now she fixed her attention on James, as if Mohammed were not speaking at all. 'Bushy,' she said. 'Densely bushy. With foliage.'

'And crevasses,' James said gravely. 'And don't forget the hills, round, full hills.'

'The plane started to fly really quite low—'

'Never forget the round, full hills,' Tracy said.

'Do you want to hear my dream or not?' Mohammed said. 'This plane – it started flying down the river valley, just above the river, by the side of a busy road.'

'How wide was the river?' Ogden said.

'I don't know – well, I suppose a sort of stream, a bit more than a trickle. Like a river in a hot country in summer. Why? Does that matter?'

'Fecundity. Carole's used to be broad and flowing,' Ogden said, flashing an open smile at the owner. She had finished her cigarette and had come over to take the order.

'What is it?' she said.

'Come on, Carole,' Ogden said. 'You remember me. We always have the same.'

'I remember you always say, "We always have the same." I can't be expected to remember everything that someone who's just walked in off the street ordered three weeks ago. Just tell me.'

'Lapsang souchong and three ordinary teas.'

'We don't have any lapsang souchong in.'

'You never have any lapsang souchong.'

'Getting it tomorrow.'

'You said that yesterday and the day before.'

'Getting it tomorrow.'

'You might as well take it off the menu, you know. It's only there to indicate that she's better than the usual greasy spoon. She doesn't fry anything and she's got tea with a Chinese name.'

'Getting it tomorrow. What do you want today?'

'Darjeeling, if you've got it. Otherwise another ordinary tea and a filter coffee. What do you want?'

He was talking to me. 'The same. A tea, I mean.'

'And two tea cakes.'

'Minimum charge two pounds fifty a head.'

'More indicators of status. Two tea cakes.'

Carole gave up. There had been no other customers all afternoon, I guessed, or any sign of any more to come. She generally stopped smoking only when customers were actually there. The room was thick with the smoke the day had conjured up.

'I don't know why we come here,' Eric said. 'Six of us at two pounds fifty a head – that would be twenty-one pounds. I'm not spending that here. I don't know how you could spend that much.'

'You'd have to buy slices of Carole's son's cake. He makes them at home, you know,' he went on to me. 'They talk about Carole's divorce and the fact that Nigel has turned out a homo, and the disappointment seeps into the cakes. Coconut, walnut, or a last one – Nigel invented it – rhubarb, lavender and almond.'

'He's making it all up,' James said. 'There might be a son but he's not called Nigel.'

For some reason this contradiction sparked something in Ogden. I've often thought since of the way the political mind needs, thrives on dissent. It will leap on any disagreement hopefully. In the best political mind, this relish of disagreement clarifies matters, rules certain considerations out of play as the argument progresses. In the weak political mind, the disagreement is carried on for the sake of conflict alone, like crowds of supporters of some sport or other, yelling assertions at each other across a square of green, a square of expensive ice. Of course Ogden was practising taking up a position that would not permit James's contribution to be just. Whether this was in search of clarity or driven by the energy rage possesses, I couldn't say. He was into James like a terrier on a joint of beef.

'He may be called Nigel,' Ogden said. 'It's a possibility, just as it's possible that Carole has a son at all, that the son is a homo, that he makes cakes, that the cakes Nigel makes are coconut and walnut and rhubarb, lavender and almond. All of these are possibilities. Some are so probable that we say that it's so. For instance, that the cakes for sale are coconut, walnut, and rhubarb, lavender and almond. We say that is definitely the case. A hundred per cent. But is there an element of probability that means they're not for sale? I mean, it says in the menu that Carole sells lapsang souchong. But she doesn't. She never has.'

'I can see the cakes, though,' Eric said. 'They have a label on them, look.'

'Still the probability fails. What if someone switched the labels with those in another café while Carole wasn't looking? And those are actually bacon-, cauliflower-, and strawberry-and-liver-flavoured cakes? Or what if a small malevolent demon has in fact created the whole world as an illusion?

What if there are no cakes, no café, no Carole, no Eric or James or Tracy or Mohammed or—'

'Spike,' I said quickly. I was terrified that Percy Ogden wouldn't know my name, or might take the opportunity to show in passing how unimportant it was.

'Or Spike,' Percy Ogden said, with a touch, surely, of regret.

'That's Descartes,' I said. I was proud to know it. My father was fond of dealing with life's difficulties by thinking of Descartes's demon, the one who might be putting all this into his head while he lay supine and unconscious in some pit of Hell.

'Very good,' Percy Ogden said. 'So that probability is less than a hundred per cent. Probability that Carole has a son – forty per cent. We know she was married—'

'But the world doesn't exist!' Eric said, leaping forwards or backwards a few points.

'No. Probably does exist. Not definitely. In the ninety-nine-per-cent world Carole was married. Had a child, probably – most married women do. Eighty per cent, halve it for sex. Probability that the son turned out to be a homo, five per cent of that forty per cent.'

At this point, I would have expected those around the speaker to start laughing crudely, but Tracy merely said, 'More than that. Look at her.' Carole was approaching with the order on a trolley – her idea, I guess, of refinement. She was, when you looked at her, wonderfully structured and controlled along certain lines. Overall she had been pushed, or pushed herself, towards yellow – her hair, skin, her jewellery, though *yellow* was not the word she would have been taught to use for any of it (*blonde, bronze, gold* ...). Her clothes hindered her, the pencil skirt, the pussycat bow, the ruffled wrist and neck, the height of her shoes. Time was made difficult for her, the measure by which we control our lives and design our own days. She wore a watch half the size of the fingernail on her little finger. She had to peer at it, and then could hardly be sure. Who was all this for, this femininity codified and pushed towards a weaponized discomfort and inconvenience? The major that afternoon had elements of performance about his masculine display, but Carole was all feminine display. There was no consensus reached with function. Her fingernails were cultivated to a length at which it was hard for her to use a pen, operate a till, type. She was incapacitated. What it was for, I could not imagine. I was struck by biological imperatives at that age. How I looked at a woman in her mid-fifties, still engaging in the formalized and incapacitating displays that femininity in this culture requires! I thought with all the cruelty of sixteen: But the menopause! It's over for you!

'Poor her,' Tracy said unexpectedly. Carole set the teacups down with no awareness that she was being discussed. 'More than five per cent. A boy baby comes out of that. Looks back. Sees all the work that's been undertaken. He says, "I love my mummy. I'm never going to love another lady as much as I love my mummy in her lovely clothes." Thirty per cent at least. Turn anyone homo.'

'Oh, you don't want to do that,' Carole said vaguely. 'Tea cakes in a minute.'

'It's all probability,' Percy Ogden said. 'Nothing is certain and nothing is ruled out. What about "isn't black" because the father of her child might more probably be white? Or "isn't disabled" because birth defects only affect a few babies in a thousand?'

'But we all say that,' Eric said, 'is, isn't, when the probability is overwhelmingly in one direction.'

'No name is anything but overwhelmingly improbable. Likelihood of child being called Nigel – less than one per cent. Do we say he isn't called Nigel? He isn't called *anything*!'

'No,' I said. 'The probability of him having a name of some sort, given that he exists – nearly a hundred per cent.'

'I suppose so. And here come the teacakes. With these sad little pats of butter on the side. One per teacake. Come on, Carole, that's not enough butter. Can we have two more?'

'If you pay for more. Five p each.'

'We'll manage.'

'I don't know why we come here,' Eric said. 'When the revolution starts up—'

'Carole's first up against the wall,' Eric said.

'No,' Tracy said. 'I want to re-educate her. Like Mollie in *Animal Farm*. Now I want to hear about the rest of Mohammed's dream. Go on, Mo. The last thing, you were taking a great big throbbing engine all the way up a tight crevasse. I'm thinking hard here. If only we had that Mrs Macdonald and her book of Dr Freud's theories.'

'I like Dr Freud's phallus,' Mohammed said idly. 'I mean theories.'

At the end of that first afternoon Eric, to my astonishment, stopped at the bike rack outside the café. He unlocked a gleaming red road bike, the uncool type with drop handle-bars. The astonishment was fairly equally divided between the fact that Eric had a bicycle, and the calm acceptance of that fact by Ogden, Tracy, Mohammed and James. And me too. At least I didn't laugh as I might have done a week before. Nobody came to school on a bicycle. It would have been the cause of endless ridicule among the student body, to know that one of their number came to school and rode home again on something so infra dig, so *spod*, to use a favourite school word, as a bicycle. Any bicycle would have been terrible, but an old-school road bike with drop handlebars would have been at the extreme edge of the ridiculous. Probably Eric knew this perfectly well. It was for that reason that he parked his bike outside Le Café Carole rather than in the school bike sheds – there were some in there, quite unused. Nevertheless it was wonderful to me that Eric just said he'd see them tomorrow, got on the bicycle and sprinted off. Wonderful, too, that they said in return nothing more mocking than they'd see him, or just a simple 'Bye', the syllable with which we end an encounter whether what follows is an unremark-able stretch of the other's life when away from us, or the sudden, unseen, violent death of our friend, something that will make us think for the rest of our lives of the inadequacy of that *bye* to say what we almost meant to say to Eric.

A manicured hand turned the sign in the café window behind from *ouvert* to *fermé*. Over the brow of the hill a number 51 bus lumbered.

'See you tomorrow,' Percy Ogden said to me too. He, James and Tracy ran for the bus, their Adidas bags with their stuff in banging against their bodies as they ran. In a moment I was alone with Mohammed. He looked at me. Perhaps he did not know who I was or understand why I had been taken into the group. I was not conspicuous in school, not famous for anything much. The name *Spike*, which I had given Ogden, was, in fact, only the slightly unconvincing nickname I had evolved for myself in solitude, which nobody ever used, not even my father or the two or three friends I had at the top end of the top English set, busy as they were mastering the recommended quotations from *The Winter's Tale*. Mohammed said, 'See you tomorrow, kid,' and crossed the road, running. In the snobbery of schoolboys, I had assumed that he was one of the Asian kids who lived up the hill with parents who worked at the university. He ran across the road and down the hill. He must live where all the Asians lived, among the grocers, the mosque, the rows of terraced houses in the part of town bang up against the city centre. All the Ogden gang had gone away from me at speed, running off or fleeing on wheels. I was alone. I walked towards the 51 bus stop. In fact, I could have caught the same one that the others had caught.

I lived with my father in a house too big for us, with two spare bedrooms, not just one. The second spare bedroom had been colonized by my father for one of his interests: in it, he made exquisite small objects, models of early industrial processes and machines. There was a lathe in the shed in the garden, where he had originally been supposed to make them. The house had been shaped by my mother's hopes and ambitions. It had then been allowed to fall apart, first through neglect and then through masculine roughness. As a sex, we have little interest in the state of cushions or curtains, and none in acquiring scented candles. In his battered workroom, once a spare bedroom, my father finished a scale model, 1:25, of an early Bessemer converter after months of labour. He picked it up. He placed it on the shelf where other scale models sat. They were exquisite, his scale models. He could have sold them for a sum not quite commensurate with the hours of delighted labour.

My mother had left us five years before. I still don't know why. I took it quite personally – I had a sense of nervous inadequacy as a child. I always felt that I was failing to interest her in any of my small doings or intimate concerns. I was old enough at eleven to search about for reasons. But I was not old enough to understand that not everything that happens in the world that affected me was also brought about by me. I didn't know that I would always be peripheral to the dramas that touched me. She had, clearly, left me because I was not good enough for her, an inadequate son. I expect my interest in social justice, or rather injustice, comes from that perception. Anyone who is left by a mother, and who has a father who takes no interest in them, is bound to end up touchy. My father's hobbies and occupations were comfortably established as modelling small engines, his job running a hospital, the Conservative Party, and ferns, an apparently fascinating range of which filled not just the beds in the garden but the space where a lawn might have been, both before and behind our grubbily curtained house. I would no sooner have expected him to show curiosity in my friends than I would have waited for him at night to read me a bedtime story and tuck me in.

There was no particular mystery about why my mother had left my father. I can't quite understand why she should have married him in the first place. She left him with no particular excuse. She went to the other side of the world, to a city called Broome in Western Australia, famous for pearl fishing.

Sometimes – perhaps at Christmas, which for both of us was gruelling, slow and immured with nothing better than the television to bring us together – my father would, out of the blue, say, 'I'd never heard of Broome before. I don't think she had, either. God knows what took her there. Hell of a long way away.' I had been once – or to Sydney, where she and I had spent a guilt-laden fortnight together. I guess there was less to entertain a thirteen-year-old boy in Broome. Or perhaps she didn't want me reporting back in detail about her daily life. If so, she underestimated the awkwardness between my father and me. He would never have been able to ask a direct question about my mother. I had never have been able to offer anything in return, except the rough and embarrassed sharing of photographs in their yellow envelope, once they had returned from Boots the Chemist.

This is a story about politics, and how some people are drawn to the political life. Politics hopes to improve individual lives. Looking back, I wonder whether anyone would ever have been in a position to make my life with my father better. Put like that, the idea is obviously absurd. You would have had to find a medical diagnosis for my father's defects of personality, justifying outreach 'workers' and health 'professionals', paying for support in the home. I imagine he could have been labelled a high-functioning autist. But what diagnosis for me? You cannot pathologize half the human race. That is what men are, unreachable by diagnosis. Politics should not talk just about lives as a diffuse and examined mass, but about ours, with the two spare bedrooms and the scale model, 1:25, of a Bessemer converter to occupy the long evenings. Politics probably thought that the life I led with my father was good enough. It was not worth remedying. It ought to have been an early lesson in the pathetic limits of current political life.

My father was in the kitchen when I got home, washing up in his bony way. He had changed from his daytime suit and tie into his evening and weekend clothes of a flannel shirt and corduroy trousers. Last night's dinner plates, the breakfast things and the dishes he had used to prepare the Wednesday dinner clanked under his thin hands like a desultory avant-garde composition. He had long ago decided that washing-up was a task that should only intrude once a day. Before dinner was the best moment, with spare time and optimum build-up of soiled debris.

'You're home late,' he said, without disapproval.

'I saw some friends after school,' I said, dropping my bag in a corner of the kitchen.

'I had an interesting issue to deal with at work,' my father said.

'What was that?' I said.

'What?'

'What was the interesting issue at work?'

'Oh,' my father said. 'A strange case. A consultant in oncology. That means cancer.'

I knew what oncology meant.

'She took time off eight months ago and said she was sick with stress. Then she disappeared. At statutory intervals the notes arrived from her GP confirming that she was sick with stress. Eight months on and she's still no better. I would like to suggest to the GP that his plan of treatment, should he have one, does not seem to be having any effect. We have no prognosis. If it's an illness, is the wretched consultant getting better or worse? Recuperating or declining? We have no word.'

My father was getting absorbed in scrubbing a pan. Round and round, up and down, the brush went; his eyes were cast with fascination into the soapy depths.

'So what happened today?'

'What?'

'What happened? The interesting decision you had to take? Today?'

'No decision. But we discussed it. I don't know what the point is going to be when we pay her off and engage with dismissal procedures. I was arguing for yesterday. Her colleagues regard her as a pretty poor doctor. Got made consultant in the end. Lucky we haven't had more lawsuits from her incompetence. Great fat woman. She was always stuffing her face with chocolate at odd times. Just after breakfast. Ten minutes before lunch. I can't understand that kind of behaviour.'

'Perhaps it's the stress she's suffering from,' I said.

'Everyone's stressed in the public service. I'm stressed. Your teachers are stressed. You don't see your headmaster or me stuffing our faces with chocolate all day long to console ourselves because someone's been horrid to us. And that's the last of it.'

He heaved a solid pan back onto the stove top where it lived. He'd cooked mince in it last night.

'What's for supper?'

'It's Wednesday.'

I pretended to think. 'It's shepherd's pie.'

'Indeed.'

'Can we have peas with it but no carrots?'

'I shall cook both and you may choose to take only one. How was your day?'

There was always something effortful about these enquiries of my father's. Somebody had told him once that you should ask other people about the details of their lives. You should pretend to take an interest. When it comes to children, it's sometimes hard to engage with their concerns, their swift and intense friendships and fallings out, their habit of trying to explain every detail and rule of each game and encounter without quite having the words to do so. By the time I was sixteen, my father and I had, in reality, given up on each other. The bridge between us was down, never to be rebuilt. In a very few years – I was still at university – the news came through to me in a note in the porter's lodge that something had happened at home, that I should contact the Senior Tutor, that my father had very sadly died, that he had committed suicide, and finally that he had hanged himself with a belt from the banisters. The cleaner he had hired when I left home had found him. (And why had he hired her? I came to think so that there would be someone to find his body.) Suicide is the most powerful way of saying to someone that they mean nothing to you. It states that you don't care what effect this ending will have on the rest of their lives. At the very least, it is a selfish demonstration that you haven't been touched, or even reached, by those who should have been closest to you. But my father had demonstrated that long before, sometimes only by saying, 'How was your day' with routine indifference.

We had finished our shepherd's pie and my father was getting up to fetch a yogurt for dessert – his plain, mine cherry. The doorbell went.

'That must be your joggers,' my father said.

'I don't think they're coming today,' I said.

'They always come,' my father said. He hopped over to the kitchen window. He looked through the blinds. 'It is they. They always come about now. I'm going upstairs.'

The joggers were my friends at the time, Matthew and Simon. They were keen runners – I don't think they would have used the word 'jog'. For about a year, their evening run had formed a large circuit of which our house occupied one of the furthest points. It was convenient for them to pause and have a glass of water. They'd been doing it every night. (This was before the rise in popularity of little water bottles, marketed by corporations. There were still water fountains in the streets.) I had assumed that Matthew and Simon would not call on us that night or, to be more exact, I had not given either of them a thought. I had been sitting with them during Major Urch's presentation, but at the end, I had got up and left them without a word about walking home. My life had changed with Percy Ogden's first words, the first jabbing of his finger. To be reminded of Matthew and Simon with this ring on the doorbell was to be reminded of a long-standing but tiresome social obligation, a visit to Grandma, a sick neighbour's dog to be walked, which offered no enchantment in anticipation or substance. I had thought they would correctly interpret my trancelike rising to seek out Ogden. I had thought they would tactfully assume our friendship was over. But what we want and think is never apparent to people around us, even the ones who know us well. They have to read us through our faces and movements and gestures if we say nothing. That is not enough to base an understanding on.

I led Matthew and Simon into the kitchen as usual. They were decent dull boys, I can see that now, boys with hobbies like my dad – the violin for Matthew, who came from a big musical family of sisters. No one could object to their son having them as friends, with their string-orchestra practice and their Oxbridge-entrance classes. Matthew was going to demonstrate commitment and idealism by spending the next summer teaching English in Africa, or packing mosquito nets, I forget which. (And the year after that Oxbridge would turn him down flat: Merton College was less interested in whether an applicant for engineering could pack mosquito nets in a warehouse in Kigali than whether he could do the sums.)

'I bet José is going to kick up a row tomorrow,' Simon said, leaning against the sink with a big glass of water.

'I bet he is,' I said. José was what some sixth-formers called the headmaster, Mr Stephens. He had once taken an English class when Mrs Macdonald was off, and had confessed that he and Mrs Stephens went to the same town in Spain every year where they were the only English visitors, and 'The fisherfolk treat us like natives.'

'There's a limit to what you can say,' Simon said.

'I don't know,' I said. 'I thought maybe that was a good thing to say. They shouldn't get away with—'

'What?' Matthew said. 'She's going to get expelled for saying that.'

'Who?' I said, thrown by 'she'.

'Beverley,' Matthew said. 'Didn't you hear? After the talk? What she said to that major bloke?'

Beverley Ibrahim had somehow found herself at the front of the hall during the major's talk, not at the back as usual. The major and the headmaster had, Simon explained, been going off stage, pottering a bit – 'You know how José is, "After you, no, after you",' when Beverley called up from the hall.

'I say, Major,' she called. 'Major.' It was surprisingly good, her imitation of a real pukka plate-glass military accent. She got his rank right, too. The major turned around. He might have thought that now he was going to get a sensible question from someone of his own sort. Not everyone feels comfortable asking a question in front of an audience of their peers – it could have occurred only now to this top-notch-sounding pupil. He smiled expectantly.

'I say, Major,' Beverley sang out. 'I don't suppose you have a squaddie chappie to hand you could lend me for the afternoon? An ordinary sort of fit private soldier? I'd simply rather like to be thoroughly fucked by a fit squaddie.' Then she went into a sort of horrible Cockney, and screamed out, ''Ave yer got one, mister?' before running out.

'José couldn't believe it,' Simon said. 'Can I have another glass? Thanks. He was left fulminating – "Mrs Macdonald! Mrs Macdonald!" – but Beverley Ibrahim was too quick. She's going to be hauled over the coals tomorrow. I don't know what she's even doing in the sixth form in the first place.'

'Golly,' I said.

'Didn't you hear any of that? What did you think I was talking about?'

'I thought you were talking about that question Percy Ogden asked.'

'Oh, Percy Ogden's question,' Matthew said. 'Golly, that went on. He's such a wazzock, Percy Ogden. No one cares what he thinks.'

'It's so immature to be rude like that to a guest, just because you've read Karl Marx and can't stop going on about it,' Simon said. 'I don't think he's going to get into trouble for it. I honestly don't see much difference, by the way, between Percy Ogden saying that armed forces oppress and murder the innocent proletariat, you blood-soaked collaborator with imperialism, and Beverley Ibrahim saying, "Fuck me now." They both seem pretty rude and immature.'

A silence followed. Simon's last sentence had sounded surprisingly aggressive, considering that Percy Ogden was not in the room. It was unusual, too, for him to use an obscenity in speech, even quoting one. He did not look at me while he said any of this. It was as if my role here was to answer, defending Percy Ogden, so that Simon or Matthew could answer back dismissively. Of course everyone in the school knew who Percy Ogden was. They mostly had the same sort of views about his phalanx of supporters. I certainly knew what those two would say about him. Though I hadn't defended him in the past beyond saying, 'He's not that bad,' now I had reached the point where I didn't feel he needed to be defended from the boys who had been my friends. To be blunt: Matthew and Simon were not worth it. It seems astonishing now that I was prepared to lose two friends of years on the chance of stepping into the world of Percy Ogden. I had only heard him speak in public, which is no guide to character, or of anything but how someone wants to be seen, and an hour in a teashop. There might be no friendship there. Even if new ones began, they could exist quite happily with other, more established, friendships.

'What happened to you, then?' Matthew said. 'We waited for you for ten minutes after that colonel, but there was no sign of you.'

He must know perfectly well. 'I got held up,' I said. 'I was talking to Percy Ogden and that lot.'

'That lot,' Simon said. 'That Mohammed Ahmed, he's an idiot. He was in my Greek O-level class. Every week another stupid question that had nothing to do with anything.'

'Everyone failed,' Matthew said.

'I didn't fail,' Simon said. 'I got a C. I'd have done better if Mohammed Ahmed hadn't spent all his time flustering Mrs Benton with questions about democracy in Athens. I don't know how he even got considered for Greek O level.'

'He lives in Markham, down the hill,' Matthew said. These points – they seem so mysterious years later, and made perfect sense when we were sixteen. 'They wanted to show you don't need to be posh to do Greek O level.'

'He's all right, that Mohammed,' I said, perfectly calmly. 'What did he get, anyway?'

'I think he got a C, too,' Simon said. 'But that was a fluke. That was definitely a fluke. No one could believe it. He was still having to learn the alphabet the week before the exam.'

'That Percy Ogden, he's definitely awful, though,' Matthew said, giving it one last go. 'Apparently he does the same – spends the whole time in economics arguing with Guy the Gorilla.' (The A level economics tutor.) 'Guy told him he'd do better to listen before striking poses out of Marx third hand. Guy thinks he isn't even going to pass the mock. I've heard he's a queer, too.'

'How far are you going today?' I said.

There was some ambiguity in what I had said. I had not given it the aggressive intonation that would have made it a response to Matthew's absurd and injured comments. Matthew looked at me for the first time before answering.

'I think we'll get up as far as the hospital tonight,' he said. 'I'm feeling quite up for it. Thanks for the pit stop.'

'See you tomorrow,' Simon said. They filed out of the kitchen. I watched them go in a sarcastic, supervisory frame of mind, as if they were likely to steal something from the hall. Judging by the way they set off, heads down, silently padding up the hill towards the mental hospital, they felt the weight of my gaze and its meaning. But that must have been a delusion.

*

They must have been talking about me on the bus home because they were ready with the questions the next morning. They were as focused as a group of matchmakers with a commission to earn. We didn't have to go out and *play* in the *playground*, as the lower half of the school did. The adherence to the infantile terms for the activity and the space repre-sented our judgement on them. Instead we tended to sit in one of the form rooms at the top of the first staircase, whether it was raining or not. Some kids walked down the hill, and that age and that generation was one that was (now astonish-

ingly) committed to smoking. Others might, I suppose, have
played football or some other game, but most went between
the dour, high-curtained form rooms like dowagers on an
evening *passeggiata*. Things had mended between me and
Matthew and Simon that morning. I think they had peni-
tently concluded that if you were angry about a friendship
declining, the way to hasten the decline was to behave dis-
agreeably. Matthew caught me up on the way to school.
When Simon saw me, he immediately suggested an afternoon
of Dungeons and Dragons at his place on Saturday. I was
alone in a classroom at lunchtime, reading Ibsen's *When We
Dead Awaken*. I guess at this distance all anyone would have
seen was that weird kid reading some book. Tracy Cartwright
and Eric Milne slid silently into the desk in front of me,
prepared and practised. They pulled the chairs round with a
screech.

'So we hear you're into radical politics,' Tracy said. Her eyes
were running over me like spotlights. 'What sort of thing?
What are you? Have you read Bakunin? What's that you're
reading? Ibsen? What's that for?'

'Mass entertainment,' Eric said. 'Mass capitalist nineteenth-century entertainment. What are they, plays? That's
the industrial system, buy tickets and sit in order in some
kind of class hierarchy, rich there, bourgeoisie there. Agree to
sit silently for three hours, yeah?'

'I'm not sitting silently for three hours,' I said. 'I'm just
reading it.'

'Bakunin would never have gone to the theatre,' Eric said
decisively. 'Too much *order*. Too much *control*. Too much
Ibsen.'

I personally doubted this, but Tracy interrupted.

'I love, love, love Bakunin,' she said. She got up. She began to dance around the empty room, her arms windmilling. 'He's incredible. He tells it like it is. He doesn't have, like, a new *system* of *control* to put in place of the old one. I love him. He's my god. Me and Eric, we're anarcho-syndicalists.' She had reached the whiteboard. She took a black marker pen. She wrote 'ANARCHO-SYNDICALILISM NOW' on the board. 'If you haven't read Bakunin,' she said, returning, 'who have you read?'

I thought, or looked up at the ceiling to give the performance of thinking. My father's bookshelves had a few political classics, wedged between the substantial biographies of right-wing presidents and prime ministers, the authorized accounts of Nixon and Kennedy, Wilson and Macmillan. He liked, he said, to keep an eye on what the enemy was up to. On those shelves I had found a good deal to agree with. More than you might have expected. Last night, too, I had wondered whether this question was going to come my way.

As I thought, Tracy was using the black marker pen to draw on my upper lip. I submitted to it. The sensation I felt was cold and wet. The sharp smell under the nose of a moustache being drawn. Only that. And the helpless look on Eric's face. I now understand he was watching a woman exploring the limits of her sexual power. We fell on either side of those borders, he and I.

'I've just read *The Nineteenth Brumaire of Louis Bonaparte*,' I said. 'By Marx.' Just read was right – I'd read it the night before. I had spent about an hour getting the title straight in my head. I'd never heard of it till then.

They were surprised. Eric Milne, who had been rocking back and forward, tapping his feet with nervous energy, became very still. He turned his attention on me with his richly sincere gaze.

'Cool,' Tracy Cartwright said, setting her marker pen down, not missing a beat. 'Cool. What did you think?'

'Amazing,' I said. 'History happens twice. The first time as tragedy and the second as farce. So fucking true.'

'Yeah,' Tracy said. 'Yeah, that's the one. That old *Nineteenth*.'

'She's never read it,' Eric said. 'Never read *The Nineteenth Brumaire of Louis Bonaparte*.'

Eric was showing off now.

'Where's the call to action in that, though?' Eric said. 'I mean, what do we do when we see history coming back as farce? Sit in the stalls like you and your Ibsen and laugh?'

I had read it: I could have said that what I had read contained a call to action, but that would have been to make Eric and Tracy stand up and walk away, affixed to their dignity. I did not say that. I went along with the principle that we had all read Marx's pamphlet, many years ago.

'Sometimes people fail when you laugh at them,' I said. 'You make martyrs when you kill them. Nobody ever turned into a martyr after being laughed at. If you'd shot that major on the stage yesterday, twenty kids would have signed up within the year.'

'We weren't laughing at him,' Tracy Cartwright said. 'We were holding him to account. Showing what that stuff means. I'm not planning to laugh at him, yeah?'

'I heard some kids today saying "Trotskyite" to each other. Then they fell about laughing.'

'I don't get it,' Tracy said.

'That's what the major said. Didn't you hear him? After Ogden got shut up. That major just goes, "Trotskyite."'

'No. You're making it up,' Eric said. 'We didn't hear that. What else have you read?'

'*The Communist Manifesto*. I read that ages ago. And some Lenin. I read the Penguin Lenin reader. And George Orwell going to Wigan.' Their eyes were bright with concentration – I couldn't tell, but it might have been glee. They could have been responding to an imminent game of War in the lower playground. Orwell was not much to offer, I felt. I had read *Animal Farm* when I was ten, first mistaking it for a book for ten-year-olds. Then, quite quickly, I had realized that the book was not about what it said. I loved these grand historical moments peeping from behind well-made screens, like the moment when a man in Lilliput falls off a tightrope and lands on a fat cushion – I remember reading about Walpole, the Act he was trying to balance, the King's fat mistress who saved him. It was probably the first footnote I ever read. I was ready for *Animal Farm*. I was probably not up to *The Road to Wigan Pier* – my form teacher asked if I was following it. I said yes. But then I asked what socialism was. Perhaps what 'socialism' meant. He laughed. And those other books – I could see that they were not quite good enough. The book that everyone read anyway, and an anthology put together by Penguin. The only thing I had been able to offer was *The Nineteenth Brumaire of Louis Bonaparte*.

What tempted me was to do on a grand scale what I had done with the *Nineteenth Brumaire* – I had started to read that brilliant spurt of a pamphlet. Then I said that I had read it. I said the thing that tempted me. 'And *Das Kapital*.' Marx's colossal *Capital*, a copy of which (the first volume) sat like a dire warning on my father's shelves. I have read *Capital* now many times, the second and third volumes as well as the first. But I am not, now, the person who was talking to Eric and Tracy in form room 8C on a Thursday lunchtime. And that is the point. When we pretend to have read something, or to have gone somewhere we have never visited, like (a boy I knew at university) Democratic Kampuchea, it strikes those around us as ridiculous, if they discover the imposture. The gap between the person that is, and the experiences he wants to claim, the knowledge he pretends to have – that is contemptible. But should it be? The person who pretends to have read *Capital* is throwing his mind forward, into the future, into a person who has the same name as him, but really has read that book, really has walked the streets of Phnom Penh. Even when I read these books, I pretended to myself that I was admiring them more than I was. A great painter said of his first encounter with Raphael's cartoons that *I feigned a relish, and the relish came*. All thinking people are like that. People who laugh at such false claims have not understood that the human animal is always in a state of becoming, is never merely what it is. Soon I would become the person in the Ogden group who had read *Capital*. 'Ask him anything about it,' Mohammed would say. 'He's read it five times.'

'Knows it backwards,' Ogden would say.

By stepping in confident deception into the person I wanted to become in the future, I helped them become the persons they wanted to be, too. Since then I have pretended to be many things that, afterwards, I became – loyal Party member, ardent lover, a respecter of the freedom of women, a creative and open thinker, a keen hiker. I don't suppose they were telling the complete truth either. It's hard to imagine Bakunin being anyone's idea of hot stuff; to describe him like that is to protect your own dignity, since it places him entirely out of the realm of what can be discussed. But, then, Tracy and Eric described themselves as anarcho-syndicalists.

I held my breath. 'You're going to have a *lot* to talk to Ogden about,' Tracy said. 'I mean a *lot*.' Her tone was menacing, but even I knew that harm comes without menaces. She was impressed.

'We're meeting up tonight with the others,' Eric said. 'You can come if you want. Ogden's going to pick us up.'

'Ogden passed his test last week,' Tracy said. 'He's driving his mummy's car. Mummy's not around and Daddy hasn't noticed.'

'We'll enjoy it while it lasts,' Eric said. 'If you're coming, be at James Frinton's pub – I mean, his parents' pub. Eight. Do you know where I mean? It's the Fox and Hounds out on Thomas Lane, at the bottom. Don't be late. We won't hang about.'

There had been nothing exactly friendly about the encounter. In fact, I had twice thought they were going to walk away. They must have heard Major Urch grunt, 'Trotskyite,' from the stage, but if they really thought I was making it up, then the motivations they might ascribe to me could easily lead them to end the conversation. But they had not. I watched the two of them slope off with some satisfaction.

In a moment Guy the Gorilla came in. He started that monologue with interruptions that passed as preparation for the general studies A level. For the rest of the day people kept saying, in a detached sort of way, 'You've got a moustache drawn on your face,' as if there was nothing I could do about it.

I knew the Fox and Hounds on Thomas Lane, where James Frinton, I had just learnt, somehow lived. The information bewildered me. Pubs in general were mysterious. Especially city pubs. The Fox and Hounds would never have seemed the sort of place that I or my father would have gone into. It was a 1930s roadhouse, broad in red brick. It was guarded by a wall that had needed mending for years. The car park was only ever a third full, the asphalt cracking and sprouting weeds. The air of unpleasantness, at odds with its picturesque name, was tangible to me at the time. Only now do I pin it down to a remembered sign at the door, the indicator of the failed business everywhere, reading *Toilets for Customers' Use Only*.

I made my way round the side of the building. I came to a door, more domestic in appearance. It even had a bell. I've often thought of that doorbell since, an idea of the astonishment that the ordinary can possess. I had never considered that the outer door of a pub might have a bell. I don't know what I thought it would have – a klaxon, a test-your-strength hammer, a flamethrower – but things outside our experience usually possess, to our incredulity, properties that could not be more ordinary. This was one of them. In just the same way, people who are quite outside our familiar experience, who initially strike us as unique, prodigious, astounding, often emerge as in the thrall of emotions that anyone can have.

They turn out to run along tracks of behaviour long and deeply engraved in our own selves. I did not know what to expect when I rang the bell, but what happened is what happens when doorbells are rung. In just the same way, even the most extraordinary people will react in the most common-place and distressing style when faced with disappointment, fraudulence, theft, malignity or betrayal. Perhaps nobody is extraordinary all the way through, even boys who turn out to live in pubs. Even pubs have doors with bells. Someone always answers.

It was a small boy I recognized. He was one of the weediest boys in the school, his skin almost blue with translucence. He looked as if he had been hauled in from the deepest cold. He was still wearing his uniform, although it was now half past seven. I had observed him in the past, but had no idea he had any connection with James Frinton. The idea that Frinton had a brother was a new one. I had certainly never seen them together.

'Is Frinton here?' I said. It was idiotic. There were a number of Frintons available, including the one I was speaking to, but this one evidently knew the idiotic codes of school life because he only said, 'Hold on.' He dashed up the stairs behind him. Waiting there in the shade of the porch, the door open in front of me, a smile fixed and stupid-feeling on my face, I gave way to that sensitivity to smell that causes children such distress. The stench of tar, of a particular obese owner of a hi-fi shop, of the brewery at a particular moment in the brew-ing cycle that covered the whole city centre with the nauseat-ing warm aroma of rotting tomato soup – these were the things that made me retch at sixteen. I could never understand how adults endured them. People had to work in the brewery even on its worst days. Standing outside Frinton's open door, I thought with horror that my first consideration, that the smell I was enduring was that of Frinton within the house, was quite wrong. Rather, that soiled-socks smell of peas boiled too long and left to sit was not a personal smell. It was the smell of his home. Frinton brought it with him in the mornings. His flesh was carefully imbued with it over-night and he carried it into the public areas of his life, like a duty.

James Frinton came thundering downstairs – not in school uniform, but in some arrangement of jeans and T-shirt. The smell did not noticeably strengthen. His clothes, however, were strange in a way I can't now reconstruct. Perhaps his T-shirt bore the logo of a firm only a father could have deal-ings with, drill manufacturers or the skimmers of detritus. His clothes spoke to me of spiritual deprivation as clearly as his small brother's gormless or pathetic failure to put on clothes other than his school uniform for the evening relaxation or festivity. In reality, their clothes should have spoken only of contempt for the idea of investing any thought in outer appearance. They were quite alike, I now think, those brothers.

'Oh, hello,' Frinton said. 'Coming out with us?'

'I thought Ogden told you,' I said.

'No,' Frinton said. 'Ogden didn't.' Then he reconsidered the value of absolute and unexpanded truth. He said, 'But Tracy did. I thought you'd be round later. Percy said he'd pick us up at eight. In his car.'

'It's twenty to eight now,' I said.

'Well, you'd better come in,' he said. As if struck by a brilliant thought, he added, 'Spike.' He gestured lavishly up the stairs. The satirical edge was as much like him, the irremovable core of him, as his smell, though what or who he was satirizing with his contemptuous pronunciation of my name and a courtly gesture I don't think he could have said.

The brother was waiting at the top of the stairs: hovering palely like an orphan. There were not many voluntary visitors in that house. The spaces downstairs were public. That public, business life must always have been encroaching. 'Shoo, flee, fly,' Frinton said to his brother, with a wave of the hands. The hallway was lined with doors, somehow all shut, and the brother, scuttling off, opened one into a kitchen landscape of abandoned supper and unwashed plates. The door shut behind him. Frinton paused, assessing me. For a moment I thought we would wait there at the top of the stairs, in a gloomy space of ornaments and one photograph of the Frintons in a frame. Our indecision was dustily lit by a single light bulb. It seemed like a long time. He said, 'In here.' He opened another door. We went into the Frinton sitting room.

It was a large room, which took its shape from the demands of other spaces. The curtains were closed, the gloom only interrupted by the light of the television. At one end was a dining table, long unused. It was half covered with papers of a business sort, invoices, correspondence, account books. No one had eaten there for weeks. At the other end of the room, squatting gracelessly on the floor in front of the dusty screen was a woman who must have been Frinton's mother. She did not react to us entering. She was propped up with cushions in a sort of nest, her hair blonde and wildly curly. A comb had been run through the mess and abandoned. It sat like a piece of punctuation at the crown of it. She was far too close to the television. I had always been told by my father that it was ruinous to the eyes to sit less than six feet away. It was an act of the greatest naughtiness to sit so close that the screen crystallized into shifting squares of colour, like gazing so hard at a word, *cabbage*, for instance, that it became meaningless and bizarre. But here was Mrs Frinton, sitting so close to the television that it must have occupied the whole of her field of vision. It must have meant nothing. She was lost in it. A singer was performing in a glittering long dress, lit by a spotlight in a television studio. I could not hear what she was singing, as the volume on the television was turned down almost to nothing, but from her stylized and intense gestures, some statement about love and suffering must have been under way. The singer's despair spread her hands wide; her fingers opened; she had known what love could do to a girl. Every few seconds Mrs Frinton reached out a finger towards the television screen, not quite daring to touch the anguished face. I wondered where Frinton's father was, before the terrible answer came to me: he was in the pub. Of course he was.

'Mummy really, really loves Eartha Kitt,' Frinton said.

I almost laughed. The idea of having strong feelings about this singer was so unlikely.

'It's best not to interrupt when she's watching one of her videos,' he said. I had been on the verge of sitting down, but I stood up again. 'Come on.'

We left the sitting room. We went into the kitchen I had glimpsed, where Frinton's brother sat, surrounded by detritus.

He, as much as we, was waiting for something. I did not know his name.

'I'm Spike,' I said. We sat down. The boy looked at me in something like terror.

'It's my brother,' Frinton said. Then he went into a more urgent style. 'How long has she been—'

'All day,' the boy said. 'She was watching when I went out and she's been watching since I got back.'

'The old story,' Frinton said. 'She gets to the end of the tape, she rewinds, she watches it again. Mummy,' he went on, turning to me in a sociable, kind, amused way, 'really loves Eartha Kitt.'

'I can see,' I said. I looked at the clock above the door, but it said twenty past three. The hands were not moving.

'What time is Ogden coming?' Frinton said, interpreting my gaze. Without waiting for an answer, he added, 'You done your homework?' roughly to the brother. The door opened. There was Mrs Frinton. I had had my ideas of what a pub landlady might look like – ideas from conventional representations of confidence and the unwavering stare, the finger pointing at the door in a way that brooked no opposition. The word *brassy* would have been of use. Mrs Frinton came in, a round assemblage of shawls and soft, pastel-coloured woolly garments. Her eyes shone with tears and transcendence. She had gone through a marvellous emotional experience and she wanted us to know about it.

'Was she good, Mum?' the younger Frinton said anxiously. He didn't know who I was, but he wanted to put up a good show in front of me. He was pretending now that she had been watching it for the first time, innocently and with a decent degree of interest.

'Yes,' Mrs Frinton said. 'Very, very good.'

'Mummy's a big fan of Eartha Kitt,' James Frinton said again.

There was embarrassment in the air. I felt the need to establish that this was quite an ordinary thing to be interested in. Across from me, Frinton's brother had spilt some water on the table. He was trying to see if he could guide it into the shape of a country, a continent, or perhaps just a square, pushing it with the edge of a table mat. Somehow I went on speaking and fixating on the shapes the water was making.

'I've never really seen her,' I started by saying. 'At least, I have seen her. On the television. I've glimpsed her. I've glanced at her. I might even have seen the programme you were watching, Mrs Frinton. But I don't think I would have enjoyed it as much – no, I mean … What I mean to say is that you only enjoy something as much as you obviously do if you pay a lot of attention to it, so that you're not really aware, I guess, of what's going on around you. Is that right, Mrs Frinton? I'm definitely sure that I'll pay a lot more attention to Eartha Kitt the next time I see her on the television, Mrs Frinton. Have you been a fan of hers for a long time?'

I said this sociably, to bring Frinton's mother in, but she only said, 'She helps me with things. When I've had a bad day or two.'

The countries made of spilt water were growing larger on the table. Frinton's brother was shaping Frances, Germanys, Spains. His head and James Frinton's were both down in steady concentration. James Frinton was looking at his watch. I was aware that the Frinton smell was not coming from Mrs Frinton either. She smelt of soap and some brownish, spice-warm perfume. The source of the smell must be behind another of those closed doors.

'My father is just like you,' I said. 'Not that I really know, we've only just met, but I can tell, Mrs Frinton, my father is a bit like you. He has these enthusiasms – he likes ferns. You know ferns? The green things in forests. My father grows them and he always likes to look at new types, new specimens, and then he's just like you, totally absorbed in what he's doing. You don't try to speak to him if he's converting spores or propagating roots. I could go in and say I'm leaving school or I've got a girlfriend or I'm marrying a girlfriend or my girlfriend's pregnant even, and he wouldn't say anything or hear at all because he'd be thinking of how to deal with this very tricky customer of a fern, and I suppose that's how the world goes on, advances, I mean, though, you know, the single fixed obsessive concentrating on the one thing, whatever people think of them and whatever's happening around them doesn't matter at all. I mean my father only knows it's time to eat because the clock says it is, and I suppose it's like that for you, is it, with Eartha Kitt? Do you only like her or do you like other singers too, because I know my dad has a record somewhere of – of – I forget her name – Bobbie Gentry. I've never heard him play it, it must have been my mum's but she left it, I expect that must be it, or Dusty Springfield, do you like her, Mrs Frinton, or is it only Eartha Kitt? I must take a look at Eartha – it's an interesting name, isn't it? I expect you know whether it's her real name, named after the Earth itself, is it, or just a stage name? She growls, doesn't she, like a cat, a big cat, a kitt, is that it? Well, good for her, and I hope you go on with your enthusiasm for singers like her or is it just her? Good for you, Mrs Frinton.'

Perhaps you have never found yourself speaking like this, going on from point to point, making no sense. The feel of panic when speech must be made but that one is not at all the person to be making it. And yet the words go on. It happened when I was sixteen, in the kitchen of the Frintons. It has happened once or twice since. If people can be divided into two (but people cannot be divided into two, can barely be divided into seven billion), then you might say that they divide into those who fall silent and those who start to speak. I am someone who starts to speak. Now I know that about myself. I forced myself to finish. I had surely finished with a question, but no answer came.

Like any well-mannered hostess when presented with a blundering guest, Mrs Frinton changed the subject.

'Your father doesn't want you to be late back,' she said to James Frinton. 'He wants you back before closing time.' The way the Frintons divided the day was quite new to me, not by mealtimes, work commitments and the nine o'clock news, but by opening and closing times. And yet it was my father, and not the Frintons' mother, who committed suicide in the years after this conversation.

'We're going out for a little drive,' James Frinton said. 'Just that.'

'Don't let your father catch you coming in at one in the morning,' Mrs Frinton said. 'You've got *school* tomorrow.'

Mrs Frinton was detached from reality. She knew it. This last observation was produced with some ebullience, as of a clinching, little-known fact.

'Coming in at one o'clock,' Mrs Frinton went on, 'you'll wake your father and your grandmother, and your brother and me.'

'And you'll wake Eartha Kitt,' I said. I don't know why I said this. I immediately wished that I hadn't. One of those spontaneous stupid remarks that come from nowhere and last for ever, giving pain whenever it is recalled. I was making some silly observation in my own head about Eartha Kitt being so constant a presence in the Frintons' flat that she might as well be thought to live and sleep there. But Mrs Frinton's ebullience was punctured. She looked at me with puzzlement and pain, as at a cruel piece of mockery. It is still giving me pain, years later, that sentence. Outside in the car park, a horn sounded, a twilit, melancholy sound echoing between the brick enclosures of the quiet suburb. We were summoned.

'That's Ogden,' Frinton said. 'In his car. We've got to go.' He wouldn't look at me. I'd said something wrong, and I knew it. I thought he was delaying the schoolboy snap of rage only until we had left his mother, who was most under attack from my remark, but I underestimated him. If he was going to respond, he would respond later, perhaps hours or days later. That was his measured style: he filed things away. We said our goodbyes and started downstairs. A bright thought occurred to Mrs Frinton. She called after us, 'You should take your brother out on one of these jaunts! Take him! But you'll have to promise something – not to bring him back at one in the morning, covered with love bites!'

We carried on walking. Mrs Frinton's remarks bore no real relation to the actual or possible world. Neither Frinton nor his brother made any attempt to reconfigure the group as it stood, one part of it at the head of the stairs, one opening the door into the quiet world of the empty car park. A single car was there, a dark green hatchback parked without reference to the parallel lines and boxes painted on the asphalt. Inside, Ogden's face loomed against the windscreen. The dashboard light had been switched on. Behind him were Tracy Cartwright, Mohammed and Eric. Eric, in the outside world six foot four, was hunched up somehow, his face forced between the two seats in front. The car was not large, but at that point in our lives, it was quite normal to set off with four in the back, squeezing together, joints and forked limbs fitting together and jolting, shrieking. It was just what you did. We opened the door, said, 'Hi,' briefly. I pulled the car seat forward so that Frinton could clamber into the back. Frinton laid himself across the three of them before somehow squeezing into a space that wasn't there before between Eric's hard angles and Tracy's softer corners. A giggle came from Mohammed, a groan of performed pain from Tracy. I sat in the front seat. I fastened my seatbelt.

'Here you all are, then,' Ogden said, starting the engine. We set off.

'Told you,' Mohammed said.

'I knew he would,' Eric said. 'I never had any doubts.'

'Knew who would what – me?' I said.

'They were betting you wouldn't come,' Tracy said. A shiver ran down my neck. A finger was being run down the side of

my head. I couldn't see, but it must have been either Tracy or
Eric. 'I knew you'd come.'

'We all knew he'd come,' Ogden said. 'We never had any
doubt. Where are we going?'

A howl burst into my ear from behind, a world-destroying
cry only slowly turning into a noise – *sbro* … It died down.
Ogden looked at me, a direct, open, confiding look. He
smiled.

'Greasbrough,' he said, crooning a little, like a gentle remi-
niscence of the howl years later.

It burst out again from behind – 'GREASBROUGH' –
with James Frinton's full force.

'We're obsessed with Greasbrough,' Ogden said. 'Yes, we'll
go through it, some time tonight, I promise. Greasbrough!
You can call your borough anything, and you decide to call it
Grease. Imagine living there, and having to spell it every time
you wanted to ask a girl round.'

'Or a boy,' Tracy said.

'Or a boy,' Ogden said. 'We're not going there straight
away, though. The Spartacists asked us round. I thought we'd
go there first. Do you know the Spartacists? You, kid? Eric
met them first, and me too. Do you know who Spartacus was?
They named themselves – their movement – after him.'

'Ancient Rome,' I said.

'The Spartacists – Kate and Euan and Joaquin if he's there
– they're our friends, they're on the right side. Do you go to
the library? The central library? You know the ones who stand
outside on a Saturday morning?'

I knew the Spartacists now. The Ogdens were about to
introduce them to me, but it might so easily have been the

Spartacists who introduced me to the Ogdens. The central library of the city was a white stone art-deco palace of monumental grandeur. It was a centre of life in a way difficult to imagine now. (I think it has recently been sold off by the local council to Chinese property developers keen on turning it into a hotel, one of seventeen planned or in existence in the city centre.) It was normal to go there to work, to read, to escape from home. Outside the library, on the pavement by the entrance, the sellers of radical newspapers often stood. I was one of those boys who take out five books every week and return them seven days later, perhaps having read two to the end. I thought I knew not only the Spartacists in general, but perhaps the very ones Ogden was talking about. I had seen a short woman, with long, untidy blonde hair, in what we then called an Afghan coat. She was sometimes accompanied by a shambling large dark man with hollow eye sockets. He always wore a green military jacket from some army-surplus store. They were selling their newspaper. I must have known it was a radical publication, produced as cheaply as possible. I might have thought of buying a copy, of getting into conversation with them. Ogden had mentioned three names, but I could only remember ever having seen two at once. Through that conversation I would have been introduced to the network of groups, campaigners, radical bookshops, men's groups, free sheets, radicals, protesters, pamphleteers, terrorists, squatters – *students* in short – that made up the life of the mind in that provincial city. They might in time have heard the name of the school I went to. They could have introduced me properly to their friends in the sixth form there, Ogden, Mohammed, Tracy, Eric, Frinton. Which is to say that my inclinations of thought were and are like water. They would always have flowed quite quickly to the same point through quite similar routes, downwards. I would always have found myself in the same place, knowing the same people. Radical thinkers are not like the uninflected children of the bourgeoisie, in their crippling and yet unspoken ideology. If you take three dull children of a provincial bourgeois neighbourhood and choose to introduce them in turn to religion, to the harp, to long-distance running, you will produce three people quite different in temperament, in habits, in the final shape of their lives. It hardly matters what you do to try to shape the lives of the radically minded. Their lives will flow, despite any impediment, to the same point, as our existences in the thirty-five years since those first meetings must show. I am talking about the lives of Percy Ogden, who was born to lead a political life, and Frinton, of course, and Eric Milne, and the rest, including me. I would always have met them, and Joaquin and Kate. My life would always have followed its particular path. Nothing could have prevented it.

'Do you like Lloyd Cole?' Ogden said. Without waiting for an answer he pushed a cassette into the slot of his mother's player. I knew it. It was the sound of that year, the way by which people like us distinguished ourselves from the mass consumers of pop culture. Then, it was the epitome of freedom, of a taste unshaped and unfunded. Ogden explained about Joaquin, Kate and Euan. I can hardly remember Euan now, and Kate is just a hairstyle and a particular coat. It's strange to think of a time when Joaquin had to be explained to me, now that I've settled into knowing him, the best of men, for thirty years. But it was in that car, driving from the comfortable west of the city towards the brutalist centre, that I was first told about my friend. Hardly anybody in the car from that day is still much a part of my life, rather than just my thoughts. But that was where I heard that there was a man called Joaquin.

Percy Ogden explained about the Spartacists during that drive. The others must have known it all, but listened with enjoyment, sometimes putting in a correction about details if Ogden forgot something, or confused one thing with another. There were three of them. I suppose there must have been more than that to get their newspaper printed every month or six weeks. I suppose they submitted the money they collected to some organization with a bank account and a hierarchy of responsibility. The three of them lived in a flat in Park Hill, where we were going now. The flats were a huge 1960s development, then very much out of fashion. For the most part they were desperately vacant. (By now they have been renovated and rendered possible for chic provincial taste to live in.) From the air, the blocks of rain-stained concrete curved in and around each other, desolately overlooking empty and threatening spaces where muggers, I believed at the time, lurked. Although there was no mistaking the dramatic force of the architecture, the idea of the designers that everyone would have a quiet patch of green to admire had not come to pass. I had never been inside the development although, of course, everybody knew its unnatural, many-jointed curve along the ridge of the hill above the railway station. If you wanted to be civil about it you called it *brooding*.

Joaquin, Kate and Euan lived there because it was so cheap. 'They're squatters, actually,' Ogden said, but Eric corrected him. They were not squatters. They paid Mr Das, their land-lord, fifty pounds a week, quite in order. 'Fifty pounds a week each?' I asked, wanting to have a grip on the situation, but, no, it was between the three of them. They were students at the university, in solid academic subjects: Kate, who wrote poems, studied English, Joaquin and Euan history. Ogden and Eric had met them first, outside the library. An argument had taken place. Ogden did not specify – 'Just a discussion,' he said dismissively – but it may have been over some now discarded piece of ideology, somehow visible on Ogden's person. I strongly suspected this of being a CND badge. Ogden's earlier dismissal of nuclear disarmament as an idea suggested to me that he had, at some point in the past, been an adherent to the point of wearing badges in support. 'How did you get talking?' I said. They had just seen them – some kind of sceptical comment had been made, the other side had defended it, a counter-argument had followed. 'Then Joaquin turned up and we all went to the pub,' Eric said. It had been half past five on Saturday. They were probably not going to sell any more copies of the newspaper. Eric had been passing as eighteen in pubs for five years, a useful accessory to the under-age even though he himself didn't much like drinking. In the winter the three Spartacists stood outside one of the town's two football stadiums. I wanted to know whether Ogden and the rest were Spartacists, too, but it didn't seem so. They were cousins, as it were, or pen-pals. There was an odd note of derision when Ogden talked about them. Euan and Kate were, he said, your typical middle-class rebels, chil-dren of doctors and shop-owners. Even at the time it seemed to me that the same could be said of Ogden.

Joaquin, too, was the son of a doctor, but there was no question over his status, no suggestion that his existence was somehow comic. I think he was the reason that the group fastened on to the Spartacists, and treated them, in the end, with respect. He was Chilean. His story was the first thing I ever heard about that country. His father, the doctor, had been a leftist radical. After 1973 he and all his like had been prosecuted, placed in jail, tortured. Joaquin's mother had left the country, going first to Spain. Then, quite quickly, she had come to England, where she had some cousins in Camden Town. She and Joaquin and her daughter Rosa had made a kind of life in London. There was no rebellion there. Joaquin's politics were just as his parents' had been. They had no idea what had happened to his father, the doctor: disappeared. He had been disappeared. That was the phrase, which hardly seems English to me. For Joaquin to have professed anything but a politics in line with the first principles of the Soviet revolution would have been an unthinkable betrayal of his martyred father. There was no arguing with that.

'He was twelve when they came in 1973,' Ogden said. 'So he's twenty now. Rosa's our age. I've never met her. She's named after Rosa Luxemburg, of course.'

I didn't then know who Rosa Luxemburg was, but I thought I'd start at another end of the story.

'What happened in 1973?'

'Oh, right,' Ogden said. 'I forget. If you hang around with us you get to hear a lot about 1973. In Chile. You forget not everyone knows about it.'

There had been a coup, and a Fascist government had expelled the democratic government of the left, imprisoning

and torturing people. It was hard to envisage. I forced myself
to envisage it. I saw men in guns bursting through the presi-
dential doors of a palace, splintering white paint and gold
ornamental baroque flourishes, shooting machine-guns into
putti-laden ceilings. Was this what revolution meant? And
could it happen in the country where I lived? In many respects
these are the questions I have gone on living with for thirty or
more years. The possibilities of revolution, I think, are always
present in a society. They must be present in the society we
live in – England now and England then. Yet the idea of a
revolution taking place or of a group of military taking over
is and always was remote from the streets, the suburbs, the
parks, schools, libraries and open spaces we live in. Major
Urch points a finger at Percy Ogden. Half a dozen soldiers
leap forward to drag the questioner off to … to where? Hither
Green police station, where PC Brewster and the other
constables are going to take time off from filling in dog-li-
cence applications to torture him to death? Really? The imagination fails. But Chile in 1973 was just as ordinary to Joaquin
as our town was, in 1982, to us. Sometimes I cannot say
whether we were closer to revolution in 1982 than we are now.
At both times it has an impossible aspect that we try to
overlook.

A conversation had been taking place in the back seat
between Tracy and Mohammed about Scritti Politti. Now she
was warbling that she was in love with Jacques Derrida, quite
ignoring the music playing on the cassette machine. We were
by the entrance to the car park by the library. Ogden was
signalling left.

'Has anyone got any change?' he said.

'Why are we parking here?' Tracy said, breaking off. 'This is miles away. James, why is he parking here?'

'I always park here,' Ogden said, which could not have been true. He had only been able to take his test in the last month or two. But lives change so quickly. We forget what they were like before those changes. 'This is a good place to park.'

'You can park right by the Spartacists,' Frinton said. 'There's a car park there. There's always spaces.'

'Yeah, right,' Ogden said. He leant out of the car, took the ticket from the machine. He drove up the ramp under the raised barrier.

'What does that mean, "yeah, right"?' Mohammed said. He sounded surprisingly outraged. 'Why can't you park your mummy's car by Park Hill flats for nothing? This is going to cost two quid at least.'

We all knew, I think, why Ogden was parking his car in the secure, enclosed, supervised space, rather than in an open area of near-darkness where deprivation roamed, bored. It was indefensible. It would have been bad enough if the car were Ogden's own, but it was clear to Mohammed in particular that Ogden was parking there for the sake of his mummy's precious car. He said so.

'Well, I tell you what,' Ogden said, as we walked down the stairs of the car park. 'Why don't *you* borrow *your* mummy's car the next time and park it wherever you like? How about that?'

'Two problems,' Mohammed said. 'My mum can't drive and neither can I. The thing with you is that you don't trust the ordinary working class. You deep-down think they'll bash up your stuff. You don't even know them.'

'Who?' Ogden said. 'The *lumpenproletariat*? If they do smash it up, set it on fire, then what if it was just a group of kids who've been sniffing glue and wanted to smash something up? Nothing follows. Not all violence is ideological. So, if you don't mind, I'm going to put my mum's car in the car park by the library.'

We had crossed the dual carriageway. We skirted the railway station, walking up into the landscape of orange lights, half of them broken, and rancid concrete doorways, deep in shadow, that constituted the Park Hill estate. There was nobody about. It was hard not to feel some fear. I had never been there before. The others were talking too loudly, in bravado. Around a corner a large, solid figure stepped, a darkly unshaven man, disappearing at once into the unlit gloom of a concrete recess.

There were no lighting schemes then. What lighting there was remained unrestored to function. There were no closed-circuit cameras to record the moment. Joaquin stepped out of thick shadows at the base of a twelve-storey block, a tender, dark face, a large, broad, muscular shape. He could have been a murderer.

I recognized him from the library steps. He was wearing the same army-surplus jacket I had seen before. His head had been shaved maybe two weeks ago. Now the hair was even all over to a length of a quarter of an inch, showing the first signs of curliness, like astrakhan fur. He had shaved his chin more recently, but not very recently. He came towards us with hand outstretched – I think Joaquin was the first person I knew who shook hands on meeting you. He had carried on shaking hands without any kind of reference to how people greeted each other in the place he now lived. The noise he made as he approached was of slapping – he wore yellow flip-flops with his jeans. He shook my hand, too, with warmth and energy, and with a burst of bright whiteness in his cheerful mouth. From his body came a physical smell, quite strong. It was a fleshy smell, Joaquin's odour, the smell of an animal who has run a good deal, but not at all unpleasant. He was perfectly clean, but never used perfumes or deodorants, either to mask or to erase what his flesh smelt of. This was an age of anti-perspirants and guilt and fretting, deodorants called Worry for Men and a pong of metal and chemicals in the mornings on buses and in classrooms. I think I can honestly say that it was Joaquin's smell – the smell of a warm human body at ease with itself – that changed my mind as much as what I heard people say. I wanted to be in a room with this man.

'Who is this?' Joaquin said politely. 'I know Eric and James and Tracy and Mohammed but this one, no.'

'I'm Spike,' I said.

'We only have tea and maybe not milk,' Joaquin said. 'I come down, I came down for you. Kate told me I must come. She says you don't know where to come. I tell her she must be crazy, you've been a hundred times to our place. Number seven hundred twelve, seventh floor. Elevator is not working. As always not working.'

'How did you know we were coming?' Tracy said.

'I came down and I waited,' Joaquin said. 'I waited for you, Tracy.'

'Oh, fuck off,' Tracy said.

Joaquin gave a brief, joyous bark of laughter. 'No, we see you coming. Don't you know that? On the seventh floor, we see all the way over the city, we see anyone coming over the bridge, you know, the footbridge on the *dual carriageway*—' this phrase produced with care and some pride, a phrase recently mastered, perhaps '—and tonight we see one-two-three-four-five-six kids coming and Kate she says who is the sixth and Euan says his friend Percy mentioned a new friend comrade and I say good, I go down and meet them, bring them up if Kate says it's necessary. Today six comrades. Tomorrow maybe we see the police and the army running over to us, come to arrest or shoot us, me and Kate and Eu-aron—' it was always touching, the lengths Joaquin went to not to call Euan Juan – 'and I tell you, we see them coming with their batons and guns and uniform, and we know *what to do*. But today it is again Percy and the good guys we see coming. Ten minutes ago.'

Joaquin burst out laughing once more, there on the second floor ascending the flights of stairs. We didn't have the same right as he did, the survivor (at twelve) of real policemen running over real bridges to take action, the right to laugh at the idea if he chose to. We waited, impressed and disconcerted. It was my first glimpse of Joaquin's lightness of spirit, the way that for him things both mattered and didn't matter, could be done away with and forgotten or fiercely engaged with, given a good slap. It depended not on their inherent gravity but on the dignity and decision of the thinking person. The spirit of laughter. There was nothing in the world like Joaquin's laughter. It came up from the depths of him, in his bowels and belly, a sound that burst out like a single man applauding in a crowded place, and could make strangers turn round and even, sometimes, join in. There was a ripple and a gurgle in it you could never forget. I loved Joaquin's laugh. I still do. Did he think that the English policemen were going to run across the bridge over the dual carriageway to beat him and his flatmates into submission because of their ideological convictions? They could not, while he could laugh at the idea. That was stronger than any policeman. And so Joaquin went out after midnight with lightness in his heart to paint walls and to smash windows. Of course he did.

'Did you come on the bus?' Joaquin asked.

'No,' Mohammed said. 'Ogden drove us. He passed his test last month.'

'He's got his mum's car,' James Frinton said, quite neutrally.

'He's parked it in that multi-storey car park by the library,' Mohammed said. 'He thought it would be *safer* there.'

This was clearly meant as a jibe, but Joaquin either didn't catch the tone or didn't see the point.

'Yes,' he said. 'Very good idea. Not to come down here and leave it. Not safe. The little kids round here, they strip it, smash the windows, cut the wheels, the tyres. Or I tell you, last week, these kids, they break into a lady's flat, old lady. Two, three flats away from us, she's sitting there, can't do anything, was watching, they take TV in front of her, take it out, throw the TV out of the window, bang, explodes. Why? No idea. I have not the foggiest. You are underneath a TV falling from seventh floor, I tell you, you know about it when it hits you, or even car, empty, bash, bang. No, that's good idea, park your mum's car in the multi-storey. Gonna be safe there.'

I glimpsed the kind of authority that Joaquin had. Nobody contradicted him, or reverted to the previous stages of the argument. The only resistance to Joaquin's sensible-sounding point was James Frinton, saying, 'Well, but they're deprived, aren't they, these kids, they're the real victims here.'

'I tell you what these kids are,' Joaquin said. 'They are the total little cunts. Mrs Gunnarsson, she's scared now all day long, and guess what, she has no TV. So the real victims – no. They are the real total little cunts. And here we are at last home. I wish they mend that fucking elevator some time.'

Joaquin jiggled at the blue-painted door. In the pane of glass, there was a small poster advertising a people's gathering with the date of a year earlier. The door stuck, then fell inwards. We all followed Joaquin in, dumping our coats on a plastic chair in the hallway. There were pairs of scuffed shoes, walking boots, old plimsolls and two more pairs of flip-flops, red and green. On the wall was a framed front page of the Spartacist newspaper – I can't now remember what it was called, although I know it wasn't the *Spartacist*. But I remember that the issue they had gone to the trouble of framing was one they had produced to celebrate the royal wedding a year or two before. Over a photograph of the happy couple in uniform and medals and massive cream finery in taffeta was a headline reading 'GET OUT THE GUILLOTINE'. Underneath, a subhead purported to claim that 2,745 malnourished children in inner cities could have been fed for a year on the cost of that one dress. A brilliant piece of fabrication, I learnt later. They had been turned away by three framing shops.

'Hi, honey,' Joaquin called. 'We're home.'

A thin wail of delight came from upstairs – it was, I realized, a two-floor flat, something I didn't know was possible.

'I got the kids,' Joaquin said, trotting upwards, his flat brown hairy feet slapping happily. 'And a new one, too! What's your name?'

A woman came to the door of the sitting room, a wide, untidy blonde woman. Her hair was up and in it, like a Japanese woman's hair-chopsticks, was a pair of biros. She had been writing. Her tools were her ornament, her display. The sitting room behind her had a long, plate-glass window, giving out onto the city centre. From here, it was a long way down to the grime and the empty, dumpy streets smelling of piss and beer. And Joaquin was right. From there you could see anyone approaching across the bridge over the dual carriage-way – police thugs, young radicals, anyone. They were up there looking down on the direction that humanity could take, whether individuals or in groups. I was overcome with admiration and envy. I wanted to be these people. Joaquin's physical presence in particular filled me with joy – the teeth, the hair, the wonderful smell of him as he cast off his jacket, dropping it on the floor, his hairy humorous feet idling and gripping the yellow flip-flops, a joy that, at that moment, I did not quite understand. If I'd had an explanation it would soon have been proved incomplete.

Introductions were made. Kate kissed each of us, including me. (But she had only just met me, I remember thinking, with a bourgeois stuffiness about intimacy rituals that I tried to suppress.) 'Welcome, Spike,' Kate said formally. Now it is clear that she was a doctor's daughter, only twenty years old, just as uncertain as any of us, trying to make up her mind how to live and how to improve the lives of people she would never meet, subject like any of us to vulgar complaints like love. She seemed immeasurably wise and experienced, like Goldberry in Tolkien. Her poetry, when I came to read it, was quite wonderful.

> *Magic can happen on a bus*
> *To anyone.*
> *On the window the mud was like filigree.*
> *And the man sitting next to me*
> *On the magical bus*
> *Which was red*
> *Said in a stagey way that he was struck with love.*
> *Like an angel he looked deeply and passionately into my*
>   *eyes.*

She would show me this poem, and twenty or thirty more, in another week's time. Joaquin was beyond anything my experience held, but even Kate was extraordinarily mature and thoughtful and impressive. I was not the only one who felt this. The others had gone silent since Joaquin had met us, walking up the seven flights of stairs in a quiet that could only have been awestruck. They were only four or five years older than us. They were separated from us by the lifespan of a pair of Y-fronts. But the awe was there, hanging in the air like the smoke-hung echo after an explosion.

We'd just missed Euan. He was out, Kate said, doing whatever he had to be doing — it was early in the evening to be painting on walls, so I guess he was at some meeting or men's group or an ecological action. 'We ought to hear about it when Euan's here,' she said. 'But I'm too excited. I want to hear about your guy the other day — the military guy?'

'The major who came to speak?' I said. 'The one who came to our school?' I was surprised by Kate's breadth of interest.

'Percy was going to smash up that guy,' Joaquin said. 'We talked about it. You used the numbers we gave you, yes?'

'The guy from the army, he didn't know what hit him,' Eric said. I felt an unexpected pressure in the side of my thigh. I was sitting on an old brown sofa, ragged and stained, though not exactly dirty, a pile of paperbacks on the arm. Next to me Tracy had taken off her shoes and drawn her feet up. It was her bare feet that were pumping and pressing against my thigh. Her attention was apparently all on Ogden and his story.

'He just saw a kid in a school uniform with his hand up,' Tracy said. Her voice was husky, almost seductive in its hoarseness. No one seemed to think her bare feet in my side at all odd or wrong. I wondered if she did it to everyone.

'That's the thing,' Kate said. 'You don't dress to stand out if you've got an action in mind, and with a bit of luck you slide under the radar. The other day – no, last month – Joaquin comes in and he sees me and Euan and I'm wearing a jumper and skirt and pearls, fake pearls from Woolworth's, and Euan's wearing a tweed jacket he found in Oxfam. And you said, didn't you—'

'I said what the hell, Kate,' Joaquin said happily. 'And they are going they tell me to a meeting, to this Fascist group, the Monday Club, is it? At the university. Euan he had a bottle of piss, he throws it at the speaker they got, it smashes, they run. I wish I go there too. But no suit, no jacket, no tie. No me.'

'And I guess they'd remember three people but two – it's just a bloke and his girlfriend,' I said. I surprised myself. 'They won't recognize you if they see you the next day. Different clothes.'

'Yeah, that's it,' Kate said. '*And* I brushed my hair. This one gets the point. We like you. You can come again. So you ask the question. Did you get it all in?'

Ogden gave a quick grin, like a chimpanzee baring its teeth, a warlike gesture. He started to give the main points of his question, but it was easier to perform it, word for word. I guess they had recited it together, practising it, here and in the houses of the group all over the rest of the city. Occasionally Kate or Joaquin said, 'Yeah, that's it,' or 'That's what I said you should say', particularly when it came to the figures Ogden had brought out. Whoever had come up with the summary of the cost of an education had been through an education that had been charged for. I wouldn't enquire, just yet, whether that had been Kate or Euan. The text of the question had been agreed in committee, as it were. Even in the context of a careers visit to a suburban comprehensive school, it was important to them to get the agreed version out. Fission, division, denunciation can follow a speaker who decides to get it more or less right, to leave space for what he himself might think. The early Church divided, after all, when one faction decided to say *homoousios* and another *homoiousios*. Ogden went through what it had been agreed that he would say with care, strictly, and without embellishment.

When it was done Kate gave an audible outward breath. 'So that was it,' she said. 'Did he give any kind of answer?'

'No,' James Frinton said. 'He didn't give any answer. The headmaster shut him down and they went away.'

Frinton had been quiet since we had left his parents' pub. Now he spoke emphatically, his eyes cast down. I could not see what he was angry about. It was unusual, I see that now, for Frinton ever to reveal that he was angry, even if he did so, as now, by restraining himself. I think in the future I was to understand that Frinton had, on a particular occasion, been angry or contemptuous, but most people would have been struck on the same occasion by his charm and likeability, turned up a notch or two. This moment of cold, closed dismissal was a rare one. It was something that (obviously) Frinton grew out of. Kate looked at him with a touch of surprise. She gave a kindly sort of smile.

'That's always the way, isn't it?' she said. She made me think what an unlikely revolutionary she was, an implausible and unsuspected hurler of bottles of piss, an innocuous painter of walls, a smooth-faced smasher of windows. 'They only very occasionally fail and let another voice be heard. But if it ever happens, they pretend nobody said anything. They really are cunts.'

It was only that last word that made me see Kate as she wanted to be seen. It made me see that she and not Joaquin was the destructive presence there, the presence utterly focused on herself and her own voice and deeds. All her energy was spent presenting herself. Her interest in those around her was a performance, made to cloak her with a sympathetic air. But at first she was not interesting. She was only sympathetic. I reached out to this sympathy. Like most men, I wanted my voice to be heard above all things.

'It wasn't the whole thing, though,' I said. 'The headmaster' – I wasn't going to say *José* with Joaquin there – 'cut Percy off, saying, "That's quite enough," and then he turns round to the major, this soldier, and the major says this one word – I guess he thinks this is going to put Percy in his place or something. He just goes, "Well, yes – mean to say – perfectly honest – harrumph – yes, well – *Trotskyite!*" And then that's it.'

The others had, some time ago, been very clear that this had not happened. But now they did not make any kind of comment. Tracy's feet in the side of my thigh paused where they were, not removing themselves but holding still. They wanted to know what the Spartacists thought of this anecdote, its plausibility in their eyes. Again I think, with consternation: Those people were only twenty-two, at most.

'I tell you,' Joaquin said drily. 'They got that one right.'

'They don't know, though,' Eric said. With that, my authority and standing were confirmed. Eric going along with the story of Major Urch saying *Trotskyite* had the same force as the group starting to echo my word of *commensurate*. They had agreed that these were words that proved a point that would have been made anyway. 'He just said *Trotskyite* like you would say *scum*. How was he to know that the term was the right one? It was a lucky hit.'

'I don't know,' Joaquin said. 'I think about it. I don't know what we're going to do with all the army. It has, you know, a purpose, real purpose. Close down the army because I mean that major, he is like an idiot, an asshole, and then what do you do with all the working-class men, all those proletariat? They leave school, no learning, they can't read. You say to me in our society, the one we build, everyone read, everyone education, but I tell you, always some violent men. They don't like to read or think or paint watercolour painting. Poems.

No. It's a good solution, the army. Not this, not the army of imperialist fighting for territory, but you attack the idea of army, you know what you end up having, excuse me, end up being? Bourgeois pacifist, no army, no nuclear weapons, your friends in Campaign Nuclear Disarm, your friends, Percy, you know what I'm saying?'

'They're not my friends,' Percy said. 'I haven't agreed with them for years.'

'Well, you lose the nuclear and you leave the Soviet revolution without defence,' Joaquin said. 'Hey, I tell you what ...'

Kate got up. Handling it delicately, she extracted a flyer from a red folder on top of the dusty old TV. It was advertising a CND rally at City Hall the following week. Campaign for Nuclear Disarmament. It's a sign of those long-gone times that an organization like the CND could, in the early 1980s, command a space holding several thousand people. There was a general feeling of doom and despair, I remember, and quite unexpected people had signed up to the proposal that these weapons should be removed from the Earth through a process of disarmament. It was even a bone of contention between my friends Matthew and Simon, the joggers. One wanted abolition, the other believing in a balance of awesome forces to maintain a tranquillity of existence. The point of view, like the Spartacists', that believed the most important point was that the Soviets not only had a nuclear arsenal but should use it at some point was, I believe, an unusual one even at the time. It didn't take long for Kate to persuade us that a good thing to do would be to go along to the CND rally the following week and fuck it up. There wouldn't be that much dressing up to do.

'Cunts,' Kate said, of the bourgeois pacifists, her eyes shining.

Somehow I found myself with Joaquin on the flat's small open space, a little enclosed balcony. I don't know how we got there. There was no alcohol along the line. I didn't feel drunk, just open to the possibility of intoxication. Joaquin must have got up in his big, confident way, carrying his mug of tea. Like a duckling, I must have got up too. I would have followed his flapping flip-flops out. I think what it must have looked like. Tracy's bare feet all at once kneading away at the space where I had been sitting. I don't think I gave it a moment's consideration back then in 1982. The world was changing.

'Have you seen the view that we have?' Joaquin said. His dark eyes were full of pleasure. He was being funny. For some reason to do with design, the balcony we stood on faced away from the city and the lights and what money could produce, and towards the steeply rising black hill that had always been there. A spottily inhabited final block intervened. Then darkness.

'You can see everything,' I said, trying to be funny. 'Grass. The other building.'

'It's interesting, you know? The fifth floor up, seven windows from the left – Spike, count, I show you, three, five, seven, okay? – there's an old man. Lives there. Very fat. Sunday afternoon, every Sunday afternoon this happens. He takes off all his clothes, walks round, one hour. Then he puts his clothes back on. Sits down again. I forget the important part, sorry, excuse me. Lives there with big fat old lady too, his wife, I guess. Sunday afternoon she goes out. She puts on hat and coat, goes out, shuts the front door, okay, then it is he takes off all his clothes, walks around, very pleased, very happy, one hour, puts back on, sits down, wife comes home. What the fuck, what, why, don't know. Can't say. Interesting, I guess. You know?'

'Maybe he just wants to have something that his wife doesn't know anything about. His naked hour once a week.'

'I guess,' Joaquin said. Then he brightened. 'Strange thing, though. Everyone knows about it. Just not his wife. We see him every Sunday, know he's gonna do this. Same with everyone in this block. They all know the fat old man naked over there, Sunday two thirty three thirty. We like it. Kate and Euan and me, Sunday lunch, whole Spartacist family, finish eating, come down and sit here on this balcony and watch the performance. Very, very nice.'

'Does he wank?'

'Does he – excuse me? Does he – oh, no. Nothing like that. Just a big pink fat baby, only that. How old are you, Spike – Spike, yes? I never heard your name before.'

'I'm sixteen,' I said.

'I see,' Joaquin said. 'And you just now start to think about things – is that the fact of things? When you are sixteen you start to think the world, it is not how I want it. How it must be. And one day you say to a man, a friend, a stranger like me, the world it can change and that friend or stranger he says …'

He was lost for a moment. I caught a whiff again of Joaquin's smell – rich, toffee-like, a sour metallic edge to it. He bared his teeth at me, a grin in the dark.

'What's Chile like?' I said boldly.

'Oh, you have discovered it,' Joaquin said. 'My English is not good because I was in England for ten years even. You have to know – my mother she kept us at home for three years after we came. They only found out I was there and must go to school when I was fourteen and then I spoke English for the first time. So, yes. I am Chilean and my English is not good.'

'I didn't mean that,' I said. 'I honestly only meant to ask what Chile is like.'

'Okay, I don't understand,' Joaquin said. 'But they told you about me, I see! So Chile it is a shithole now. There is no future there, it's all gone. My father he had friends, and now they are in Canada or Australia, Spain, maybe one in Nicaragua. Another shithole. Portugal, here in England. I don't know where they all go in the end. When I am a kid, they meet every week, twice a week, your house, my house, his house. Ten-minute walk from where you are living, two minutes in the car, or you ask your driver to stay where he is and finish his dinner, you are happy to walk. That kind of life. But now they are never going to see each other ever again. Those are the lucky ones.'

'What do you mean?' I said.

'The lucky ones are still alive, you know. My father was not so lucky. He is buried – his body is buried, excuse me – behind a police station somewhere. I guess. Maybe most of his body, not all the finger bones. They cut those off earlier. The usual story. He must have suffered before he died. My mother, she brings us to England.

'That was strange to me. The only time I go out of Chile before that was when I was eight. My father he is invited to East Germany. He is a hero of the German Democratic Republic and they ask him to come and bring his family, two

weeks' holiday and an award for international friendship. I
remember that very well. And then we are in England,
everything very strange, with my mother in this house in
London. All the time she is saying that he escaped, he is fine,
he is in Guatemala or in the – I don't know – Seychelles
maybe. She thinks he doesn't phone us because then, ring-
ring, the Chilean government guys they are listening in and
then they know where to find him. I have a sister. To her, too,
she says that when we are safe your father comes and finds us.
I don't know that she believes what she says. She says that all
the time we are in the flat, three years, just us in London,
Camden Town – you know Camden Town?'

'I'm sorry,' I said.

'Oh, sorry? Sorry is still to come,' Joaquin said. He was
quite calm, even with the appearance of enjoyment. He was
fixing me with a look of real concentration. From inside the
flat came a yell of disappointment – I think it was Percy
Ogden, groaning over some false or implausible move in an
argument. He hated to lose an argument, and he pretended
to hate an inadequate challenge in argument. Joaquin must
have heard this sound many times before, probably more
often than I had. He went on with his own familiar story.
'What happened, okay, is that a guy comes one day to our
house in Camden Town. I know this guy, I see his face from
the old days, and he comes in and sits with my mother for
two hours. Me I get told, go away, take your sister Rosa, nothing to hear. Then he goes. What I think now is that this guy
he shows my mother something, tells her something that
afterwards she doesn't think – no, she knows that there is no
husband in Guatemala or Seychelles. Hiding until the time is

safe. Then she understands, no question, he is no longer living, not writing because he is beyond all that. So the little family goes on. It has to. I don't know how my mother goes on. I guess if you have son, twelve, thirteen, and little girl too, then you have to, you must go on. So there it is. What happened to you?'

Joaquin's tone was guileless, apparently a real question. It was what people said when they noticed that a stranger had injured his face, for example, or torn his clothes, nothing more than that. In a moment I understood what he meant, perhaps enquiring about what series of injustices had set me off on the radical path, to be standing with a South American revolutionary on a balcony so small that, if either of us moved, our bodies briefly brushed against each other. But there was no injustice. The injustices were yet to come. Everything had been comfort, indulgence, opportunity, and the usual comment of the sixteen-year-old that none of this was *fair*. It wasn't fair, but that, I felt, would not keep me on the balcony with Joaquin. I said something absurd. It had worked before.

'I read *Das Kapital*,' I said.

'No,' Joaquin said, with amusement. 'No, you didn't read the *Capital*. It doesn't matter, but you don't need to say that. You like those others? You like the boy James, James Frinton?'

'Well, yes,' I said, surprised, adding lamely, 'He lives in a pub.' That was the most interesting thing about him.

'He's a strange one,' Joaquin said. 'I don't know why it's him who's the leader of that group you're in.'

I looked at him, amazed. 'He's not the leader,' I said. Then I remembered the world as it should be. I said, 'The group doesn't have leaders. How should it?' But of course I had been surprised, not because Joaquin had thought the group had a leader but because he had identified the wrong one. Ogden was the leader, the guiding political spirit.

'He listens to everything,' Joaquin said. 'Then maybe he says something. Everyone likes him. I guess I like him. His mother, you've met the mother? Kate says she's crazy, the father bastard only interested in money but can't make money. He's on his own, he knows that. Kate goes to see him once, just wants to see. What makes this guy? I tell you. If I am sixteen and woman, twenty, comes to see me, my mother very concerned about it. Those parents they don't care. He's on his own. He's going to make his life his self. It's like he's an orphan and, believe me, an orphan sixteen years old, that's a dangerous thing. Like me, an orphan. We say whatever we need to say.'

'Would you ever go back to Chile?' I said. I could see Joaquin at the head of an army of widows, orphans, exiles, revolutionaries, standing in a hurtling jeep in the hot sun, hurtling under arches of white bougainvillaea and hibiscus, his arms outspread in acknowledgement and welcome.

'Chile, no,' Joaquin said, bright with hilarity. 'That is over for me. Someone else can deal with it. Put it right. What I have to do is here and now. You know what I mean?'

What astonished me was to discover that Joaquin and I were exactly the same height. He had seemed so big, and so physically substantial with bone and hard flesh. I hardly knew how to place myself in relation to that physical scale. It was only now that I discovered our faces were in the same place, exactly level, six feet above the concrete floor of the balcony where marigolds, scarlet geraniums, marijuana plants, purple, pink, aquamarine and yellow snapdragons sat in pots, one warm evening, within the all-including rich, masculine smell of Joaquin, the revolutionary. Joaquin's kiss, when it came, was a fact of inevitable nature, like a warm front predicted on the news bulletin and then experienced without surprise, recognized rather, a fact quite external to our characters. I had no idea, or not much, that it was in me to kiss a twenty-two-year-old Chilean Spartacist until it was actually happening, and once it started, I had a moment of shock, almost alarm, that *I am a male and I am being kissed by another male* before a more certain and individual sense that I was meant to be kissed like this, with the solid arms around my back and shoulders, the thick trunk of the tongue in my mouth, pushing back at my own tongue, the rough rub of Joaquin's face against mine and, I knew, my right hand gripping the short curly hair on the flat back of Joaquin's head. His odour was all around me. I closed my eyes and was within it. I had kissed girls before, but I had never, it now seemed, *been* kissed. Everything in the world that was soft and tentative, pink, blushing and yielding was gone from my life in a moment. I had no idea where I found myself in this new world of definite statements and solid certainty. I had no idea where I was. From now on I resolved to devote my life to the liberation of the urban proletariat.

Joaquin pulled back for a moment, his arms still around me. His beautiful face was filled with laughter and amused joy.

'The way you were *looking* at me,' he said, and he plunged once more at my face.

Some sign of the alteration in me must have been there when we came back into the flat, and went upstairs again.

Those ten minutes changed everything, rerouted my neural pathways, told me where I stood in relation to happiness. Of course I had thought of men in such a way before, in ways that could be ignored or dismissed as a normal part of the development of the adolescent male (I am quoting). But I had not thought of Joaquin in all his detail – the rough texture of the skin on that arc between thumb and forefinger, the surprising pinkness his dark flesh produced at mouth and nipple. It was just Joaquin. He was not there on my mind until he was there in front of me. Then, of course, I should have seen him coming a mile off. The change in me would have been obvious to anyone, a brightening, an opening up, the way I looked around me and (I suppose) the way I was holding my arms as if something large and important had just been taken from them. Certainly, too, there was the more obvious truth that my face must have been rubbed raw and red by Joaquin's unshaven chin. It is the superficial and apparently insignificant physical facts that are essential in this world, the ones that last in the mind and that matter. Abstract principles, on the other hand, shift, alter and dissolve without anyone thinking twice about them. Joaquin came in off the balcony. Straight away he discarded his flapping yellow flip-flops. He walked in front of me barefoot up the stairs. Nobody in the upper flat could have heard when he stopped walking, barefoot, halfway up, and seized me for one more kiss, just by a poster of a monument. I now know it was of Vladimir Tatlin's tower for the Soviet revolution, the Monument to the Third Internationale, a tower a thousand feet high that was never built. It never could have been built.

In the sitting room, too, they were talking about the Soviets.

'We have to give up on Poland,' Kate was saying, her fingers working – I saw afterwards that she had a roll of Sellotape. She was rolling the end into a kind of ball, an anxiety-solution for her. 'I don't see the way forward.'

'There is always a way forward,' James Frinton said.

'Well,' Kate said, 'there's a choice between this so-called trade unionist, the imperialist-funded guy in Gdansk. And the government. They've run out of ideas. They've run out of trust. They've forgotten what they're there for. They're sclerotic. Seized up. Stalinist dinosaurs. Everything okay?'

'Yes, everything just fine,' Joaquin said. 'Fine, fine.'

Kate gave him an inscrutable look. It was the egotism, the solipsism of sixteen that made me believe she could know nothing of what had just happened to me. It is the wisdom of late middle age and my knowledge, extensively acquired through Joaquin's ribald narratives, of Kate's character that now makes me say she knew nothing of what had happened because she was not very observant or curious. If an event happened out of sight and it would not bring her to the fore in some substantive way, it hardly touched her. Her notion of love came in literary phrases, ones she had heard before and then chosen to write down to flag up her sensitivity.

Like an angel, the man on the bus
looked deeply and passionately into my eyes.

No bus, no man and nobody said anything. Her eyes passed over Joaquin and over me.

'The thing I wonder about,' Frinton said, 'is the Pope.'

'The Pope?' Ogden said. 'What's the Pope got to do with anything? That's your way forward, is it? Fuck the Pope!'

'The Pope, who's Polish,' Frinton said, explaining slowly.

'I know who he is,' Ogden said, matching him for a patronizing leisureliness of tone. 'I don't see what he's got to do with the Polish *problem*. He's essentially a head of state, a foreign state, a sclerotic one.'

'He turns up and he inspires the man from Gdansk,' Frinton said. 'He says one sentence and the government in Warsaw is fucked. Do you know what he said? *Don't be afraid.*'

'Means *Be afraid. Be afraid of me*,' Joaquin said. 'I know these motherfuckers. They were on the side of Pinochet in Chile.'

'There's a lot of Poles who call themselves Roman Catholic before anything else,' Frinton said. He didn't want to contradict Joaquin directly. Again I glimpsed the power Joaquin had within his lightness.

'It's insane,' Kate said. 'Why are they hanging on to that? These old fairytales! Lovely, lovely sugar-coated Candy Mountain where you can eat toffee apples for free from the trees forever, waiting for you when you die …' She was sitting down, but she pranced with her arms and torso, saying *for fwee fwom the twees fowever* to indicate that this wasn't her talking. 'And in the meantime here's your life – fifteen hours a day down a mine so that the owner can get rich. Most of the world's forgotten about God and all that. Humanity grows out of it. Not in Poland. Why?'

'Euan is not agreeing with this,' Joaquin said. 'Euan thinks—'

'Oh, Euan thinks,' Kate said, with a flurry of action through her loose hair. A biro tinkled to the linoleum floor as she rummaged over her head. 'Euan lives in the world as it should be, not the world as it is. The Pope Wojtyła comes to Poland. Two million people come to genuflect before him in Warsaw, another two million in Kraków. You know what Euan says? There weren't two million. At the most twenty thousand. Black propaganda by the Western media. They were the same people at every stop.'

'What Stalin said,' Ogden said. '"The Pope!" Do you know this? Somebody said something about the Vatican, what will the Vatican do about something. And Stalin said, "The Pope! How many battalions does the Pope have?" He had a point.'

'The Pope doesn't have battalions,' Joaquin said. 'He doesn't need them. You see – I know. I come from a country that knows about this crap. And we never had a Chilean pope neither.' By now he had, quite naturally, slipped away from me. He was perching on the arm of the sofa where Kate and Eric rested on each other, somewhat entwined in a comradely way.

'Nobody can say it isn't a problem,' Kate said. 'There must be a solution.'

'Define your question,' Tracy said.

'And get an answer,' Mohammed said, in catechistic response. 'Why doesn't Moscow act? They've acted before.'

Eric was bursting with laughter, I think unfeignedly. 'Define your question,' he was saying. 'Tracy, I love it when you strike a pose.'

'They think it's under control,' Ogden said, ignoring Eric. 'The general has taken charge. The puppet of imperialism is in jail, isn't he? Memory of the Pope is going to fade. What is there for the Soviets to do? They're busy in Afghanistan. They don't want to open up a second front. Snipers in Kraków? I don't think they're keen on that.'

'The imperialist puppet,' Frinton said, as if throwing Ogden's words back at him. 'He's called Wałęsa. Lech Wałęsa.' There was a touch of scorn in the precision with which he rendered that middle consonant, the difficult Polish crossed-out *l*. It would not be for some years that I would realize that, for him, too, this evening would change the world – this evening we were spending in a scruffy flat, its furniture mostly stolen from skips, posters on the greying wall from radical bookshops, stuck up, against the landlord's explicit prohibition, with Sellotape.

'The thing you need to remember,' Kate said, in the emollient, understanding tone that was her main means of control, 'is that it's Moscow holding the whole thing together. Threats and money. Or, to be precise, it's Brezhnev doing it.'

'Kate's a great believer in Brezhnev,' Joaquin said genially.

'I think I am,' Kate said bravely. 'Maybe we all should be. Brezhnev is the only thing holding all this together. He's not acting when he could act. And the Poles are pretty grateful for that, believe me. Do you know what Polish television was showing all last December? Films about Hungary 1956.'

'Do you know what Polish television was showing all January?' Joaquin said, trembling with laughter. '*Sissi*. Ten-part film for TV about the life of the Empress Elisabeth of Austria Hungary, the one the anarchist kills in Geneva. Make you cry. They fucking love that, you know.'

'Wałęsa's in jail,' Frinton said.

'Criminals in jail shock,' Kate said. 'Treasonous felon sent to prison in surprise government move.' Kate had comic voices. Like all of us, she sometimes spoke in mock tabloid headlines to ridicule the political positions of other people. 'Maybe he would have been shot a couple of decades back. I tell you one thing – Brezhnev's being very tolerant but he's not going to be around for ever. The next generation down in the Kremlin are real hardliners to a man. In ten years' time, with one of them in charge, you're not going to see anything like this Polish chaos being permitted by Moscow. One other prediction from me and that's your lot – a socialist Yugoslavia within the Soviet sphere of influence and control. It's only Tito keeping them on this whimsical path. They're going to face up to realities when he dies. What do you think, Spike?'

I hardly needed to think. I was spilling over. My tongue had no hesitation. I was speaking to Joaquin, and not to the woman Spartacist who had addressed me. 'I'd send in the troops. To Warsaw,' I said. 'Don't put up with that crap. Set the whole thing in order. If you let one have its way, before long the whole thing is going to fall. We can't have that.'

I don't know what I was expecting – perhaps applause – but not this embarrassed shifting of feet. 'Well, yes,' Eric said. He was still chuckling.

'We love your hard-left friend,' Kate said to Ogden. 'It's the sort of thing we like you bringing into our house.'

And I was their friend. Perhaps my expertise in constructing friendships had never developed. But my friendship with the Ogden lot and even with the Spartacists was progressing along lines that I felt I was in a position to understand. I had felt so secure and confident in its progress because in some ways its development had been defined from the start. It had aspects of fairness and merit about it. This was unlike most friendships. The process I had been experiencing over the last few days, leading me from Urch to Joaquin, had been much more like a job application. I had been auditioned and the possibilities and range of my conversation had been sampled. The only thing that was irregular was the impulsive gesture of Joaquin in kissing me. And then, of course, the whole thing was revealed as irrational, based in inclination and whim like anything else, including the application for jobs. There is always a Joaquin, whose likes and urges everyone knows about and understands. He always changes everything.

'I thought you were going to make us a cup of tea,' Tracy said.

'I'll make you some tea,' Joaquin said. 'Just for Tracy, though.' He left the room, something saucy in his walk.

'He's so sweet,' Tracy said, but she looked, smiling, only at me. I sat next to her again. 'You went to James Frinton's, right? Did you go in?'

'Yes, he came in,' James Frinton said, from the other side of the room. 'It's not so weird. My mum said hi. My brother was doing his homework. Then you lot turned up and we came here.'

'Next time,' Ogden said, 'we can pick you up at your place. It wouldn't make much difference.'

'If—' James Frinton said, then stopped himself. 'When's the next time?'

'Were you going to say if there's a next time? James? Were you really?' Tracy Cartwright said, her slow eyes blinking. 'What's going to happen?'

'Of course there's a next time,' James Frinton said, as if repeating what somebody had just said. 'We like having Spike around. He can come any time.'

'Spike's a find,' Percy Ogden said. These tributes were dutiful, but my eyes were on the door. I was waiting for Joaquin to return. I knew in my bones he would come with a cup of tea for me too. At that moment everything depended on the answer to this question: would Joaquin, in the kitchen, consider that I, Spike, might like something? The world turned on that question, and no other. But Ogden was continuing to talk. 'What's the best thing to do? Are we on for that CND rally next Thursday? Is there anything before that? Anything at all?'

I waited. In less than a minute Joaquin would come through the door. I would see if he had thought about me, and about what I wanted. Now I see something else about that minute. What would have been started by Ogden's question, *anything before that*. Even then it was not an innocent question. Friends did not engage with each other in the time-tabled way that the question implied. There was a lack of innocence from my side, too, in wondering whether there would be anything before the agreed disruption of the CND rally in less than a week's time. I wanted to be with Joaquin. I guessed that the thing shaping the answer to Ogden's question was whether I could be included, and in what. The activities of the Spartacists were large set-piece movements and gatherings, but also smaller engagements, often in pairs. Those larger gatherings included participation in or, more often, disruption of substantial protests. Organized large-scale suggestions to the authorities, we thought of them, like three thousand signatories to a petition, turning up in the same place. Those would be my next stages of engagement. Beyond that were the paired-up actions, which at this moment I humbly accepted I would not be invited to, still less undertake on my own. I did not grasp the reasons why, however.

It was not quite clear to me why the others in Ogden's group did some things but not others. None of them, for instance, stood and sold the Spartacist newspaper outside the library or at football matches, even though I guess Ogden, Eric and perhaps Mohammed would have been happy to. From the Spartacists' point of view, this was not a moment of retail exchange but an opportunity to express the collective opinion seamlessly and correctly. There was no possibility that an anarcho-syndicalist like Tracy would have done the job, or a bourgeois single-issue obsessive like Frinton. (They liked both of them. They shook their heads over them.) And even for the others it was a lot to ask, insulting the outraged Tories, telling supporters of the parliamentary fucking Labour Party where they should think again, explaining in close detail what the important facts here were – that would be to intelligent, curious, open people with a Trotskyite bent like me, I suppose. Too much to expect.

But other things restricting my future input were not so apparent to me yet. I don't think I understood how much the group protected Joaquin. His confident swift presence seemed so little to need it. He laughed at what might be thought vulnerabilities. But the group mostly understood that it could be catastrophic for someone in a fragile immigration status to be arrested for any reason. We were to take responsibility, and Joaquin was going to leg it. I saw what this meant three months later when Joaquin's manner had persuaded the others that I could come out with him and Euan on a sloganeering jaunt at three a.m. on a Friday night. (It hadn't taken my father long to give up on me. My Friday nights were always for Joaquin and Park Hill flats. Sometimes now I wonder if my father knew how old I was.) The rule about sloganeering turned out to be this: never fewer than three if Joaquin was there. One held the can of white paint. Another was the writer of the slogan with a brush. Joaquin stood back and directed and watched out. He had to be able to run. He must not have any of the incriminating properties on him. That evening, the other two had to run purposefully into the arms of the police, who were sweatily bounding out of their panda. We had to make it look convincing, too. I was no good at it, and got away. Euan did it shamelessly. He was well known to the police. They never knew a third person was involved. He was in bed when I got back. The paint on my hands was soon smeared all over his chest. The slogan had been his idea. We had nearly managed to finish it. At lunchtime the next day, I saw it from the bus going home up West Street. 'ARM THE POOR', it almost completely said.

In the end, I was one of them, the one who stuck around, and not just because of Joaquin. The others drifted off. Ogden and Frinton, of course, Mohammed I don't know about, and Tracy died. This morning in the year 2020, I was woken by the radio alarm, switched, I'm afraid, to Radio 4 these days. After the summary of the news, a guest started to speak. It was the anniversary of the murder of the London teenager Stephen Lawrence. Another event, this time a gross and public insult of a woman Somali refugee, had taken place three weeks

earlier. The distinguished campaigner, barrister and community spokesman Lord Milne was being interviewed.

'Is this helpful?' the interviewer said. 'These calls for
extreme and direct action? In these tragic circumstances?'

'I am not making these calls,' Eric replied grandly. 'I merely
state that I have sympathy for those who do make such calls.
What, you may ask, are we expected to do when history
repeats itself in such a way? Are we to sit in the stalls in the
theatre of history and applaud? When it repeats itself, not as
tragic circumstances but as Marx said it would, as farce, what
are we to do? Should we perhaps laugh?'

'I taught him that,' I said. 'Introduced him to it. Joaquin,
I introduced Eric Milne to what he's talking about.'

'What's all this?' Joaquin mumbled into his pillow.

'*The Eighteenth Brumaire of Louis Bonaparte,*' I said. I got
up. The dogs were clamouring for their morning walk.

The lives that we were to lead were set in those days in the
early 1980s. The lives that we now follow are not shaped by
the commitments and principles we then endorsed. Most of
them were ridiculous and impossible. I can hardly remember
the rationales that justified them. But the paths were entered
upon. The lives of politics, of saying what the world might be,
as well as putting on a suit and kissing the Queen's hand,
being admitted to her Privy Council. What to make of it.

I feel that these public lives began, in some sense, the
Thursday after I first went to the flat in Park Hill. Many
things had happened in the meantime. I had returned to the
flat on my own, two days later. Joaquin and I had fucked for
six hours. (I am now fifty-three. Joaquin is the only person I
have ever fucked.) I had bought another copy of Marx's

Capital, so that my father would not see that his copy had been read. I had told Tracy about Joaquin. I was sixteen. I had to tell someone. She was sixteen. She had to tell someone. She told the school. And then I was properly in the Ogden group of outcasts.

We went to break up the CND rally. We didn't dress up in any special way. The faces pouring into the City Hall: clear, open, trusting, clean-scrubbed. These people were dressed quite as the Spartacists were dressed. Sometimes a 1950s tweed jacket. Otherwise the usual stuff. A lot of army surplus, a couple of dozen women in Afghan coats. There was an excited buzz within the hall, a decent ladylike excitement, like a mass gathering of Sunday schools. It was important that we were in the middle of a row in the balcony, in two quite separate groups. It should be as difficult as possible for the organizers to evict us. We reckoned we could get three solid uninterrupted minutes of disruption, given a good start.

A lectern was placed at the front of the stage. Nine chairs stood in a row behind. Nine chairs! But this was CND's high point. They had, in 1982, nine speakers prepared to spout their sanctimonious rubbish, aimed at depriving not just the West but the Soviet bloc of its means of support and defence. They were queuing up for their opportunity to speak to an audience as stupid as they were, back then in 1982. Of course we weren't going to be allowed to listen to all nine. I looked behind me, quite casually, at the stewards. They were amateurs in tabards. The nearest were a pair of weedy teenagers. What contempt I had managed to acquire! The speakers filed in to bursts of applause here and there. More organized applause followed when the convenor told us to applaud. It was all like the headmaster's plan to tell selected members of the audience what questions they were allowed to ask. Ogden was next to me. His face was red. He was biting his lip. His full concentration was on the stage. I thought, But this really matters to him! The same thought, too, that had come to me in the first moments of Joaquin's touch, that I was doing it, I was actually going to do it. The applause died down. The first speaker was introduced. They had not been able get the monsignor who ran the whole shebang: he was in Middlesbrough tonight. That monsignor had never known such a fucking triumph. He had never been in such demand, the whore. But he had sent his friend, a Roman Catholic priest too. Joaquin was quite calm in outward appearance from here, but I knew what joy this announcement must be giving him. I do not know how he stopped himself giving a little groan of pleasure. He wanted to fuck with the Roman Catholic Church almost above all things. They were the ones who had fucked with his father. And I wanted to fuck with them too. My hand was on the handle of the device in my bag. My bag was a school satchel. It was on my lap. Innocent days. Nobody in 1982 had thought to search any of the nine bags that the nine of us had brought in.

The priest came up to the lectern. I almost said pulpit. The lights in the auditorium dimmed. Another piece of luck. It would take them a bit longer to identify us in the pious semi-dark. He began to speak. He had a dry, practical voice that you couldn't imagine praying. It had a peremptory, impatient quality. I was glad he was down there. He began by saying how happy he was for the turn-out – the idealism – so many young people – the importance of peace – the importance of love—

The word *love* was so preposterous in his voice.

—and he thought he would start not with a prayer but by remembering all those who had been killed in war and other episodes of violence in the thirty-seven years since the first nuclear weapon had been dropped on Hiroshima. The millions of dead. He suggested that we remember them in a two-minute silence.

What a piece of fucking luck.

The silence began. After eight seconds Joaquin broke in. I didn't think he would last even that long.

'Fuck pacifism!' he yelled. 'Fuck your fucking Pope!'

'Fuck your disarmament!' I could hear Tracy screaming.

'Fuck you! Fuck you! Fuck you!' a voice was shouting. It was mine. It felt like the day I became a man. The football rattle was out of my bag and making a din. The others had theirs – Eric's klaxon, Mohammed and Kate on football whistles. The others were throwing bags of flour, some breaking up in mid-air, showering the pacifists in the stalls with clouds of powder. This was one of the reasons to be in the balcony. The noise was immense. The priest looked up at us with weary distaste. He said nothing. The flour was not going to hit him. It was as if he was not going to break with his promise that two minutes' silence would be held. It was absurd, too, that the stewards, cast into the exercise of reverence, were looking about them. They were only tentatively coming up to throw us out.

'Arm the fucking poor!' Mohammed yelled. 'Arm the global fucking poor! Arm the revolution!' They reached him first. I thought our time was up. I kept on sounding the football rattle. All around me were angry or frightened faces. I caught a glimpse of Joaquin, his set, determined jaw. Some poor sap started hitting him with a copy of a newspaper – *Peace Times*, I bet. Oh, you fool, you child, I thought. As I knew he would, Joaquin drew back his fist and hit the pacifist in the face, hard. Bleating broke out. Now Joaquin was running for it, over the backs of chairs, his size-thirteen boots in the laps of the two-minute silencers. All the time he was blowing his whistle. Ogden and I pushed after him. 'You're not going anywhere,' a timid teenager in a tabard was trying to say to us. 'This is a police matter, this is a—' Kate and Tracy were behind us. I hit the teenager as hard as I could. I had seen how it was done. Afterwards, the man you hit stands shocked, his hands to his bleeding nose. The last thing I saw was the smooth face of James Frinton, still in his seat by the aisle. He had brought no bag. I supposed now it had been agreed that he would not protest. Instead he was going to stay there. He would report back. We were not interested in what the idiots were going to say from the stage. We only wanted to know what effect the action had had. Nobody would have thought he had anything to do with us, the Spartacists. He caught my eye. He gave an immense, reckless grin and a massive wink, his face almost folding in half. There was nothing discreet about the gesture. But if you had seen it – if a pacifist in his seat were to have seen it – I'm pretty sure he would have thought a satiric point was being made. James Frinton was giving me a Norman Wisdom wink in support. Anyone who saw it would have thought he was saying, 'You dickhead.' But in detail, from my side: 'Don't you ever take the piss out of my mother, you dickhead.' In still more specific and admonitory detail: 'You – you poor fool – you are going to stay like this for ever. A boy, with a boy's principles.' James Frinton gave a wink. He thought he knew what growing up meant. I was to see that gesture again. Only years later did it occur to me that in no circumstances could anyone ever say that James Frinton had smashed up an orderly political movement in 1982. He was there. He knew that disturbances were planned. That was all that could be said of him. He knew that disturbances were inevitable.

Part two

I have always been interested in the processes of friendship. Dr Johnson said that friendship was a stuff in need of constant repair, which makes me think of my oldest friendships, the ones of decades, as objects that have been nailed, pinned and stuck together, stitched up, altered and added to without any ultimate plans. Probably in the end you notice that the thing has seven wheels of different sizes, a length of yak wool is loosely nailed to the rear corner (one of thirteen corners at different levels) and the coat of purple paint has only been applied here and there. It holds together. It makes me think, this aphorism of Dr Johnson, that if friendship had been put together solidly, with foresight from the start, these ad hoc staplings and patchwork would not be necessary.

I was bad at friendship when I was a child. This was the case even before my mother packed her bags and left. You can see the causes of both my incompetence at friendship, and my mother's departure. My father never really saw the point of human connection. He had a wife not because he much liked her but because he thought that a wife was what you had. Perhaps my mother was no better at human connection, or could not teach it. She was warm and open, but her friendships were intensely begun and petered out quickly, I think, as she took to venting her complaints. I had to analyse what friendship was made of from first principles.

There was a boy in my class at junior school. I was crazy about him. He dressed much as others did, a white shirt, grey shorts, grey knee-length socks and brown shoes, but there was something about his presentation that set him apart, a kind of crispness. I was crumpled and untidy by the end of the day, but the boy I admired remained bright, clean and sharp-edged. Did he not sweat? Some things about him must have been his mother's contribution – unusually for that time, his hair was neat and short – but his personal immaculacy could only have been attained because he himself valued it so. He seemed to me extraordinarily distinguished in all things, not least in his name, which was Ivan.

The construction of friendships must be simple. You see the substance that results around you all the time. I asked my mother to invite two friends round for tea: Ivan and some other boy. There was a small craze at the time for having friends round in this way. My mother was surprised. My father openly thought that those extra-curricular social exchanges should be limited to annual happenings. He admitted the necessity of birthday parties. Ivan and the other boy came round. I don't think it was a success. Certainly the next day someone who hadn't been there asked when my parents were going to get divorced. I have a sense of the kitchen door being slammed. An invitation quickly followed from Ivan. In retrospect it was too quick. An obligation was being taken care of. The matter was closed. At the time it filled me with happiness. I loved to walk next to Ivan. I loved to hear his faint, non-committal tones. He was my very best friend. I went to tea. No other boy from school was there, just Ivan's three elder brothers. I shrank back, daunted. Nevertheless the structure of friendship had been erected, within which future incidents could play out securely. Ivan was my friend.

At some point after that, a couple of weeks later, I was standing next to Ivan as some playground crisis reached its peak – some kid pushed a girl's face into the mud. The bully ran away screaming with excitement.

'What do you think of that?' I said feebly to Ivan. 'Him doing that to her?'

Ivan turned to me. His expression was astonishing: full of loathing and utter resentment. He felt passionately about me. My attentions to him, my proximity to him together formed a shocking injustice.

'Why the hell would I tell you what I think?' Ivan said. He didn't even push me. There was no urge to waste physical energy on pushing me, or fighting. We were not friends. The encounter was over.

*

'And this is your room, my dear sirs,' the lady said. She was clean, bosomy, wearing an apron over a white cardigan and black skirt. The apartment-pension was on the third floor of the quiet street off the Kurfürstendamm. We had taken a clattering brass-framed lift up to the front door. She had let us carry our own suitcases from the front desk of the pension. 'This is the breakfast room,' she said, gesturing with a turn and a smile. 'Breakfast from seven thirty to ten, but it would be a kindness to Marlene, who helps, if you would try not to arrive at two minutes to ten. A hard-boiled egg. If you would like anything other than that, with cheese and ham and the usual, please inform me the night before. That will be fine? Very good. And here is your room.'

Ogden followed her in, making no comment, not matching the smiling and nodding that I was offering. He dropped his bag. He flung himself on to the bed by the window without taking his boots off. There was a clean white counterpane. It was a beautiful room, clean and airy, a wide window giving on to the thick sunlit foliage of a lime tree in the street. The proprietor's smile hardly changed at Ogden's muddy boots on the bed. Perhaps it fixed a little. 'And you are here for two nights,' she said, switching to English. She must have guessed that I was the only one of us who could speak German. Perhaps she politely put Ogden's roughness down to not understanding something.

'No,' Ogden said. He massaged his temples, his eyes shut. 'We're leaving tomorrow. One night only.'

'It's actually two nights,' I said. 'We have stuff to arrange tomorrow, Percy. I don't know how long it will take, to be honest.' I was on the verge of apologizing to Frau Dittberner for my friend. I settled for smiling warmly. It was Percy, after all, who I was going to be spending the next two weeks with. She smiled warmly back, withdrawing.

'It's pretty nice,' I said. Ogden lit a cigarette. There was no other response.

I was in charge of the arrangements. The first of these had been to find a place to stay in West Berlin. It was only for two nights. Still, I was concerned about my choice. This fortnight was the first time I had been away with Percy Ogden. Things had happened since we had last spent much time together. I wanted the journey to begin well. The tone of the place in West Berlin was important to get right.

Ogden had arrived at the airport at the utmost pitch of lateness. I had long ago given up. I had got on the plane when he was escorted on by officials. A couple of people in business class even gave an ironic burst of applause. We had been sitting there for some time.

'A close-run thing,' Ogden had said, sitting down.

'I'm sure you had important things to do,' I said.

'There was a phone call out of the blue. Went on and on. Had to be dealt with.'

'Well, you're here now.'

'Looking forward to it.'

Our lives were quite different now. Ogden had gone to London after university. He was working for a Labour MP. I had gone back to the town where we grew up. I was a year and a half into a PhD. I was starting to be given teaching work. I had all the time in the world. The suggestion that we go together for a two-week trip to East Germany had come out of the blue. I had agreed. I had actually never spent time in a socialist country. We would do it as holidaymakers. I had suggested going by rail, ferry and road, which would be cheaper. In the end Ogden had got his way. We had taken a plane from London, changing in Frankfurt. This was the requirement on commercial flights to Berlin reached by agreement between the four powers who had divided the city between them in 1945. There were other oddities about the formal arrangements, including the interesting fact (I had spent an hour at the airport in London reading a guidebook) that German residents of the three Western segments were not subject to call-up for military service by the Federal government in Bonn. This part of Germany was physically separated from the rest by a large wall.

We had arrived at the pension in West Berlin. I had found it by luck. A Germanist colleague of mine from university, when appealed to, had said, 'Oh, anywhere in Charlottenburg should be fine.' I had acquired a greasy catalogue, both flimsy and thick, containing long lists of the hotels and pensions of West Berlin. I had dismissed the childish temptation to book a place that would demonstrate some fact about capitalism. An exploitative fleapit where the unemployed moaned through the walls at night. Or a palace of vulgar luxury, shining our own faces back at us from the spotlit mirrors in the lifts. I think we had passed the age when everything needs to prove a large point about society. I had plucked the Pension Dittberner from the page at random. The places we would be staying in the DDR, for the next two weeks, had more or less chosen themselves – there were fewer options. The price categories had been clearly indicated.

'Why don't we set off tomorrow?' Ogden said. He put out his cigarette in the bedside ashtray. He rubbed his eyes with his fists. He sat up on his bed.

'I don't know how long it's going to take at the Reisebüro,' I said.

'The – oh, the office in charge of stuff over here,' he said. 'Isn't it all arranged? I thought you'd arranged everything.'

'You need to show them your itinerary,' I said. 'They look it over, they check the hotel bookings in the places you're going to, they give you a visa, then you're off. I don't think it's complicated. We'll go first thing tomorrow morning. I think they issue everything you need the same day. I was being cautious, I expect. In case it's an overnight thing.'

'International co-operation,' Ogden said. 'Or lack of it. The Westerners sitting in the office here, looking over your application. Taking their time. Don't want to be too speedy and efficient and helpful to their opposite numbers. Or anyone proposing to go and visit the other side of the Wall.'

'They're not Westerners,' I said. 'I don't think they are.'

'They're over here, though,' Ogden said. 'What, do they live in the East and come here to work every day? And then go back home at night?'

'I expect so,' I said. 'I can't think what else they would do.'

'They don't—' Ogden said, but checked himself in what he was about to ask. Then he smiled brightly. 'I don't know about you but I'm a bit starving. I haven't had anything since break-fast. Phil always says you should never skip lunch if you want to get work done. It's nearly five – well, four English time. Let's go.'

At the time, I thought nothing much of Ogden starting a question before thinking better of it. It was not hard to work out what he was about to ask. He was thinking of the DDR office workers who, every day, crossed the border to come to work in the West, and every evening went back over the same border. In time, I was to discover that in fact many inhabitants of the DDR had the right to travel in the West for professional purposes. It was not as unusual as we had been led to believe. Ogden's question, if he had posed it, was one based in more human and irrational urges. He had been about to ask why the clerks in the Reisebüro didn't just leave their office in the West, walk out into the street and never return. The answer would have been a simple one. These clerks had stable and well-supported lives. They certainly believed in their country. They could understand that human happiness was not a universal condition in the other Germany, or beyond. Of course they returned home each night. I would have had no hesitation in being able to explain that. The aspect of Ogden's restraint that I might have paid more attention to was why he did not want to ask this question now, of me. Perhaps it was a delusion, but in the past no question had been out of bounds. I should have understood straight away that his behaviour had changed – had been changed by university, by a year working for a Labour MP, or something else entirely. The name of the Labour MP was Phil.

We left the pension building, walking down the wide flights of stairs. Almost immediately we were on the Kurfürstendamm, which I understood was the main shopping street of West Berlin. It was a beautiful afternoon, warm and bright. The street was foreign in striking ways. The pavement was immensely wide. In the centre of it were placed glass vitrines in a row, containing objects from the shops that stood behind – exquisite little arrangements of hats and socks, boxed photographs of people having good times in restaurants. I would have liked to pause to examine them.

'Is it too early for dinner?' Ogden said. 'This looks like a bit of a tourist area. We ought to find a district where ordinary people live. Where's your map?'

Together we examined it. It was uninformative, giving only the names of districts. One was called Wedding, which struck us as funny. But that was too far. In a practical way, I hadn't done much investigation of the shape of West Berlin apart from the location of the Reisebüro.

We would not be spending much time in this part of the city.

'Do any normal people live in West Berlin?' I said. 'It isn't a normal city.'

'I expect some people do,' Ogden said. 'They go about their normal lives. They take their children to school. They watch game shows on TV. They go for walks on Sunday in the countryside.'

'I don't think they can do that,' I said. 'The Wall goes all the way round. There isn't any countryside that they can get to.'

'We're getting off the point,' Ogden said. 'Where's the nearest underground station? What do they call it – U-Bahn, is it?'

We carried on walking in the same direction. The atmosphere was unusual. The street was made up of one luxury Western business after another, with cinemas, hotels, clothes shops and other retail experiences. It was very much like the main shopping streets of a rich British city, but the width of the pavement gave it an empty feeling. There were few people walking along. They were lost in the space. They hardly had anything to do with each other. Nobody was shopping or, rather, buying anything.

Some of the businesses were cafés and restaurants, jutting out onto the pavement with covered terraces. They were the busiest parts of the street. Waiters were standing at the back of each, looking out for a customer who needed something.

The one we were now coming up to was called Androvič, the name of the restaurant spelt out in a neon sign above the awning. It had a menu on a pedestal at the entrance to the terrace. I veered over to take a look at it.

'To be honest, I'm starving,' Ogden said, following me after a thoughtful pause. 'What does it look like?'

'Not too bad,' I said, meaning that it was not obviously expensive.

'There ought to be rules about how to discover a good place and stay away from rip-offs in places you don't know,' Ogden said. 'I need a me.'

'What do you mean, "I need a me"?'

'I need someone to sort me out the way I sort Phil out. I need a me. What sort of food is it?'

'They have pork and sausages,' I said. 'And – oh. I think it's from Yugoslavia. Serbischen is a part of Yugoslavia, isn't it? Serbia?'

'That's right,' Ogden said, not sarcastically but encouragingly. 'It could be good. I'm hungry.'

We went in. We stood there until a waiter at the back noticed us. He was wearing the traditional outfit of his profession, a white shirt, a bow-tie and a long black apron over black trousers, though his shoes were American trainers. Waiters walk a good deal in the course of the day. Those shoes must have been a practical solution. He hurried over to us in an impatient way, gesturing widely across the terrace. There were several empty tables. I think he was suggesting without saying anything that we should take our pick and sit down. We did so. In two minutes another waiter came over with menus that had the Serbo-Croat names for the dishes, but also translated into German and English. The prices were very reasonable. We began to relax.

I had seen Ogden regularly since we left school. He had chosen to go to Manchester University to study economics. Three of us had got into Oxford – me, James Frinton and Tracy Cartwright. Ogden, like Eric and Mohammed, had maintained that Oxford was not the place for people like us. He had not applied. We had argued about this a good deal at the time. But Ogden and I had still met up in the vacations. When my father committed suicide, Ogden wrote a kind letter. He had asked if I wanted to go to stay with him 'to get away from things'. I actually had somewhere to go to get away from things, but it was thoughtful of him. Tracy and James Frinton, with whom I had gone to university, were the ones I was not very close to as time went on. Ogden, who had gone somewhere else, had carried on making an effort. I had made an effort in his direction, too. Sometimes a phone call would come late at night, and it would be Ogden saying he had thought about it, and that I should move my PhD to a college in London, where I could live with him. Or he would suggest that we should go on holiday to India together to look at temples. I was touched but puzzled by these kind suggestions out of the blue. Often, when he rang, Ogden was calling from a phone box. He would go on talking until he ran out of ten-pence pieces, persuading and cajoling until his final sentences were blotted out by the telephone system's warning bleeps. Quite frequently he was drunk when he called me. He could begin, without saying anything else, by howling down the phone, '*GREEEAAASBROUGH*,' whether it had been me or Joaquin who had picked it up. Joaquin would hand it to me without comment. He would go back to his book. The excitement from that end would die down; comments about the horrors in the House of Commons would run their course; Ogden would make an enquiry about my work; derision-flavoured advice about ideology and theory would be swiftly run through. Finally the sequence of suggested trip, lyrical evocation, cajoling, encouragement, disappointed reiteration, insistence. Then the beeps from the telephone system. The next time he rang it would all have been forgotten.

'Maybe he loves you,' Joaquin said from time to time.

I had once agreed to a suggestion, and had spent a weekend at Ogden's place in South London when there was a big demo planned. His flatmates were away. There was no suggestion that Joaquin could come – it was one of the things that had been established between us that Joaquin's name was not going to be mentioned. The flat was a conversion, and the conversion had been adapted again by a greedy landlord – it would have done quite well for one person, or a couple in a bedroom with a tiny boxroom and a small sitting room. The sitting room had been turned into a bedroom that the others had to walk through to get to the kitchen. Ogden had the bedroom, which stank of old cigarette smoke. I stayed in the tiny, foetid, barely windowed boxroom that his flatmate Sue normally lived in from Monday to Thursday. On the Saturday morning, lying in bed waiting for sounds of movement to come from Ogden's part of the flat, I found a half-empty tub of hummus just under the bed, thick with mould. Just by it, there was a more recently abandoned used condom. It was what London living for people our age was like. We went to an Irish folk night on the Friday; we went to the demo; we had a dissection of it in the pub the rest of Saturday with some kids we'd marched alongside, who I'd never seen before and never saw again (I can't speak about Ogden). Late Sunday morning I got on a coach after a big fry-up breakfast in Tooting. I turned down another couple of suggestions from Ogden, but a year after that I agreed to go with him for two weeks to the German Democratic Republic. To see socialism, Ogden said.

'In two weeks that one is never going to mention my name,' Joaquin had said. 'And you know why?'

'Ideological differences, these days,' I said. 'He believes in parliamentary democracy and working for change through mainstream party policy. He doesn't have anything to say to people like you.'

'Bullshit,' Joaquin said. It was true that my ideological differences from Ogden were also quite marked. We overlapped. But I had not yet got to the point where I thought bourgeois voting rituals would ever change anything. There was a quality of the unspoken whenever I was in the same room with Ogden. Was it down to unresolved differences in ideological assumptions? Joaquin had reached his own conclusion. He thought love was at the bottom of it, or something that thought of itself as love. I didn't think so. Ogden and I had agreed to save some money by sharing a room (with single beds) all through the trip. The Interhotel network that Western travellers were required to stay in was quite expensive.

The menu in the Yugoslavian restaurant on the Kurfürstendamm had been simple but puzzling. It asked you to choose a meal, all straightforwardly priced, its components described in a succession of lists. Although the menu was long, and the number of possible meals was high, this was because the twenty or so items the restaurant provided could be permutated in a lot of different ways. We had taken a long time to choose. We thought we had gone for two quite different meals. But, in the event, the food that arrived looked very similar. It was served on strange dishes, with numerous indentations for different items, each filled with either meat or vegetables in a thick brown sauce. The waiter placed them in front of us with an exaggerated flourish. It might have been satirical. I comforted myself with the thought that after this we would no longer have to think about the problem of finding food until lunchtime the next day. I started to eat.

'Look at that man over there,' Ogden said. He lit a cigarette.

It was hard to do so, because Ogden was showing an interest in someone behind me. I turned. The man was in fact at the next table, no more than eight feet away. He was so close that he looked up at me, startled. He was neatly dressed, completely white hair brushed with a parting and a white moustache. He had a German newspaper in front of him folded vertically. His face was very pink. He gave the impression of cleanliness. I made an embarrassed pretence at calling the waiter over to ask for some salt, as if I had turned to look for him: the waiter was surprised, partly because there could hardly be anything saltier than their food, but also because, as he pointed out, there was salt in front of me. I apologized.

'How old do you think he is?' Ogden said.

'That man? Sixty-five, seventy? Why?'

'I'm looking out down the street and seeing all these Germans. They look so nice and neat and happy. The retired ones, I mean. He's really enjoying his dinner. But if he's sixty-five he would have been twenty in 1943. Look at him shovelling in his Serbian pork stew. Do you think when he was our age he was shovelling dead bodies out of gas chambers?'

'Hard to say,' I said. I thought he was eating neatly and carefully, not shovelling anything in at all. 'He might have been a resistance fighter, I suppose. Maybe he was just a fireman or something like that.'

'Or look at her – this one. She's just stopped to have a look at the glove display, over there, the one with the two terriers. She's just the right age, I reckon.'

'Right age for what?'

'Hitler Youth. Or she could have been Goebbels's mistress. That fur collar and the dogs' little tartan coats. She likes things just so. Always has done. You can tell. It was tough after the war for her, but Goebbels gave her a painting by Renoir. One he'd acquired from a rich Jewish family – they'd tried to bribe him with it. He didn't much like it, but it would do for – what's her name?'

'Ingrid.'

'Ingrid liked it. And she liked it much more after the war when she could sell it to an American collector. Lived on the proceeds for five years. During the difficult times.'

'Lovely. Do you think they know each other?' I made a backwards gesture of the head, indicating the dapper man at the table behind me.

'They do, but they're not going to greet each other in public. That would be fatal. They'll see each other at the annual party for the old gang, the one to celebrate Wolfi's birthday. They'll kiss each other then. Talk about old times.'

'Who's Wolfi?'

'They don't refer to the Leader by name. Mr A. H. Not even in private.'

'Oh, I see,' I said. I always relished Ogden's ability to spin speculation out of nothing. It was with beady enjoyment that he watched the neat and, surely, completely respectable woman in late middle age trot off with her two terriers, one black and one white, like an advertisement for whisky.

'This food is terrible,' Ogden said. He spoke quite mildly, without much in the way of disappointment. In fact being able to dismiss the food, coming after his indulgence in an elaborate and baseless fantasy of war criminals, definitely cheered him up. His manner from the airport to now had been veiled in some way, covered with a layer of assertive self-importance, performed bored indifference, of a clear intention not to engage with me. In short, he had been stiff. But now that the food had been agreed to be terrible we could move on. He looked at me, apparently for the first time. His gaze was blue, wide, intense and blank. He could have been looking at a monument. 'This is going to be fun,' he said.

West Berlin, even then, had a reputation as a late-night city, but all that we experienced that evening was a walk past old-fashioned cafés with pink signs in the cursive writing of giants, a pause in front of a cinema to work out that the apparently poignant German melodrama with a poetic title was, in fact, the very ordinary American film now playing at the Gaumont at home, extravagantly translated. We saw some sights: we walked past a church that had been ripped to pieces by a wartime bomb, its fragmentary tower supported by a modern shell. We supposed they'd left it there to remind people either of what they had done or what had been done to them. One of the two. We found ourselves standing in front of a preposterous Chinese gate, the entrance to the zoo. On our way back, my map in my hand, we were walking through the bus station. We found ourselves in the middle of an unadvertised market of dereliction, dozens of victims of the savagery of capitalism selling themselves or vials of oblivion. The centre, or one of the centres of heroin and prostitution in this money-making island city, kept going by the artificial support of the imperialist powers without much thought for the lives of the victims. We had a lot to say about these final results of historical forces, in ways that afterwards turned out to have been abstract and impersonal.

There were so many bars. We thought we would go into one, called the Old-timer. We thought it might have more retired National Socialists in it for our entertainment (I've since learnt that 'old-timer' is what Germans call vintage cars). In fact, it was a gay bar, which we realized, embarrassingly, after we had ordered two beers. For different reasons we had to get through the following half-hour without referring to this. We spent the time going over our planned itinerary, in more detail than we probably needed to. Our heads were lowered over the sheet of paper, which I had in my jacket pocket in an envelope – the Reisebüro would need to look at it the next day. It should not be crumpled.

We walked back to the Pension Dittberner, with a lot of pauses to consult the map. We were two or three streets away when Ogden suddenly said, 'What do you think happened to her?'

Perhaps sometimes people have a telepathic sense of what old friends are referring to, and not just in films. In reality it is not so. I had no idea who Ogden was talking about.

'I have to say – at the time I heard I couldn't believe it. She changed her name at Oxford, didn't she?'

Then I understood. He was talking about Tracy Cartwright.

'A lot of people changed their name,' I said. 'It was a weird kind of Oxford thing.'

'But she kept it up afterwards. It must be hard,' Ogden said. 'I mean, you've had twenty years of hearing people say, "Tracy," when they want you. I mean, if I said I wanted to be called Stephen I wouldn't automatically respond when I heard the name. I just wouldn't. What did she want to be called?'

'Alexandra,' I said. There was something sad about the change of name, let alone how the story had finished. I didn't see her after the first term – in the end Tracy wouldn't have wanted to hang out with someone like me. Not just because I would probably have forgotten and called her Tracy. It took me a day to realize what had happened. The girl who had died, in a shared flat in London, was called Alexandra Cartwright. That was not someone I knew. It was a year after we'd left university. I didn't understand until the evening I opened the door of the flat and found James Frinton standing there apologetically. In my memory he is holding a hat in both hands, but I think that is just what the bearers of bad news do in films. I hadn't seen him for years, either. He had come, he said, because he couldn't think who else there might be to let me know that Tracy had died.

'These things happen,' I said weakly.

'I couldn't work out,' Ogden said, 'whether it was because

she had turned herself into someone completely different – into Alexandra Cartwright with the smart friends and the ballgowns and stuff – or whether it had happened because she was always like that. I can't remember any more whether she was always crazy. She was an anarcho-syndicalist. But I don't suppose she was even that towards the end.'

'Why were you thinking about her all of a sudden?' I said.

'Seeing you, I suppose,' Ogden said. We were at the pension. I produced the key to the street door, though it was not particularly late. Frau Dittberner was probably still around to let us in. 'Partly that and partly, I guess, seeing those kids at the bus station earlier.'

'But she wasn't like them,' I said. 'She wasn't injecting heroin behind bus shelters. It was all – oh, I don't know. I hadn't seen her for years.'

'On the other hand,' Ogden said, 'she died and those kids at the bus station, they're still alive.'

I didn't think that Ogden's argument was as much of an unanswerable point as he seemed to think. Of course the heroin users we had seen were alive. There were certainly plenty of heroin users who had hung around the Zoo Station in West Berlin who were now as dead as Tracy Cartwright. When it came to it, it would be hard to conclude that a dead Tracy Cartwright was more unfortunate than a dead Berlin heroin user of the sort we had seen. Ogden's points of comparison were too selective. His argument was fundamentally unsound. In our room, I got quickly into my pyjamas while he was in the bathroom putting his on. We both read the books we had brought for a while. My reading was light, a classic German novel of the 1930s. His was a detailed history of the German Democratic Republic, written by an American historian and published by an American university press. Although the room was unfamiliar to both of us, it was clean. The beds were comfortable. The scene was quickly safe and agreeable, even domestic. I started to think that the tensions I had felt earlier and the awkwardness that had arisen once Tracy Cartwright had come up were superficial. They would soon disappear.

    Then
     the I
      was maybe school
     yes this was
    the school I was at and my
brother there in the classroom my brother Joaquin having to learn to fly because because outside a group of tigers will get in and in here the doors being bolted the windows shut Tracy blocking gaps with thick black cloth and everywhere through a gap the mouth the teeth wet white shining the growl of a tiger and the phone in the classroom rings a tiger is in here somehow in here somehow and Joaquin turns and his eyes are wet with tears and he says because now I am going out and the sacrifice is mine it is not important and it must happen and he walks out and down and around me these people they celebrate but who are they where are the tigers and I hear downstairs a door opening and the noise of running tigers towards up
  and tigers towards
    and towards
     and

I woke up. It was dark. The room was unfamiliar. I could hear snuffling breathing. I was gulping for breath in a panic. After a few moments I knew where I was. Some machine was making a hum, not in the room but not far from it. The sheets were crumpled under me. My pyjama top was around my armpits. I had thrashed around in my nightmare. I was in Berlin with Percy Ogden in the bed next to mine. Joaquin was safe in our flat in England. I waited until my heart had stopped pounding and I felt confident that the dream would not return. I closed my eyes. The next day we would make the final arrangements to travel into the German Democratic Republic. The day after that we would begin our interesting holiday. I opened my eyes. I shut my eyes. The blackness was the same in each case.

We got up at half past seven. I washed and dressed first. I went to the breakfast room. It was a pleasant space with three tables already occupied, and a long side table laid with a variety of cold meat, cheeses, a large basket of bread and a small device with hot water to cook eggs in. The other guests were respectable German couples, talking in lowered voices. I ordered a pot of coffee from Frau Dittberner. In five minutes Ogden came into the room. He sat down.

'It's a change getting someone else to fetch your coffee,' he said, when he had given his order. 'It's always me fetching Phil's coffee in the morning. And for the rest of the team. I can do it blindfold now.'

'Who's doing the coffee while you're away?' I said.

'Oh, Phil's in the constituency,' Ogden said. 'It'll be his agent. Or even Marion. That's his wife. Parliament's in recess now.'

Two more Germans entered the breakfast room, a small, dark, neat couple. The wife had a polished patent leather handbag over the crook of her arm in a curiously medicinal shade of pink-brown. '*Guten Morgen,*' the man said confidently, and the three occupied tables all said, '*Guten Morgen,*' back, echoed by the man's wife. They sat down.

'I didn't say anything when I came in,' Ogden said. 'Did you say good morning?'

'Well, no, I have to say I didn't,' I said. 'It didn't occur to me.'

'It's important to be polite,' Ogden said, lighting a cigarette. 'It's going to be more important when we get to East Germany. It wouldn't be right to behave as if we were in England and ignoring strangers. We're going to a socialist country, remember? It's all about belonging together. We should definitely say good morning to strangers. I'm going to start doing it when I get back.'

The Reisebüro of East Germany opened its doors at nine o'clock. We were there at ten to nine. It was on the second floor of an anonymous office block in the back streets behind an enormous department store. I had not expected that. For some reason I had thought it would be in a shop, with windows carrying photographs of beaches and historic towns to lure people in. I had thought of Torremolinos. This was my first direct encounter with a socialist state. Back home, we had often talked about how a socialist state would function, but our concepts had been broad and principled. We had not really considered what it would be like to work for the state and hold a responsible job. As if to confirm the essential mystery of what it would mean, there was no noise behind the door and apparently no movement. A light was on, but no other signs of life. Just as I was starting to think we might have chosen to arrive on a holiday, there was a rattle of a key in the lock. The door was opened. It was nine a.m. precisely. The woman opening the door was in ordinary clothes. She walked back into the office around a screen without saying anything. We came in. We found ourselves facing a man wearing a grey uniform. He was sitting behind a desk, quite bare apart from three rolls of tickets, the sort you might use in a raffle, one red, one yellow and one white.

'Next, please,' he said.

I had been practising. I said in German that we were undertaking a trip in East Germany. We required permission for a trip of two weeks, starting tomorrow. He tore off a ticket from the red roll. He drew out a drawer of his desk with careful attention, and gave us a form each. He indicated that we should go into the waiting room and fill in the form. We should wait until we were called.

There was nobody else in the waiting room. Nobody else had been waiting behind us. Ogden took both forms and began to fill them in, so that the details would be the same on both. I found myself paying attention to the man who had given us our tickets – our tickets of admission, I found myself thinking, as if to a funfair or a place of entertainment. He and the woman who had opened the door were the first citizens of the DDR I had knowingly looked on. His uniform was clean, neat but frayed around the edges. I tried to reconstruct his day so far. I thought of him getting up with the aid of an old-fashioned alarm clock, and washing himself. I thought of him sponging himself down from a bowl of cold water by the side of the bed. For some reason he lived, in my imagination, in a sort of barracks. A wife in a pink nylon nightie lay with tousled blonde hair in the bed, ignoring the summons of the alarm. His uniform lay neatly on the back of a chair, white shirt, grey official tie, tunic, trousers, socks and the shoes he had polished last night before bed: he put them on quickly. He went through to the kitchen, turning on the kettle before brushing his teeth in the square, stained kitchen sink. Out of the kitchen window was a view of a bleak square of grass on which two chickens pecked behind a wire fence. He would collect any eggs when he got home in the evening. He made a cup of ersatz coffee from powder and dried milk. He took a piece of black bread from a wooden bread bin. He drank and ate standing up in the little kitchen, to save washing up: he leant over the sink while eating. Then he brushed himself down and rinsed the plain white mug. He left the flat.

I looked at him. He was only a little older than we were. He was blond and square-faced, his jaw substantial and his eyes weakly blue. His cheeks were reddened as if he had stood in a brisk wind. There were no children of that marriage to say goodbye to, I decided.

His journey: a walk through streets of high tenements with people heading in the same direction. Occasionally he would greet a colleague or an acquaintance or a friend of his parents, since he had grown up in this suburb, I felt. His greetings were formal, saying good morning to Frau Schoolmistress and Herr Engineer, Herr Doctor, Frau Architect, with a nod and no smile. Everybody in the state going to their purpose and accepting their duty, a place that worked.

We had been waiting for some time now. I brushed away the thought that the guard in my head had a blonde sleeping wife who had no intention, it seemed, of undertaking any activity. He had left her sprawled and asleep. I could not think what she had done, or what she would be doing.

But he was at the railway station now – yes, I was sure of this – holding a neat, polished briefcase. I reversed, I rewound: I made him pick it up before he left the kitchen. Those initials under the handle were his father's; he had now retired from his job in the civil service. They would be proud of each other. He was standing on the platform. The train came in with a pleasantly familiar hum, the doors opening with an agreeable musical note, like a harp being plucked. He had been familiar with that all his life. It was busy but not too crowded. A small boy in a Scout's uniform sprang to his feet to offer the sixtyish lady who had got on at the same time his seat, but she declined it, being as fit and healthy as anyone else. The journey was smooth. In six stops my guard found himself at his destination. He walked down the platform and out onto a busy street, with shoppers, office workers going to work, a group of small children heading to their nursery school in a well-ordered phalanx, holding hands in pairs. Everyone would be dressed according to their station in life, not just my guard in his uniform. I thought now his name should be Klaus, no, Kurt. The border crossing was not far away. Kurt waited at the road with other busy people before the signal let them across. The cars on the street were all white or blue, and all the same shape. He entered a neat little building of glass and steel in front of the wall. There, a group of colleagues greeted him before he offered his permit, dated today. He was allowed to walk through, his jaw jutting, his bag swinging. He had a purpose. I saw the West through his eyes as he walked to the desk where he now sat: the drug-taking, the chaos, the permitted filth and mess, the idle many, the confusing and idiosyncratic ways people dressed and presented themselves, the purposelessness. It seemed impossible. But he had a job to do.

He and I had come to this room along different routes. I had chosen it, as if the idea of society and a way of living were two quite separate questions. His orderly and rational life, supporting a society that worked in every respect as well as existing within it, was something different. Perhaps he did have children. The state would trust a family man with responsibilities to return home each day. But perhaps they would trust Kurt to return home having seen what life in the West was like on a daily basis. But I was troubled by his wife, Brigitte, no, Gerda, still lying in bed. What was she doing? She was quite idle. She was no schoolteacher, she was not ill. She was simply lolling. Her hand ventured under her pillow. There she found a box of chocolates, half finished. She would get up in a while, and go in a cloud of red chiffon into her pink bathroom to wash and soak and spray herself with perfume. Gerda was a problem in my idea of the East German state. She obstinately lay on a purple velvet sofa in my imagination: she hung there waiting for her lover to appear, an unemployed intellectual with big shoulders called Günther. What was he doing in my DDR? Why did she have no occupation? The doorbell rang. It was her lover. In my mind she said one thing, murmuring in the hallway before she opened the door and gave herself up to unlegislated ecstasy. She said only, 'I forgot to make sure that Kurt had a bowel movement before he left the house.'

The guard looked up. There was another man to give a ticket and a form to. This time the ticket was a white one. The form came from a different drawer. The new applicant looked us over before plumping down on a moulded plastic chair with a sigh.

'It's always the same,' he said in English.

'Have you done this before?' I said.

'I've been doing it every three months for the last two years,' he said. He started to write on the form. 'I'm doing some research in their archives. I'm a historian.'

'My friend's doing a PhD,' Ogden said, looking up. 'But we're going over on a sort of holiday.'

'Good luck,' the historian said. 'They make it as tiresome as they can. The whole process. Every time there's a more searching interview and every time it turns out that they got the wrong end of the stick last time. When I came last time, they began by saying, "So, Dr Clark, you are researching the history of the Australian embassy in Berlin." I had to tell them, no, I was researching nineteenth-century Protestant missions. The Australian embassy came into it because I'd submitted a letter from them supporting my application. I think somebody just thought they had to write something to satisfy their superiors. You're adventurous, going on holiday in the DDR. Where are you planning to go?'

I ran through our itinerary. 'We both wanted to see a socialist state in reality,' I finished. 'We've been supporters of socialism in the UK. But you can't understand the full detail of it without spending some time in a socialist system that's established itself.'

'In different ways,' Ogden put in. To my surprise he gave the impression of being somewhat embarrassed by what I had just said. 'What's the process? How long does this take?'

The historian was looking amused. I suppose in retrospect what I had said was absurdly idealistic, and probably not at all what most people would say when in a bureaucratic waiting room. The officer in charge of handing out tickets had paid no obvious attention to what I had said. 'It's a same-day thing,' the historian said. 'If you've got all the papers they ask for you'll be sorted out in three or four hours. Don't be intimidated by them making you wait like this. It's all a performance. They want you to be a bit frightened. Just act unimpressed. Good luck. When you're in Weimar go to see Goethe's house. It's beautiful. And in Berlin I always have a beer at the bar at the corner of Kollwitzplatz. In Prenzlauer Berg. It's been there since the 1920s. Top tip.'

The historian was saying goodbye because a voice had started calling over the sound system, a voice I was only slowly resolving into *dreihundertzweiundvierzig*, the 342 printed on our ticket. It was our turn. I gathered up my folder of documentation. We went through.

'I'll do the talking,' Ogden said. 'There's no need for you to explain anything.'

Our number was flashing over another desk, quite unoccupied. We sat down in two moulded plastic chairs, fixed in pairs, and waited.

'I'll have to talk if it's in German,' I said.

'Just translate what I say in that case,' Ogden said. 'I don't think it'll be as bad as all that. Just don't say anything about how wonderful the socialist DDR is. They'll think we're spies or something.'

Then a woman was in front of us, brisk and unsmiling. She held out her hand. She took our two completed forms. It was the woman who had opened the door to us half an hour before. She turned and left.

'Should we go and sit down in the waiting room?' I said. 'While they check the details?'

'Are they done? Was that it?'

'They would have taken our passports too,' I said. A brisk shout came from the man I had called Kurt. 'We need to go back there, he said.'

The historian had disappeared. The waiting room now contained half a dozen new arrivals, all of them filling in the form. We sat down again.

Time passed.

'We should have gone to Romania,' Ogden said at one point.

Outside I thought I heard the sound of rain at one point. It was more likely something – some substance like iron filings – being dropped in the stairwell.

It occurred to me that I had forgotten to return a book to the university library. It was a novel by Primo Levi. Returning the book had been one of my tasks on Tuesday before setting off. It was due back on Monday. Fines would shortly be mounting up. I considered sharing this with Ogden before deciding against it.

Three people were summoned as we had been, to hand over their forms. They came back as we had done. The others sat there with their forms, waiting.

'How long do you think this will be?' Ogden said, but there was no point in replying.

The waiting room filled up further. By eleven o'clock there were fourteen or fifteen people standing or sitting. 'They should have posters up on the wall,' I said. 'Pictures of the beauties of the DDR.'

'It's not a travel bureau,' Ogden said.

'It is a travel bureau,' I said. 'That's exactly what Reisebüro means, travel bureau.'

'Well, they're not here to tempt you with fancy advertising,' Ogden said. 'This isn't a money-making scheme, like it would be in the West.'

'Excuse me,' a woman sitting next to us said, leaning forward. She had the plump russety quality with red hair and a squashed nose that I always associate with the name 'Moira'. 'Actually, it is a money-making scheme.'

I looked at Ogden. This was an unexpected statement from a stranger in a DDR office.

'The whole business. They want to raise currency for the DDR,' she continued. She was not lowering her voice at all. 'The requirement to change money. Twenty-five Deutschmarks per day. The requirement to stay in government hotels and pay in Westmarks. Have you stayed in the official hotels? They're not worth the money, I can tell you.'

I smiled weakly and without any real encouragement to the woman. I did not think direct criticism of the DDR was permitted or wise on its premises, in front of its citizens.

'I'm sick to death of it,' the woman said. 'I wouldn't go if I didn't have to. My boyfriend. He comes from there. We met at a conference in Trier. It's where Karl Marx was born but the conference was nothing to do with that. The conference was about what I work with, about Christina Rossetti. Georg works with the Rossettis too. We're both members of a team, him in Leipzig, me in Bristol. He's working on a concordance. I'm helping to prepare her letters for an edition. I'm English. You're English? I'm English. He gave a paper about the prevalence of colour words in Rossetti's verse and I showed him some unpublished correspondence. We suit each other. He's fifty-eight, twenty-seven years older than me. I know I look older than that. He has permission to travel for these purposes but not often enough. I go over to visit him three times a year. We meet and stay in hotels. They're horribly expensive. I pay for them. I don't think he wants me to come and stay with him. I went once and his flat was full of the sense of somebody else's life. Sometimes I think it wasn't his flat at all. He hardly knew where the knife drawer was, where the cups were kept in the kitchen. The photographs had been removed from the table top before my visit. But he loves me. What would you do?'

'I really don't know,' Ogden said. 'I don't think I can give you advice.'

'They might be divorced,' I said. 'It might simply be that he didn't want to talk to you about previous relationships. That's the advice, isn't it? When you meet somebody, don't talk endlessly about the relationships you've been in before?'

'Why are you going?' she said, ignoring what I'd said. 'Nobody goes unless they have to. What's your reason?'

'We want to travel a bit and see what we can,' I said. 'We're going to be tourists. I think it's going to be interesting to see a country that's organized in a completely different way from the West, and perhaps to meet some of the people who live there.' I smiled at her.

'This is my seventh time,' she said, not smiling back in the slightest. 'Every time Georg tells me that he loves me and we should go to visit a different beautiful town with historic sights. Once I could no longer go on. I broke down and cried in front of him in the Zwinger in Dresden. He has never once asked me to bring anything across. I think that's unusual. Why does he have no desire for anything from the West? He says he has everything he needs. It upsets me to have to go through this questioning before I can see Georg. I want to settle down with him but I don't see how that could ever happen. He has friends who live in the UK. They visit me whenever I come back. They need to pick up the things that Georg gives me for them – he always gives me something for them – but they stay and talk for a couple of hours. They're called Rudi, Anja, Monika, Gerhard, they're nice people. They asked me if I'd like to come along to their discussion group – they have a political, I think it is, discussion group. They live in the UK and Georg one day could live in the UK too. I said to him last time that if he asked me to marry him I would apply to come to live with him in the DDR. But I don't speak German. Only *guten Morgen, guten Abend, gnädige Frau, ich liebe dich*, just that. He didn't answer when I said I wanted to come to live with him, come and live in the DDR, but he wrote me such a beautiful letter. I have it, look, here. What do you think I should do?'

She had plucked an envelope, a letter on pale blue paper, from her bag, a black patent-leather handbag with a gold clasp. She stabbed at it with her forefinger.

'Do they usually take as long as this?' Ogden said.

'But what do you think I should do?' the woman said.

'I don't think you can do anything,' I said. 'The only thing you could do would be a negative thing. To stop seeing him and coming to the DDR. I don't think you can advance the situation on your own. We have no experience on which to advise you, I'm afraid.'

The woman sank back in her chair. She thrust the envelope into her bag. She clicked it shut. Everything about her was neat, apart from the form she had tried to fill in. She had crumpled and torn it, resting it on the side of her handbag. She placed her hands over her eyes, making a wiping gesture. I realized with horror that she had actually started to cry. Nobody else in the room was paying any attention to her. Her story had been retold in a low, warm, serious-sounding voice, not at all in accordance with the madness and despair she appeared to be experiencing. I had given her a firm response, which had taken into account the possibility that officials of the DDR might hear what I was saying. It would not be helpful to say, as I wanted to, that there was surely something underhand about the way she had met this man, that he was not telling her the whole story. He must be using her for purposes of his own. I wonder, now, what the story was, and what happened to Georg after the breakdown of the DDR – she must have known his real name, since they'd met at an academic conference. I had not asked what she took to his friends in the UK. Did he have some official status? Was his relationship with her a matter of public scrutiny? Or had he seen a pretty woman, plump and russety, and seen no reason not to make a move on her? I have sometimes thought of that woman and her edge, barely concealed, of romantic despair. I never saw her again after that moment in the DDR Reisebüro.

I have always thought afterwards that it was politicians who had their way with her. Georg was their tool, whether he knew it or not, and so was she.

The tannoy came into action. '*Nummer dreihundertzwei-undvierzig, bitte,*' it said. It was our number.

There was already a man sitting at the desk above which our number flashed. He held out his hand, unsmiling. Ogden understood what he wanted. He handed over our passports. The man took them and flicked through them, pausing at a stamp in Ogden's – it was an Egyptian visa, I discovered after-wards, from a holiday Ogden had taken with his parents after his A levels. He placed them in front of him. He began to ask his questions.

     On
       what dates
      do you want
     to travel, From the
    fourth of April to the
  seventeenth, What is your itinerary, From
Berlin on the seventh to Leipzig and to Weimar on the tenth to Dresden on the thirteenth and back to Berlin, What is the reason for travelling, For tourism, What is the reason for choosing the Democratic Republic for your tourism, An interest in the historic sites of the country and an interest in your country's traditions, Where do you live, As it is stated on the form, These cities are different, why is that, I live in the town I was born in where I met my friend but he now lives in London, in the capital, What are your occupations, I am a student writing a

doctoral thesis, Are you coming to the Democratic
Republic for research, No, for relief from hard work, This
is not the opportunity for humour, sir, I understand,
What is the subject of your research, briefly stated, It is a
historical account of the literature surrounding the anti-
Catholic riots in Yorkshire in the 1780s and its relation to
the seeds of proletarian resistance movements, Where are
the funds for your travel coming from, From personal
means, What are the sources of your income in general
terms, Grants from the government, What grants from
the government, Grants for my research, Are you in
receipt of government funds enabling you to travel in the
Democratic Republic in particular on this occasion and
have you received any instructions for tasks to be
undertaken during your travel, No, not at all, the grants
are made for living expenses and research purposes over
three years and the government has no reason to know
where I am taking a holiday, How is a student grant
sufficient to allow you to consider a holiday of two weeks,
I have some private savings which I am using for this
holiday, What is the source of these private savings, My
father died last year and left me some money and I am
using that, How did your father die, I do not see the
relevance of this question, How did your father die, This
is a private matter, I ask again, how did your father die,
As you insist, he committed suicide, How much money
did he leave you, I am sorry, but I do not see the relevance
of these questions, Nevertheless these questions are being
asked and are relevant and necessary, how much money
did he leave you, He left me fifty thousand pounds,

Where do you live now, In the town where I grew up, I
would be grateful if you would try to answer these
questions in a calm fashion, Please continue, Do you live
on your own, No, Who do you live with, I live with a
friend, What is the name of your friend, Joaquin
Gorriategy, is that his full name, No, Joaquin Anibal
Gorriategy, That is not an English name, No he was born
in Chile, Please write down his name and age and contact
details in full, where did you learn German, At school,
And have you been to a German-speaking country before,
Yes I have been twice to the Federal Republic and once to
Austria when I was a child, Please describe your itineraries
in those countries and the dates of your travel, I was in
Austria in April 1973 when I was six years old, we went to
Vienna for a holiday of five days at Easter and our
itinerary included performances by the Vienna Boys'
Choir and the Spanish Riding School as well as going to
see the Prater, and my parents went to the opera although
I was left in the hotel room, I believe they saw the opera
Tosca and my mother wore a long blue dress, These are
serious questions and I must warn you again against
answering them facetiously or with mockery, I am sorry,
sir, If you hope to be granted entry to the Democratic
Republic then mocking the officials and citizens of the
Republic will not be looked on favourably, so I ask again
if you would outline the itinerary of your trips to other
German-speaking countries, in the first, you remained
entirely within Vienna, and the others, please, The second
trip was to Bavaria with my father when I was sixteen,
and we visited the towns of Munich, Würzburg,

Nuremberg, Bamberg and Rothenburg, Is that all, Yes, I
believe so, And the dates of the trip please, August 1983,
Could you be more precise, I think it was the two weeks
before the return to school but I am not sure, And the
third trip please, The third trip was with a youth orchestra
I played with in the town I grew up in and it was an
exchange with the youth orchestra in Bochum in the
Ruhr Valley, And your itinerary there, please, We
performed concerts in Bochum, in Essen, and in Münster,
And the dates of the trip, September 1985, it was at the
end of my second year of university, What were the names
of those in charge of issuing the invitation, The invitation
was one to the orchestra and I do not think I ever saw
those names or met the people involved, What is your
interest in travelling to the Democratic Republic, We are
interested in its history and its culture and the people, Are
you planning to meet with any particular citizens of the
Democratic Republic during your trip, No, What are
their names, We are not planning to meet with anyone,
Are you a member of any political party in your country,
No, Are you planning to overthrow your government
through violent means, No, Have you ever undertaken
any subversive action or distributed anti-government
publications, Anti the government of the United
Kingdom you mean, Yes, I am a supporter of socialism,
That is not what I asked, Could you repeat the question
please, Have you ever undertaken any subversive action or
distributed anti-government publications, An election
pamphlet by an opposition party could be viewed as an
anti-government publication, but I have never taken part

in any activity outside the normal range of ordinary
political activities in my country, I would like now to ask
some specific questions of Mr Ogden, He does not speak
German, I will ask my questions and you can translate
them to him, and afterwards translate his answers for me,
is that understood, Yes, Where does Mr Ogden live, In
London, Who does he live with, They are tenants who
answered an advert and not friends of Mr Ogden, What is
Mr Ogden's profession, He is a personal assistant, Who
does he work for, A British Member of Parliament, What
party does he represent, The Labour Party, What is his
name, Philip Cawston, Has Mr Ogden ever visited a
German-speaking country before now, Never, What is Mr
Ogden's means of financial support, His job, What is his
income, Ten thousand pounds, A month, No, a year,
Who do you plan to meet with during your trip to the
Democratic Republic, We have no plans to meet with
anyone in particular, as I said a moment ago, Has anyone
given you anything to take into the Democratic Republic,
No, Has anyone given you a message to pass on to a
citizen of the Democratic Republic, No, Are you planning
to overthrow the Democratic Republic by any means, No,
You realize that any false answers to these questions would
result in serious consequences,

    I understand that, I would like
      to see the reservations you
        have made with hotels
          on your itinerary,
            if you
              please.

We were dismissed. Soon we stood on the street outside the office building. It had the weightless, brilliant look of a town seen for the first time in weeks by a confined convalescent. Ogden and I looked at each other. My stomach began slowly to unclench. I realized that I was very hungry.

'Should I have left Phil out of it?' Ogden said. He lit a cigarette. His hands were shaking a little.

'I don't know what else you could have done when they asked what your job was,' I said. 'What would you have said?'

'I guess I could have made something up,' Ogden said. 'I could have said I worked in my uncle's shoe shop or anything. I just don't like the idea of them phoning Phil up and quizzing him. Or deciding that they'll let the *Daily Mail* or the *Sun* know that Phil's got a member of staff who likes going to the DDR on his summer holidays. They could make that look terrible.'

'I don't much like the idea of them phoning Joaquin up either,' I said.

'Be that as it may,' Ogden said.

'I don't think there's going to be any problem,' I said. 'They like being terrifying, if they can manage it. In the holidays, claiming the dole – don't you remember how those juniors in the dole office tried to frighten you if they were really bored? Tell you that your dole would be stopped if they couldn't see evidence you'd been looking for jobs? This is the same. He was bored and he wanted to frighten us a bit. It'll be fine when we're over in the DDR. Not everyone in East Germany wants to devote time to scaring students.'

I wasn't sure I meant this. It was surely a mistake to have brought up Ogden's employer when he had not mentioned the fact that he worked in Parliament on his application form.

'Anyway, it's lunchtime now. We should go back around four, four thirty. They said three hours and they close at five.'

'I told Phil I was going to East Germany,' Ogden said. 'He said fine, good idea. He gave me the names and phone numbers of a couple of people he knows in Berlin and somebody he met from Leipzig. They're party stalwarts, not subversives.'

'You should have told the bloke,' I said. 'You should have said. He asked three times. I translated at least once. You must have known he was asking.'

'It's just an innocent meeting,' Ogden said. 'It'll only take half an hour. He wants me to give them copies of his book.'

'Oh, come on,' I said. 'The man asked whether you'd been given anything. You said no. We're in big trouble now.'

'It's just his book,' Ogden said. 'You know his book, a sort of manifesto about achieving socialism in the UK, what needs to be done from within the Labour Party. He's been writing it for years. He wanted it to come out before the 1983 election, so Foot would have had to give him a job when they won. Then that didn't happen. So he went on writing it. It's ended up explaining everything that's gone wrong and how they need socialism again.'

'He ought to leave the Labour Party,' I said lightly, 'and join someone a bit more serious. Do you think the comrades in Dresden are that interested in where Kinnock went wrong?'

'I don't see why not,' Ogden said. 'I've actually come to think that you're not going to hold the same beliefs that you had at sixteen all your life. Not if you want to grow up at all.'

I ignored this. 'I don't suppose it'll get that far,' I said. 'You know they're going to search your bags. They're not going to let multiple copies of the same book through.'

'Phil asked me to,' Ogden said briefly.

'I'd prefer it if you didn't say, "Be that as it may," when I mention Joaquin,' I said.

Ogden looked startled; flushed; looked away. There was nothing much for him to look at. A strikingly beautiful woman, dark, with a black fur collar on her coat, was walking a substantial pug. An empty bus drove by. In a moment Ogden said, 'Let's go and find something to eat.'

I have been to Berlin since then. It has been a united city for nearly thirty years now. It's hard to remember the appearance of the Reichstag then, like an old cow lying sick in a field, abandoned, and just beyond it the photo opportunity of the Wall running in front of the Brandenburg Gate. You could have gone anywhere to see the Wall, but that afternoon, looking for something to do, Ogden and I went to the place that all visiting politicians went to. We made the sort of remarks, half jeering, that you would expect people like us to make – remarks about photo opportunities. About the loss of nerve of the DDR in building the Wall, since the opportunists who wanted to run away would have tailed off by now. Ogden knew that the numbers of people who had illicitly crossed, or tried to cross, the border had diminished over the years. It was now statistically insignificant. We had a reasonable discussion. I felt, nevertheless, that it was going to be hard to stay with Ogden for two weeks. One of the first things that anyone had said to me about him was that he was 'a queer' – one of those boys I used to hang around with,

Matthew or Simon, had made the observation. There had
never been any sign of a romantic attachment in Ogden's
case. He quite liked it if some other people embarked on an
attachment, so long as it was clearly and absolutely ludicrous,
and conducted for a reason of public policy, as it were. The
summer before we all went to university, he encouraged
Tracy Cartwright to go to bed with Mohammed at the end
of a long night. It was so strange, that summer: for the first
time ever, we had nothing to do, scholastically speaking,
between handing in our final A-level papers and packing our
stuff into the boots of our parents' cars, driving off to university at the beginning of October. Those three months, irre-
sponsibility set in: we never drank so much, plotted so
ingeniously, wrote on so many walls. When Tracy and
Mohammed were found to be snogging each other, it seemed
hilarious, preposterous, inevitable, a good idea all round. I
think Ogden hoped that it would affront either set of parents.
A point could be made here. In reality Tracy's mother didn't
care, and the distance between Mohammed and his parents
was immense. Their polite, bearded, veiled, monoglot world
was already far removed from what he did and wanted. A
blonde girl who slept with him was not the strangest thing
they had seen or envisaged. He got a tattoo that summer, as
well. The encouragement and excitement died down over the
course of a couple of months. Mohammed came to visit
Tracy at Oxford three weeks into term. She had changed. It
was over.

Now we were walking the immured streets of West Berlin.
Ogden was still unable to make any reference to Joaquin, the
position he held in my life. My own madness, that summer,

had been subdued. I had been with Joaquin for two years. He was often described as 'crazy' by the others, but his madness was circumscribed, formally distinct, taking place within certain hours and for particular purposes. It was a festivity like Christmas, starting and finishing on a timetable. When Joaquin had decided that he would break out in this direction, whether to smash up a political gathering, to get hopelessly drunk, or to take hold of me, seizing me, tearing his own clothes and mine off, falling onto the nearest bed or just some horizontal surface, the madness he had decided on looked unbordered, unplanned, terrifyingly limitless. You never felt you knew what Joaquin might be about to start doing. But this was misleading. Whatever he was going to be capable of doing, he had decided that it would carry on for the next two hours (say) and stop short at a certain point. Whether I was walking with Joaquin towards an estate agent's shop window with a pot of paint and a bag full of half-bricks, or bent over a chair, mid-afternoon, with my face pressed hard against the floor, my books and papers thrown aside, my trousers looped around my ankles, feeling Joaquin's pulse and heartbeat hot and hard and unrelenting within me, the pressure and heat of his blood inside me, I was certain that his animal madness had formal and respectful limits. Animal: a very good thing for other people to be. He knew more exactly how far I wanted to join in with something than I did myself. Just then, walking with Ogden through the streets of West Berlin, I thought it had been a mistake to come here with him. I had nothing further in common with him. I wished I had come away with Joaquin – that I had stayed where I was with Joaquin, that I had decided to continue my daily life or to take a holiday, whichever it was, to be with Joaquin yesterday and today and tomorrow. I was homesick for a Chilean refugee.

'I think we ought to clear the air,' Ogden said carefully, 'if we're going to be two weeks together.'

'I think that's right,' I said. I was surprised. I didn't think Ogden would raise anything in this way.

'There just seems to be some tension here,' Ogden said. 'I don't quite understand, but there definitely seems to be some tension here.'

'Maybe it's just that we aren't used to each other,' I said. 'I mean, we don't see each other every day.'

'To be honest,' Ogden said, 'I wish you'd make a bit more of an effort. That's what would improve things.'

'You wish I'd improve things? I mean, you wish *I*'d make more of an effort?'

'Yes. That's what I said. I don't want to be rude but, you know, you've hardly said a word for the last twenty-four hours. It's a bit like walking round with a large inanimate object, like pulling a fridge on wheels or something.'

'That's not fair.'

'Look, I know what this is about. I'm really sorry. But responding to what I say, then shutting up and looking at the ground, then once in a blue moon making some kind of cold, rude observation, "I'd be very grateful if in future you'd refrain from referring to ..." you must see what that sounds like.'

'I don't know what you're talking about.'

'I'm trying to be sympathetic here, after what you've been through.'

'What do you mean, after what I've been through?'

'Well, I mean – your dad. Anyone can see that's going to have a massive impact on anyone. You've never even mentioned it to me.'

'My dad?'

'Yes.'

'My dad was just a bastard.'

'I meant about him dying like that. I'm sorry. You're just in shock in some way.'

Sometimes as humans we decide without consultation what would be best for people. We consider human nature in general. We then think about what might be most likely to be driving the human animal in particular. Ogden's was a political mind, for whom the individual case would always be encased within a range of the most likely general responses. He took it for granted that my emotional response would be much the same as the emotional response of anyone whose father had been as detached and simply disapproving as mine. Anyone, that is, whose father had chosen to commit suicide in such a way. In fact, my response had been my own, and in response to nobody but my father. Of course, everybody in the world whose father committed suicide was likely to be overwhelmed with grief. It might be everybody but one. My response was my own. My father was who he was and nobody else. I was not even sure that I had responded at all. I didn't think I needed to. I didn't know what Ogden was talking about when he said that I had not engaged with him since we had met. I thought we had been talking perfectly well when it had been necessary to say anything.

'I don't understand why you're not living in the house,' Ogden said. 'Surely it would make more sense to live in your house than where you are.'

'It's not my house,' I said. 'It never was. It was my dad's and he left it to the fern society. You know he was keen on ferns. It went to them.'

The gardens at the house were a little marvel, two hundred different ferns – quite similar-looking, I think – embedded in mosses, under trees. It took, I understand, some skill to get them to propagate, the moss to do whatever moss does. My father might have hoped that the Pteridological Society would open the garden as a visitor site. There was a sentence in the will about a visitor centre. But the society took the bequest. In time, long after this trip, they were to sell the house, and use the proceeds for their own festival purpose, probably paying the salary of a new chief executive for a decade. There never has been any question, for them, of a visitor centre.

'What did you get?'

'Fifty thousand of my dad's savings. I kept a bit of that and I gave most of it to the Communist League. The Revolutionary Communist League, I mean, not the other lot. They needed it.'

'But I thought you resigned from that?'

'Over their stance towards the Soviets in Afghanistan. Yes, I did. We both did. There was no real way of reconciling their position and our positions on that. We left. We weren't the only ones. There's five of us who take the same position. The RCL's in the hands of a reactionary cadre. It's us who kept things going. I gave them the money before we broke away.'

'Well, that was sensible.'

'I got them to buy a van with some of the money,' I said. 'And then after the meeting that resulted in the split—'

'You drove off with it.'

'Well, yes. I was the nominated driver. I had the keys.'

'At least you got something back.'

'I honestly don't care about any of that,' I said. 'I didn't want the money. I don't care that my dad's dead. It was pretty thoughtless of him all round. The cleaner he'd taken on complained that she'd lost a job she was counting on – he got her to come in three days a week for three hours a time. The fern society got in touch to ask if I'd do all the work of putting the house on the market and just sending them the cheque.'

'What did you say?'

'Joaquin told them to piss off. They'll think twice about calling us up next time. It's just standing empty while they decide what to do with it.'

'You should go and live there. Sounds like they don't want the trouble.'

'I don't want to live there.'

'Well, I can see that. Your dad, though. He wasn't like Frinton's mum with her Eartha Kitt and the crying fits. I'm sorry.'

It seemed to me then that, as a depressive, it is actually much easier to be really, publicly, effortlessly crazy and insistently noisy about it. Frinton's mother never had to do anything. She never had to go downstairs to open up the bar or do the accounts or make breakfast for Frinton and his brother. Depression gave her permission to sit on the sofa in a dressing-gown eating Dairy Milk bars and yawning and scratching and watching all those old Eartha Kitt videos.

'It's fine. My dad goes to work every day and shouts at his underlings and comes back and does what needs to be done in the line of housework and ensuring that I get fed and his little hobbies to blank out whatever there is to be blanked out and then one day he does what his voice has been telling him to do twenty times a day, all his life. He didn't leave a note. My mum said she didn't have a clue either. That's why she went. Anyway. Shit happens.'

'And now Frinton's got a job working on a London newspaper owned by a foreign billionaire.'

'Writes the third leader every day. The funny one.'

'On his way to the top. Let's go and pick up the visas.'

'I don't think there are going to be any visas,' I said. 'I think they're about to turn us down. He looked pretty unhappy with what he was hearing, that bloke.'

'Revolutionaries, eh?'

'The revolution was a long time ago. There's a bourgeoisie that's reformed itself within the revolutionary society.'

'But how can a bourgeoisie even function in a free-floating way outside the paradigms of a society? How does that work?'

We carried on all the way back to the Reisebüro. It was like old times. On the second floor I handed over the red ticket I had been given when we had left. The man at the desk – I had christened him Kurt or Klaus – performed a short, satisfied nod. He handed over our two passports and a pair of stamped permits indicating our agreed itinerary. It had all been for show, after all.

'Was it Eartha Kitt Frinton's mother liked?' Ogden said. 'Or was it Dusty Springfield?'

'Definitely Eartha Kitt,' I said. I began to sing an old number.

'God, you gays,' Ogden said, quite warmly. 'You love your torch songs, you really do.' We turned into a bar. It was only five o'clock, but they served us.

In the morning, we had breakfast at Frau Dittberner's – '*Guten Morgen. Guten Morgen!*' – in an atmosphere of slightly doomed hilarity. It was the morning of an examination that had been inadequately prepared for. The tense wariness between us had lifted the night before. We paid Frau Dittberner. We travelled to the crossing point by U-Bahn. It was a famous crossing point. As foreigners, we were required to cross at the celebrated 'Checkpoint Charlie'. 'It's only famous,' Ogden said, 'because *Americans* have to cross here.' The different checkpoints used by citizens of the Western part of the city or the Federal Republic had never seeped into the public consciousness. The crossing point was temporary in appearance, with low-built offices spanning what must once have been a busy road. There was a chevroned path for motor vehicles, blocked with barriers. The signs indicated the paths that military vehicles and others should take: the specific and yet inadequate information that 'YOU ARE NOW LEAVING THE AMERICAN SECTOR' was written in huge letters above everything else. We had been full of excitement and fun, even giggling, at breakfast. Now we were quiet. In the crossing post itself we handed over our documentation with our passports, which were stamped. We changed the regulation twenty-five Deutschmarks into the same number of Ostmarks. We opened our suitcases, which were gone through by different agents. I had a copy of Ogden's boss's book. He had another, as well as one in his overcoat pocket. The searching was not so thorough as all that, or as coordinated, and nothing was confiscated. We were through.

I was in a socialist state for the first time in my life. The streets were empty, apart from the fast-dispersing tourists and day-trippers who had come through Checkpoint Charlie with us. There was an unfamiliar smell in the air, which I now know to be the brown coal that the DDR burnt everywhere. It was long forbidden in the West.

In five minutes we were in a busier place. The cars that were driving the streets were white or baby blue. They were all the same in appearance. The people looked no different from the people in the West. We were not in any way of interest to them. Their orderly and contented quality was not apparent at first glance. They had seen people like us before.

The hotel admitted our reservation, under a show of reluctance. There was a long, frowning consultation in a heavy ledger. But the time of check-in was at two in the afternoon exactly. Could we leave our luggage here until the time of check-in? The woman clerk had hair disconcertingly similar to Mrs Thatcher's blonde helmet, a neat pale blue uniform glistening with artificial fibres, a stripe of matching pale blue eyeshadow. She looked at us unblinkingly, not evidently thinking. In the end we paid our hotel bill in full, in advance, in what the guidebook called 'hard currency', by which it meant Western currency. On this condition she agreed that we could leave our bags. We would return at two o'clock. It was now ten.

I realized, as we left the hotel, that I had no real idea where we should go in Berlin – Hauptstadt Berlin, as we should call it. Our task, of assessing and experiencing the life of the state, was, I understood all at once, an impossible one. The life of the state is only to be experienced by those who are not idle. We were idle. We could experience only a simulacrum of being busy. A guidebook was in my hand, and a map of the whole city. The possibilities of museums, monuments, historic objects lay in front of us.

'Let's just go for a walk,' Ogden said, understanding that we were unexpectedly at a loss. The hotel, a glistening white 1960s construction, was on a sort of central artery of the city. We left and turned right. Huge stone buildings lined either side of the road, and a parade of shops, mostly of women's fashion. They were beautiful and unconvincing, like museum displays of women's clothes from a remote civilization in a state of perfect preservation. The colours were perhaps slightly strange. The cut was perfect in its own way, but inconceivable on a human being. Where the extravagant displays of shoes, gloves, hats and ballgowns in the pavement vitrines on the Kurfürstendamm had clearly been waiting only for the right rich woman to arrive and bring them to life, these creations had been made only for display. This was all the life they needed. They reminded me of the scenes in 1950s Hollywood movies where an ordinary girl is swept up by a millionaire and, in a showroom, seated on her own, learns that Paris couture can turn her into Audrey Hepburn, Doris Day, anybody. These clothes would never leave the window on anyone's back. They bore no prices. They were meant only for the eyes of visitors even more naïve than we were. Opposite stood, in colossal self-assurance, the embassy of the Soviet Union.

'That twenty-five Deutschmarks we changed,' Ogden said. 'We're paying in Western money for the hotel, aren't we?'

'It's the regulation,' I said. 'You have to change twenty-five Deutschmarks every day. So keep the receipt every time we do it. I guess it doesn't much matter where you change it.'

'Wait a second,' Ogden said. 'We've got to change twenty-five marks every day? Each? What are we going to spend it on? Is food expensive?'

'You could buy a pair of shoes,' I said. 'Or anything. They've got pretty well whatever you want to buy. It's good for books.'

'Books in German,' Ogden said. 'That's no good for me. Are you sure – twenty-five marks every single day?'

I showed him the information in the guidebook. We were outside the Opera House, facing a large open square. Just there was a café with a terrace. We had fifty marks to spend today. We sat down. A shy-looking girl, toothy and pale, hovered at the door. In a moment a savagely hairy stout supervisor came out. He encouraged her to take menus to us. She might have been given a push, so jerky and unconfident was the movement in which she came over.

'I don't really want anything,' Ogden said, having looked at the menu. 'Why is she standing there? I might want to read the full thing.'

'She's doing what she was told,' I said. The girl – we should say *woman*, I know – was frail and nervous, straight from school. Perhaps this was her first day in the job. She was standing by us, casting looks back at the hairy supervisor. A couple of tables away, two groomed, efficient civil-service types in suits and ties were paying her close, humorous attention. In her hand were a notepad and a small, neat pencil. She waited. She spoke no English, I could see.

'I think I will have a *Kaffee Komplett*,' I said in German to her. I had plucked the name more or less at random from the list of coffee options. She wrote down my order in full, slowly and neatly.

'I don't want anything,' Ogden said. 'I suppose I'd better start spending. What did you order?'

I told him.

'What's that?'

'It's some sort of coffee,' I said. 'I don't know exactly. Look, it's there. One mark forty-seven pfennigs.'

'What did you order it for if you don't know what it is? It might have hazelnut or brandy or anything in it. I'll have the same. Mind you, I'm only having it because I need to change money. Twenty-five marks every day.'

The waitress took our order. I watched her go with sympathy. I saw her life stretch before her. She had gone to an East German school for catering and tourism. She had studied hard and had got the top place in class. She had applied with diligence to the most prestigious of all East German cafés, the one by the opera house that every rich Western tourist stopped at. She was determined to make a success of this, and one day she would apply for official permission to open her own café in a suburb of Berlin. I saw her as a well-trained alternative to what Carole used to be. But was that how it worked? Or were all cafés and restaurants in the Democratic Republic supervised and controlled by a central authority? Could this girl do anything but rise up the ladder until she occupied the space taken by the furiously gesticulating man with the fat moustache standing in the open door, by the cupboards of forks and knives? I didn't know. For a moment I thought of the question posed by an official Soviet visitor to the United Kingdom, much enjoyed by an academic economist I used to sit next to in hall: *Please to tell me, who is the official in charge of the supply of cake to Central London?* Who was that? And who was the official in charge of the supply of beer, of comfort, of a sense of security, a man to love? I felt I wanted to ask these questions in the Democratic Republic of Germany, where they would have a reassuring answer. Just now I did not have anyone to ask. The task was to investigate, not merely to be a tourist, snapping away at interesting monuments, museums, and the preserved or restored wonders of long-dead Prussian emperors.

Ogden had opened the guidebook. He was reading drearily about the history of the square we were in. Books had been burnt in it. Two tables away, one of the business or civil-service types had got up, hardly saying goodbye to his colleague or friend, and hurried away. The other pressed his napkin to his mouth in a gesture of preparation and anticipation – cleaning himself, like a cat about to go out seducing. He looked in front of himself levelly for half a minute. I saw that the friend had left a ten Ostmark note in the saucer, not waiting for his change. The man got up, stretched his shoulders – had he been there a long time? He paid no attention to us. It was a surprise when he abruptly stopped by our table and sat down on the third chair. Ogden raised his eyes from his book; he stopped reading.

'It is indeed something to think about when travelling in our country,' the man said in English – his consonants were precise, his accent a little American. 'The changing of money. This law! Our great government has determined it, the changing of twenty-five marks of hard currency every day. If your currency is hard currency, what is ours? Surely not soft. It seems harder than your currency. It never changes. It is exactly the same as the mark in your country. Or not in your country. *Over there*. This is the land of one to one. But what if it were not one to one? What if a gentleman were one day to approach you to suggest that he would be very happy to give you two marks in exchange for every one of yours? That would be very nice, would it not?'

'It would also be illegal,' I said. A thrill was running through me. We had not been two hours in the German Democratic Republic. We had already unearthed an enemy of the state. I felt that this was an interesting experience, an improvement on listening to Ogden reading out about the Nazis burning books.

'Ah, legality,' the man said. 'Legal – illegal – legal – illegal. It is so pleasing, the way the state decides that one thing shall be illegal today, and a matter of being sent to prison, and tomorrow it shall change its mind, and the same thing is quite permitted. But again, I ask my question of you two intelligent gentlemen: you would be very happy, would you not, to be offered two of our marks for every one of yours?'

'Happy up to a point,' Ogden said. He folded his arms. He sat back in the chair. The man fell silent. I thought he had been stymied by Ogden striking a make-me-an-offer pose, a pose I hadn't thought he had within him. But in fact he had seen what I had not, that the girl had emerged from the café door with our two coffees on a tray. He waited until she came.

She set them down. She cast him a look. He remained seraph-ically calm, apparently unaware that she was there at all.

'But I am not offering two of our marks for every one of yours,' the man continued. 'Today you will give your friend Mario one hundred Federal marks and he will give you four hundred of his East marks back. You are rich, gentlemen.'

'Who's Mario?' I said.

'That is I,' the man said.

'I don't suppose you can give us a receipt,' I said lightly. 'I mean, it wouldn't help us with our requirement to change twenty five marks a day.'

'I am so sorry,' Mario said. Could his name be Mario? He looked unremarkably German. 'Unfortunately I have mislaid my book of receipts, even if I could lay my hands on a pen.'

'Well, thank you, but—' I began to say.

Ogden interrupted me. 'I don't see why not,' he said. 'I'll give you a hundred Western marks. Can you give me five hundred Ostmarks?'

'That is too much,' Mario said.

'Five hundred,' Ogden said.

'Four hundred and fifty,' Mario said.

'Fine,' Ogden said. He took out his wallet and, with complete openness, counted out ten ten-mark notes. In return, Mario, much more quickly, counted out forty-five notes from an envelope he produced from the breast pocket of his jacket. In a moment everything was swept away. Mario was rising to go. I had said nothing. The problems that would arise if I made a fuss here in public were insurmountable. I saw worse than embarrassment.

'Where shall we go?' Ogden said, as if nothing at all had taken place. 'This is sort of the historic centre. I guess we could go and see some museums.'

'There's plenty to see,' I said.

'I'm just going to the loo,' Ogden said, 'and then we can go and see some of it.'

Ogden got up and went inside. I called the shy waitress over.

'To pay, please,' I said. Then an inspiration struck me. 'I don't think people should use your café for black-market activities. Do you know what just happened?'

'Please?' she said, her forehead crinkling with the scriptless quality of my question. It occurred to me that she might not actually be very intelligent, her sweetness being enough even in the Democratic Republic for a frontline tourist job.

'A stranger approached us and offered to change money illegally. At a black-market rate. I got the impression he was sitting here waiting for tourists to show up. Is he here regularly? I can describe him to you.'

'I am quite new here,' the girl said. 'I don't know the answer to your question. Please, write it down,' the girl said, gesturing at the book on the table. It was the guidebook to the Democratic Republic, but it had a few blank pages at the end. I wrote a telegraphic version of what I had just said. 'And your names, please.' I wrote both our names. I felt that some kind of obligation had been fulfilled by her request, that nothing further would come of it. Some kind of obligation on my side, too. I had placed myself on the other side of the law, and of principles, to Ogden and his black-market Mario. I had done the right thing.

'What was that all about?' Ogden said, returning.

'Just chewing the fat,' I said. 'Here's the bill. You could leave three marks.'

We checked into the hotel. We lay about for much of the afternoon reading our books. Towards evening, we found ourselves talking about James Frinton. It was not predictable that he would have left university and gone immediately into a job in the commercial mass media, writing reactionary comment for a million-selling right-wing newspaper. We remembered him from school; from those afternoons at Carole's café, until she was closed down for tax avoidance; from sitting around at Joaquin, Euan and Kate's place; from direct action. We had done a lot of shouting, of throwing things, of painting slogans on walls, of punching people who deserved to be punched. All that still went on, but those times were our most unified, our most directed, our most significant.

I had never been caught by the police, but my criminal record should have been long and doleful. Ogden had actually been prosecuted. He had been discovered using old paint cans to try to dam the foul-smelling but shallow river that ran through the city centre. It was impossible for Ogden to run away from the police when they were standing with disbelief watching him, knee deep, midstream, kicking cans into place. It was on his fourth night constructing it that he'd been apprehended. The scale of the dam he seemed to be attempting drew the police's curiosity. The question of why he had so many paint cans persuaded him to give a detailed answer of political conviction. That was when we were in the sixth form. Kate's spare room was successfully cleared of the hundreds of paint cans she'd been complaining of. Ogden had his day in court, told twenty times to sit down and be quiet by the judge, was cheered from the gallery by fifteen Spartacists and their friends, had earned his spurs.

But had Frinton been in the gallery? I wasn't sure. There had been no criminal conviction to disclose when he applied for the *Globe*'s graduate programme. (Ogden's MP, the famous Phil, had laughed about it at the interview. He had his own record of painting on walls, digging up cricket pitches, sending human shit in boxes to the South African High Commission.) Frinton had come along sometimes. He had been the girl in the pub fight who always offers to hold people's coats. Perhaps only when the doors were closed and the company was known did he talk seriously, and with any appearance of commitment, about revolution and the future, and what action might be taken before socialism appeared on the Earth. I had heard him do so. Now I wondered.

It had been a long time since I had seen him. It had been the day that he came to knock on my door to tell me about Tracy Cartwright. He had changed a lot – changed his clothes, mostly. He was wearing a tweed jacket and what D. H. Lawrence describes as 'a little red rag of a tie'. His shoes were brown brogues, and polished. I had seen him about before, with his Trumper's haircut close to the skull at back and sides, and floppy on top. He had turned himself into something different from the first day at university. It had not, it seemed to me, been a complete success. But had his appearance and behaviour towards us in the sixth form been a success? Ogden and I were talking in Berlin towards the end of an afternoon, in a hotel room whose warm, damp and disinfected atmosphere spoke of the night-time solitary sexual pleasures of Bulgarian delegates to conferences of unimpeachable ideological purity. We thought we had got Frinton quite wrong. We would not be so naïve now. We had thought he was on our side when he was standing there in order to examine us more closely.

The true Frinton should have been apparent when we went to his place – the father's rage-filled account books, the mother, the brother, the stench of the grandmother behind closed doors, the sense of mother-love reaching out beyond Eartha Kitt on the television to an object that had long gone somewhere else. The conviction that you could achieve anything, that bad luck and malice were keeping you in your place. Frinton wanted most of all to grow up into a man, I now believe, not to remain in the hell of boyhood. That was what was in the air at Frinton's place. We hadn't understood that, or that manhood, for Frinton, would always require the renunciation of principles.

I had kept my principles. I had remained what I was, a boy. Our lives had not had enough experience to be other than awed and stunned by the superficial strangeness of the set-up. We all subscribed, too, to the belief that it was Frinton's mother, in reality hard as nails and living within the successful coping mechanism of declared and performing depression, who would be the one to kill herself. I almost said 'living happily'. But happiness was not the point.

'I heard Frinton joined the Tory Party,' Ogden said. 'What is it with Oxford, what it does to you?'

'Christ knows,' I said. I had no idea.

That evening, we decided to go to the bar we'd heard about, the one on the corner of Kollwitzplatz. Kollwitzplatz turned out to be a little distance north of the historic centre. The immaculate presentation of the historic, or idealistically future-looking façade, fell away quickly. We got on to the U-Bahn at Alexanderplatz, a statement of achievement and gleam. When we got out three stops along, the city had decayed into rotting tenements. The stone fronts were blackened and decaying. The once grand front doors were dissolving and fraying at the bottom. Former palaces of bourgeois comfort sprouted trees from cracks in the wall thirty feet high, rotting and breaking apart, like stale old chocolate cake. We made our way past an ancient brewery, neighbourhood shops generically labelled *Lebensmittel*, cobbled streets where the nation's only domestic cars sat parked, in the three colours that were all the nation needed. When we entered the dark brown space of the bar, lit with candles and half full of muttering people, we remembered where we had heard about it.

We had hardly come in when a drinker stood up and greeted us. It was the Australian historian who had been waiting with us in the Reisebüro in West Berlin. It was an immense, a geological, stretch of time between then and now; no more than a day, but a colossal era. He asked us to come and sit down with him and his friend, who, he explained, was a bit of a dickhead. We agreed. It was a surprise to find out that the friend was a citizen of the German Democratic Republic, like our new friend a historian in a university. It surprised me that the Australian felt able to criticize individuals in this way without much lowering his voice.

This bar was a bar that only had regulars – that was made up of regulars. The substance of their lives and habits, their rules and restrictions, their small desires and their short-term futures were present in the space like the wood of the stools and the smoke-darkened red paint on the ceiling. A lot of these people came here every day. There was a smell in Berlin in those days that you never smell any more, a smell of flesh long steeped in beer, and of what happens to clothes when they are deposited in an old-clothes shop. That smell: it appeared to me to be the smell of disappointment, and not just the result of particular molecules in combination. The centre and origin of that smell must have been in the bar at the corner of Kollwitzplatz – I never knew its name, or even if it ever had one. Nobody looked long at us, though they assessed us in their quiet way for what needed to be assessed. They knew what we were. They knew what each other was.

'A friend of mine has greatly suffered from this increased capacity to permit travel,' the Australian's friend, the dickhead, said. He was called Uwe. He had started as soon as we sat down. 'Do you know that some of us are given permission to travel? Me – no. Never. I do not know why. But my colleague Dr Müller, my colleague Professor *Sütterlin*, as we call him, my neighbour Braun, who works for the central government sporting agency – and so on – they have all started to travel. A week in Paris. A weekend in Madrid. A conference in Rome. A month residency in the Scottish countryside, in a house belonging to the old aristocracy. And then some of them do not come back. And others of them come back and they decide they do not want to return to their old lives.

'Two years ago, if you had come into this bar, you would have seen a very different group here. Not a solitary boring dickhead, as my friend here calls me, sitting alone with his *Schwarzbier*, but a whole group of friends who have been coming here since they left the *Gymnasium*. There is my friend Ingo, and Dieter, Wolfgang, Thorsten and Thomas. And there is our friend Matthias. We have all been at the *Gymnasium* together, and we all have our jobs. And every evening when we meet we talk about what we have been doing since the last time we met. And every morning afterwards our friend Matthias writes a report on each of us for his friends in the large white building off the Stalinallee. You understand what I mean by his friends.

'Now, Matthias has been doing this since he was at school. It is his hobby. He enjoys it. We all know that he does it, and since none of us has ever done anything or thought anything that could interest anybody, we are quite happy that he does it and that it makes him feel important. If there is anything that is significant in our lives about to happen, then perhaps we think about mentioning it only when Matthias is not in the room. Everybody understands and everybody is happy. Matthias does not have a very important job. He is the assistant in a little library in a small town in Brandenburg, I will not mention which one. And this gives him something to do, to write reports about all of us.

'And you have to understand another thing. We are not in a democratic society, though we call ourselves that. We do not have a line of communication with our government through voting, as you do. It is helpful to have somebody in your circle who talks to officials every week. That probably does not occur to you. An *informal colleague* of the friends in the large white building just off the Stalinallee can be a nice thing to have. How do you think Herr Honecker will ever hear about what I have been up to? A friend of friends – he is a very nice conduit to authority. He tells them about all the hopes and dreams of our whole circle. Once a week he tells them this.

'One day Ingo tells us that he has been approved to have a permit to travel, and will be going to Hamburg in the Federal Republic the next day. And he goes. This is quite a new thing, and we are often talking about who has the permission to leave the Democratic Republic in this new system of rewards. Him, him, her, not him, not her, but him. And soon the same thing happens to Thorsten, who in a month in Madrid meets a Spanish girl who teaches him how to speak Spanish, not like the Spanish as Thorsten has learnt it from books and Frau Tranchell at the Language Institute of the Humboldt University, Berlin, but how to speak Spanish when you are in bed and horizontal and with some pleasure. And Thorsten stays. And then in a month or two permissions are granted to one of the others, and then another. Some of them come back. Most of them come back after their trips. But the strange thing is this. When they come back, they do not appear at the bar in Kollwitzplatz. It is only by chance that we find out that they have returned, and when I go to call on them, they are quite friendly, and say that they will come down to meet with the gang some time, and they do not come.

'The place and their friends do not work for them any more.

'So the group becomes smaller and smaller. I am given permission to go abroad, too. I am the last of the group to make a trip like this. The last except Matthias, and for

Matthias the permission will never come. He is a deputy librarian in a suburban public library. Some evenings we are only two, he and I, in this bar. Something terrible is troubling him. This is one night in February. I cannot bear this. Matthias is my friend, after all, and I ask him to share the problem that is weighing on his mind. And Matthias says, with great difficulty, and even with some tears, "Uwe. I have done a terrible thing. I do not know if you can forgive me. For years I have been writing reports about you – not just you, but every one of our friends. I have been classified as an informal colleague by the security services. Every week I have scuttled home and written a report about what you have said, adding a paragraph to a dozen reports on a dozen friends. And tonight I am going to do exactly the same thing about what we have talked about tonight."

"'I hope that you won't tell them that you have admitted this," I said.

"'No, of course not,' Matthias said.

'You could see that he was startled that this was my first reaction. "The truth is," I went on, "we have all known this for years. Nobody was in any doubt that you were busy writing reports on all of us."

"'But what must you have thought of me?" Matthias said.

"'It made no difference at all,' I said. This was not quite accurate, but it was true that it did not persuade anyone to stop meeting with Matthias, or to treat him differently.

"'The fact is," Matthias said, "that they are growing impatient with me. Two years ago, I could supply reports on eight people, just by sitting in this bar once or twice a week. But now—"

'"Is it only me?" I said. Matthias nodded. He was filled with shame and inadequacy. It is true that the world judges an individual by his success in the world – by which I mean his success in forming connections and friendships. A man with many friends makes more friends. An ugly and boring man who has had one beautiful girlfriend will find it quite easy to find another beautiful girlfriend. This is a fact of existence, and I believe that the individuals in the security services are subject to it. They are not impressed by an individual who has, it now appears, only one friend. And, believe me, I do nothing interesting, and say nothing interesting. Matthias's reports on me must be very disappointing.

'But I do not see what I can do. As I explain to Matthias, I cannot turn myself into a dangerous criminal in order to raise his reputation. He quite understands that. He went away in a disconsolate mood. But tonight, it occurs to me, I can, after all, help him out. Would you mind very much if I introduced him to you? It would be quite harmless. Make sure he gets your names. By the time he writes his reports, I am sure you will be out of the country altogether. It would make him so happy.'

The Australian historian was laughing. 'I'd love to,' he said. 'I've always wanted to think I was being watched by those guys. I was never convinced they'd even opened a file on me.'

'Why not?' Ogden said. 'An interesting experience. Let's meet him.'

A middle-aged man passed in an old tweed coat. The whiff of second-hand clothes was strong on him. His hand shook as he pointed. 'There's too many foreigners in here tonight,' he said. 'Berlin for the Berliner. I don't want foreigners in my bar.'

'Fuck off,' the Australian said briskly. '*Ich bin kein Ausländer. Ich bin Schutzmacht.*'

The man, who had been opening his mouth for further denunciations, closed it again. He looked old, frightened, drunk. He turned away.

'That's how you deal with them. Remind them that you're not a foreigner, you're a protecting power. They hate that. How long are you here in Berlin?' the Australian said. 'Watch out for strangers in mackintoshes following you.'

'We're going to Leipzig tomorrow,' I said. Before we knew it, the Australian had decided that he would come too. He needed to go there some time for his research. It was tedious to travel on your own. We agreed on a train to catch. And soon a large, shambling fellow came in, with an untidy, patchy beard and pink skin. His clothes gave off that smell of beer and mould. He greeted his friend Uwe briefly, without warmth. To us he paid the special attentiveness that consists of looking elsewhere, only flicking us a brief glance when Uwe introduced the three of us. I looked at him with interest and curiosity. He was, after all, a direct agent of government, of the politics I had a degree of admiration for. He was about to explore our lives. He was hoping to gather information about individuals. We did not live in this society. We were not subject to its borders. We were consenting to engage with its structures of power as a change from the structures of powers we normally lived within. That would be our holiday. For a moment, as he began his halting, unconvincing small-talk, politics appeared to me as an activity that had profoundly mistaken its own nature. It thought of itself as something that was done to people. In reality politics was much more like the situation as we conceived it. We were aware of the postures of power, more aware than the person who was concealing it. We were going along with it for the moment. We were giving it just as much information as would make it feel in tune with its existence as it conceived it. We were humouring it. They would find out about the hopes and dreams of two foreigners, visiting. And once the second beer arrived – it was good old-fashioned beer, well worth the journey into Prenzlauer Berg – I began to relax. I started to tell Matthias, with all the vividness I could muster, everything about the Spartacists: what we had done, what we wanted to do, the things we had smashed, the things we had written, the fun we'd had.

We got back to the hotel as drunk as drunk could be. We had spent five marks and twenty-eight pfennigs. 'That was fun,' Ogden said, as we fell into the lift. 'That was as much fun as – what time are we up in the morning? The train?' But I was through the door and into the bathroom and two pints of water from the tap and then onto my bed. Someone was taking my shoes off – an incompetent fumbler. The bed underneath me was spinning, the whole room, too bright. Black.

    In
      the end
    I am in
     a room with those
      huge windows and who is
    it by my side no facing me
  talking my mother with tears in her eyes don't worry my
  time's up I've had my life it doesn't matter and I'm crying

too because above in the sky full of ships the crowds
running past us on a hillside she is holding me the aliens
say everyone must die tomorrow the ships in the sky great
beige globes and my mother saying if I die it doesn't
matter and not understanding that everyone dies these
crowds die all England dies she dies and I die and it
happens tomorrow my legs running but won't move won't
move and my mother crying her face big in mine and her
arms around me embracing holding me down love and I
can't move I can't run the death ray is coming I hear its
hot scream
   I hear its hot scream
    I hear its hot
       scream I hear
      its hot
        scream

The curtains were already drawn. The day was bright. In the
bathroom the shower was running. I prised my eyes apart. In
fact, I didn't feel all that bad. I had followed Joaquin's practice
of making sure to drink as much water as I possibly could
before going to bed drunk. Today we were leaving Berlin. We
were going to Leipzig. Leipzig, where Bach came from. There
was historical stuff there and the real DDR, not just over the
Wall with the Potemkin façades for the benefit of the day-trippers. We were going with the Australian historian. I remembered it all now.

'This is OK,' Ogden said, when we were sitting in the
Interhotel's restaurant for breakfast. 'I don't think it's any
worse than Frau Dittberner's breakfast.'

'I don't know why you would think it was likely to be worse than Frau Dittberner's breakfast. This is a big international hotel,' I said, but the breakfast was undeniably worse. The salami was a brilliant shade of pink; the bread had been sliced yesterday; the smoked salmon, laid out reverently and with a minatory serving boy standing by unsmiling to make sure you didn't take more than your fair share, tasted of exactly nothing. The hard-boiled eggs had been sitting in hot water for too long. Each carried a ring of deep grey around the yolk, like Victorian mourning paper with an edging of black. But it was important not to comment on trivial differences like these. 'I bet you know exactly what breakfast in big international hotels is like.'

'Because of Phil, you mean,' Ogden said. 'A few. I don't go on all his trips. I tried to get him to take me to Venezuela with his select committee. But the rules had been changed and it wasn't allowed.'

'How long are you going to stick with him?'

'Might not be up to me,' Ogden said. Then he went on, in pompous tones, 'It's the wishes of the electorate that have to be taken into account.'

'What's Phil's majority?'

'Twenty-four thousand seven hundred and twenty-seven,' Ogden said.

'So twenty-four thousand seven hundred and twenty-seven people would have to change the habits of a lifetime to throw him out. I would call that a safe seat.'

'Nothing's safe in this world,' Ogden said. He leant back in his chair, his eyes professionally hooded and knowledgeable; he lit his first cigarette of the day. 'And it's twelve thousand three hundred and sixty-four, the figure. They'd go off and vote for someone else. Twelve thousand fewer for him is twelve thousand more for someone else.'

'Twelve thousand – oh, I see. So then what are you going to do?'

'Well, I'd consider my position,' Ogden said. 'I see everything that Phil's done, and the select committee is great, but it's not actually achieving anything.'

'It's not power,' I said.

'No. There's some interesting people in the leader's office. I think I might make my case there.'

'You'd work for Kinnock?'

'You don't have to believe everything your boss says in public.' Ogden stubbed out his cigarette rhythmically, making his point with it. 'And they don't say exactly the same behind closed doors. Believe me, he's an interesting sort of mind.'

'But Kinnock – after what he's done. You might as well cut your differences and take up a job working for Thatcher. There's no ideological divide between them.'

'Bollocks. Anyway, it won't happen. They're still suspicious of people who come from where Phil's come from. I mean ideologically. So I guess it's going to be a job in a non-profit for two years and then ...'

Ogden made a huge gesture with his hands, as if describing a round sexy woman, the explosion of an atomic bomb over the table with its uneaten breakfast. I started to place the detritus in the miniature rubbish bin at the centre of the table.

'I don't know what that means.'

'I mean a safe seat. Somewhere in the north ideally. I want to stand up and get my voice heard. You can see that. Not just getting a third of what I suggest to Phil read out by him. On the select committee he has questions written for him by the clerks on the committee and then I write some for him. And of course he's got his own. So they come first and mine sometimes get asked but maybe not. It's frustrating. I want to get my own words out in my own voice. The only way to do that is to become an MP. And when the socialist government's in place – next election's 1991, the one after that 1995 – I'm going to get listened to. Believe you me, I'm going to get listened to. Bag carrier, junior minister, Cabinet minister, I'm not going to stop until I'm chancellor.'

'What's your deadline?'

'2003,' Ogden said, and then, again, made that explosion gesture, his fingers spread wide, his hands moving apart to a noise in his mouth. It was a gesture new in Ogden's repertoire. It must have been borrowed from an important and impressive figure in his life. Perhaps Phil – Dr Philip Cawston MP, the ex-steel worker and, under the counter, the Militant activist. Or perhaps someone still more impressive, somebody who as yet was hardly aware of Ogden's existence. I had that impression. Ogden was going to become who he would become. His plans had been dwelt on, evolved, shared with few. I was privileged.

'Of course, things might change,' I said. 'Circumstances might not be the same in 2003.'

'What do you mean? Revolution, you mean? Do you know? I think there's never going to be a revolution in this country. England, I mean. I think it's just going to have to be done through the usual methods. Parliament, constituencies, elections. They won't notice a revolution's happened until it's there. We're going to bring it to them so nicely wrapped that everyone will welcome it. A bomb buried in flowers.'

That was not quite what I had meant. In my head were the last remnants of my dream. I still had the feeling that at any moment large forces could assemble in the sky and order change, or an ending for everything we had known. Ogden had not learnt the same lesson I had learnt. For him, still, politics consisted of what politicians choose to do to the people. Their agreement must be extracted, or the appearance of an agreement. Then the politician is free to do what he wants to them. For me political life is a matter of objecting from the floor, of making the individual voice heard. Had I made a great mistake? When Ogden had spoken from the floor that time the army major came, I'd admired him because I thought he wanted to make his unimportant voice heard. He wanted to encourage all the other unimportant voices to be heard, too. It did not occur to me that Ogden had spoken at such length because he wanted to take the place of the major. He wanted to speak from the stage, to tell the rest of us what to do. There, in the East Berlin breakfast room in 1987, I heard Ogden's career path laid out for the first time. He modestly restricted himself. He was going to be chancellor by 2003.

'What time's the train?'

'I bet that Australian doesn't turn up. He was a bit drunk.'

'Let's pay the bill and get off. We need to change our twenty-five marks too. The daily requirement.'

Ogden folded his arms and shook his head at the reception when he discovered that the hotel bills in the Interhotel group could be paid only with hard currency. That meant running into his 1000-Deutschmark stock. He handed over the daily twenty-five marks to be returned for twenty-five Ostmarks with a very bad grace. It was added to his 520-odd Ostmarks in the wallet – even with all that beer, we had only managed to spend about ten marks between us the day before. Even the train tickets to Leipzig, which Ogden paid for from his illegal stash, made only a very small dent. The socialist policy of making public transport affordable for everyone was for once not welcome. We had to go shopping, I thought. Furs, I thought.

I was sceptical that the Australian professor would turn up, but he was waiting on the sooty platform by the third carriage of the train. He leapt up from the station bench with a big smile and his hand outstretched.

'Got your tickets? Got your permits? Got a book to read?' he said. 'Here we go. Never taken one of these? It's an adventure. A slow sort of adventure. Sometimes you think you're not going to get there the same day, or it would be quicker to walk. But you get there. Hungarian rail's better. See if we can find three seats together.'

We found three seats together.

'Give you a hard time, did they?' he said. 'The permit people at the Reisebüro? They like doing that. It's all baloney, though. They tell you that you need to get a permit before you move two miles in that direction but I never bother.'

'Haven't you got a permit to go to Leipzig?' Ogden said, impressed.

'The thing is that before they give you a permit you have to tell them where you're staying,' the Australian said. 'I'm probably going to stay with the lady I usually stay with. She rents

out her spare room to whoever – she's the widow of a professor of physics so she likes a scholar – and she's in that bit of
town by the Opera House. It's pretty nice and she only charges
twenty marks a night.'

'Doesn't she know you're coming?'

'I'll just turn up and if it's taken I'll find somewhere else.'

'Why don't you phone her?' I asked.

The Australian looked me over, kindly but amused. I
blushed to be so immediately forgiven for my naivety. 'She
hasn't got a phone,' he said. 'There aren't many who do. It's
not like it is in the West. Haven't you noticed? Your room in
the hotel doesn't have a phone in it, does it? What you do here
– you phone up, you book, you make arrangements, you fall
in with the arrangements. Everyone has these intricate kind
of interlocking arrangements. But here – I don't think they
hand out phones very readily. You can get one, but it takes
years and plenty of people just don't bother. So – you turn up
and ring the doorbell and say, "Hi, Frau Bayer, is your spare
room available tonight?" and she says yes or no, *leider nicht*,
I'll walk round the corner with you to see if my friend Frau
Kapossy can help. Did you have fun last night?'

'Spinning a story,' Ogden said.

'Yeah, I was kind of listening to your quiet friend here,' the
Australian said, nodding at me. 'He's good value when he gets
going. That friend of crazily boring Uwe – the guy Matthias
with the *clients* just off the Frankfurterallee – those clients are
going to be thrilled with the stuff they're getting from
Matthias. Maybe too thrilled. If I were one of the *friends* I'd
be asking Matthias how it is exactly that after months of
reporting on the blameless home life of Uwe and how the

beans are growing in Uwe's allotment in Pankow that he's got all this red-hot material about radical leftist terrorism in the West. It was a good story, though.'

'Where do you come from in Australia?' I asked. I didn't want to get into the substance of what I had told the informer the night before. I had been drunk during most of it. I had the impression I had been quite exuberant. If the Australian thought I had been making it all up, I wouldn't put him right.

'I can honestly say that a vast fog of mid-Pacific oblivion has now arisen between me and Australia so that I hardly remember one thing about it.'

'Seriously.'

'I come from a town called Sydney. I learnt German at school. I was one of those weird kids who shut the curtains against the sunlight, never went to the beach, dressed in black, practised adjective endings and tried to read Karl Kraus. Dreamt of living in Vienna or Munich or Berlin. The other kids thought I was so weird I didn't even get bullied – you know how a pack of dogs will steer well clear of a dog that's acting seriously strange. I moved to Germany when I was twenty-one, as soon as I could get someone to pay for some research project. It's harder to be one of those kids in England, I guess. But your German, it's pretty good. You don't get to speak good German by learning it unless you're a bit weird.'

'Have you ever been to a town called Broome?'

'Bruhm? A town in Germany?'

'Broome, Australia. Western Australia. My mother lives there.' It was comforting even to say 'Western Australia'. I still wrote WA on an envelope once a month, an envelope filled with warm and funny incident. Once a month I got a warm and funny letter back, bouncy with news and details of my mother's life in the pearl-fishing capital of Western Australia. They were strangely impersonal in their warmth and comedy, my mother's letters. Mine were too. Sometimes I made stuff up about Joaquin if he hadn't said anything worth reporting or done anything interesting all month. Sometimes I made stuff up if what he had done was too interesting or, from my mother's point of view, hair-raising. This is what is called the art of letter-writing. My relationship with my mother had improved a good deal since I'd stopped seeing her altogether. My feelings towards her, embodied in the words *Broome, Western Australia*, were delightful, affectionate, and ultimately indifferent.

'Your mother comes from Broome? Seriously?'

'No, she moved there. She got divorced from my father and she moved to Broome.'

'That's an interesting thing to do. I don't mean Broome's interesting. You move to Broome and there's about twenty people living there and if you don't much like them then you'd have to go about two thousand miles to meet anyone else.'

'I suppose my mum gets along with anyone. She's been there for ten years now so it must suit her. Interesting's an interesting word.'

'Nobody in Broome would think it was weird that someone wanted to move there. Moving to Germany would be weird to them. You can't move to the Democratic Republic of Germany, though. Actually, the East Germans would think that was really weird. They think it's weird even them living there. That's why they're so obsessed with which of them has the right to travel. The ones who go abroad and come back to

Erfurt after a week in Munich at some conference. They call their whole family together and say they have an announcement to make. You know, they say, that we all thought it was weird living here. Well, I've gone somewhere else and I've eaten their food and I've seen their shops and I've talked to the people who live there and guess what. We were right. It really is weird living here. They all like that. I've got this friend in Berlin – in West Berlin. I'm not annoying you, I hope?'

'No, no,' I said. I didn't know why he would think that.

'Do you know Kreuzberg? In the West? It's where the dropouts ended up. And the Turks. All the anarchists and the draft-dodgers and the plotters and the radicals – they're all in Kreuzberg. When Reagan came on a state visit to Berlin the police thought it would save a lot of trouble if they just put up a big barrier round the whole of Kreuzberg and stopped anyone getting out. A walled city within a walled city. It's up against the Wall itself, and on the other side of the Wall there's a place called Friedrichshain, and Friedrichshain's exactly the same. There are anarchists and troublemakers and kids who wear nothing but black in East Berlin and they all live in Friedrichshain, some of them fifty metres away from the kids in Kreuzberg. Anyway.

'There's this guy I know a bit in Kreuzberg called Christoph. He's Bavarian but he came here to dodge the draft and he's been here for years. He works in a museum two days a week. He's a really fantastic tango dancer. They're crazy about the tango here, those anarchists. I don't know why. Christoph's the best of the best. He teaches an extra-mural class at the Free University in tango. He drinks at Rose's on the Oranienstrasse and Bierhimmel and Würgeengel, and there's an abandoned boat on the Landwehrkanal that someone broke into a couple of years ago. Now it's got fairy lights and electricity and a working bar. It plays seventies German hits at top volume and it's called the Pick-As, the Ace of Spades, which is a kind of joke. That's what a really awful bar would be called in suburban Paderborn or somewhere. And it's usually got Christoph Egger in it. He likes his wheat beer, his *Hefeweizen*, just like your quiet friend here, and his four beers and his tango class once a week. If you want to find him you go into the Pick-As and you ask the barman if the professor of tango has been in.

'That's his life in total. He never goes anywhere. He's sort of famous in Kreuzberg for never leaving Kreuzberg even. And one night in a bar around four a.m. someone says to him, "Christoph, you'd be better off in the Democratic Republic." It's a joke but they start talking about it. They have a point. Christoph would be looked after. He'd have somewhere to live and a job that would be worth doing. They might even find him a wife or something. Christoph wakes up the next day and this conversation makes perfect sense. He goes on considering it. No one can think of anything against it. So one day, after a few weeks, he goes into the East German embassy in West Berlin and tells them he would like to emigrate to the Democratic Republic of Germany. The man whose job it is to interview applicants – I don't think he has a very busy life. They talk to him all day, they take his details, they send him away. Christoph is over the moon. He's practically giving his landlord notice. Then the letter comes. They won't have him.'

'Just one question,' Ogden said. 'Most people who'd think of moving to the DDR would do it because they believed in the project, not for an easier life. Why didn't he do it for that reason?'

'That's what they would have said, I believe,' the Australian said. 'Not that they give an explanation. They just turned him down.'

I looked out of the window of the train. It was passing a thick-wooded landscape. It was artificial, neat and regular in its arrangement, like a plantation. There was some mist about, clinging to the trees. There were forests like this by very similar train lines in this country, and the other country over there. There were different political systems governing each of them. Yet the trees grew. Politicians took charge. The trees grew in any case. What is the name of the politician in charge of the growth of trees in this region of the country? Germany. Sleep was overtaking me.

The door of the first-floor apartment was opened a crack. A face, round and brown and suspicious, was there just above the level of the door handle. I explained who we were. We were here with friendly greetings to pass on to the minister from Dr Philip Cawston, the Member of Parliament from England. She opened the door wider. Without any words she gestured us into the hallway. I entered with interest.

We had decided that we should visit Ogden's contact as soon as we reached Leipzig. We had left our suitcases at the hotel, just by the station. We had come straight away to the address Ogden had, with a copy of Cawston's book, suitably inscribed. After that, we would go to the central police station to register ourselves as visitors to Leipzig, as required by the authorities.

The flat was heavy with past glories. Facing the door was a ceiling-high glass case filled with miscellaneous objects – statuettes in polished silver of flag-bearers, an African object made out of a fat tuft of hair sprouting from a beaten bronze globe, a mock-Meissen plate bearing a scene of fraternal greeting, its rim obscenely bubbling with glistening fruit like cysts. Although this was the minister's house, each beautifully dusted object carried a typed label in front of it. These were gifts to the minister, or ex-minister, in his official capacity on his travels around the world – Cuba, Nicaragua, North Korea, Albania, Romania, Zimbabwe. The flat itself was faded in the way that flats become after thirty years of being lived in by the same people. Everything was dusted and clean and muted and worn, and dimmed by time. Someone had chosen this floral wallpaper with love, some time when Erich Honecker was inspiring his new nation. No new painting would be added to the twelve watercolours of insipid rural scenes that lined the corridor. Even the books gave the impression of a completed collection. They were sets of collected classic authors, the neatest bookshelf imaginable. We followed the small woman who had let us in. She had done this before today. Was she his secretary or a housekeeper? She wore a very respectable brown suit. Her hair around the neat, wrinkled face was tight and careful, that of a professional woman.

We were led into a large salon. The minister was sitting in a corner of the room with a pair of people, a woman and a small girl. He paid us no attention, going on with what was evidently a very amusing conversation. The secretary indicated that we should sit quietly in another corner and wait until the minister was ready for us. She promised us tea. She marched off. The flat had high nineteenth-century ceilings. A chandelier hung in the centre of the room. There were three double windows in a line, with shutters open. Heavy dark blue William Morris curtains were tied back. The room was large enough to have a number of groupings of furniture, all modern, or 1950s at least, all gathered around a standard lamp and a coffee-table or card-table. There were rugs on the amber-coloured parquet. The furniture was oatmeal. On the wall over the black grand piano there was a portrait of the minister, holding a scale model of a building, looking up with a disconcertingly inexpert sparkle in his eye. The minister had been in charge of major projects in Saxony-Anhalt, some put up mostly for prestige, for a quarter of a century. I couldn't be sure, but I thought the architectural model he was holding in the painting might represent the Leipzig Opera House. The painter had been told, late on in the process, to incorporate a visionary gleam in the eye, a visionary socialist gleam as the minister envisaged the future. The people of Saxony-Anhalt flocking straight from work, paint-stained overalls next to insurance suit next to pinny, for a wonderful evening of Wagner. The visionary gleam had been supposed to convey all of that, but all the painter had known how to do was to dab a brilliant blob of white on the subject's iris. It looked unusual, like a Hollywood leading man in the light of a magnesium glare.

We sat down quietly. The secretary returned, handing the minister a piece of paper. I compared the portrait with the original, sitting in the opposite corner of the room, charming two ladies who were charming him back. His hands disposed of the piece of paper into his pocket. He was busy with the

Meissen teapot. Little cakes were beautifully arranged around a Meissen tower of plates. He was dark in the painting. His hair was white now, and he wore glasses. The painter had conveyed quite well his lean and purposeful aura, I saw, even if now that purpose was directed mainly towards a glamorous woman and a small girl. They were very dressed up. The woman was in a suit of nubbly pink tweed – you felt she lived her life beautifully dressed. The girl, around eight or nine, had been told to prepare for a special treat. Her dress was baby blue with lace ruffles at the neck, puffed sleeves, and ruched with scarlet ribbons. She even had a little handbag. She wore it all with panache and even pleasure. It seemed to me that special treats were a regular part of her life, cosseted and petted and charming the great. She was pink and delighted, not showing off but beautifully behaved. She had her own teacup. She took a cake only when invited to do so, eating it in tiny bites, setting it down on the Meissen plate in between. I could not be sure, but her conversation appeared to be asking questions of the minister – polite, neutral, ladylike questions, observations about his holiday and his grandchildren. She had been trained well, and trained all her life, not just trained for this afternoon's encounter. She was, surely, with her grandmother, not her mother. The personal perfection and the air of relaxed irresponsible indulgence were too marked for motherhood. The grandmother and the minister were both delighted with the little girl. The minister, from time to time, leant forward to give the child a pat, even a pinch, on her thigh, on her upper arm, on her cheek. Nobody objected. Nobody acknowledged there was anyone else in the room. I grew self-conscious of what Ogden and I were wearing, could almost feel the dust of the train falling from our old jeans and unwashed sweaters. We waited without speaking, a sort of beginning of a smile on my face.

Some sort of mock-altercation was taking place at the other side of the room. The minister asked the little girl to ask her grandmother something. The grandmother declined, with a smile and a wave of her hand, as if shooing away a fly. But the minister asked again, with a smile, and this time she shook her head and agreed. The minister got up, followed by the woman. To my surprise they came towards our corner of the room. He nodded to us genially. The woman gave a sort of smile that might have been intended for the portrait on the wall to our side. He sat down at the piano. He began to play. The music was not very hard. She began to sing. I know when greatness reveals itself, and here was greatness, in a Chanel suit, and a granddaughter in a dress with ribbons.

Du holde Kunst ...

The little Schubert song came to an end. The granddaughter burst into applause – solitary applause: I think Ogden and I both felt we were eavesdroppers there. With a shock I saw that the secretary in the brown suit had quietly entered the room when the minister had begun to play. She stood for a moment as the minister and the great singer, now retired from the concert stage altogether, congratulated each other; she gave a nod; she went back to her work. In five minutes the woman and the little girl had said their goodbyes, submitted to having their hands kissed, and were gone. They were free in their lives, I understood. They lived, both of them, in a world where borders and decisions from above made no difference, a world in which Schubert meant the same anywhere, whatever politicians wanted to do. *Du holde Kunst ...*

The minister came over to us. We stood up. He made a small wave. I could not tell whether this meant 'Sit down' or 'Stay where you are'. With a frown, he took the piece of paper from his pocket. He looked it over. 'Gentlemen,' he said finally, in English. We sat down. I felt that this was the second-rank position in the saloon, around an empty card-table. Over there was a tower of cakes. Perhaps tea would come.

Ogden explained that he had come with greetings from Dr Philip Cawston MP, who remembered with great fondness the week he had spent at the conference in – I forget now. I started to translate, but the minister cut me off.

'Not necessary,' he said. 'Mr Cawston, a very distinguished member of his party. I remember meeting him. We had some pleasant evenings in each other's company.' He could not help it. As he said this, very charmingly, he cast an eye down to the piece of paper on which his secretary had typed an explanatory paragraph.

'Mr Cawston sends his best greetings,' Ogden said again. 'The party is changing, in some respects, but Mr Cawston represents its future, as well as the past.'

'I am pleased to hear it,' the minister said. 'I myself retired from political life three years ago. I thought I would be much less busy, but—'

Ogden took the opportunity to hand over Philip Cawston's memoir, or programme for political change, or manifesto, or whatever it was – I had looked at some of it on the train. The minister thanked him with a delightful, boyish, practised smile. He set it down quickly on the card-table.

'May I ask,' I said, 'who was your guest just now? I seemed to recognize her. And she sang so beautifully.'

'An old friend,' the minister said. 'I have known her for many years.' He showed his teeth. He might have been waiting for the next move in the conversation, but I had none. Ogden, too, was overawed. He leant forward as if to make some comment, but thought better of it. He leant back. The silence was broken by the door to the salon opening. The small woman in brown entered with a sheaf of papers. A glance passed between her and the minister; she nodded; he stood up. We found ourselves saying goodbye with, again, assurances of fraternal greetings.

'I don't know what I expected,' Ogden said, at lunch the next day. We had made a tacit agreement that we would not discuss it until then. 'It wasn't what I would have done – what I've seen Phil do.'

'He's retired, though,' I said. We were sitting in a beer hall in the central square of Leipzig. A historic building was on one side of the square. On the other, a bold piece of bright blue modernist fantasy from the 1960s bore a mosaic of the triumph of workers. We had two beers in front of us, and two schnitzels. At the bar, two waiters leant against the wall, half attending to the nearly empty room. One was using a beer mat to pick his teeth.

'Phil always finds times for foreign visitors. Gives them tea.'

'He needn't have seen us at all.'

'He was more interested in flirting with that old opera singer and the little girl. Done up like Violet Elizabeth Bott.'

'She was his old friend. He had no idea who we were. How often has he ever seen Phil? He must have met thousands of foreign socialists in his life.'

'People like that – they just don't care. About what's going to happen to the world. Retire, and dribble your time away having tea with celebrities. Those people – they're as bad as English Tories. So long as they're all right.'

'Oh, come on.'

'And this food is awful.'

'Well, yes.'

There is a play by Chekhov called *The Cherry Orchard*. In it, the characters are gathered and talking when, all at once, in the remote distance, a sound is heard. It is inexplicable, like a great string being plucked. No one can explain it. It changes everything. What happened to us after that lunch was like that. There was no explanation for it. Afterwards my life was never the same.

We left the beer hall. We were walking down a street of shops and offices. We were supposed to go to the police, to register our presence in Leipzig. There were a few people about, but not a crowd. One side of the street was covered with scaffolding. Ogden and I were passing the occasional remark when, five yards in front of us, a small but heavy piece of luggage – a small rucksack, I thought – fell with a thud to the ground. It had fallen from high up. Pieces of glass fell with it, shattering across the pavement. A worker must have dropped it, or had it been thrown through a window? We were lucky not to be struck by it, or by a shard of glass. Immediately afterwards, a much bigger piece of baggage hit the ground. It was an unusual shape. For a moment I thought the bag had split open while falling. The two objects lay there. The larger one had tubes, almost like sleeves, almost like limbs. At my side a human voice made a sound. I understand now it was Ogden's throat. The sound he made was like a man who has been punched – an outburst of air. Nothing had fallen on him. He had understood a second before I did what had dropped from the sky.

A sheet of glass was being lifted by a crane. The support had failed. It had somehow fallen on a workman. The man's head had been immediately severed. The smaller object, which I had thought was a small rucksack, was the man's head hitting the ground. The larger one, which was a stranger shape, harder to understand, was the man's torso, his trunk and limbs.

We had seen the death of a man. A life had taken place before this moment. What lives contain had run its course.

Around us people were beginning to scream. Ogden's arms were around me. I could not understand it. But his concerns were for me. He was hustling me away.

I never knew the name of the man who died. There was no reason why I should ever have discovered it. Perhaps, in the old German Democratic Republic, the victims of industrial accidents like that were not made publicly known. There was no connection between me and him – between me and that body divided in two, between trunk and limbs, and sightless head. The only connection that was made was that I was there at the moment of his death. The connection is slight and trivial. The event took place, now, thirty years ago. Nothing about it should have made any change in my life. But those two objects falling heavily to earth are, to me, the same as the sound of the string breaking, far off, in Chekhov's play. My life divides into two. There is the part of my life that happened before a decapitated man fell from a height, in Leipzig, in the year 1987. And there is everything that happened afterwards.

We were back in the hotel room. I was not quite sure how we got there or what time it was. The curtains had been drawn. I was sitting on the end of the bed, looking at the wall.

'Everything will be fine,' my friend was saying to me. 'Everything is all right.'

I agreed with him in some way.

'I'm sorry you had to see that,' he went on. 'Nobody should have to see something like that.'

'I thought it was luggage,' I said. It was a strange remark he had made. He had seen what I had seen, and understood what he was seeing before I had.

He looked at me directly. I found his expression difficult to read.

'Falling luggage,' I said. It was as if I had said something that made very little sense to him. I lay back on the bed, looking at the ceiling. It would take me for ever to sleep. Perhaps it was not time to go to sleep. That time called night. I did not think I would ever sleep again. I felt giddy. There was something in my head, something important I wanted to think about. I would forget it. It would never go away. I could not think what it was. A voice in the room was talking, saying words. I thought I would shut my eyes. The voice has come closer. Somebody is taking the shoes from my feet. They are unbuttoning my shirt. I stay as I am. I am not going to sleep.

                    What
                  is it
                 what is it
               something there what a
              finger hard in my back
             no a face bony there on mine
            and a mouth a tongue hard sour
          stink where in the dark where at home
no where who no his hand on tugging my balls who a
tongue in my mouth pressing down and then dark a
weight on me a body bones, a corner, a joint, a stab in the
side smell of sweat old beer belch come on don't don't
come on relax I always wanted he named it who and I'm
fighting come on we're in Berlin no one will know yes it's
Berlin and no it's not it is it's Ogden a tongue in my
mouth a hand on my dick my balls and there in my side a
dick hard and pushing a stab a hand forcing under me
and a forearm on me on the chest and I can't push and
something wet something greasy under me and a push
and there Ogden is behind me and his forearms around
my shoulders somehow and he's inside and pumping and
I am no longer

    there.

    I feel nothing.

    It occurs to me that Ogden has forgotten where we are,
too.

    We are actually in Leipzig, not Berlin as he said.

    There is a body with a hole somewhere in the German
Democratic Republic.

    A man puts his thin hard little dick into it.

It hurts.

Nothing matters.

It will go on for a while.

I can think about other things.

I wonder what time it is.

The male orgasm is an act of violence, connected to the erection, which is connected to the collapse of the erection after orgasm, which is connected to impotence, which is connected to failure, and happens once before everything comes to an end

in an instant

and renewable

death.

Think of this interesting proposition.

The orgasm of the active partner, of the top, is death.

The orgasm of the passive partner, of me, is of the willed pleasure or the withholding of it.

There in that bed too narrow too hard too borrowed the men are put together and one rapes the other. But I can stop Ogden raping me so easily. I can stop him in a second. I can stop him by saying *fuck me* and wanting to be fucked and then I have consented. And then he is not raping me. Instead we are having sex together. The thought might make me laugh, in a parallel universe.

Or I could stop caring, or never start caring, whether Ogden in his misery and secrecy fucks me or not.

It will not take long.

There is no doubt in my mind that Ogden does not love me. I am quite certain that the man he loves is Joaquin. This is a fuck of punishment, a fuck of frustration.

It will not take long, Ogden's fucking.

In the city outside a torso with splayed limbs like a broken spider lies by the side of a head. I am to blame for it and I am being punished for it.

It does not take long, Ogden's fucking.

He has his orgasm and falls back onto the bed. Lord, Ogden is going to have a miserable day tomorrow and my day will be just fine. It is four thirty-seven in the morning. It is too narrow a bed to lie on, the both of us, and after four seconds I get up and go to lie in Ogden's bed. Four seconds is not very long; I mean it to be rather rude. His bed smells of him. It is not very long before Ogden starts crying, quite loudly. It is a disturbing noise and it takes me longer than I would have liked to go back to sleep. The noise of Ogden crying is the noise of a thin whining voice asking *please* and *sorry* and *I never meant to* over and over again. Outside the streets are silent. Only once in this aria of grieving self-pity do I hear a thin whining noise outside. A German Democratic Republic car on some early errand. It actually interests me, the consonance between the thin whining voice inside, trying to say words, and the thin whining engine outside,

  meaningless, purposeful, filling the empty street
    with its music. After a while I
      fall into a harmless what a
        harmless dark and quiet
          and silence and
            sleep and
              nothing.

In the morning I woke up to find that Ogden was staring at me. He was in my bed. I was in his. I yawned in a performing way, arms upright.

'Have you had a shower?' I said.

'No, not yet,' Ogden said. 'Do you want to go first?'

'I'll only take a minute,' I said pleasantly.

'I thought we might go to Weimar today,' Ogden said. 'I think we were supposed to go tomorrow. But we're done with Leipzig, don't you think?'

'The hotel was booked from tomorrow. But I suppose we can say we made a mistake, got a day wrong.'

Through breakfast, we talked about travel arrangements. We paid the bill in hard currency. We discovered there was a train to Weimar in an hour's time. We walked to the station. We bought tickets. We had plenty of time still. I reminded Ogden that we had not yet changed our daily twenty-five marks, as required by the law. We could do so at an office by the ticket counter.

'This is getting too much,' Ogden said. 'I shouldn't have changed anything with our friend in Berlin. We're only spending ten or twelve marks a day. I've got hundreds of Ostmarks. This is really a terrible situation.'

'The state requires it,' I said. 'There's no point in complaining about it. You shouldn't have gone above requirements like that.'

'Do you think our friend would change them back?' Ogden said. I didn't think it was worth answering.

We took our seats in the train, both facing forward. I thought of saying to Ogden, 'You raped me,' but decided against it. The carriage was half full. I was submerged in a rich, almost soup-like boredom. I carried out an experiment of discovering exactly what I could see without moving my head in any way. To the extreme left was a stretch of empty platform out of the window. To my right was a sliver of Ogden and the table on the other side of the aisle. There was a smell of old clothes and the pungent, inescapable brown-coal atmosphere. Probably people who lived here were quite unaware of it.

A man, a handsome, alert-looking man in a pale grey suit, asked if the seat opposite was taken. He sat down.

'This train is late,' Ogden said, looking at his watch. 'This is the right train, isn't it? Can you ask?'

'I'm sure it is,' I said, but asked the man opposite if this was the train to Weimar.

'Are you visiting?' he said politely, once that had been cleared up.

'On holiday,' I said. 'We are from England.'

'How interesting,' he said. 'I read many English novels when I was younger. I had a teacher who had an enthusiasm for your writer Dickens.'

'Your English must be good,' I said.

'No, I hardly speak one word,' he said. 'I read everything in German translation. Of course my teacher read the originals.'

'What is he saying?' Ogden said.

I ignored him. 'We're travelling to Weimar, and after that to Dresden,' I said. 'Do you live in Leipzig?'

'Yes,' the man said. 'I was born in Leipzig.'

'What would you advise us to do in Weimar?' I said. 'We're first-time visitors.'

'There are many historical sites to visit in Weimar,' he said. 'I do not think you will be at a loss for something to do.'

I felt very happy. This man was alluding in the most friendly and delicate way – *historical sites* – to the thing that lay at the base of his country, and of his whole existence, the establishment of a liberal political system, seventy years ago, that was always called the Weimar Republic. It was pleasant to meet a kindred spirit on a train journey in this way. 'It helps to understand history when you travel to the places where it was made,' I said. Something came innocently into my head. It was the possibility of action, like going to the restaurant car – if there was one – for a cup of coffee. Out of the window I could see another pair of tracks, for trains going in the opposite direction. I could get up now. I could go to the end of the carriage. I could open the door to the sideways hurtling air. I could step out into nothing. I would fall at great speed to the inert tracks opposite. I could lie on the tracks bloodied and groaning for some time, until a train in the opposite direction came along and severed my body in two or three. I could commit suicide. The thought was a peaceful one, and very detailed.

'I have travelled very little,' I said to the man. 'I know that travel abroad is difficult and limited for citizens of the German Democratic Republic. But I have travelled so little that coming here seems like a large adventure. I went on holiday with my parents when I was a child, and we went half a dozen times to Austria and Germany, the other Germany over there, as well as to France and once to Portugal, but I was young and there-fore self-centred and I think I now understand that when you travel with children your gaze must be constantly focused on

them, rather than on what you are travelling through. Does
that make sense? I know I said that citizens of the German
Democratic Republic can't travel, but that isn't quite correct,
is it? You can travel to other Warsaw Pact countries, and I
believe that you can go even on Mediterranean holidays in
Bulgaria, as well as spa breaks in Czechoslovakia and bracing
hiking holidays in southern Poland, these must be very enjoy-
able, so I suppose that you quite understand what I mean
when I say that to holiday with a child in tow is not the same
as to holiday. Or perhaps you do not have children, as indeed
we do not. I have also travelled to Australia, once, but that was
not really a holiday, that was to visit my mother, and it hardly
seemed like travelling at all, apart from the discomfort of the
twenty-four hours in an aeroplane. This is by far my most
adventurous holiday, this fortnight in the German Democratic
Republic, and we are finding it very interesting and exciting.
It is very interesting to meet citizens of a different system, who
live according to quite different philosophies, and to hear their
experiences of life, and I think it is interesting for them, too,
to meet people like us who are open to experience and who
indeed find a good deal to admire in the German Democratic
Republic and its culture. I would be very interested to hear
about your experiences of life, because the reason we travel
here is not so much to understand the past of Germany, the
beauties of the countryside and the interest of the historical
towns, but to form links with other human beings and to
understand the ways in which those other human beings look
out onto the world and try to organize it. That, I feel, is the
purpose of travel, not to go to a beach in Portugal and lie
looking at the sea for a fortnight, and after all, even there, the

waiter who brings you your drinks, if he is over thirty years old, has memories of a savage dictatorship impinging on his hopes and his possibilities, which the casual traveller has an obligation to explore in conversation, and not just to say *please bring me another piña colada*, would you not agree? Europe is full of recent memories of savage dictatorships. Some very recent, like Portugal's. And this is very much not a piña colada sort of holiday that I and my friend Ogden are undertaking. It is very good to meet someone and talk like this.'

'Will you excuse me?' the man opposite said. He took his briefcase. He stood up. He went to the next compartment of the train. There was complete silence in the compartment once I had stopped talking. The two seats opposite Ogden and me remained empty.

'What was all that about?' Ogden said, after twenty minutes. 'You were saying something to him about piña colada. I don't know how you got on to that.'

'You raped me last night,' I said.

Ogden looked straight ahead. He did not blush, as I'd thought he would. He had prepared his response for exactly these words.

'I'm going to have to find something in Weimar where I can spend five hundred marks,' he said. 'Even if it's a painting of Erich Honecker or something even worse. I bet there are marble busts of Goebbels and Himmler still hanging around. It isn't just in the West that old Nazis run the show. I have to get rid of at least five hundred marks.'

'I thought about furs,' I said.

'Caviar all comes from the Soviet Union, doesn't it? What about that?'

I thought of turning up at our flat; of unpacking my suit-
case; of presenting Joaquin with a big round tin of caviar. His
delight! I had not spoken to Joaquin since I had left home,
although I had written him a postcard from West Berlin. I
planned to send him another from Weimar. I would very
much have liked to telephone him this morning. There were
no telephones in the room, either in Berlin or in Leipzig. We
had agreed to let it go. It was not important, not speaking for
a fortnight. I would, however, have liked to speak to him.
That is all human weakness. We can deplore it, but we have
to live with it.

We had not succeeded in changing our daily twenty-five
marks at Leipzig station. When we got to the hotel in Weimar,
I asked if it was possible to change money there. The receptionist, a pleasant blond man in his thirties, had admitted us
a day early without demur. He agreed that it was possible, but
it was not necessary.

'I don't understand – it is not necessary?' I said.

'This obligation to change twenty-five marks daily, it does
not apply to visitors paying more than twenty-five marks per
night for their hotel room,' he said. 'I have to inform you, that
rooms in the Hotel Elefant do cost something more than twenty-five marks a night, and you are required to pay in your own
currency, or in Deutschmarks from the Federal Republic rather.
I hope that will not be a problem to our honoured guests.'

'What is he saying?' Ogden said.

'Are you sure?' I said. 'We have been changing the required
amount every day now, both of us, for six days.'

'If you have been paying your hotel bills in Federal marks,
you have been changing money to no purpose. Not necessary.

There is a possibility that you may be permitted to change money back, but it is quite a complicated procedure. If I can advise you, the best thing to do is to spend it.'

'What is he saying?' Ogden said. 'Why won't he change money?'

I explained.

'Do you mean to say—'

'Thank you, thank you,' I said to the receptionist, leaving the hotel through its heavy glass doors. 'Very helpful, thank you.'

'I needn't have changed – do you mean to say I needn't have changed twenty-five marks—'

'It was one of those little misunderstandings,' I said.

'I thought you were in charge of all that,' he said. 'I honestly thought that. And look ...' We were in the central town square, or what looked like it. There was something approaching a bustle underneath and around a statue of a couple of guys, looking forward bravely into the socialist future. 'Look how much money I've got. This is crazy. Look, fifty, one hundred, two hundred, three, four, five—'

'Put it away,' I said.

'There's no point in putting it away,' Ogden said. 'It's just worthless pieces of paper. I can't believe that through your basic incompetence you've put us in a situation where I've got all this paper. I can't spend it. A beer here costs one mark twenty-eight pfennigs. There's nothing I want to buy with this crap. It's totally fucking worthless. So thanks a lot. You know what I think of this money?'

'Don't do that,' I said, because Ogden had taken out his cigarette lighter. He was holding a bunch of DDR marks, perhaps a hundred marks, spread out like a hand of cards. He was attracting attention.

'This is the only fucking fun I'm going to get out of this fucking currency,' Ogden said. 'It's not worth anything, apart from this stupid fucking government they've got claiming that it's worth five times what it's really worth. We have to give them all our money, except that we've given them a lot more than we even needed to, thanks to you. I don't see the fucking point of it.'

'Really don't do that,' I said, but it was too late. Ogden had lit his cigarette lighter. He was holding it up to his money. It had never occurred to me that anyone would burn money. For years we had agreed, we Spartacists, that money did not matter, that it was a product of the capitalist system held up by false consciousness and the assertions of the capitalist state. And yet we did not burn it. We used it and preserved it. To see Ogden insisting there was no point to this money, and in this public square to set it on fire – the money burnt easily, like the paper which was all it was – to me that was deeply shocking. Money, after all, is what people mostly think they're made of, their nationhood, their families, their existence. Who is in charge of the supply of money to the cities of England? Why, the government is, of course. Money is not like doughnuts, to be supplied by whoever thinks they can get something out of it. And to confirm that people are only made of money, all around Ogden now there were people shouting. One huge-bellied fishmonger had left his stall, his wet red arms outstretched. He was trying to wrest the lighter out of Ogden's hands. The back of the fishmonger's hand struck my face. I felt the wet and something hard and cold hitting my teeth, a wedding ring on his finger perhaps. The scenes in the German Democratic Republic had been orderly and subdued. Now Ogden was burning their money. We were surrounded by noise and a remonstrative behaviour by the crowd that was not far from violence. Order was being restored quickly, however. In a moment we found ourselves facing four police officers. There was blood in my mouth. They were unsmiling. They asked for our papers.

I was in a cell on my own for more than thirty-six hours before anyone paid any further attention to us. We were in a police station, not a prison. I thought Ogden might have been taken to somewhere more serious. I suspect in reality he was in the same building, two cells away. I can't be exact about how long it was that I stayed in the cell, because they took my watch, along with a ring that was never returned, and the laces in my shoes, which I did get back. The ring was a nice one – my father's, as it happens. I was certainly there for two nights before anything occurred. Meals came at intervals, in the same sort of moulded trays that we had eaten from on our first night in West Berlin, in the Serbian restaurant. The food was no worse than that. In the evening it included something I was pleased to recognize as *soljanka* and a block of something labelled Süsstafel, which might have been an alien's attempt to create a chocolate bar, it having seen them only on intercepted earthly television broadcasts. I ate it all. Returning the tray, I tried a joke with the guard about ordering a *Kaffee Komplett* to round things off. He remained entirely silent, as he did when I went on to ask when I could see the British consul, as was my right. I was away from everything and safe.

I had done nothing. The bed was hard and narrow and the room was cold but I slept well. A man of my convictions must get used to sleeping in jail. It was disappointing that my first night in one was due to the frivolous and insulting actions of another, and not through the demonstration of those convictions. But it was a start.

Those hours were my revolution in Germany, the revolution without which, Lenin tells us, we are lost. I understood at the end of them what politics did, and the narrative it imposes on us. We live in other people's ideas of our narratives. Shortly a gentleman I had never met would start to tell me that narrative, quite convincingly to anyone but me.

As far as I can judge, it was late morning on the third day that the cell door was opened. Two guards gestured impatiently for me to follow them. I did not appear to be dangerous enough to handcuff or frogmarch. I walked with them along a corridor, a glimpse of a busy office where everyone was in uniform. Then we walked along another corridor. A blue-painted steel door was opened. I was told to sit on a chair on the left-hand side of the table. I sat down. The door was closed.

Time passed.

The fluorescent light was nearing the end of its life. It flickered painfully, like the beginning of a migraine.

After a while, I noticed there was a clock on the wall. I tried closing my eyes and counting to sixty to see how reliable a grasp of time I had. First I was ten seconds slow, then ten seconds fast. I was borderline cheating by saying *one thousand, two thousand, three thousand*, which is what a second takes. But it seemed admissible to me, waiting in that interview room.

I had been there an hour and ninety minutes, solitary, in silence. It was hard to understand why they had extracted me from my cell before they were ready. I hoped it was because the British consul was not immediately available.

Two men entered. They sat down. The taller one placed a thin Manila file in front of him. Neither of them looked at me. The taller one opened the file. Before doing anything else, he squared the papers inside it with the heel of his hands.

'I need to see the British consul,' I said. 'Where is the British consul?'

'That is not necessary in this case,' the shorter, fatter one said – he had eyebrows that, in another situation, would have been classed as comic.

'It is my right,' I said.

'You sound like a little boy,' the man said, 'calling for his mother. But you are not a little boy. You are a man. Kindly listen.'

'I would like to ask you some questions,' the taller one said. 'It would be best if you answer them honestly and fully.'

'Best for you or best for me?' I said. I was suddenly furious.

'Please,' the man said. Then he started to talk.

What
   is your
     name, What is
   your address, What is
   your age, When were you born,
 Where were you born, Why did you come
to the Democratic Republic of Germany, I came because,

Who asked you to come, Nobody asked me to come,
Why did you come to Weimar, I came to Weimar
because of its historical interest and value, What do you
mean, I mean the history, the Weimar Republic, Please
explain, I also mean the cultural history, What does that
mean, I mean the great figures who came here, the
Bauhaus and Goethe and Schiller, And yet you were
observed to be sitting with your back to the statue of
these two figures eating, eating an ice cream, I did not
know that was not permitted, This is even before you
started burning the currency of the German Democratic
Republic, I did not burn any currency, Do you think that
is respectful, It does not affect my respect for these poets
and thinkers, the ice cream I mean, not the currency-
burning in which I took no part, Where else have you
travelled to in the German Democratic Republic, We
have travelled to Berlin and to Leipzig, Who did you
meet in these places, We spent time with an Australian
professor of history who travelled to Leipzig with us,
Who else, We met a friend of his called Matthias, Who
else, In Leipzig we met a friend of my friend's employer,
Who is this employer please, His name is Philip
Cawston, What is his business, He is a Member of
Parliament, his name is Dr Philip Cawston, Were you
given anything by Dr Cawston to give to his contact,
No, I ask again, what were you give to this contact, We
gave him a copy of Dr Cawston's book, What is this
book, I don't know, I haven't read it, What was the name
of this Leipzig man who you were told to hand material
to, I don't know his full name, I only called him Herr

Sussmann, my friend will know his name and address,
Who is he, I believe he was a minister in the state
government, It is better for you if you tell the absolute
truth and not resort to fairy tales, These are not fairy
tales, but we visited Herr Sussmann in his home, You
must tell me the real people you have been in contact
with and not pluck the names of famous figures from
your copy of the state newspaper, we are not idiots and
know that you did not visit a figure like that, What was
the purpose of your stay in Berlin, There was no purpose
other than to see an important city of historical and
current interest, We have evidence that you engaged in
activity against the criminal code of the German
Democratic Republic within an hour of entering the
country, do you deny this, Certainly I deny this, And yet
it is reported by a reliable witness that you engaged with
a black-market money trader in public, we have your
names and addresses in association with this, I have
nothing to say in response to this, We will move on, We
understand that you have engaged in acts of political
violence by your own confession, I do not understand
what you are referring to, You boasted to a stranger that
you had assaulted individuals in socialist and pacifist
organizations many times and you had destroyed
property in a wilful and violent fashion, do you think
this is acceptable behaviour, I have only done so in order
to further the options for socialism in my country, I did
so out of solidarity you might say with your country, My
country needs no such acts of solidarity, Yes I understand
that now, Did you plan to carry out acts of political

violence against the German Democratic Republic, No
of course not, I am on your side, that is to say my acts of
solidarity as you describe them were always to further the
same goals that your government is pursuing with such
success, We will leave that there for the moment, There is
nothing more to say, We will discover that, but now why
did you play with an orchestra when you were young, I
liked music, Do you still play with this orchestra, No of
course not, it is an orchestra for schoolchildren called a
youth orchestra, we had to leave when we were twenty at
the latest, And this youth orchestra travelled abroad on
one occasion, you told a colleague when you were
applying for a visa, Yes, that is correct, to Germany, the
Federal Republic, Why did your orchestra visit these
places, they are not very picturesque or cultured places,
or so I am told, I believe the city I grew up in had twin-
town status with Bochum, So this was an official trip, Yes
although I had little to do with that, What was the
inspiration for this trip, I do not know, Who suggested it
in the first place, I expect it was suggested by the
organizers of the orchestra, Would they have been in
contact with the local politicians, I do not know, Can
you list the names of those Germans with whom you
came into contact, I stayed with a family called Meier,
the father was a doctor, Who else, I talked with a boy
called Wilhelm who played the flute in the Bochum
youth orchestra at a party they gave for us, Who else, At
the party I was asked to say hello to the mayor of
Bochum because I could speak some German, So this
was a propaganda visit to establish links with the political

establishment of Bochum, No that is not it at all, Can
you explain what the difference is between what I have
described and what you have described, It is complicated,
The minister Herr Sussmann's wife has informed us that
you forced yourself on her husband, demanding
refreshments, But I thought you did not believe that we
visited Herr Sussmann at all, Kindly do not speculate on
what I know or do not know, it will be the better for
you, We paid a short visit and handed over the book and
left, there were no refreshments, You should speak of
Herr Sussmann with more respect, I am sorry I had no
idea I sounded disrespectful, If you were in Leipzig why
did you not fulfil your legal requirements and register
with the police, we have no such registration, We saw a
horrible accident on the street, an industrial accident and
saw a worker killed, we did not want to stay in the town
any longer, it is distressing to see a man decapitated, We
have no record of such an accident, the safety record of
our country's working practices must not be maligned,
and so without explanation we find you have gone to
Weimar, That is so, Again without registering your
presence with us as you are required to do, We would
have done so in time, And then you burnt the money in
a provocative and insulting way, I did not burn any
money and I tried to stop my friend doing so, We have
witnesses who say that you were holding the notes while
your friend lit his cigarette lighter, That is not true, We
have witnesses who saw you laughing as the money was
burnt, do you think that is acceptable behaviour, No not
at all but it is not true, What is true is what I have stated

to be the truth, why do you refuse to accept what I am
saying, This will not go well with your case, What case,
have I been charged with anything, We will make an
official protest with the British government about your
behaviour, What case, I haven't done anything wrong, it
was all him, it was all Ogden, Any or all punishment will
be carried out in the German Democratic Republic, But
I haven't done anything wrong, I am ending this
interview now and returning
    the prisoner to his cell, I want to see
       the British consul, I am ending
          this interview now and
             returning the prisoner
                to his
                   cell.

I was in the police station for three days. I was questioned a
number of times. Once I answered every question with the
sentence 'I want to see the British consul.' If they did not
think I was a little boy, they should have stopped playing
childish games with me. The interview was no shorter than
any of the others. My questioners betrayed no impatience. All
that time I had the sense that I was walking on a very thin
piece of ice. These few holding cells were the thin surface
above a vast and unknowable darkness. There was nothing in
my cell that could not be found in a similar cell in the West,
even in England. But I knew that if I were to be moved from
this holding cell to another part of the system I would be in
something that did not exist in the West. I had, previously,
dismissed the existence and extent of that punitive system as

lies, propaganda, invention by capitalists. I had laughed when people had used the phrase *The Gulag Archipelago* – the first time I heard it, or saw it on the front of a paperback, I didn't know what either substantive word meant. Now I knew. It was strange that I knew, because I had no evidence at all for it. The only evidence I had was that the British consul did not arrive.

I grew very calm.

I thought things through.

I hardly thought at all about Percy Ogden. He might be in the same building, or he might be somewhere else.

I thought about justice, and about Joaquin.

I thought, too, about Joaquin's father, and the cell he must have died in.

I thought about them a lot. I had an immediate explanation when, on the fourth morning, I seemed to hear something that the guards could not possibly know or recognize or imitate. It had certainly come from my own thoughts, a hallucination. Such things happened to prisoners held in solitude. I should grow used to them.

The door of the cell was opened, with much clanking and the confident banging of bolts. A guard stood there. I did not recognize him.

'Follow me, please,' he said. I was aware as I moved that I smelt bad. I had not changed my clothes for some days, though I had been given the opportunity to shower twice. I followed him. Instead of turning towards the interview room, we continued into the corridor that ran by the office space. None of those working there looked up. They saw this regularly. The officer opened a door with a large iron key. I was at something like a reception area. On the other side of the desk stood a man. He was exactly the same size as me, exactly the same physical shape. He was examining a form laid out on the desk top in front of him, frowning.

'Herr Joaquin Anibal Goriategy,' the guard said.

Joaquin looked up. His gaze met mine. He shook his head, tightening his lips.

'I can't understand this form at all,' he said. 'I am what you call your *deus ex machina*. I am the cavalry, you know what I mean? One thing, though. I can't remember any of my German and I tell you, Spike, this is what I cannot understand. You have to look and explain before you sign. This is all your stuff, yes, okay?'

As it happens, it was not all my stuff. There was a ring missing. I expect now the son of an ex-police officer of the German Democratic Republic wears my father's gold ring on nights out in newly renovated Weimar. (Perhaps I am being unfair: perhaps my father's ring sits in an envelope in a filing cabinet in some archive somewhere, detached from any explanation.) But I did not notice that the ring was missing. If I had noticed, I would not have cared. Idiotically, I started to shake Joaquin's hand. Something about his name, offered days ago in a Reisebüro, had triggered an official response from the structures of power, and not a hostile one, either. The invitation to his father as an honoured guest of the state had not been forgotten. The name Joaquin Anibal Goriategy had been recorded years ago, though then it had referred to a small boy. It had summoned a friend of the state with some swiftness. He had come to get me. I was safe. I had no idea what I thought any more. What I believed. Ogden could wait until the interrogators got round to calling the British consul. My hand-shaking went on and on. In a moment Joaquin put his second hand on mine, to calm it.

'What is this?' he said.

'Herr Goriategy,' the officer behind the desk said impatiently.

'I don't want to join the Labour Party,' I said. 'I don't want to join the Labour Party. I just don't want to. Joaquin, I want to join. I want to join Labour. I don't want to do this any more. I don't want to.'

'What's this? My man, the democratic parliamentary socialist? You want to, or you don't want to?'

'I've got to say—'

'Not now. We go home. Is that all right with you? You got everything? This thing all right to sign, okay?'

When we were outside the police station, it was raining. There were clouds and sun. I had forgotten that was possible. I had had no sense of the weather, or anything outside, for days. I was dazzled by light and by the idea that water could flow from the heavens, falling wherever it chose. Nobody had ordered it or arranged it. The police station was in a central part of the historic town. It looked beautiful. All around it beautiful just *was*. The lime trees shone with rain in the sunlight. There was a heavenly smell, as perfume on a woman is meant to smell. I would love Weimar for ever, for the sake of this moment, and I would never come here again. The most beautiful thing of all was that it was over. Joaquin had come to fetch me home. Everything would be all right from now on. I clutched my passport. I hardly listened as Joaquin explained what we were going to do, the route we were going to take to get home again. As he went on talking, he began to smile.

Part three

I have lived a quiet life. My name is unknown, and I have not tried to achieve any public status. The quietness, and the overlooked corner I have lived my life in, was in part of my choosing. When I look back at the last thirty years, its avoidance of the limelight strikes me as having a moral quality. I would not sum up my existence in the priggish sentence at the end of *Middlemarch*. I am not somebody whose life was made up of 'unhistoric acts', as George Eliot calls them, because there are no such lives. All acts are historic, in the sense of belonging to history, contributing to history. My contributions, however, were anonymous. I did not publish what I wrote; I did not make speeches in Parliament, argue in Cabinet; I did not hunger after fame. I had been at school with those who did. I was that familiar figure in a group, the forgotten friend. Nobody knows the teacher in a provincial university with a pile of marking on his conscience; nobody knows who writes the slogans on the wall of the Territorial Army headquarters, unless they get caught.

My life has, in part, been quiet because of necessity. My doctoral thesis was interrupted for a year and a half, some of which I spent undergoing treatment in seclusion. I returned to my studies only when I was quite well, and I finished my thesis. My examiners were as kind and sympathetic as my nurses had been, most of them. My work was excellent, they said. I was turned down for every academic job I applied for. That gap of eighteen months always had to be accounted for, and always proved decisive. The faculty I had studied in gave me some teaching work. After some years, they appointed me to a permanent job. Five years ago, I was promoted to senior lecturer, where I expect to remain until I retire. I have published almost nothing. Nevertheless people like me have their uses. I return my marking on time. The individual assessments I make have never been queried by any external examiner. I am appreciated, as far as my existence merits appreciation. As the writer I love best in the world has said, the rule is that some people eat figs, and others sit and watch.

And perhaps we have eaten some figs, in any case. We are not old farts. We keep up with stuff. We like an argument. We were both expelled from the local LGBT group, as it now calls itself, for shouting at a man in a dress who called himself a lesbian. When the chair told us we had to leave, Joaquin, thinking he might as well be hanged for a sheep as a lamb, punched the man in a dress who called himself a lesbian. (He came with his wife; he had told two real lesbians to sit down and shut up. We are now rather the heroes of the real lesbians. Not that they have heroes.) We like Childish Gambino this year and we liked Lomepal last year. When a branch of Foxton's estate agents opened up near us, trying to sell cheaply renovated flats to property speculators, we went down on a Friday night and threw a brick through their big plate-glass window. We wore balaclavas. There are CCTV cameras everywhere.

We keep up hope. Nothing ever has a permanent triumph in this world. Things can improve. In recent years, the students I teach have grown more like the student I was. They read less, and the wall they write on is Twitter, but they want to change things, as we did. The two of us keep up hope for ourselves, too. One development of our middle age is an enjoyment of walking. Every week, we drive our ancient van out into the countryside. We walk for five hours, whatever the weather. Sometimes we vary things and walk through the oldest bits of this early industrial city. Neglected by the side of canals, the monuments of the first years of industrial capitalism crumble. Over the years, we have become well versed in the history of this place. It is astonishing, what you find out by walking, and standing, and staring, and wondering what it is exactly that you are looking at. That picturesque ruined wall by the canal now sprouts buddleia. It once contained the daylight lives of labouring nine-year-olds, some of whom died on the floor, here, gasping for air. That noble wild stretch of land, purple with heather, is not a blank wilderness, but bought and carefully controlled by a ducal corporation to shoot grouse on. We tramp on, understanding how the world is through disillusion and enlightenment. At the end of the day we are the better for it. Probably once a week somebody is startled to discover that I am fifty-three, and Joaquin nearly sixty. We don't look it. We are big, leathery, outdoorsy; our eyes are clear; we have the same teeth, and the same trousers, that we had thirty years ago. We have the same springy walk as each other, the same gleam. The word springs to the mouths of strangers – *boyish*. We glow with health, as the departmental secretary once said to me. We like that in each other, too.

Once a year we go away for a fortnight, walking somewhere in Europe. We tried a number of destinations. Switzerland was ruinously expensive; Portugal's walking paths were so badly signposted that your head was never out of the map; the Peloponnese one year was just too hot.

For the last ten years our annual walking holiday has been in Germany. The culture of walking is well established there. It is quite rare that you need a map, so well signposted are the paths. Even the cheapest hotels are clean and often pleasant. When we went in 2008, it was the first time either of us had gone to Germany in twenty years. The country had changed an enormous amount. Of course we both felt some disquiet, getting off the plane in Berlin. The last time we had passed through that airport, in 1987, Joaquin had walked me through, gripping me tight, both of us pale and silent as ghosts. I had cried on the plane home. But at this distance in time I hardly know why I cried. As it turned out, when we returned in 2008, my feelings were not stirred up by the sight of landscapes which, in any case, I had hardly taken in before. It was a great success, that first walking holiday in rural Brandenburg. We have gone on to explore different parts of Germany every year since.

We have often gone to the lands in the former German Democratic Republic. Saxon Switzerland, where the party leaders once had their villas. Thuringia. The Wartburg, that faked-up palace on top of Eisenach's hill, where Luther threw an inkpot at the devil; the ink stain on the wall is carefully renewed every so often by discreet guards, paid by the hour. We have even been back to Weimar. It is a beautiful city, after all. Some people might think it strange that we go so lightly to the former German Democratic Republic, given my history with the place. But history is what most people succeed in ignoring.

This year, the island on which we were born or made our home tried to extricate itself from the continent. Went sailing westwards, to borrow a metaphor, like a raft of stone. We went to Germany, to the Harz mountains. We based ourselves in Quedlinburg. It is picturesque; beautifully preserved; a half-timbered medieval city of imperial extent. People have admired its picturesque quality for years. There is, for instance, a photograph of Heinrich Himmler with his storm troopers entering the cathedral for a picturesque pageant in 1936, celebrating a thousand years of German purity.

'Mountains' is an ambitious word for the Harz lands. They amount to substantial hills, no more than that. They are ideal walking country for us. They possess the right level of historical and cultural interest. One day we took a steam train up to the top of the Brocken, the largest of the hills, and walked all the way down. The Brocken was closed to citizens of the German Democratic Republic for decades. It was a large hill situated very near the border with the West. For this reason, the government sited a listening station at the top. On the day the Wall was opened up, tens of thousands of people walked up the Brocken, perhaps to see where Goethe set an act of his *Faust*. Over the years, I have come to think that the collapse of the German Democratic Republic and the unification of Germany was not altogether a bad thing. In any case, that long walk down the hill in the heat of the day was the sort of day we always dream of. When we got back to the hotel room, Joaquin started to take his shirt off. I wrestled him to the floor. We fucked. He licked my neck, my shoulders, with a sort of fury. I was burnt, as he was, and the salt of me was like a necessary mineral to a wild beast. Only then did we have a shower. The smell of Joaquin after a hot day walking – the taste of him on my tongue – is something I never want to be without.

On the Saturday morning, we decided that we would go to visit the former border. There was no particular reason for this, unless wanting to do the unusual thing is a reason. Everyone has seen the old border in Berlin. Bits of it are preserved, and tourists of every sort flock to it. I can't say I had ever heard of anyone visiting the long land border that contained the whole country. Our motivation was not very strong – this was a border that was needed for some time. Then it stopped being needed. Now it is not there any more. But when you decide to go on a walk, it is often a good idea to have some aim in mind – a listening station, Goethe's birthplace, tracing the line of a national border. Otherwise you end up trailing around after some other person's idea of the picturesque, and admiring what you are told to admire.

We took a bus from Quedlinburg to Wernigerode. After three stops, a whole class of schoolchildren got on with their two teachers – maybe for some weekend nature observation. To my eyes, the thirty ten-year-olds were disconcertingly uniform, all white and almost all blond. They were very well behaved. They chatted to each other in a decent, engaged way. None had a mobile phone. At Wernigerode there was a wait of an hour. We filled our water bottles from the public fountain in the main square.

'This is a long trip,' Joaquin said, once we were on the bus, not complaining but with the beginnings of disgruntlement. 'Another hour before we get there?'

'Something like that,' I said. 'Just enjoy the ride.'

The bus was empty. We were sitting directly behind the driver. It was a pleasant ride, through forests and along rivers, stopping peaceably at crumbling and isolated concrete shelters every so often. At one point a very old lady got on. The bus driver, a cheerful soul, got out of his seat, helped her on and dusted her down before setting off again. Three stops later, she got off again with the same ceremony. That was her daughter, she confided to us, waiting for her, and her granddaughter, too, look! She wasn't expecting that! Her joy was touching. The granddaughter, slab-bosomed in a Slipknot T-shirt, had been cajoled and threatened into coming out.

'Going all the way to Sorge?' the driver said, over his shoulder. 'You'll know when you get there for two reasons. One is that this bus stops there and doesn't go any further. The other one is the English dog that'll be waiting to say hello to the bus. Lying in the middle of the road, he'll be.'

'It's a strange name for a village,' I said.

'There's a town called Kotzen and another one called Fickmühlen too. No one knows why.'

I thought it was probably something to do with a mishearing, way back. An eighteenth-century mapmaker asked some passing agricultural labourers for the name of their settlement. They had difficulty understanding what had been asked. The mapmaker had difficulty understanding what they said in return. He wrote down a word that was similar. In the end, the village was called Vomit, which is what Kotzen means, or Sorrow, which is the town called Sorge that we were going to. Fickmühlen, or Fuck Mill, can really only have been some delinquents seeing what they could get away with.

'Strange town, Sorge,' the driver said. 'I think it's only the English dog that likes it.'

'Why do you call him an English dog?'

'Well,' the driver said, thinking the question over, 'he's a gentleman, that dog. He's got an English passport and he's got English manners. If you ask me, that dog voted for Brexit and he's quite happy about it. You don't hear so much about that any more. When are you leaving our family of nations? Is it this year or next year?'

Some time passed in silence. Nobody had taken any offence.

'History in the making,' the driver said.

'We're better off as we are now. Not everyone round here would agree with me,' the driver said.

'The town's perfectly all right,' the driver said. 'Sorge. It's the people who are a little bit unusual.'

'What are they, tribal?' Joaquin said to me, when I had explained. 'Are we going to visit some people in caves to find out their ancient inner wisdom?'

I sniggered.

'This is just like where I grow up, or where my mum's dad lived – we went there when I was a kid in the summer. Doesn't look like this, all this green and trees and stuff, but the same place in fact. All people living on their own and at seven it's night and there's nothing to do except sit and complain about everything. You know, I don't even have to get off this fucking bus to find out – the people in these places, they exactly the same the world over.'

'Come on, Jo,' I said. 'We're only going for the day. You don't have to talk to anyone.'

'Not gonna talk to anyone, not even you, I tell you,' Joaquin said. But then he brightened. 'One good thing, though. This is so late a start, it's like time for eating lunch before we start off walking. That is one thing I like about today already.'

The driver announced with a flourish that we were arriving at our destination. He turned with a broad sweep from the main road. A glamorous blond dog leapt up from his resting place in the middle of the street. This was not somewhere he would be disturbed often, and he was going to make the most of it. A bus shelter; a couple of houses; a notice-board; a hotel or bar of some sort, all quite run down and unpainted in the middle of spurts and half-acres of uncared-for grass. It was unlike Germany, with its cared-for air. It looked abandoned. 'And there he is,' the bus driver said, switching off his engine. 'Come to say hello to you. Might have known you were coming.' The dog, by contrast with the village, was beautifully groomed and glossy, its blond tresses falling about an intelligent and amused face. This was the promised English dog. He sniffed around us, taking in our boots, socks and tucked-in trousers in a friendly way that promised to leave nothing out.

'If you want something to eat,' the driver said, settling himself on the bottom step of his bus with a cigarette, 'that's your only option round here. The English dog lives there. See you on Monday.'

We didn't ask why he said this. He was recommending, as a place to eat, the hotel, or bar, or clubhouse, a tatty mock-Tudor confection, like a barn, with an indecipherable sign hanging outside. Two tubs of last summer's plants stood outside, straggling collections of jasmine and fuchsia. The dog led us in. Inside, the hallway was dark and wood-panelled, an old reception desk with framed certificates of legal responsibility, a couple of abstract acrylics in amateurishly brilliant colours and a photograph of Sorge in the old days. Someone had left a paperback novel on the reception desk – it looked completely unread. Joaquin picked up a menu that sat on the counter. He started to read it out loud, phonetically. I understood what he was saying. There was soup of the day; there was sausage with potatoes; there were herrings, also with potatoes; there was goulash. Nobody was about. The dog had had enough of lying on the ground. He was trotting around sniffing. From time to time he looked over his shoulder at us, placing his forepaw on the seat of an ancient armchair before moving on to a pile of old tabletop games and jigsaws, the door to what must be the kitchen.

'You've met the employee of the month,' a man's voice said from above, at the top of the stairs. 'I'll be down in a second. He'll show you the place in the meantime.'

I understood then. The dog was walking around, not exploring, but indicating his favourite spots. He had our worried welfare in mind – this is where you might like to sit down, in this comfortable armchair with the interesting smell deep in the seat, this is how you might entertain yourselves while there is nothing else to do, here is the door out of which food to sustain you might emerge. It was a thoughtful dog, full of obeisance and consideration.

'I'm just airing a room,' the voice said. 'And now I'm done. Now. Welcome to Sorge, gentlemen.' The owner of the voice came down the stairs. He was straggling in appearance, with a beaky nose peering out between curtains of long, greying hair. His clothes were unusual: a huge black shirt, which swamped him, and loose baggy black trousers, tugged together at the waist with a brown leather belt. He was shoeless in black socks. His gait down the stairs was slow and careful, like that of a very old man, but he could only have been in his forties. He gave me, and then Joaquin, a warm but incisive look as he reached the bottom of the stairs, looking at us a couple of seconds longer than usual. 'Welcome to Sorge,' he said. 'How can I help you? A couple of rooms? Or lunch and a beer? Or' – the man's look had assessed us by now, placed us in another category of being than customers to be polite to – 'just a sit down and a shit before you set off on your hike? We wouldn't charge you for that.'

'Lunch would be nice,' I said. I wondered what we had done to deserve this matiness. He was clearly in charge and not an employee. 'Who is this?'

'That is Nala,' the man said, stressing the second syllable. 'He comes from Romania. He was a street dog, but very intelligent, as you are going to find out.'

This explained the bus driver's label. To a country bus driver, all foreigners were English, a Romanian dog much the same as an English one. I had heard about this habit before, in accounts of rural life by early travel writers.

'What is he, the waiter?' I said.

'No, your tour guide for the afternoon,' the man said, chuckling with an air-filled smoker's laugh, wheezing itself out into a few shakes of the shoulders. He had a curious accent I couldn't quite place. Oddly, it made his German very easy to follow, a musical up and down and vowels that were almost English in their purity. I didn't think it was a local accent. 'You're here to walk the Wall, I take it. Very nice. It's Nala's afternoon walk. He gets very excited if there are walkers on the noonday bus. He doesn't expect any on Saturday, for obvious reasons, but he comes out anyway. Who knows? Perhaps he doesn't know that it's Saturday, and the bus comes, but usually no walkers. Or perhaps he quite enjoys the disappointment. That's what I mean by excitement, the absence of disappointment, which is as good as it gets around here. Take a seat. Our waitress will be with you shortly. Any seat, any seat.'

His conversation was that of someone wondering how he was going to fill the long hours of his day. The way he walked away, stopping to take out a handkerchief to brush some imaginary dust off a china ornament on a shelf, was the same. We sat down at a dark-stained oak table with twisted legs, very like an old English pub table.

'What did he say?' Joaquin said. I summarized, leaving out the bit about the obvious reasons for no one coming on Saturday. An unpleasant thought was forming in my mind. The bus we had come on had stopped for five minutes, then had started up and left. He had said that he would see us on Monday. Our host had said that no walkers came on Saturday for obvious reasons. And yet there was, clearly indicated on the timetable, a bus from Sorge at 18.30 p.m. We would go back to Quedlinburg on that bus, later this afternoon.

A wail, or a groan, issued from the kitchen, as if somebody had been rudely woken up. The door slammed open. The waitress emerged.

It is hard to explain this woman's appearance now because so much commentary passed between Joaquin and me about it later that day and in the days that followed. We dissected it as if we were ever going to be drawn to it. It is wrong to talk about the beauty of women, but this woman's beauty was a compelling fact that needed analysis. Was she fat but beautiful, or beautiful because fat? Was her beauty of a sort that exerted itself even through her physical substance? Would it have been still greater without it, or was she only beautiful because of the expanses of her creamy flesh, the uncanny smoothness of her complexion and wide blue eyes above a pair of fat pink cheeks? She was lovely, no doubt about it. She had the sort of loveliness that went against what the observer thought he knew about physical loveliness. You would debate it. We did. It is common when people mention a fat person to say that they moved with surprising lightness, or something of that sort. Such a description has made many fat people jump about on the spot, and perspire, attempting to live up to it. The waitress did not move with surprising lightness. She moved like the Turandot of my dreams, a woman who regretted the brutal fact that, in the world that was and the world that should be, she was not to be carried about in a palanquin by four sweating slaves, her feet never touching the ground. Imperial feudalism has its romance, I admit. Even Brecht, in the *Kaukasische Kreidekreis* seems susceptible to it. In middle age I no longer resisted the charm of what must go from the world. Her beauty was of that sort, one that could not exist in a just society. For that reason I was drawn to it, her bare slapping soles, the sigh and huff of her breath as she walked, the beautiful shine of her hair, the red flash at the end of her fingers and toes. What did we want, she said. She held out no kind of promise that she would do anything to meet those wants, or even a pencil and pad to write them down. Her absence of anything resembling flirtation or charm – her solidity of assurance – was total, and compelling.

'I don't want to wait about here,' Joaquin said, once she had left – his most flirtatious smile had been brought out for her. 'I want to get out and be walking. I want to see the border.'

'Me too,' I said. 'We'll eat the sausage and pay and set off. The bus back's at half six. We've got five and a half hours to walk if we want a beer at the end.'

'One day we're going to come on a holiday and we're going to bring the van or, you know, hire a car, like the normal people.'

'The normal people don't know how good public transport is in Germany. There's no need to spend a fortune bringing your van over, and two full days driving.'

'We could sleep in the van too.'

'Sometimes I think you never gave up being a student.'

Joaquin gave me a brilliant, vulpine grin. His hair and beard were mostly grey, but his teeth were white. The food arrived. The fat girl brought us two orange plates with sausages and potatoes on them. It was almost the same as what we had ordered. She set it down with unmistakable resentment. We ate it.

In five minutes, the time had come to set off. The proprietor appeared again to take our plates away.

'The dog will follow you, whatever you do,' he said. 'He likes the walk. I say he'll follow you, but in reality he'll be showing you what you need to see. He's done it a few times before. And then he'll bring you back safely.'

Nala, the dog, leapt up when we started to gather our Nordic poles and rucksacks together. He was quickly through the front door, looking back impatiently, like a tour guide with a schedule to meet. We left the hotel. We followed him through the village towards the beginning of the path along the old Wall. At one point, an old man with an Alsatian came out of a house on the other side of the street. The dog Nala started to run over, but something stopped him. He returned to our side as if the other party did not exist. It was an exquisite, almost Regency lesson in the art of social snubbing. The old man went on his way without greeting us or acknowledging Nala, in the direction of the bus stop.

'So, they are shy, or they are rude, then?' Joaquin said. It was the continuation of a discussion we had started the day before, when five different sets of walkers had bluntly refused to return a greeting. I had said that there were different standards of engagement with strangers in different cultures. Joaquin maintained that even if you'd grown up in the German Democratic Republic, you would know that it was good to say hello back when a stranger greeted you on a forest path. The conversation continued. It was a beautiful day. Soon we were off the village street and into a track between fir plantations. The air was both fresh and heady with resin. Nala was running ahead of us two or three hundred yards, pausing, looking back, waiting for us to catch up, sometimes diving into the woodland to investigate something. We came to a gate that stood open, announcing that here was the historical territory of the border between East and West Germany. The woods rang with birdsong. The trees were wilder and older than the firs, older than the Wall itself, elm and oak and beech. Underneath the canopy the dappled light was alive with butterflies, feasting.

'But a girl like that,' I continued, 'she doesn't know that she's beautiful, these days, because every magazine, every television show tells her you have to be sixty kilos maximum to be beautiful.'

'She knows she would be more beautiful if she is thirty kilos less, that is the truth.'

'Rubbish. She was beautiful because she was the weight she was. She'd look like anyone else if she was thin.'

In ten minutes, we came out into a wide expanse of grassland, and the preserved centre of the old border. There was a watchtower, and a twenty-foot stretch of the old Wall, bare of the graffiti that now covered both sides of the preserved fragments in Berlin. The double line of the Wall was marked in stone, either the original foundations or (I thought) laid down by some heritage organization. It looked as if it would form a satisfying basis for our afternoon walk, leading off into land where meadows and trees were growing more thickly. Nala came into his own. You could see that, as the proprietor of the hotel had said, he had done this before. He led us to the base of the watchtower, where he very deliberately pissed.

'Dogs, they are all such reactionaries,' Joaquin said. 'I never met a dog that doesn't make racist judgements, too.'

Then the dog led us into the forest shade on, we thought, the former West German side. A few yards in, quite well hidden, was an old sign saying that this was the *Grenze*. The dog sat down, decorously posing. He waited until Joaquin had pulled out his old camera from my rucksack and taken a couple of photographs.

'Very much like Mr Jingle's sagacious dog Ponto,' I said – I very much like *The Pickwick Papers*, and Joaquin, too, had read it in snatches over the years. Nala went on, leading us with careful consideration to a bench by a sculpture installation.

'He thinks we need to rest,' Joaquin said. 'He's crazy – we're not as old as that.' But I thought he wanted us to admire the work of an official sculptor, arranging shards of slate in a perfect circle. That seemed to be it as far as the tour was concerned. Now Nala streaked off along the line of the Wall towards a meadow, alive with wild flowers, maiden pinks and cowslips, yellow marsh marigolds, red poppies, snake's-head fritillaries, white frothing flowers on the surface of the waving grass as high as your waist, uncared for and untrained, a European meadow alive with flowers and butterflies, taking back the land from what, after all, had been there for less than thirty years. By the time we were old, hardly anyone would remember it. Even now nobody much under forty-five had any adult memory of what it was, and what it hoped to achieve, and what the society whose edges it marked meant, after all.

We walked for twelve miles in total, six there and six back. We followed the line of the Wall all the way, hardly discussing it. What was there to say? I think we can say that we were more ambitious walkers than the dog Nala was quite expecting. His runs off into the forest wildness in search of fox and badger stopped; he kept to our side; towards the end he even took to flopping down and taking a rest. The signs of his early-afternoon exuberance were all over his coat. Not just burrs and fronds, but a thick coating of mud from the streams and bogs that had so urgently needed investigating. There had been nothing that we could do.

'That guy is going to be so cross with us,' Joaquin said, 'returning his dog looking like that. He will need such a bath.' But we underestimated Nala. Just before the edge of the village, a stream ran by the side of the road under a bridge. Nala dashed down the bank. He plunged into the fast-flowing water, clear as gin. He was out again, shining, soaked and half his size. After shaking himself thoroughly, considerately distant from us, he was as clean as if he had spent the afternoon dozing in a chair.

'This is the most sagacious dog I ever met,' I said.

When we got back the proprietor was outside the hotel, not waiting for us but passing the time in his long, empty day. He looked quite satisfied, as if two customers were all he asked for.

'That was a good long walk,' he said. 'He'll want his bed now. Good for you. Do you want a beer or something?'

We thought we did – it was still half an hour before the bus was due. Walking is thirsty work, as we now commented to each other. (We always say this at the end of a walk.) We sat down on the bench next to the entrance. The beer was excellent. The proprietor hung around.

'Did you see anyone on your walk? Just someone in the village? That guy, the guy with the big dog, he's typical. You won't get Nala within ten feet of that dog, since the guy hit him with his walking stick. It's the descendant of one of the border guard dogs, that one. It's hard on Nala not to have any company. He likes it when walkers come – he waits for the bus.

'Do you know about the village? Well, you know about the Wall, anyway. Nice walk, isn't it? Because it's so close to the Wall, the only people who were ever allowed to live here were Party stalwarts. The Wall came down nearly thirty years ago and still the same people are here. That old guy you saw, he believes in Marxism-Leninism like crazy. They talk to each other but they do not talk to me, I can promise you that. I don't know if they would talk to Sybille or not. The boot's on the other foot there. She won't talk to them. Too old, apparently.'

'Why don't they talk to you?' I said. I didn't quite feel like starting to talk about ideology. That is sensible middle age starting to bite. When I was young, I wouldn't have cared that the bus was going to arrive in ten minutes, that it wasn't worth starting an argument. I would have condensed my crisp judgements and opinions still further. I would have changed minds in ten minutes. Joaquin was cleaning the grass from the bottom of his boots with his Swiss Army knife. I knew he was listening to try to make out what we were discussing.

'This place, it's an old youth hostel for the Party. The kids came down here for a holiday. They had uplifting games, went running in the forest, all that. After the changes, it sat empty for fifteen years. Nobody wanted it. I heard about it and I bought it for really nothing, twenty thousand euros. I could have put it on my credit card. I was going to turn it into a luxury hotel – I had all sorts of ideas. It's in my family, the hospitality industry, it's what my father did and I grew up in that world. But we did up two bedrooms and two bathrooms, out of twenty-four, and then the builder disappeared and the whole project ran into the sand. For that lot, the place was like a showcase for them. It's like the most perfect piece of German socialist design. It was criminal to doll up those two bathrooms as far as they're concerned. I'm using those rooms for storage. Do you want to see the old rooms?'

'I don't know that we've got time, actually,' I said. 'The bus back to Wernigerode is due about now.'

'The bus? There's no bus today,' the proprietor said, in English for the first time, turning to Joaquin to include him. His English was excellent, hardly accented at all. 'Did you think there was? The next bus back is on Monday morning.'

I gaped at him.

'Show him the timetable,' Joaquin said. His mouth was set. 'Show me the timetable, too. There's a bus, definitely, I saw it.'

I got the timetable out of my rucksack. Together we showed the proprietor the 18.30 bus from Sorge, its many stops carefully marked in minute- or two-minute gradations until it reached its destination in Wernigerode.

'I see,' the proprietor said. 'You didn't notice the little C in the box at the top.'

He pointed with a grubby fingernail. There was, indeed, something that might have been a C, a superscript to the four-figure bus number that indicated the route. I followed his finger down to the footnotes, in tiny letters. I just about succeeded in reading the words *Montag bis Freitag*.

We are normally good at analysing bus timetables, their exceptions and their hidden inconveniences. This was a catastrophe. For some moments my mind refused to accept how bad the situation was.

'It has actually happened once or twice before,' the proprietor said. His voice – I started to think, with that *actually*, that I had made another mistake here. Was he, in fact, German at all? 'There was another group who came on the Saturday bus – went for a walk, just like you – came back, I offered them a beer. In the end they had to call a taxi. I kind of wondered, actually, when you turned up. The trouble is ...'

By now I was sure he was English. Joaquin was frozen, his knife poised over the muddy bottom of his boots, staring at the proprietor.

'The trouble is that there's no taxi to call. It's only Markus who sometimes helps out, ten miles away, and he left for Mallorca this morning. I would drive you, but the van's in the garage. There's a company in Wernigerode, but I don't think you'll get them to come out here on a Saturday night, and it would cost you a good hundred euros, maybe a hundred and twenty. Half as much again if they come out on a Sunday, too. The best thing is probably to stay here. It's only thirty euros for a room. I tell you what, I'll do you two nights for fifty euros. I was airing a room when you got here. I'll throw in an overnight wash of your clothes, tonight and tomorrow too, for five euros. Sybille will do it, no trouble. Give her something to do. Can't say fairer than that.'

He had us over a barrel. The dog Nala came out of the hotel. He had not, after all, been sleeping just yet. He came up to us where we sat. He laid his head on the table. He observed the empty beer glasses. He returned to the door of the hotel. He turned his head, waiting for us. He wanted to show us our horrible room.

It is fair to say that Joaquin was not at his most cheerful that evening. We had had the sausages at lunchtime. I had the goulash that night. Joaquin had the herrings and potatoes. They were brought to us by the fat girl, who had adorned herself in a flouncy green and yellow dress and a black feather boa. She remained barefoot. She had the beginnings of a bunion. A couple of times I thought of commenting on her relationship with the proprietor – was she his daughter or his girlfriend, because no connection of mere employment could possibly be sufficient – before deciding to leave it until tomorrow. Joaquin stirred his herrings with dark disdain. A couple of times he started a comment: 'Okay, so maybe we could, I don't know …' before trailing off. The expense and complexity of arranging a return from Sorge before Monday morning was more than we could overcome. We would just have to accept the waste of paying for two nights in a hotel in Quedlinburg for a room we weren't sleeping in.

Perhaps the worst of it was we had nothing to read. We had not thought to bring our novels along on our day trip. The only books on the hotel's meagre bookshelf were tawdry German thrillers and the equivalent of joke books for children, and the teenage love story someone had left on the reception desk, the book that was everywhere this year. It was lucky that we were in the habit of carrying a change of shirt on walks like this. That would have to do for tomorrow. After dinner, we sat in an old leather sofa. We started to look through the four-day-old copy of the London *Daily Express* that we had found yesterday at a newsagent in Quedlinburg. Joaquin rang a china bell that was sitting on the side table. It might have been for decoration, but it fetched the fat girl.

'*Zwei Bier, bitte*,' Joaquin said. He had folded the newspaper back. Having said this, he started to raise it again. His ordering beers in German was a deliberate attempt at antagonism. I wasn't the only one who could speak German, it said. My heart went towards my man, but I kept my face dour and cross, just to humour him.

The girl pointed at the paper. '*Mei Freind hatt oamoi von ihm gewusst*,' she said. She padded off. I looked at what she had pointed at. It was the photograph at the head of Percy Ogden's twice-weekly column. Ogden had 'come out' in print a year before, saying that the time had come to 'admit' that he was homosexual. It was as if he were a criminal in the dock, facing a bundle of new evidence. His standard fare as a columnist was ecological tragedy, predictions of catastrophe when Britain left the European Union, and the urgent need for a new party, occupying the middle ground of UK politics. It seemed utterly footling to us. Even more absurd were his occasional ventures into sexual politics, taking on the new role, at fifty-three, of an undisputed leader of 'queer politics' as he called it. We definitely didn't call it that. This was one of those weeks. It began, 'It's time that gay guys like me took the lead, and drove the disease of transphobia from queer politics, where it's got no place at all, and never did.' Somewhere deep in the hotel was the noise of television applause and musical outbursts, too muffled to identify, the sound of a glittering Saturday-night extravaganza. Outside, the silence of the woods and the village was broken only by the rustle of night-

time wind. We were stuck in a remote village at the far western borders of Saxony-Anhalt until Monday. There was
nothing else that would have persuaded anyone to read to the
end of Ogden's nine hundred words. In that sense we were
Ogden's ideal audience. The last time I had laid eyes on him,
he was setting a cigarette lighter to a fanned-out fistful of East
German banknotes in a market square in Weimar, in the
summer of 1987. I had followed his subsequent career, turning
away from politics into know-it-all journalism, with patchy
and decreasing attention. It must have been disappointing to
him. Sometimes I remarked to my colleagues in the university
common room, 'That bugger raped me once.' They would say,
'We know, Spike,' with resignation. Sometimes Ogden would
bring up his ten days in East Germany in 1987 as a badge of
honour, writing in his awful column that he had seen
Communism and had been subjected to interrogation in the
cells of the gulag. That made him think admiration of Mr
Tony Blair was the principle 'we must' adhere to, *en masse*. I
never gave him a moment's thought. It wasn't important
whether that columnists' *we* succeeded in including me and
Joaquin, or not.

The proprietor emerged from the kitchen door. His walk
towards the bar at the far end of the lounge was not at all
proprietorial, or like a hotel owner, but like that of a man in
his own house who has forgotten just what he came over for.
'Another two beers, then? Good idea,' he called, by now talking to us in English. He was already pouring himself one.

He brought the three beers over on a tray. He sat down in
the leather armchair across from the sofa. 'I shouldn't drink
beer,' he said. 'It's against the programme I stick to. You

wouldn't think it to look at me now,' he went on, 'but I was immensely fat until a year ago. Then Sybille had a go at me. Said I was making her put on weight with the way I ate. She's not fat, not at all. It's just the way women talk about themselves. But I was fat. It's growing up in a pub that does it. That was my childhood. Self-indulgence was never far away. But I've lost fifty kilos since last August. What do you think about that?'

'Well done,' Joaquin said.

'The good old *Express*,' he said. 'I haven't seen a copy of that for years. I thought it had probably closed down by now. Leave it when you go, I'd like a look at it when I get a moment.'

'Read it now if you want,' Joaquin said, laying it down. 'I'm finished with it.' He put it on the table just as it was, folded to the opinion page.

'I'll put it off and enjoy it more,' he said. 'It's nice to have company on a Saturday night. That one – you see that bloke there writing – I used to know him. I was talking to Sybille about him the other day, strangely enough.'

Mei Freind hatt oamoi von ihm gewusst. The girl Sybille's comment, left uncomprehending where it lay, slowly resolved itself in retrospect from, what, Swiss, Bavarian, into German and then into a statement I could understand. *My friend knew him, once.*

'Well ...' he went on. He had an odd air, as if he were about to make a terrible confession. He was assessing our reactions closely. He was looking at me, but not looking at me in a normal way, more going over the surface of my face for possible imperfections. '... I say I used to know him. He wasn't my friend, really. He was actually my brother's friend. They were in the same year at school together. They used to hang out a lot. He used to come round. I heard he's a big-shot journalist now.'

'I know him too,' I said. 'We both did. He was an arsehole. I would have known your brother. I was at that school too.'

'You're kidding,' the proprietor said. 'What's your name? Maybe I know you.'

I told him.

'No,' he said. 'I don't remember your name. There was a black boy and a sexy girl that used to come round with Ogden. The black boy's a lord now, someone told me. Tracy, the sexy girl was called.'

'What's your name?' Joaquin said.

'I'm Pete Frinton,' he said. He was the little brother, the boy in the pub, the one peering at us, scared, and lost, the one taking care of his mother, the one his mother had said we should take out with us, but not bring back at one in the morning, covered with love bites. It came back to me, Eartha Kitt and all. In the depths of the hotel, somewhere beyond the kitchen door, in Pete Frinton's private quarters, the sound of a star and her Saturday-night spectacular echoed from tiled floor to whitewashed ceiling. We must have gaped at him.

'But then your brother—' Joaquin said.

'My brother's the important one,' Pete said. 'Sometimes I see him at Christmas if we go over, or just a phone call. The last time I saw him – maybe seven years ago. He hasn't been here. You couldn't expect it – it would take three days out of his life. You don't get three days spare in his position. Home

Secretary. I don't think anyone would have predicted that one. Apart from James himself, of course. The papers call him Jimmy, I've heard – *Nice One, Jimmy!* – when he's locked some immigrants up or something. It's as if they're talking about someone else.'

'He turned into a Tory,' I said.

'He had to do that before he could be turned into the Home Secretary, I would say. Some people were more shocked by that than others,' Pete said. 'Turning Tory, I mean.'

'Spike knew,' Joaquin said. He was getting interested now. His foul mood with me was dissipating. The idiocy of overlooking that superscript C had condemned us to two whole days in Sorge. He was forgetting it. He leant forward. 'Spike always said that Frinton, he's following what he wants to do.'

Mei Freind kannte ihn oamoi. And that was true.

'They all changed, though,' Pete said. 'They all stayed political but I know some of the people my brother knew, and they were quite far-left. But teenagers, they'll believe in anything. The one I remember was the girl called Tracy. She was always talking about political theory in this very, very sexy way. She almost got me to read it. She died – you know she died? It was a five-days wonder. By the time she died she'd stopped being political. She wasn't going round saying, "Darling, you have to read Bakuvenitsky, you have to read the Russian anarchists, I love the Russian anarchists," to the little brothers of her friends. My brother kept on being friends with her right to the end, I know he did.'

'The last time I saw your brother,' I said, 'it was when he came to my house to tell me she'd died. I was always grateful for that. Otherwise I'd have first seen it in the papers.'

'Well, that was kind of him,' Pete said dismissively. 'She just stopped being one of the political types, all at once. She went to that girl's wedding – what was she called? The older girl, the student.'

'Kate,' Joaquin said. 'She was my flatmate. She married my other flatmate. He was called Euan.'

'Well, you'll remember it,' Pete said. We didn't. We hadn't been invited and hadn't gone to it. Kate and Euan had moved out of the flat. I had moved in. 'My brother wasn't asked and I don't think any of the others were asked – it was just Tracy. I suppose that time between school and your first job, it's a time when people like to turn themselves into somebody different. Growing up. You wouldn't have said that Kate's wedding was going to be like it was. It was sort of arty-bohemian, but all that meant was that she walked up the aisle barefoot, a garland of wild flowers round her head instead of a bouquet in her hands. You can imagine what the dress was like. It was very pretty, really. A country church in the village her parents had retired to – her father had made a packet and stepped down before he was fifty-five. The one blunder was that Kate had said everyone should dress exactly as they liked, including the smallest children. She had half a dozen cousins and nephews who would carry flowers behind her. She wouldn't impose a uniform on them. She had something clearly in mind, however. I don't think she expected to be followed up the aisle by half a dozen kids in lurid pink Cinderella ballgowns and Spiderman outfits from the toy shop. That's what happened. But it was a nice event.

'Tracy hardly knew anyone. She wandered round at the reception saying hi to people, getting into conversations that fizzled out. Everyone was at least six or seven years older than her. It was hard to explain how she fitted in here. She'd been sorted out with a lift back, or she would probably have left early. Who were these people? They were all in couples, some already with a baby in a basket, howling, and all so good-looking. The ones who had got their outfits right were in soft, floppy, pale clothes, the men with white silk scarves tied anyhow round their necks, the women bareheaded or with straw hats over loose white dresses. After a while the music started. A folk band dressed in the same way, a lot of Marie Antoinettes with mandolins and squeezeboxes. Half the party kicked off their shoes, like Kate. They started to dance in an improvised, expressive, flailing style. None of them knew or cared about dancing. To Tracy the ugliness and strangeness of their dancing was inexpressibly alluring. She just wanted to dance like that – no, she wanted not to care about how her dancing looked and go on dancing anyway. She tried – they let her in – she drank some more and tried again. She had thought that, whatever she wanted to be, her friendship with Kate and with Euan had prepared her for it. She didn't know why she had been invited.

'The music stopped. A few speeches followed. Anyone who wanted to could stand up and say something. There was no best man. Kate started. She clasped her hands together, she said that she was just so happy she felt like crying. Then she read a poem she had written that morning. Euan had got a job with the BBC two years before. I think he's still there, producing documentaries, winning prizes. Or perhaps he's got some admin job, Head of Outreach. Who knows? Tracy listened as best she could to the dozen or so speeches by friends of Kate and Euan. She felt her inner core clenching painfully. If you stand at the top of a great waterfall, see the river run smoothly to the edge before toppling in a thunder of waters, a temptation seizes you to leap in and be swept over in that huge collapse. A huge collapse is what the human race always dreams of. It's so banal, the human imagination. Hearing all those friends bear witness, some beautifully, some awkwardly, some with the appearance of improvisation and some with the sad and embarrassing reality, Tracy felt sure that if it went on much longer she would throw herself at the stage and seize the microphone. She was the most marginal guest there, she knew, the one who might just as well not have been invited. She felt she would not be able, in the end, to resist the temptation to introduce herself and gabble on about everything she'd discovered about love, from Kate and Euan. The desire to speak to a crowd from a platform, to tell them what's what – that's as strong as the death-wish above Niagara.

'Of course she didn't. At some point in the late evening, she found herself dancing with Kate, who was dancing with a dozen of her women friends in a kind of improvised *khorovod*, a round dance. The women drew her into a kind of stately stomp where a rhythm of claps and simultaneous hand-raisings was starting to emerge – they were all learning the dance and inventing it at the same time. It felt tremendous. It must have looked ludicrous. It fizzled out in a snake-train of women, threading through the rest of the party, and Tracy, who thought she was leading someone, found herself being led by Kate out of the tent into the warm bluish dark of a hot English September. Kate squatted and then toppled over with a little cry, bringing Tracy with her. She brought herself upright again. Out of some fold or pocket in her mud-streaked cream dress she produced a spliff, which she lit. "I've been promising myself this," she said, passing it to Tracy. "I tucked it away, planning for just this moment. No one's going to miss us for five minutes. I'm knackered, I can tell you. Never get married. Are you having a good time?" Tracy was having the best time ever, she told her.

'But she had forgotten that Kate liked to make a parade of her analysis. It was all part of Kate's belief that she was interested in other people. In reality Kate wasn't interested in other people. She was only interested in herself, and showing off how much she had understood about other people was just a way of exhibiting her own wonderfulness. She hadn't mentioned Euan in her speech, or anything other than how happy she was. Now she started to perform her incisiveness. She wondered whether Tracy was really having such a good time. She worried about Tracy. She felt that she was always on the verge of doing something to please other people, to fit in with them. Those kids she had hung round with, did they really admire Tracy, see what a fantastic person she was? Or did she have too much to bear in that situation? All that talk – the books she read, the arguments they started up. All that wasn't over for Kate and Euan but, you know – said Kate – the time comes when it all starts to sound a bit like students rabbiting on. There isn't going to be a revolution. The time comes to grow up. Tracy just had to find herself now. She was lucky. She'd gone through the time of pleasing other people, of pleasing *men* with the right thing to say. Gone through it years before most people did. Now she could leave home. She could become anything she wanted to be. No one at Oxford would have any idea about who Tracy had been. She could just turn herself into someone new who didn't give a shit about what people thought of her.

'The spliff was finished. Not everything Kate said made sense. But they pulled each other to their feet. They went back to dancing. Tracy thought she was right. Up until that point she had kept an eye on everyone, wondering what they were thinking about her dancing, whether she looked right in the dress she'd chosen – there was no one else there in a tight dress, let alone a black one. Now she kicked off her shoes and set about it. From that moment she was free. At the end of the evening she got into a car with a boy she'd met an hour before. She drove with him to Manchester. It was a hundred miles from where she lived. Where her parents lived, I mean. There was a bit of a row about it when she got home five days later.

'My brother. Nobody knows what happened to him that summer. He had a job in a solicitor's office in Leeds from the day after his last A level to the day before he went to university. I don't remember how it was fixed up. My mum and dad wouldn't have done it. You were in James's year in school. You might have heard people talk about what our home life was like. I think we were both embarrassed about it, to tell you the truth. And here I am, living the same sort of life now. If I had children, I'd expect them to be embarrassed about this place in their turn. And independent. James fixed it up for himself. Went off. Lived in the back bedroom of a shared flat. I don't think he knew anyone in Leeds or anyone he worked or lived with when he turned up. It must have been there that the damage was done. Who were those people?

'My brother. In May we couldn't get through a meal at home without my brother jeering at my dad, explaining how justice should be done in the future in society. It quite often left my mother in tears. You know, I think he believed in revolution, socialism, all that. Kate and Euan, he knew them too. I know when *they* were students they were signed up to some loony-left organization. They grew out of it, of course. Everyone does.'

I said nothing to Pete Frinton's easy belief that adulthood consisted of renouncing your principles. It was quite likely that Joaquin at some point would get up and walk away. This belief, that the passion and intensity of adolescence has a date stamped on it, like a borrowed library book, had infuriated me when I was an adolescent. I couldn't see why you can't maintain that fury for justice and right – for isn't that every child's first complaint, *it's not fair*, a glimpse of the inequalities of the world? The idea that that solipsistic cry at six grows into a demand for social justice at sixteen makes perfect sense to me. The further claim, that the journey always progresses with an understanding of the world and an understanding of other people, and the dulled subject votes Conservative at thirty-six, is a supercilious explanation. Rationalizing after the fact. If it ever happens – and I think some of those placard-bearers were always really Tories – then all that has happened is that the subject has got hold of a little money. And wants to hang on to it. No: it doesn't always happen. And yet there was a word that every new acquaintance of Joaquin and mine disavowed, apologetically said they wanted to use when they talked about us: 'I'm sorry, but I always think of the pair of you as *boyish*.' We believed much what we did when we were boys together, sixteen and twenty-two. We had light hearts, a little savings, no children and no debts. We looked to the world like boys on a hot day swinging from trees, boys falling with a cry of joy into rivers.

'I came to your house once or twice,' I said. 'I actually remember you, I think. There was one time, I was leaving with your brother, and your mother suddenly said something very strange.'

'That wouldn't surprise me.'

'She said, "Why don't you take your brother with you? Only don't bring him back at one in the morning covered with love bites."'

'That sounds like something she would say. Of course she was talking about my dad, really. The coming back covered with love bites, I mean. His evening off he spent with Wendy. That was his girlfriend. It was a hard school for the emotions we grew up in, James and me. We were too much admitted to my parents' bedroom – not literally, I mean. We just knew far too much about what went on between them and what had stopped going on between them. My mum told us everything. And all that love, it got ladled out onto us. A lot of fondling and cuddling and crying and her making us promise that we would never do to our wives what Daddy had just done to her. I don't want to call it abuse. All that love pouring down on us. It did its damage, though. We both got away.

'My brother's a mystery to me. I would say that I'm probably a mystery to him too, except that you don't need to wait for me to confess anything before you know everything about me. I ran away from university, never finished my degree.

Twenty years in Germany, first in Bavaria. Then here, mostly stuffing my face and pouring drink down my throat. That's Sybille's summary. It's not hard to understand. But the thing our childhood taught us both is *you don't share stuff.* I've wondered what happened to my brother that summer working in Leeds. Was it somebody? I don't think so. That's not his style, to be persuaded of anything. I think he was alone quite a lot, and thought things through. He came to a particular conclusion. I know he wrote a few letters to Tracy. It seems incredible now, a teenager sitting down and writing letters on paper with a pen to another teenager who was only living fifty miles away. That was actually how things were. In any case the answer might have been in those letters. I don't know what happened to them.

'My brother changed in a single moment. I know roughly where and when it happened. My parents couldn't drive him to Oxford – my father couldn't take a day off, he said, and my mum could barely drive. So James put whatever he needed in two suitcases and a shopping bag. He took the bus to the station. When he left home, he was wearing what he always wore, a pair of jeans, a T-shirt, trainers, a windcheater. The T-shirt would have had some band's name on it. He got on the train – it wasn't full at that time, late in the morning. Some time after Nottingham, he went to the toilet at the end of the compartment, taking the small bag with him. He locked the door. He undressed. He put his wallet and his keys on the shelf by the window. His clothes he let drop on the floor. In the mirror, a thin, determined boy in underpants and socks. He opened his other bag. He started to dress. It was a green tweed suit he'd bought in a Leeds second-hand shop, some cast-off from the widow of a duke's gamekeeper. He had a graph-paper shirt from M & S, a plain tie, a worn and scuffed pair of brown brogues. His socks weren't quite right – they should have been loud and red, like the tie he now put on. Instead, they were the black socks he always wore with trainers. He would have to do something about that tomorrow, but tomorrow would not be the first impression. He picked up the old clothes. He opened the narrow window in the toilet. He forced them through. The T-shirt and jeans and windcheater scattered in the backwind of the train and were gone. There, somewhere between Nottingham and Birmingham, the clothes – the outer signs of what had been James Frinton lay on a railway track for a while. James Frinton as he would be from that day onwards made his way back to his seat. A middle-aged woman sitting opposite him gave him a puzzled look. But then she went back to her book, unable to place the immense change that had happened in the last few minutes. Most people are not that observant.

'So he turned up at Oxford like he meant to go on. All the other kids would have been coping with embarrassing parents, dressed up, hoicking pot plants out of the back of the hatchback. James Frinton got out of a taxi in an old-fashioned tweed suit, tipped the driver to bring his two suitcases into the porter's lodge. He was ready to go. He made an impression. He went on making an impression. That's why he's Home Secretary, you see.'

I, too, had gone by train to Oxford, probably arriving on the same day. I remembered it perfectly well, for a reason we went on talking about for a week. Some kid turned up who hadn't been offered a place. He'd pretended he'd been accepted to his parents – he'd told them that the college had phoned while they were out. Everything else had inexorably followed, until it was down to the college to turn the three of them away. The scene was occupying the porter's lodge when I turned up. The parents had the exterior trappings of wealth: a Range Rover with the hapless boy's initials on it, RVW1, stood in the car park. An opulent gift, a reward when he had told them he'd got in. Of course their son must be on the list. In the end the Senior Tutor was sent for, I believe. They drove away. I don't think my arrival made much impression.

'What happened to you?' I said. 'Ending up here, I mean.'

'Oh, nothing interesting,' Pete Frinton said. 'My brother was the brilliant one. That's what everyone decided. Me, I had a year abroad that never came to an end. I met Sybille – a little town in Bavaria. Actually, she was still at school when we started seeing each other. It made a bit of a stir in a small town like Bad Schlangau. In the end it was easier to start again, somewhere else entirely. And that's all there is to say about me.'

'Oh, I see,' Joaquin said. He was extended full length on the sofa by now. The walk had been a long one. At nine o'clock, after three beers, he was dropping with tiredness. 'I see you have said that before. The brother of the Cabinet minister, he says this to the people who you know maybe come here to find, you know the journalist, he arrives in Berlin, he finds his way here, hello, hello, I wonder, is it good to talk today maybe, you know, and so there is all there is maybe to, well, there is nothing to say about me the brother of the Home Secretary the Tory or if I can say go back and I never talk to anyone like.'

He snapped into wakefulness. He gave a wide clean smile, as if he had fooled both of us, and had not been saying anything.

'We might have an early night,' I said.

'You go to bed when you like,' Joaquin said. 'I'm just getting started. What's the time? You're crazy. It's nine o'clock. I don't go to bed at nine like an old person.'

'Well, don't go to sleep on the sofa,' I said.

'We go to bed early round here,' Pete Frinton said. 'I think everyone does. Sybille always was a lazy cow, but it's unusual she's not in bed and snoring her head off by ten. There's nothing much to do round here, you see. I can't understand why I don't remember you. Where did you go to university?'

'I went to Oxford too,' I said. 'I went at the same time as your brother and Tracy. I never saw them, though. It was how much they changed. I remember that. I hardly ever saw them after I got there, just in the street from time to time. Your brother was better at stopping and having a friendly chat than Tracy was. I don't know why.'

'That's it exactly,' Pete Frinton said. 'Having a friendly chat – he was always good at that. I don't want to sound embittered, and he's my brother after all, but the last couple of times I saw him, I wondered whether there was any difference for him between seeing me and Sybille and seeing a long-standing constituent. Every time he sees her, he asks her the same thing. He makes me translate it, about what she thinks of – oh, I can't even tell you the question he asks, it's so far away from whatever Sybille thinks about. The famous Frinton charm. It's probably quite good if you only meet him once. That first day at his college was like a first meeting that went on for three years. It would probably only have worked at that point in time, the early 1980s. There was a sort of movement among young men to dress up as if they were fifty, and to admire some pretty dull things. They called themselves "young fogeys". There was all sorts of dressing up going on. Even at the university I was at, I had a friend who everyone called Daiquiri. Used to go round digging out platform shoes and flared trousers from charity shops and jumble sales a decade late. When they first saw my brother, in his bright green scratchy-looking tweed, those neat John Lennon NHS round glasses, his very sharp haircut slicked down with Brylcreem, I know what they'd have thought. They'd have thought here was someone ahead of the game, in tune with the time and the place he was coming to.

'He must have felt as if he'd made quite a success of Oxford. Well, he did. He made a completely different person out of himself. He ended up president of all sorts of things, university societies. The story that ends up in all the newspapers – the one of how he mistook the famous philosophy professor for a tramp and gave him fifty p for a cup of tea. Not everyone thinks it's that funny. Well, I think in reality it wasn't charming vagueness. I believe he probably did it for a bet. He got to feel he could do things like that sometimes. He'd built so many bridges that he could afford to burn a little one, here and there. The success he made started the very first night. There was a drink for the first years.'

'I remember those drinks,' I said. 'I went to the one in my college. It was the noisiest room I'd ever been in. Eighty people, braying away. I was quite a confident person, I'd always thought, but ...'

'My brother was confident,' Pete said. 'For some reason the confidence he'd developed was attractive rather than daunting. Probably everyone he knew at Oxford has worked out since what he wanted to achieve, but only because he achieved it, or almost. Those desires weren't transparent at the time. He seemed genuinely interested in meeting everyone. He moved on to talk to someone else. They felt pleased to have been singled out for five minutes by the bloke in the tweed suit. "Were those your parents this afternoon? What are their names? Your father – he looked quite at home. Are you one of those old Oxford families? Isn't there a pub where they've been stapling ties to the walls for decades? Is your father's tie up there? Admit it!"

'He fitted right in. He was a little pet, at first. They fed him, and he grew. Then he ate them.

'Three days later – my God, he was a star by the time those seventy-two hours had gone by – he went up Turl Street, asked a question at the porter's lodge in, what was that college, I can't even remember, Trinity, Lincoln, what was it called? He found his way through two quads to a staircase with the word "CARTWRIGHT" painted on a board at the bottom. The porter he got the information from, he'd remember my brother next time. The charm he'd cultivated! Those days, in the old colleges, there was a thing that people did. They had a double door. You left one open, the inner one shut, if you didn't mind visitors. If you were working or in private, you shut both of them and no one would bother you. James was climbing the staircase. He could hear music all the way up. At the top, Tracy's room had both doors wide open. Motown was pouring out. There was a boy lying on her sofa in his underpants. Tracy on her desk, by the window, in her bra and pants in the dust-strewn sunshine, dancing to "Where Did Our Love Go". James knocked on the open door with a bright smile. Tracy leapt down and rushed to him.

"'This is *divine*," she said firmly. "How *sweet* of you to come straight away. I've been simply *longing* to see you. Now I do hope you're going to stay and have some gin. Last night we went to a howlingly drunk cocktail party – this university society called the Campaign for Real Gin. Glorious, isn't it? They had sponsorship and we stole all the sponsorship. I think the sponsorship was just bottles of gin and a poster. We left the poster. Have you had your gin today, *darling*? Marcus says – this is Marcus – Marcus says a day without gin is like a year without sunshine, is like Laurel without Hardy, is like the Bible without Leviticus. *So sweet.* Now – let me take a look at you …"

'She took a look at him. He took a look at her. Perhaps she had prepared this speech, or something like it, to impress the little man who had argued with her about ideology and read Marx with her that she was no longer there for him. But she got through about half her speech before she saw that the James Frinton in her room had undergone a change, too, that, like her, the prospect of Oxford had persuaded him to become a different person. Clothes, hair, accent, manner, behaviour, belief, all that surface was changed. Nothing of them remained except the steady assessment of the gaze, and what they had both gone through together.

"'Look at you," she said. She stepped back. She reached for a silk gown lying on the back of an armchair. "I've been waiting for Marcus to go, actually."

'My brother knew when to take action. He took the prostrate sleeping boy under the armpits. He dragged him out onto the landing. He returned and picked up the pile of black clothes by the sofa – it looked like fancy dress, and included a cape with a scarlet lining. Whether or not it belonged to the boy Marcus, he would have to do the best with it. He shut both doors, one after the other. Then he started making a cup of tea for them both. The Young Fogey and the Flapper, but they'd known each other for ever. It was like a chance meeting of the Happy Shades in the afterlife.'

Without much warning, Joaquin raised his head. He reached out to the table in front of the sofa where a box of the game Risk sat. He pulled off the lid. He was suddenly and briskly sick into the box, in two or three spasms. I leapt up. I did what I remember my mother always doing when I was a child being sick, and rubbed his back in circles.

'I'll get a towel,' Pete Frinton said. 'Bad luck. Too much walking in the sun, I suppose.'

When he came back with a towel and a bin-bag, Joaquin needed to be taken up to bed. He drank a big glass of water and took his shirt off. He sat on the edge of the bed. 'It was not the sun,' he said. 'I am not troubled by walking in the sun.'

'What was it, then?'

'It was listening to all that crap about going to Oxford and Cambridge and your *Brideshead Reunited* crap.'

'Oh, come on,' I said. '*Revisited* not *Reunited*. Don't you remember Tracy Cartwright and James Frinton? Aren't you interested?'

'No, no,' he said. 'What happened to them always happens. Weak, stupid people.'

'You didn't always think that,' I said. 'You liked Tracy, I know you did. James Frinton's not a weak person.'

'Weak people,' he said. 'You can become a leader and still be a weak person. You know that's true. How he becomes up the greasy pole of your parliamentary politics, up and up, into the Cabinet, into government, he's Home Secretary now and goes everywhere with six bodyguards. You know how – by being weak and saying stuff that agrees with the last powerful person he met and talked to. Everyone he ever meets thinks he agrees with him. What a nice person, how nice, and then he does something that shows he's met someone else in the meantime. Like a little boy wanting to please his mummy and all his aunties, but in fact he is Home Secretary. Fuck. And Tracy, she was so nice but weak too. I make her a cup of tea, I cuddle up with her, I know she likes me because I'm there, that's all. In a moment I leave the room and then she forgets I was ever there. They all change at the first chance. You know who is strong, Spike? I am strong and you are strong. Nothing has changed for you and me since that first day. That is the life of politics. Changing your mind, like this man and that woman, forgetting what you thought a week ago, deciding, okay I'm a Tory now, libertarian, not anarchist, changing what you wear to fit in and the books on your bookshelf. What everyone does. You know something, though. I tell you a lie. It's not the listening to the stories about Oxford Cambridge, make me puke, whatever fucking place. It was the herring I ate, I promise you. That herring was shit. Don't kiss me. Okay, I'm going to wash my mouth and clean teeth and then you kiss me, you don't want to kiss me now, don't kiss me, what's wrong with you.'

We slept well. The next morning it was Sunday. By eight o'clock there was no sign of Pete Frinton. The girl Sybille gave us something like breakfast – I think it was probably exactly the same thing that she ate for breakfast, a bowl of muesli, a couple of supermarket croissants and some instant coffee. 'He knows you too,' she remarked, making a bit of an effort to speak in normal German. 'He won't be up until lunchtime. Are you going out? I can make you a couple of cheese rolls. Potato salad. Herrings.'

It was the decorous way the dog Nala was sitting by the table that made us accept. He wasn't in a begging stance but, all the same, he made it plain that anything we wanted to reach out to him would not be refused. If Nala came, he could eat the herrings. I always believed that dogs' digestive systems were stronger than humans'. We planned to walk the Wall in the different direction, and see how far the dog would come. In my mind I thought of finding a river to swim in – Joaquin, the dog and I.

'Did you maybe blame me?' Joaquin said, once we were out in the country. 'For losing all those people, those friends.'

'I'd have to think about that,' I said. It is our style, I think, not to offer an easy answer to the other in order to soothe or give way. And it is true that after Joaquin came along, quite soon none of the others from the group had stuck around. Tracy and James Frinton had transformed themselves. Perhaps everyone else transformed themselves. For each of them, there had been a small window in a train. An opportunity had presented itself. They had forced the remnants of their previ-ous selves through it, like old clothes, abandoning those

previous selves for ever. It was just Joaquin and I who never
had. They would hardly have wanted to sit down with someone so different, someone who was just as they had always
been. In any case, Euan and Kate had been Joaquin's friends.
They had taken a stern, inventive line, in the end, about me
being in the flat all the time. You would have thought that
Joaquin had misled them from the start. Sometimes, after
they had gone, we heard hair-raising stories about things that
he or I were said to have done. (Only last month an activist
asked us whether it was really true that we'd had three-way sex
with a policeman who was trying to arrest us, back in the
1980s. We'd heard the story before, but not for years.) Ogden
had stuck around, really until the trip we took to Germany
after university. Eric was perfectly pleasant whenever we met,
until one day it occurred to me that I hadn't laid eyes on him
for five years. I hadn't missed him at all.

I think my time at university was a lesson in solitude or,
rather, a lesson in the fact that solitude was not a punishment
for me as it would be for most people. I doubt that I appeared
especially solitary. I joined a couple of organizations – not
university political societies, but radical town organizations. I
made some connections there that have gone on being useful.
I was friendly with the six other kids who were doing my
subject in my year. They were fine. I had people who ate
supper with me. I had friends from home who came to stay.
Joaquin came twice a term, sleeping in my narrow bed – there
are times when even two big men of six foot three don't object
to sharing a single bed. I went back to the place I was born,
once a term, and I stayed with Joaquin. My father did not
know that I had come back for those weekends. One day I

heard from the college porters that my father had killed himself. I had friends. I enjoyed my subject and did well at it. I dressed much as I had dressed in the sixth form. The day I left that university I was much the same as the day I had arrived at it.

It was a hot day, that Sunday. After three hours we sat down under a tree, Pete Frinton's dog at our feet. We drank from the water bottles we'd filled up after breakfast. We'd thought to bring a plastic dish. We filled it for Nala the dog to drink from, too. We were shirtless in the hot sun. Now Joaquin took off his boots and thick walking socks to massage his feet. It was only eleven o'clock. There was no reason to hurry back to the hotel. I felt full of energy, buoyant, thrilled. There had been days when our walks had lasted for ten or twelve hours; days ending in a tiredness so heavy that there was something luxuriant about the physical sensation, a tiredness so wonderfully overbearing that it could keep you from sleep, like pain. Comfortably, our thoughts were running along the same lines.

'This dog has no idea,' Joaquin said, 'what he has let himself in for, walking with you and me.'

'He's going to find out,' I said. 'How are you feeling? After the herring, I mean.'

'I was thinking last night,' Joaquin said. 'That James Frinton. He used to come round to our place. Our place before it was our place, I mean. Didn't he? There was a group of them. I can't remember, though, who was the first to come round, how they got involved.'

'You thought James Frinton was the leader, I remember,' I said. 'I was really surprised when you said that. For me it was

Percy Ogden who was the important one. James Frinton never really said anything. He was just the guy who agreed with things, or not that far from it. A sort of camouflage ideologue, only not that, because he's conspicuous, he's on a stage, he looks like a hero … Those politicians. They aren't driven by principle. They don't believe in anything that can't be erased. They're not like us. Are we political, Jo?'

'Of course we are,' Joaquin said. He lifted one of his walking socks to his face. 'Hey, you know something? These socks – they fucking stink. Two days' walking. I love it. You know we know what we think about all that shit, politics.'

'But everything changes,' I said. 'What use is it thinking the same that we thought in the 1980s? Everything has changed so much. Why shouldn't people change everything they think, like James Frinton, once they start being surrounded by different people?'

'It didn't happen to you,' Joaquin said. 'It hasn't happened to me. That university you went to, the one that people say, oh, it changed me, changed everything about me. It didn't change you. You knew what you thought when you went there. That's okay too. What do you think it was like, when, you know, like the brother was saying, when James Frinton knocks on Tracy's door? I liked that Tracy. She was crazy but she was okay. And he comes in and she's changed, like she's a party girl with nothing in her head, just wearing her bra, knickers, and he's dressed up like it's the 1920s. What do they say? Do they say, "My God, what happened to you, you crazy?"'

'The one thing I know,' I said, 'is that James Frinton wrote her a lot of letters during that summer. Pete Frinton was right

about that. Maybe two a week, all summer. He wouldn't have
carried on if she hadn't loved getting them. She showed them
to us, whenever she got one. I don't think she'd have shown
them to you. Those letters, I bet she kept them. She'd have
told him she'd kept them, too, straight away. He'd have been
pleased at first. She was seeing Mohammed all that summer.
He would have hated that. She'd have taken the first chance
to let him know it was him that mattered. That first meeting,
they'd have read some of them together. I reckon he was
thinking things through in those letters, talking to her about
why they'd smashed stuff up with the Spartacists, what they'd
been thinking of, maybe saying he wasn't sure he was in favour
of nuclear war any more.'

'That is what is called the young love. He's come round in
a big circle,' Joaquin said. 'He wanted a nuclear war then
because, you know, the workers' paradise in the ruins, you
know. These days, he wants a nuclear war because that's what's
needed, he thinks, him and his friends in America, waving
weapons at North Korea, whoever.'

A thought came to me. I couldn't share it with Joaquin. It
was too inchoate. In the newspaper we had brought with us
there was a photograph of James Frinton, the British Home
Secretary, with the new Saudi prince who was supposed to be
running things. The fat prince had had some journalists killed
last week. On the other hand he was supposed to be thinking
about letting women drive. (Give a head of state the choice
between doubling the size of a consumer market and his
mental religious convictions – the money wins.) They were in
some opulent interior. In the photograph, Frinton was grin-
ning wildly. His stance was not conventionally statesmanlike.

He was actually winking in an exaggerated way, his face half folded up. Some comment had been made in the press, I knew, which described Frinton as embarrassingly sycophantic on the basis of this gesture. I had seen it, and instantly remembered the insulting wink Frinton had given me, years before, as we were being carted out of the CND gathering. Behind the fat prince was America, paying for his genocidal war in Yemen. Did Frinton have any American friends in the sense that Joaquin meant? Was he under any illusions about the fat Saudi twat? That photograph made me think he was taking the piss. It gestured over everyone's head at those who had known him years ago. *Look at this wanker*, the wink said.

'I guess he wouldn't see the connections,' I said. 'You love oil. You love the genocidal maniac who owns it. You love the Americans who fund them. You love the nuclear threat the Americans have.'

'They are fucked, those guys,' Joaquin said.

Those letters. I wondered what happened to them. The next time I saw them, she mentioned them to us, again, but this time it was in front of him. I got the sort of impression that she'd been dangling them in front of him. I don't know why – whether it was like a gesture of fondness, *I've loved seeing what's in your mind*, or whether it was a kind of threat. I don't know what she was going to get out of the threat. Did she even know she was threatening him? Or was it more like a tease, in her mind? Hey, you big Tory – my God, I've got some funny stuff you wrote to me, two years back. That CND meeting we smashed up! And kicking that monsignor in the head, the peacemongering friend of capitalists! I love that letter you wrote me about it – it's so funny. The gap is small between blackmail and recording what has been done and said. It depends not on what has been done and said. It depends on how we have changed ourselves in the interim.

Two weeks after arriving at university I had a letter from Mohammed. He was probably the one in the group that I felt least connection to. He lived down the hill, you see. There is so much difference between the espousal of principles and the living of lives.

That last summer before university, Mohammed and Tracy had had their affair. It was engineered by Ogden. Sometimes Tracy performed in front of Ogden, and the rest of us. Perhaps Mohammed wasn't performing. She definitely made what might have been passion our entertainment. Mohammed couldn't help himself – he might have preferred to snog in private, but a look would pass from Tracy to Ogden, a look of innocent temptation. Her arm would snake out around Mohammed's waist, a head descend on his shoulders. She would start pecking, licking, groping, a full-on snog. Around us, strangers looked away. I never understood whether she was doing it to please Ogden, or whether he had gone as far as giving her instructions. There was no doubt in my mind that it was for him. That initiating look was always quite clear. Mohammed was lost. Each time, he tried to continue with whatever we were talking about for a while. Then her tongue and mouth silenced him. She would continue to snog him, her arms around his torso, until his little dick rose stiffly in his pants, a solid presence, stabbing upwards in his loose cotton trousers. The end had been attained. She sat back in her chair, wiping her mouth, smiling. Ogden, Eric Milne and I would carry on talking all the while – I remember that summer we were all reading Lenin's *What Is To Be Done?* Those ancient arguments about whether the coal miners could ever spontaneously generate a fundamental change hit the wall of their lechery, their not listening. Sometimes I almost reached the point of carrying on the debate on my own. "'Without a revolution in Germany we are finished,' I said, quoting. 'This is our Germany. It really is.'" There was no answer. James Frinton was in Leeds. Both Eric and Ogden were, in my memory, distracted by the spectacle of those two snogging, forgetting that breathing was necessary to life.

There was no question that Mohammed was swept away, even if he understood that his passion was being observed and dissected at every stage. Some time in August we all took a day trip to Scarborough in Ogden's car. At some point during the day, Ogden arranged matters so that we all found ourselves outside a tattoo parlour. We should all get tattoos! Wouldn't that be great? In the year I left school, I knew nobody at all who had a tattoo. The only people you ever saw with one were very old men, bikers, sailors and labourers. But somehow Tracy was saying to Mohammed in an exaggerated way that if he really loved her, he would get her name tattooed on his arm. He laughed: she wasn't serious. She was serious. If not her name, then something that would always mean something to the pair of them. Those roses he had given her on her birthday, they were beautiful. A rose on his arm, around her initials. He wouldn't go for the initials, but wherever Mohammed is, thirty years later, he has a badly drawn tattoo of a rose on his arm. I imagine that he is a father and a grandfather by now. He would never have shirked that responsibility. He did what people asked of him.

He wrote to me, saying he'd like to come to visit the following weekend. He wouldn't stay with Tracy – it had finished in
an okay way, but he thought it would be weird to sleep on her
floor. He had told Frinton and Tracy that he was coming, but
I dropped them a line in any case. I picked Mohammed up
from the bus station at five o'clock on a Thursday. He'd
decided to skip his Friday classes. We walked back to the
college. That walk through the town, or maybe through the
university, was one of belonging or not-belonging. There were
those, I remember with shame, who made a performance of
who they were, or what they had become, a kind of uniformed
embodiment of status that extended beyond clothes to the
way they stood, carried themselves, spoke, looked about
them. In retrospect they filled the streets. Mohammed and I
walked along, talking quietly, like manly revolutionaries. I
don't suppose the sort of people I'm talking about saw us like
that, or saw us at all. 'There's a hell of a lot of idiots around,'
Mohammed said at one point. 'It's only Thursday night. It's
not like this on a Saturday at home.' I had to tell him that it
was like this all the time. There were idiots in the university
where Mohammed was, too, but they mostly had the excuse
of being drunk. This lot – were they all rich? 'You don't have
to have anything to do with them if you don't want to,' I said.

Like me, Mohammed had joined a couple of university
political societies, but most of his attention was with radical
groups in the town where he studied. There was a Spartacist
group he had signed up with. Joaquin and I had left the
Spartacists in the course of the summer – for once it had been
a decision based on personal matters, not on ideological differences. If we left, then Euan and Kate could stay in, Joaquin

said, with a remnant of that Latin consideration of private connections. We'd been talking to the Revolutionary Communist League for a while. They had a division in Oxford. I explained all this to Mohammed as we walked. I'd been along twice to the group. The leader was only a couple of years older than me, but he'd taken a trip to Democratic Kampuchea. He knew all about it. When Joaquin came to visit, the week after, we would go together. He thought he knew the chair from a congress in Salford in 1980. It was the congress that had broken up in a fist-fight. Mohammed had already taken part in a piece of direct action – he'd thrown a bag of his own shit in a branch of Barclays Bank, a popular target of the time for its investments in South Africa. The RCL had its own approach to direct action, but they were a bit more cautious. They hadn't talked to me yet about what they'd done. I got the impression, too, that bags of shit were lower down their list of priorities than other strategic aims. When someone arrived out of the blue, they would have been crazy to open up on the spot. You need to have some trust before you start explaining what you hope to achieve in twenty years' time.

We walked along, the braying rich flailing around us. From time to time I cast a sideways look at Mohammed's left arm. His rolled-up sleeve displayed the stem and thorns of his tattooed single rose.

'What's the strategy?' Mohammed said. 'Have you got any sense of that?'

He was talking about the Oxford group.

'I get the impression it's more interested in gaining power and influence than smashing windows,' I said. 'The first thing they said – are you a member of the Labour Party?'

'Fuck off,' Mohammed said.

'That's what I said. I thought they were asking whether they could trust me, or whether I was just another bourgeois socialist who's made his peace with multinational corporations and the stock exchange.'

'But they meant it.'

'Yup. They think it would be good if someone like me joined the Labour Party. In ten years, fifteen, people from our segment of opinion are going to be in a position to influence thought.'

'Have you joined the zombies, then? Call yourself a democratic socialist? Vote for Roy Hattersley? What's Joaquin say?' It was one of the nice things about Mohammed that other people's domestic arrangements appeared much of a muchness to him. For some time I had thought he didn't know that Joaquin and I were going out together. In fact he'd known at the same time as everyone else. It hadn't been that important to him.

'There's a rude word for the tactic. Entryism. I'd rather be smashing the windows of Carole's café again.'

'She deserved that. And Frinton and Tracy. Are they in the RCL too? What have they joined?'

I didn't know, but half an hour after leaving Mohammed's bag in my room we were climbing the staircase to Frinton's. I hadn't seen Frinton since I'd got there. I'd thought I would go to see him, then Mohammed's letter had arrived. I decided to save it until his visit. His outer door was swinging open. I knocked – knocked again more loudly. There was a conversation, or rather speech, going on inside. We went in.

For a moment I thought we had come to the wrong room. I didn't recognize the person standing up, making broad gestures with his arms. This person saw us. His eyes flickered between us and someone sitting in an armchair. His words bore no kind of relation to the scene. He made no acknowledgement that anyone had entered. He was talking at top volume about something being a goddamned lie. He was addressing someone called Martha, though there was no Martha in the room, only us and the boy in the armchair with one leg draped over the side. Mohammed and I stood apologetically. For the first time I felt like a suppliant in Frinton's presence.

The speech came to an end. The boy who had been speaking made a huge gesture of dissatisfaction. He had been facing us, but now he acknowledged us. Only now did James Frinton turn his head. He smiled. His charm, afterwards so famous, was a work in progress. I got the impression that there were always people knocking and entering. James's smile was the one he produced for everyone. It swept over us like a searchlight.

'Bloody hell,' he said, but only after a moment. 'Spike. Mohammed. What are you doing? I didn't expect that at all.'

'Thought we'd surprise you,' Mohammed said. But in fact Mohammed had written to James Frinton. I had sent both Frinton and Tracy a note through the internal mail. Neither of us had had an answer, but we hadn't attached any importance to that. We had been Spartacists together.

'This is Simon,' James Frinton said. 'He's going, though. I was just hearing his lines. He's George in *Who's Afraid of Virginia Woolf?* Everyone else on the staircase is out doing important stuff. It might as well be me. Go on, Simon. Push off, there's a little love.'

'Bye, Jimmie,' the actor said. 'Coming to Claudia's bash, I expect.'

'Not sure,' James Frinton said. 'Developments, as you see. See you later.'

The actor went away, leaving James Frinton with the developments. He got up and hugged first Mohammed, then me. What were we doing there? It was great to see us – of course he could see Spike any time, but it was always great to see Mohammed. (I think as he started to talk he had remembered that I was at Oxford, too. He hadn't seen me since A levels at school. That was a world away.) We'd have a cup of tea and then what? The pub, a pizza? He was at our disposal.

At our disposal. A chilling phrase of society and *politesse* – I hadn't anticipated James Frinton's change of expression. There was nothing until that phrase that couldn't be explained away, that wasn't compatible with James Frinton exactly as he had been. The grand room was just the college he was at. The flailing actor had taken him as his victim. Even the clothes he was wearing, the tweed waistcoat and trousers and thick shirt with rolled-up sleeves, could just be a change of style. We all wore different clothes from time to time. Some of the Spartacists dressed like farmers and went to folk nights at the student union. But the expression *at our disposal* was not something we had heard James Frinton say before. It had not been wished on him.

'How long are you here?' James Frinton said. 'Are you staying with Spike? When did you get here? I've got a lot of plans for you, this weekend. Ogden's not here, is he? Not a complete reunion?'

'Have you seen Tracy?' I said. It was a kindness on my part. I thought it was the question that Mohammed was holding back from asking.

'Seen her, yes,' James Frinton said. 'Half Oxford's seen her. A bit of a spectacle. Last time I saw her she was drunk. And the time before that. And the time before that.'

'She likes a drink,' Mohammed said bravely. 'So what's it like here? You're only here for the library, right.'

'No,' James Frinton said. 'I'm not just here for the library. There's other things. It's bollocks, the whole thing. It's mad. But there's a reason people want to come here.'

'That's what Spike said. He's here for the library. What's so great about the library?'

'Don't ask me to pass judgement on the whole place,' James Frinton said. 'I've only been here three weeks. It's beautiful to look at. You can have some fun here. That's all I know.'

'I've been here an hour and I'd put a bomb under the place,' Mohammed said. I gave a faint cheer. 'This fucking library – who's allowed in it? I tell you who's allowed in it – people who've got into this fucking university. Who gets into this university? Rich kids, mostly. That library ought to have its doors open to anyone who wants to read a book. They ought to be teaching kids how to read and lending them any book they want to borrow.'

'Yes, well,' James Frinton said. 'There might be a few logistical problems with that. It's a lovely idea. Do you want a cup of tea?'

'Yes,' I said. 'Let's all have a lovely cup of tea.' I meant it to sting. But James Frinton was at our disposal. He had made himself available. He had plans for our weekend.

Talking to Joaquin about the weekend, thirty years before, when Mohammed had come to Oxford to see us, some things had become clearer. The dog had abandoned us, running deep into the forest after a fox or some other powerful scent. I expect he knew his way home. The day was a hot one. We were following the line of the Wall without any shade or shelter. Both of us had our shirts off, our walking trousers rolled up around our knees. The waist of Joaquin's was dark with sweat. We were glad to have filled the rucksack with litre bottles of water. The more I walked and talked, I began to draw energy from the effort of my own expounding. There was no reason why we should not have walked for ever, northwards along this forgotten border to the Baltic, to turn and walk back again until we hit the border of what had once been called Czechoslovakia. The blood and the joy of action arose from action. The meaning and the joy of talking came from all the talking we did. That day, in the sun, it made perfect sense.

'It's all changed so much,' Joaquin said. 'When I see that man, the Home Secretary, in the newspaper, or I hear him explaining, so gently, gently, sensibly, nice, on the *Today* programme that, yes, Mishal, you say what is true, but I tell you, the people of this country they want to have strong borders, only strong borders when we leave the EU, choose our destiny, shoot foreigners, okay? When I hear that shit, I only hear the Home Secretary. I don't hear the boy used to come round with you and Ogden. I don't even remember that boy. He's gone.'

'I'm just trying to remember the last time I saw any of them,' I said. 'Ogden, it was in Weimar.'

'I read that piece in the newspaper Ogden wrote,' Joaquin said. 'It was so bad. And him it was who wanted to be politician, supposed to go out and rule the world. Prime Minister by the time he is forty and here he is, writing little, little pieces, *A gay guy like me knows how things really are, okay,* for newspapers that nobody reads. And those others.'

'Not everyone was like Percy Ogden. He was just a narcissist, thinking about where he could put himself, how he could listen to the sound of his own voice. *A gay guy like me.*'

'The narcissist. He always has to find out that his love is unrequited. Trying to love someone who never loved him. Himself. *I love myself so much because I hate myself.* Poor Tracy. Her I am sad for.'

We fell silent for a while. The rhythm of our steps was enough. After a while I passed a bottle of water to Joaquin. He swigged from it.

'The one thing about James Frinton changing like that. He never tried to change the past, as far as I know.'

'Like God,' Joaquin said joyously.

'Like God?'

'That's the one thing God never does in the Bible, go back to change things that have happened. James Frinton and God!'

'I mean he never lied about his past.'

Everyone else was lying about where they had come from. I don't think he ever did. Apart from the Spartacist part, of course. There was a strange little business when he made us tea that once. He said, after a minute, 'You're in luck. I've still got some of Mummy's fruit cake on the go.' His mother had got her act together. She had done what mummies were expected to do at that time. She'd made him a big fruit cake to take to university. The idea was that you would meet somebody. You would ask them back to your room, and be able to offer them not just a cup of tea but a slice of delicious home-made fruit cake. Without this, how would you ever make friends? Frinton's mum had made him a fruit cake – I can't imagine all the poring over recipes, the anguished weighing of currants and sultanas, the tears when it looked as if it wasn't going to work. He got it out of the tin. There was about a quarter left. She'd tried to ice it, but there was just a fat blanket of shop-bought white icing laid over the top, pressed down with fingers whose prints you could see. She'd decided, with all the mother-love at her disposal, to decorate it with glacé cherries, one at each hour of the clock. At least, I suppose so. There was only one left on the remaining quarter of the cake. The cake sticks in my mind. He was quite proud of having it. It reflected well on his mother. That was the most important aspect of it. Frinton wouldn't have pretended a bought cake was his mother's creation. The other thing I remember is that Frinton asked us if we would like a slice of cake. He cut three slices, one of which had the glacé cherry on top. It sounds a bit childish, but I was honestly shocked when he took the slice with the cherry. He did it quite casually.

'Oh, for fuck sake,' Joaquin said, when I had told this aspect of it again. 'That is the most important thing? Really? The thing he did with the cake? He took the cherry?'

'He's greedy,' I said. 'I think he's learnt to hide it in every way apart from one, the most obvious way. That glacé cherry was his to take.'

And then we had gone to see Tracy. I never saw Mohammed again after that weekend he came to visit. I don't think it was anything to do with me. In fact, I don't believe, at this distance in time, that he was visiting me at all. He came that weekend for Tracy and he cut himself off from all that lot because of her. Her rooms were open to the world. Music of some operatic sort was playing, filling the staircase. The three of us went in, led by James Frinton. The rooms were so lived in, so full of comfortable and ostentatious knowledge. They were unlike my room, bare, with a single poster, twenty books, and the contents of two suitcases not filling the wardrobe. This room had a table with drinks on it – bottles of gin, whisky, vodka, brandy – and cushions, throws, a banana palm, a huge voluptuous nude in oils over the fire. Mohammed went over to the mantelpiece. It was thick with invitations, cream and white, scribbled on with the italic hand of privileged education.

'Are these, what, birthday parties?' Mohammed said. 'People send you invitations? Like when we were seven years old? No one's sent me an invitation like this ever, I don't reckon. They're not even like party invitations, they're like wedding invitations, like once-in-a-lifetime, pay to print them, sort of thing …'

He trailed off, picking one off the shelf.

'We're not in the right place,' he said. 'This isn't right. These aren't for her. Someone else sharing this room with her it must be. Or, right, has she, I don't know, taken all these invites, nicked them from some stupid posh girl as a joke? Why's it say Alexandra? Look, "Alexandra darling, do come," it says. I want to get out of here.'

I said nothing. Mohammed was in the wrong place. Soon events would set the mistake to rights. But he put the invitation back where it had been, behind a lump of crystal. His hand rested on the crystal. It was that stone called Blue John that you could pick up in odd places in the countryside near where we had grown up. Something must have been recalled to him. I could reconstruct it easily. They had spent the whole summer together, those two. We had all done the same thing at some point: a day out in the hills. At some point one of them had overturned a rock. There was a wound of blue crystal in the limestone. You took it; you put it in your rucksack; you kept it as something from that day. This was Tracy's room. Mohammed remembered this exact stone, where it had come from. Still he was in the wrong place. The crystal had come in handy to hold an invitation upright, an invitation from a pair called Stella and Johnny.

'I suppose we'd better wait,' Mohammed said. He sat down on the sofa, pushing cushions to one side. 'Do we have to have that on? I can't stand that crap.'

James Frinton bent down. He turned off the cassette player – what people called a ghetto-blaster, back then. There was a lightness, even an amusement, about him. I thought he knew that Tracy's rooms were like this. The silence was abrupt. In the quad below an aggressive call came, some sportsman hailing another.

'I think she might be—' he started to say. The door to the bedroom opened. Tracy was there, yawning.

'You woke me up,' she said. 'I was doing my reading, or trying to. And then I thought I'd have a lie-down. I'm so knackered. Mohammed. Spike. What are you doing here? What a joy. And James Frinton too. You should have—'

'I wrote you,' Mohammed said. 'Doesn't matter. I'm here now. Look at you.'

'Give me five minutes,' Tracy said. 'I'll be with you in five minutes. James, what happened last night? Were you there till the grisly end? I love, love, love that bar. I don't even know whose bash that was. The one we went to after the politicos. Somebody scribbled it on my wrist in the middle of a lecture. And I went and there you were too. Give me five minutes.'

She floated – I think I can say floated – back into her bedroom, leaving the door open. We stayed in the sitting room, not talking, listening to Tracy. She was calling out the odd remark to us, or muttering curses to herself. The tap in the bedroom ran; an aerosol sprayed lengthily; she opened and shut the doors of wardrobes, the drawers of cupboards.

'I won't be a second. I'm a quick dresser. I'm not ironing anything.

'I should be writing my essay, really. I haven't even made a start on it. Looks like an all-nighter.

'It's Sophie's fault.

'Do you know Sophie, James? Awful girl. Dragged me out three nights running. I love her really.

'This is such a strange place. I don't know what I'm doing here. It's like I'm here observing this strange tribe – I want to take my notebook out or something.

'It's so nice to see you three. I'm so happy you're here – it's like old times.

'Where is that fucking thing?

'Almost done, almost done, almost done.

'There's something on tonight in college. I was looking for an excuse not to go, and now I've got one, I'm so happy. You three and a pizza and a good old gossip. I can't tell you how nice. And now ...

'Ta-da,' Tracy said, standing in the doorway, her calves crossed, like a pantomime boy's, her arms upright, like a star making an entrance. Her whole essence had somehow changed, but how? It was just clothes and hair. She had always been passionate and chaotic, had always declared herself in theatrical ways. That was just the same. When I think of her now that she has been dead for thirty years, I think of a girl with wide eyes, stretching back on the sofa at Joaquin's to knead her bare feet into my side; a girl glittering with a joyous rage, lifting a bag of flour with both hands to throw it into the stalls, a girl saying *ta-da* in fancy dress with her arms upright in a doorframe in Oxford. It was all performance. She was always there with her arms and hands above her head. That gesture, of her arms above her head, was the thing about Tracy that would never change – everything else, her name and her beliefs, would change in a heartbeat. But when she came into contact with another human being who had once been important to her, she was afraid. She raised her hands like Eartha Kitt about to sing.

We went out for a pizza. It was not the same. She talked about people. There were no principles to be gone over any longer, just individuals – people she had met, people who were shagging other people she had met, people who had made a name for themselves, and people who were only famous within a tiny circle of twenty or so. There was nothing really to contribute. That was the point of her conversation.

James Frinton kept it going – he knew the people she was talking about, or knew who they were. He could encourage her with an occasional 'Didn't he get arrested in Pakistan, trying to join the mujahideen?' or 'I thought her brother worked for BP,' or 'They were at school together.' From time to time she threw us a bone, a 'Do you remember that time when we …' And we dutifully remembered. But it went nowhere.

Once she gave a little shriek and clutched Mohammed's left arm, pushing his rolled-up blue shirtsleeve towards his shoulder. 'Look, look,' she said. 'You had that done – you had that done in Scarborough. I remember! It took so long! I thought it was going to be in and out but we must have been an hour standing outside. And there it is, your rose. I love it. What a charming thing to have, a souvenir. I almost envy you. I do envy you. I do.'

'You held my hand,' Mohammed said. 'I thought it was going to hurt and you said you'd hold my hand. It was the others who were standing outside waiting. And my hand was really sweaty and I worried it was disgusting, but it did hurt, and you did hold my hand.'

The smile grew bright, the eyes were wide. The target of Tracy's expression might have stood ten feet behind Mohammed. 'Happy days,' she said eventually. The saddest part of that pizza was that we all knew exactly what the others would order – we had discovered Pizza Express some months before the end of school: Mohammed a Marinara with no cheese, me a Four Seasons, James Frinton a Margherita, to save money. Tracy had that strange one with onion and sultanas, of which ten pence of every pizza went to help save

Venice from Peril. Venice is still where it always was. The strange pizza still sits on the menu at Pizza Express. But Tracy is long gone. We had a bottle of wine. Tracy had a gin and tonic as well. Nothing had changed. Mohammed still ate his pizza from the inside out. Frinton still carved his into neat sixteenths before rolling them up and eating them. Tracy was still the last to finish. And everything had changed. We saw that.

On the pavement outside, I said I thought we could go to the King's Arms or to the college bar. Something barely perceptible passed between Tracy and James Frinton. The smooth surface of charm that he later developed was still incomplete. I saw this exchange. She lowered her eyelids and let him take control.

'I've got to get on with a couple of things,' he said. 'But we'll see you tomorrow. Maybe tomorrow night. Come round about six, yeah?'

'I'll be in terrible trouble if I don't finish this essay. Start it, even,' Tracy said. 'I can't believe you've just turned up on a Thursday, you two. It's crazy. You're mental. I love it. We'll see you tomorrow.'

'I'm going to walk Alexandra home,' James Frinton said.

'Walk who?' Mohammed said. 'Half those invites in your room – to Alexandra. Who the fuck's Alexandra?'

'I guess it's just what people call me here,' Tracy said. 'It's just … I guess they thought it suited me better, like a kind of nickname or …' She trailed off. She smiled brightly.

'Are we supposed to call you Alexandra now?' I said.

'See you tomorrow,' Tracy said. James Frinton put his arm around her shoulders. It was a gesture of consolation after a friend had suffered a terrible experience of some sort. They walked away. Mohammed and I went to the pub.

At some point that evening, Mohammed looked at me directly – we had been talking about our disgusted reactions to the pair of them – and said, 'Fuck them. Let's do something else tomorrow.' And we did. It was the last time I spent any time with Tracy. I saw Frinton only once again. Friends of my youth.

'I love this story,' Joaquin said. We were finally on the walk back to the hotel in Sorge. 'And most of all I love that tomorrow we are going to be able to get on a bus and go back to the hotel we are paying good money for, back in Quedlinburg. We say goodbye to James Frinton's brother and we say goodbye to the girl, Sybille, that's her name, and then they are with the friends of our youth, we never see them again, okay?'

'But Nala,' I said. The dog was tired out. He was no longer running off into the forests. He padded by our side, sometimes giving an incredulous look upwards at us. 'I don't want to say goodbye to Nala. Nala's great.'

'Oh, no,' Joaquin said. 'We aren't saying goodbye to Nala, no way. We are kidnapping Nala and taking him home with us. Nala is getting on the bus with us tomorrow, I swear to God. Nala is the best. Nala. Nala.'

Nala raised his head at each iteration of his name, wearily acknowledging, like a film star at the end of a tour, his fame and celebrity. He knew how far it was, still, to go to his bed.

'That girl Sybille,' I said. 'I bet she wants to come with us too. I can't work it out.'

'What I can't work out,' Joaquin said. 'Is she beautiful even though she is fat? Or is she the sort of beautiful that depends on being quite fat? Would she be not as beautiful if she were thirty kilos the less?'

'What does she do all day long?' I said.

'What you are saying is this question,' Joaquin said. 'Why is she here? And this question is the same as the big question, what is it that women should do with their lives?'

'And in this particular case.'

'Oh, the particular case, I am not invested in the particular case. But, yes, she is not going to come away with us. But why is she here? She wants to leave her village where she grows up. But anywhere will do. She applies for a job in the capitalist military complex, in an oil company in Berlin, and she gets on a train. That is what women do, the same as men do. They insert themselves into the capitalist structure. Then their life is over.'

'It's not much of an improvement, running away with Pete Frinton,' I said. 'She's here with nothing to do. Do you think she fancied him? Hard to imagine.'

The question, what did she do all day long, was in fact a real one. There could be such a thing as a purposeful life that was nevertheless quite unoccupied. I thought of Lenin, kicking his heels in Geneva. I thought of the lives of painters, sitting still and gazing, thinking. Perhaps it is wrong to extrapolate from a single glimpse, but in the way this woman emerged from the kitchen, her flip-flops slapping, to find out what this pair wanted now was not quite what it appeared. She was impatient with us, but not with her life as a whole. Our demands had taken her away from something that mattered to her. Soon she would return to it. She knew what she was about. If one could observe her for a week, unseen, what that *about* consisted of would emerge.

'Do you know what Pope said about women,' I said.

'Pope? What pope? This pope?'

'No, a poet called Pope, an English poet. He said *Most women have no characters at all.*'

'Your poet sounds like an asshole.'

'I think he was making a subtle point.'

'Hit me with your asshole poet's subtle point.'

'I think he was saying that women aren't allowed to take charge of things – they have to fit in with what's expected of them.'

I thought of something I could never say to Joaquin, that twenty years ago his mother had returned to Chile, and his sister had felt obliged to go too. Joaquin had taken charge of his life, and there was no question of going back with the women. Men want women to do something, and if they want to eat, they go along with it. They just perform one thing after another. When they're seven, they have to be sweet, innocent little girls. Then when they're seventeen they have to be innocent but sexy. Then they have to be like a geisha or something. Then suddenly they have to be strong, capable women but still sexy, so someone will give them a job. And so it goes on. A total change every seven years, I would say. But Pete Frinton's woman hadn't done any of that. Somehow, in this corner of Europe, she had settled herself down to do nothing more than she wanted to do. She ran her own show.

We got back to Sorge around six in the evening – a ten-hour walk sustained by a couple of cold sausages, two cheese rolls and a boiled egg that we had eaten at the midpoint. Nala had eaten the promised herrings. We were ravenously hungry. In the front garden of one house, a small, wrinkled, fit old man was trimming a tight-bushed shrub with a pair of angry shears. It hardly seemed to need it, but he was dedicating a good deal of energy to the task. He stopped to watch us approach, fixing us with a baleful blue stare. We passed; we smiled; we were on the verge of greeting him. But we did not greet him. He watched us go until we were quite out of sight. I am sure of it. In the door of the hotel stood the woman, Sybille.

'I cleaned your room,' she said accusingly. 'Do you sleep in the same bed, like gays? Peter had to replace the beds when he bought this place. They were all single beds otherwise. He thought people would like a double bed. Do you like a double bed? You could have had two rooms. There's no one else staying here.'

'We prefer to sleep in the same bed,' I said. Joaquin sat on the bench by the door. He began to take off his boots, inch deep in mud.

'Oh,' Sybille said. A silence fell between us. She had been struck by something. For a while she examined me quite minutely. It was hardly polite by any standards. From a hotel owner, it was the sort of examination that might be trying to work out whether a guest is going to be trouble or not. All at once the scrutiny switched off. 'It's Peter's habit to cook an Indian dinner on Sundays. He likes it. He said I am to ask you if you want to eat with us. Also, he used to know you once.'

'Thanks,' I said. 'We'd like that.'

She turned to go with a satisfied nod. Then something occurred to her. 'We won't charge you for it,' she said. She walked off.

So much of the significant lives of women is hidden from us. When I say *us* I don't use the word as Percy Ogden used the pronoun, the first person plural. When he wrote in his columns that *we* must do something or believe something or sign up to something that he approved of, that *we* was somewhere between *we the human race* and *me and the people I approve of.* When I use the word *us* I use it, confidently, only of Joaquin and me. We are friends with women. At the end of the evening we say goodnight to them and leave. Not all the important things in a woman's life could be shared with us.

But now I think I know what happened to Tracy, and what happened after Mohammed and I left her and James Frinton on the pavement outside Pizza Express in the early 1980s. They said goodbye to us. They started to walk in the other direction. He would have said something noncommittal, perhaps about a party they'd both been at. She would have said she really did have an essay crisis. He would have said there was always an essay crisis – the whole of Oxford was one long essay crisis interspersed with gross amounts of drinking.

'And then you're stuck with these people for the rest of your life,' she would have said.

'Hm?'

'The people you get to know here. They're the people who are still going to be around in thirty years' time. That's what they say.'

'I don't know about that.'

They would have carried on walking, talking companionably. By the time they got back to Tracy's room, they were laughing about something everyone always said, that you made friends here in the first two weeks that you then spent the next three years trying to get rid of.

'I'm really one of those people who everyone can't get rid of,' Tracy said. James Frinton followed her in, throwing himself down on the sofa. 'I'm your general embarrassing friend.'

'Oh, rubbish,' James Frinton said. 'Have you got any gin?'

'Go on, then,' Tracy said. 'Friendship, eh?'

'Friends,' James Frinton said.

'It all seems a bit of a long time ago,' Tracy said. 'You know the slightly embarrassing thing?'

'Mohammed's a nice guy,' James Frinton said reprovingly. 'He's a bit … earnest. But he's a nice guy.'

'We were all earnest,' Tracy said. 'But you know the slightly embarrassing thing? I actually had forgotten that Spike was at Oxford too. I was carrying on for about half an hour as if he'd come for a visit with Mohammed.'

'I know what you mean,' James Frinton said abstractedly. 'Thanks. Cheers. Did you put *any* tonic in that? No, doesn't matter.'

'It all seems a very long time ago,' Tracy said. 'Spike, though.'

'As you say,' James Frinton said. 'Spike. He was Ogden's idea.'

'And whatever happened to Ogden? Cheers,' Tracy said. She drank her gin in one – a theatrical effect that is always amusing.

'I'm going to stick around,' James Frinton said. He held up his glass as if toasting her. She refilled hers.

There was a pause. Sometimes people have to face the possibility of their conversation moving into a different place, like a surprising change of key in a song. That shift into a place of intimacy was, for all of the Ogden group, often a move into explorations of general truth. The specific human case, talk of one man or another, was a trivial exchange that could happen with anyone. The consideration of wider humanity was a bond almost of secrecy, an understanding that some grand perception linked two people together.

'The thing is,' Tracy said, 'some people move on and some people stay as they are.'

'In my view,' James Frinton said, 'the fatal thing about this evening was that neither of us felt we could tell those two where we'd been last night.'

'Oh, no way,' Tracy said. 'They wouldn't have understood. They don't understand just how awful it would be to go on thinking the same things that you did when you were fifteen.'

'Still,' James Frinton said. 'The fact remains. We went to a party hosted by the Oxford University Conservative Association last night.'

'Isn't it awful?'

'Those two, they're going to believe the same things when they're fifty,' James Frinton said. (I'm sure he said this. He was correct if he said this. There was no reason for him to say it with an edge of amused disgust.) 'It's not even the principles they believe in. It's membership of one club or another. I don't feel as if we've lost any of our principles, you and I. What am I?'

Tracy smiled. That *what are you* had meant only one thing, back at school, when one of the Ogden lot said it of someone else. 'You're overly committed to the single issue. You don't have a complete and consistent ideological framework.'

'Exactly. And what are you?'

'I'm fascinated by the principles of anarchy. And I like a drink.'

'Well, it seems quite clear, doesn't it?' James Frinton said. 'On pure ideological grounds, our most appropriate home is where we went last night. Political home. I've got the bonnet up and I'm addressing all sorts of technical questions in a fix-it way. And you've seen the value of creative disruption and the possibilities of a state that has withered away. Bakunin.'

'I love, love, love Bakunin,' Tracy said, just as she always had. 'He's got no home in a party that wants to bring all economic activity within state ownership. Are you mental? Of course we went to their cocktail party. I wouldn't have thought Spike gets free gin at the Spartacist caucus in Cowley.'

'Of course it was fun,' James Frinton said. 'They're much cleverer than the old lot. Last night, talking to those Monday Club boys, it was really as if you could say anything. One of them wanted to privatize the army.'

'Could you sell shares in it?'

'Of course.'

'And when this country went to war with Germany, what would the German shareholders think?'

'Of course I'm saying what those boys were saying last night. Bakunin would have loved it.'

They were on the sofa together. Tracy had kicked off her shoes. She was kneading James Frinton's hips. Beneath the soles of her feet, his joints were hard as stones. He was looking ahead.

'That big girl over the fire,' he said. 'The one with no clothes on. Is that you?'

'No, you idiot,' Tracy said. 'Of course it's not me. Look, she's got ginger pubes. And she's a lot fatter than me. Idiot.'

'I thought those might be just modern-art touches,' James Frinton said with simplicity. 'Picasso painted women with three eyes, didn't he?'

'You're such an idiot,' Tracy said. 'I've borrowed it from the college art collection. You can take a painting away for the term. It's brilliant. Nobody else wanted that – it's too rude. Doesn't Trinity have anything like it?'

'God, no,' James Frinton said. 'I couldn't have that in my room. I'd do no work. I'd just wank all day long.'

'When did you think I could have had it painted, apart from anything else?'

'You could have had it done in the summer,' James Frinton said. 'I suppose you might have mentioned it. In your letters.'

'Did you keep my letters, James?' Tracy said.

'Of course.'

'I kept yours. I loved your letters. They were so funny. I almost wanted to get on a train to come to visit you in Leeds, but then I thought, there's no chance at all that Leeds is half as much fun in reality as it is in James Frinton's letters.'

She leant over and gave James Frinton an immense, wet, smacking kiss on his cheek. He turned and looked at her, amused.

'Oh,' Tracy said. 'Oh, it is nice to have you here. The best letter you wrote me, you know, it was the one about – oh, what was it about? – the night out with the solicitors for the senior partner's birthday. What was her name?'

'Mandy,' James Frinton said. 'Get off, will you? We were supposed to call her Amanda, but everyone talked about her as Mandy.'

'And in the middle you just said you didn't think you were a socialist any more. In brackets. And I remember reading it and just giving a big scream. I was glad I was on my own. I was glad I hadn't been reading your letters out loud to Mohammed, too. I loved that letter. But how could you think …' Tracy picked up her glass, drained it, put it back on the table. 'I won't be a moment,' she said.

She went through into the bedroom. When she came back, two minutes later, she was naked. In her left hand, she held a few sheets of writing paper. She must have hoped to do something unforgettable, but it was she who was surprised. James Frinton, too, had taken all his clothes off. They were placed in a pile on the side of the sofa.

'I wanted to show you that the painting couldn't possibly be of me,' Tracy said. 'Look. Ginger pubes. Look. Black pubes. Not me. So what's your excuse?'

'I want to fuck,' James Frinton said.

'It's normal in polite society to ask before you get it all out,' Tracy said. 'I wanted to read you something first. It's a letter you wrote. I love it. Listen.'

The two of them, naked, among all that stuff! The paraphernalia that Tracy had contrived and collected to show what she wanted to become, the stuffed toys, the silvery bottles and cocktail shaker, the trophy invitations, the books and paintings and the fur coat lying across an armchair. James Frinton and Tracy looked so innocent in their nakedness among all of it. They looked like victims. Their thin pale bodies, their touching little powdery puffs of hair here and there.

'This was the letter I liked best,' Tracy said. As she spoke, and read, she came towards James on the sofa, swaying. 'Or one of the letters I liked best. The one after the Mandy letter. I was waiting for it. I snatched it from the postman's hands. *Dear Tracy, It's so strange to have changed my mind. I think I was wrong all the time. I think I'm going to go on being wrong, but I know from now on I won't stop myself finding out what's right.* That's such a beautiful thing to open a letter and read. You could inspire people, you know, James. And then it has such a funny version of that time we went out with Euan and Eric to that Tory MP's house, remember? When we took a bag of horse manure and a package with a clock ticking inside it? That was the best. It was so funny. Listen. *I really thought there were better things to be doing on a sunny Saturday afternoon in April, and it was my birthday, too. The plan was just to dump the horseshit in the driveway, put the fake bomb through the letterbox, and scarper. I'd have been quite happy with that. But then bloody Euan thought there might be better possibilities. Off he goes round the side of the house and comes back with the news that there's a conservatory with a door open. Why not go into the house and dump a sack of horseshit inside? In for a penny in for a pound, think I, and so there I am, celebrating my birthday by pouring half a ton of horseshit onto Sir Brindley Roth's best draw-ing-room carpet. Maybe it was at that point, or maybe it was reading all about it in the paper two days later, that a thought comes into my little head. Is this the best use of my time? I mean, not that Sir Brindley and his lovely lady don't deserve to come home to a big pile of manure.* It's so funny, all of it. I just loved your letters. In a way,' Tracy said, plumping herself down beside him, 'I wish we weren't in the same place so that you'd write to me every day.'

'I can write to you,' James Frinton said. 'I could send you a letter from Trinity to Lincoln. I could get the university's internal mail service to deliver it.'

'It's only three hundred yards,' Tracy said. 'You could walk it and give me the message in person. Are we going to fuck now?'

'I never saw those letters again,' James Frinton said. 'I'd love to read them. Can I borrow them? I'll give them back safely.'

'No, James,' Tracy said. 'They're mine. It's the rules of letter-writing. Now can we fuck? I may be wrong but it looks to me as if you're getting a bit of a hard-on there.'

'Two Tories fucking,' James Frinton said. 'It probably happens all the time.'

Occasionally they saw each other. In that world, they were not in quite the same place. Tracy would have been taken to parties at the Union, that Victorian debating society. She would have sat through the odd debate, but she would never have been asked to contribute. In a couple of terms, James Frinton had made a few speeches. Even I heard about them, from the university newspaper. He had been asked to have dinner with one of Mrs Thatcher's Cabinet ministers, down to propose a motion about economic policy. He must have been clever and funny about the urgent need to privatize – what? The university, the army, the Queen, or something that afterwards was indeed taken out of the public sector, such as the railways or the post? Somebody noticed something about the boy with a northern accent at the end of the table. Somebody would have suggested that he run for some job or other at the Union, that he might like to pop in and say hello to the guys in Central Office – just tell them that Norman had said they should show him the ropes. That's how it goes. Norman was the Cabinet minister. Tracy was an ornament and a spirited girl, good for a drink or a race backwards round the quad after dinner. She wouldn't have been quite right for dinner with a Cabinet minister. As for me, I heard enough about them to realize that I didn't want to see either of them any more. I didn't see any difference between them and the famous skinhead at Merton, who had a swastika shaved into the back of his skull, or the boy in the Monday Club who wore a badge that read 'Hang Nelson Mandela'. Those were celebrities in the university at the time. Tracy and James Frinton had passed into the world such people inhabited. The difference between them was not one I would have cared to understand. Only later did I understand the difference between their two existences.

But all the same, despite that difference, they did find each other in the same place quite regularly – a party, a big dinner, a jazz concert, going round the job-interview circuit with capitalist companies known as 'the milk round', I don't know why. At the end of their third year, after their final exams, they bumped into each other at a ball at Trinity, James Frinton's college. He was actually on the committee. Tracy had been taken by a boy she knew, a fellow drunk from another college whose uncle was a duke. She couldn't decide whether he was a prize or not. Quite soon she had left him in the drink tent with all the other nephews of dukes. She went outside to see if she could find anyone she knew. She could. It was James Frinton. I have no idea what these events were like. They cost over a hundred pounds a ticket. I had no dinner jacket, and no friends who would have wanted to go. So the only idea I have of it is from photographs, and from the glimpse of people going along, in pairs, or coming back, singly. I can see what the conversation would have been like between James Frinton in his dinner jacket and Tracy in a huge, midnight-blue rustling taffeta ballgown, which she'd paid for who knows how. I knew them, you see.

'You're already a little bit hammered, aren't you, Tracy?' James Frinton said.

'James,' Tracy said, leaning against him, 'where's your date?'

'I sold her to the highest bidder,' he said. 'I had to pay for all this somehow.'

'I hope you got a good price for her,' Tracy said. 'You're the only person who calls me Tracy. I love it.'

'I try to remember,' James Frinton said. 'Mostly I do remember to say Alexandra. But it's nice to talk dirty to you when no one's around. You're looking radiant, by the way. What are you doing next year? I forget.'

'Oh, marketing. Cheever and Spark. In London. Soap powders, shampoos and, for some reason, butter substitutes. God knows how I got it. You? Oh, I know – you're going into journalism.'

'You're looking radiant, by the way,' James Frinton said.

'You already said that, but thank you. It's my skincare regime,' Tracy said. 'You have to do it religiously. You should do it. Everyone should. It's a three-part thing. Cleanse. Tone. Moisturize. Can you remember that? You'll look much better at fifty if you do that twice a day now. Cleanse. Tone. Moisturize.'

'Cleanse. Tone. Moisturize. I'll try to remember,' James Frinton said. 'But what about exfoliation?'

'Exfoliation,' Tracy said, getting through the word with some difficulty, 'is bollocks. Don't tell Cheever and Spark I said that. I want to go off into a corner with you.'

'Will a dance do?'

'No, James,' Tracy said. 'It has to be a corner, a nice dark corner. Promise me. When I look at you I can't remember who it was I came with. It was somebody, I know. Do you like my dress?'

'Not that much,' James Frinton said. 'I look forward to tearing it off you, a bit later.' He smiled. She was in the glow-ing, wide-eyed phase of drunkenness that is only sometimes recognizable as drunkenness at all; he had his hair smoothed down, a new white shirt and a dinner suit only six months old, shining with cleanliness. Anyone would have thought them engaged in the most charming and well-schooled cock-tail-party chatter.

'Shall we make a date?' said Tracy. 'Half past three behind the Stranglers' tent?'

'We don't need to,' James Frinton said, with the utmost old-fashioned charm. 'We are going to be drawn towards each other by irresistible gravitational force.'

How to account for that irresistible gravitational force? In reality, gravity is a weak force, and puzzles physicists. From time to time Tracy and James Frinton did come together. There was no resisting it. At least, they did not resist it. They were never an item, a singularity, to use another term from science.

Then they were in London. Living within walking distance of each other, too.

'This flat suits you,' James Frinton said.

Tracy had got lucky. She was sharing a solid, respectable mansion flat in an Earl's Court block. As if in an extension of university existence, people dropped in without notice, and a couple of times, one of those people was James Frinton.

'Well, your flat is quite nice too,' Tracy said primly. James Frinton was living behind the exhibition centre, in a flat that had been carved out of an old house during some previous boom.

'I miss that painting you used to have,' James Frinton said.

'What are you talking about?' Tracy said. 'Oh, that nude. The college demanded it back. They were rather strict about it, darling. Do you want a drink? I was going to have a whisky.'

'It's too early for me … Oh, what the hell?' James Frinton said. 'Give me two fingers of Scotch, dollface.'

'I've got something much naughtier,' Tracy said. 'Ludo and Blaise, they're rather party animals and they keep something in that little Indian box for a wet afternoon.'

'Who are Ludo and Blaise?' James Frinton said. 'Oh, the flatmates. I keep forgetting. Do you have threesomes?'

'Of course,' Tracy said. He knew perfectly well that Blaise was her boyfriend. 'They're so sweet. Do you want some?'

'I have no idea what you're talking about but, no, I don't think so,' James Frinton said. 'Save it for your fast set. I'm just a boring younger brother that you were at school with. Think of me like that.'

'You're so adorable,' Tracy said. She picked up the little Indian box from the table. She disappeared into her bedroom.

James tapped his feet. He might even have whistled a few notes. In two minutes she returned, abstracted, a wild look in her eyes. She ran her fingers through her hair. 'You never wrote to me,' she said. 'You said you were going to write more letters to me and you never did.'

'Yes, I did,' James Frinton said reasonably. 'I wrote you a long letter about all the goings-on in Central Office last summer. I know you got it. I'd love to see all those old letters again – the ones from before Oxford too. Have you still got them?'

'Somewhere,' Tracy said. 'I packed them up and put them in a special file I remember. I read them all over again before I moved here – they were such fun. James Frinton the Trotskyite, destroyer of worlds. They're in a box somewhere – under the bed or in the wardrobe.'

'Do go and dig them out,' James Frinton said. 'Darling. It would be such fun to see them again.'

Years later, perhaps ten years after this, James Frinton would start to be famous for his personal charm. Those who had close dealings with him shook their heads afterwards. They wondered at the fact that, through sheer politeness and apparent interest in them, he had persuaded them to do something they had previously ruled out. So often, people said, they had left a conversation with James Frinton, the Home Secretary, with the exhilarating illusion that they and he had agreed something harmoniously. And then a subsequent telephone call from a ruthless, charmless underling. It became apparent that the human warmth of James Frinton was something he performed. What was so often called his charm had to be analysed. I had seen only small unremarkable glimpses of that charm at school. He was not much more likeable than anyone else. It was at university that he developed that smoothness. Even now, in his first year in London, it had not yet attained perfection. People saw through it from time to time. This was one of those moments, and even Tracy, mildly drunk and somewhat addled in the middle of a Sunday morning, saw that he was not entirely saying this out of warmth and love for her. That affected turn of phrase, *Do go and dig them out again*, that debutante's imperative form of the auxiliary verb, *Do*, was not James Frinton's own turn of phrase. The vocative *Darling* sat strangely on his tongue. I dare say in saying things that he had heard others say, he discovered, stumbling over it, that he was the wrong sex for the phrase. His charm failed.

'I'm not going to give them back to you, James,' Tracy said. 'I know perfectly well you'd rather I didn't have them. I'm not going to show them to anyone. You needn't worry.'

'I don't know what you're talking about,' James Frinton said. He tried to laugh. 'All I meant was that I'd love to see them again some time. It was such fun, that time before we went to university. Don't you think?'

'I was going out with Mohammed,' Tracy said. 'And you were in Leeds, working. And not having much fun, according to your letters, anyway. Go on, James. Piss off. I think I want to take some drugs on my own. Off you pop.'

He didn't piss off; he didn't pop off; he stayed. They had sex all afternoon. (Ludo and Blaise were looking at horses in Oxfordshire.) From the outside, anyone could see they were drawn together. They had an understanding of each other that easily burst into flame. They made each other laugh. They knew what the other wanted. There was not much to be said for Blaise in bed. He lay there on top of her. He buckled away unrhythmically. From time to time he would put both his hands on her tits; rotate them; push himself up while his entire bodyweight rested painfully on her thorax. It was over quickly. That was all that could be said for it. So the connection between her and James Frinton was easily explained. Passion and understanding will do it.

But at this distance it seems to me that James Frinton was not driven by passion, though he certainly liked Tracy. He might have chosen to seduce her once. It might even have been a thing that suited the three-year stretch of university, finishing quickly afterwards as circumstances changed. The recurrence of it, every few weeks for three years, seems uncharacteristic of him. I believe there were two reasons why he easily gave in to the pleasure that these encounters undoubtedly contained. The first was some sort of experimental spirit. He wanted to see what became of a person subjected to a particular process. The experiment had begun at university, but the important question must have arisen – what would happen to this process outside the institution, once *loco parentis* had walked away, and what would come to be called a *safe space* had been dissolved? To understand that, he needed the privilege of intimacy. The process was one of progressive intoxication. You could map out Tracy's progress through the substances, until she met one that had a progress of its own to chart, through the bodies of its adherents.

The advancing stages of Tracy's discoveries were a mirror of James Frinton's advancement through the ranks of society. In his three years at university, he went from post to post, society to society, rising in visibility from likeably incompetent student actor to treasurer of the political society to president of the junior common room and, finally, president of the debating society, the Union. And at the same time a kind of progress inwards: private dining societies in white tie, invitations out to lunch with people's rich uncles, a seat next to a Cabinet minister in town, a quiet trip up to London on the first cheap train to set out his stall in somebody's private office. Now, with a job on the *Globe*, it was all beginning in earnest. One day it would all be made beautifully clear by some investigative journalist or authorized biographer. The stages were like Tracy's journey. What at first was thrilling, audacious, unimaginable, a shock quickly became banal. The extremity of the situation was absorbed into the life. At the beginning Tracy would decide to get high; James Frinton would take steps to go to meet the government chief whip, or a leader writer on *The Times*. After a while those were not diversions from the mainstream of their existence.

I'll come back to the second reason why James Frinton kept returning to Tracy – kept badgering her, as she came to think. It is not a very honourable reason.

James Frinton's existence at this time. It had seemed perfectly unimportant to him where he lived. He had taken no more than a morning to look at rooms in flats and decide to take one. 'Where on earth did you find it?' people asked. The answer was that he had found it in the classified adverts in *Time Out* magazine, like someone who had moved to London without knowing anyone at all. The flat was owned by a middle-aged set designer, whose boyfriend, a painter, had died of AIDS a year earlier. (This was not specified in the advert.) James contributed to the household budget, sleeping in a spare room that was still lined with the painter's grey-to-brown abstracts. No one could understand why he hadn't taken a flat with friends, like Tracy or anyone else. But returning to a domestic setting of tears, muddle and Eartha Kitt spectaculars (I am guessing) was inexplicable. Perhaps, like a novelist, James Frinton was gathering material. At the *Globe*, James Frinton quite quickly became the graduate trainee in the green tweed suit – the one who lives with the old queen – no, but last night in the pub he was saying – fending his landlord off – preserving his honour – barricading the bathroom door with a loofah – you'd have to ask him, it's a good one. None of it was true – the set designer was aloof, chaotic, incapable of action. But the stories were good. In one year the general agreement would be that something must be done about James, and the top floor of a Notting Hill villa would be his.

That all lay in the future.

Some friends of Tracy who lived in Parson's Green in a beaten-up old terrace were having a party, the first Saturday of January. There was some kind of funeral theme. The invitations were black-bordered. The hosts regretted to announce the long-expected passing of their old friend and constant companion, Fun. Guests were requested to attend in deep mourning. Tracy scored a personal victory by turning up in a white sari, a vivid presence in the little rooms among everyone else in black. She had even managed to part her hair down the middle, and score the parting with cochineal. At one point she was on the little terrace behind the house. It was really too cold to stand outside in January in a sari, but the house was

simply too full. Why was it the end of fun? Who knew? The
end of Oxford, of private dining societies, of fancy dress? This
year, in London, they had declared themselves both wage
slaves and hopelessly broke. They had even asked people to
bring bottles. The door opened. It was James Frinton, in an
outfit that had survived the evening's demands, a Victorian
mourner's coat and stock, and even a cane. She had had no
idea he would come.

'What are you got up like that for?' James Frinton said.

'It's mourning in India,' Tracy said. 'Widows in India don't
wear black. They wear white. It's very, very sad, if you think
about it. I've just been in India. We went to India for six
weeks. It was full of widows. Most of the widows you never
see. This is in India I'm talking about.'

'Have you just been to India?' James Frinton said, smiling.
'I thought that was last year.'

'I went with Blaise,' Tracy said. 'Just now, last year. He's
always wanted to. So we went. He said we were going to take
ourselves off to an ashram. There is this very, very holy place
in the hills that we were going to. It's so holy. It's not the
Himalayas, it's the other place. The Ghats it's called. And it's
so holy that they all smoke this very holy opium, very holy,
very pure.'

'I hadn't heard that bit,' James Frinton said. 'Did you get
to see the Taj Mahal, Tracy?'

'Yes.'

'I'm glad.'

'So we went to the ashram with our suitcases and everyone
else had backpacks – it was so awful I could have died. And
then we sat cross-legged and listened to people talking and sat

some more and looked into the trees, and after thirty-six hours Blaise asked an Australian in the queue for the vegetarian dhal when the holy opium came out. And it turned out they didn't have holy opium. Only it was all right because it turned out that a lot of people came to this place hoping to experience this holy opium. So when on the third day we walked down into the town nearby there was somebody who straight away could sell us some holy opium.'

'Oh, good,' James Frinton said. 'Would you like to know something? I missed you terribly when you were in India.'

Tracy looked at James Frinton, focusing. He had never said anything like that before to her.

'But that was a long time ago now,' Tracy said.

'I wish you'd written me some letters,' James Frinton said. 'Letters from India. That would have been so interesting, to read about things while they were going on. Are you having a good time?'

'Now, you mean? Good-ish. I'm cold, but it's too crowded in there. And I really, really don't want any more to drink.'

'Do you want to go home? I'll walk you home. I wasn't going to stay long.'

'Blaise was going to come but I don't know that he did in the end. We had an awful row on Tuesday and he left. I think he's at his mother's.'

'I was thinking about you,' James said. 'You were the person I really wanted to share things with, you know. I mean, to tell things to. Every time I see you I want to be on my own with you. Can we go back to your flat? I think I'd really like that.'

'We could go back to yours,' Tracy said, not meaning it.

'No,' James said. 'Yours is best.'

There was an unusual urgency about James Frinton's tone. She tried to dissect it. We know, on the whole, when we're talking to someone who wants the same thing that we want. I think about the moment, so long ago, when I found that my face was in exactly the same place as the face of a twenty-two-year-old Chilean. We had been standing, too, in a narrow outside space with a party going on inside. Tracy might have realized, at this moment, that her head was a foot below that of the man she was talking to. What he had said ought to coincide with what she wanted. In many ways it did. She wanted to go back to her flat, too, to shut the double door and have marvellous sex with James Frinton one more time. But what James Frinton had said did not coincide with what she wanted. He seemed to have forgotten that she had another flatmate called Ludo, a good friend of her boyfriend. There was no possibility that she could take James Frinton home with her. She felt terribly alone, and badgered. He would badger her until he got what he needed. At least he would be close to her all that time.

'Come round tomorrow,' Tracy said. 'I love it when we have tea and chat. Chat about old times. Get out all those lovely old letters you used to write to me. They were such fun. I'd love it if you came round.'

James Frinton smiled the gauche, charming smile of the good loser. She watched him go back into the party. She lit another cigarette. In five minutes a girl she knew came out.

'Aren't you simply freezing?' she said. 'So brilliant of you. Mourning in Asia. White. Did you see, Jimmie Frinton came.

I love him. He's such fun. I honestly think people have such a strange idea of him. If they got to know him—'

'I know him,' Tracy said.

She got up quite early the next morning. There was still no sign of Blaise. Ludo hadn't come home, either. She knew that James Frinton would be round as early as he dared. She estimated what he would estimate her time of getting up to be. She didn't think he'd be round before eleven, but not much after that, either. She tidied the flat in a brilliant frenzy, picking up her clothes from the floor and putting them into the laundry bag. Two rubbish bags were filled. She walked to the flower shop and bought some yellow chrysanthemums; to the French patisserie and bought two éclairs, one chocolate, one coffee. (The joy of discovering at Oxford that an éclair could be coffee-flavoured! She would never go back north to the town she had grown up in, as long as she lived.) She went to the bedroom. She took the shoebox out from the bottom of the wardrobe. As a final touch, she thought she would place a pile of James Frinton's old letters to her on the little table. He would appreciate that.

The flat was on the second floor. It looked out onto Earl's Court Square. She saw him coming down the street. He was wearing one of his famous green tweed suits and, astonishingly, a trilby – she realized that it was, unlikely as it seemed, his seduction outfit. It was exactly five minutes to eleven, as Tracy had exactly foreseen. His walk was determined. He knew what he was coming for. Tracy went into the kitchen. She quickly made two cups of coffee. She brought them through and set them on the table. She took the opportunity to put herself down at the desk, open a file of papers she had brought home from work, spread a few sheets of financial summary about. There was no reason for James Frinton to know she was in trouble at work, had been given a warning that her probation period might not have a successful outcome if she didn't knuckle down. This morning, for James Frinton's sake, she would pretend to be hard at work.

'Hello, my darling,' Tracy said into the entryphone. 'Just push hard on the door.'

'It's me,' James Frinton said, over the intercom. 'Before you say something you regret.'

'I knew it was you,' Tracy said, opening the door as he hurtled up the stairs. 'I saw you coming, actually. Strangely enough, I don't have a hangover this morning. Did you stay long?'

'No,' James Frinton said, flinging himself down on the sofa. 'I might even have left before you did. What's up? Is that for us? That lovely-looking pink box?'

'It's got éclairs in it,' Tracy said. 'I was saving them for Blaise, but do you know what? I think I'd rather eat one now, with you. Would you like a cup of coffee? Have that one. I only just made it.'

'What on earth is that?' James Frinton said, poking at the pile of his old letters. 'God, my handwriting was so awful then. It's awful now but in a completely different way awful. Do you like your handwriting? This is like the writing of a nine-year-old.'

'Put them down, darling,' Tracy said. 'They're only there because when I got back last night I had a sudden urge to read them again. What fun they are.'

'Happy days,' James Frinton said. 'If you wouldn't mind, some time I'd really like to—'

'All that smashing windows and posting poo through letterboxes and painting Trotskyite nonsense on walls. And smashing up other people's meetings! I can hardly believe we used to do any of that.'

'It's an oddity, isn't it?'

'And no one would believe it now. It's so extraordinary that we never got caught, either. The truth of the matter is – I know it's amazing – but the only real solid evidence that any of that ever happened is really here. I mean in your old letters. I don't know why, but it was obviously preying on your mind, up there in Leeds. All the window-smashing and so on. Ah, well. Happy days.'

'Happy days,' James Frinton said. He eyed her, neutrally.

The reason she had made him a cup of coffee before he arrived must have become apparent. She was not going to go into the kitchen, and leave James Frinton alone in the room with his old letters. If she gave them to him, or let him take them, she would never lay eyes on him again. It was the one thing that would continue to draw him to her, she understood. He smiled back. He changed the subject. They began to talk about his plans for his career – by which I mean, if you think about it, that he did not change the subject at all.

We had eaten almost nothing all day. Our expense of energy had been tremendous. The girl Sybille had invited us to have our supper with them, but had not mentioned the time. It is fair to say that both Joaquin and I hoped that it would not be too late. Pete Frinton had the bohemian air that you might expect from his history. His girlfriend Sybille had the uphol-stered, blonde, comfort-accustomed appearance of someone who did not wait for dinner. Between the sort of person who had grown up scavenging and one who had eaten meat promptly at six all her childhood, we preferred the sensible German bourgeoise.

We showered and changed into the shirts from yesterday, laundered by Sybille. We rinsed our by now unspeakable socks. We went downstairs barefoot. There was a good smell of cooking, and a cosy sound of television laughter from somewhere in the back.

'Hello?' I called.

'Here,' Sybille shouted. 'Come through.'

There seemed no change in atmosphere between the public parts of the hotel – the wood-panelled bar and restaurant, the painfully orange cheerfulness of the rooms – and the private. We went past a chaotic office, a bathroom and a bedroom that, unused, looked much like the room we had been sleep-ing in. We found Sybille in an L-shaped sitting room, watch-ing the television with absorption. An open box of chocolates lay on the sofa beside her.

'I'm watching my programme,' she said. 'He's cooking tonight.'

There was a strong echo of the past in Sybille's absorption. I thought of Pete Frinton's mother, in the shabby private quar-ters of a public business, soaking up an ancient diva. Sybille, too, was watching a musical programme with total attention. We sat down and looked. It was a religious programme. A choir of women was singing in a self-satisfied, unprofessional way about the love of Christ. They were in a church in the south of Germany. The camera kept cutting to the exterior, among alps and meadows. But there was something different about Sybille's attention. She was both detached and intensely aware. She was not being swept away by this, but following the detail of the ladies' outfits and dental work with considerable fascination. She pushed the box of chocolates towards me and Joaquin without a word. We took one each. In a moment the song came to an end, with a thundering organ, and the credits of the programme began to roll.

'There you are,' Sybille said, with a satisfied sigh. 'He's cooking his speciality – it's chicken in an Indian way. He likes it and I think it makes a change. He'll be happy to be cooking for someone else. He thinks I don't appreciate it properly.'

'We like a curry,' I said.

'So are you going out together,' Sybille said. 'Like boyfriend and boyfriend?'

'Something like that,' I said.

'Can you ask her now how long the dinner is going to be because you know I think I am going to die,' Joaquin said. I patted his knee.

'That's what I thought,' Sybille said comfortably. 'But then I thought if you were like that you would have nicer clothes to wear.'

Pete Frinton came through. I was touched to see that he had changed, perhaps in our honour. He was wearing a bow-tie with his cook's apron. He was carrying a tray with three drinks on it and a very welcome bowl of nuts.

'Gin-tonic all right?' he said. 'I'll only be five, ten minutes. Welcome to our humble abode. I don't know the last time we had anyone to entertain. It's a bit of a treat for us.'

'We'll be sorry to get on the bus tomorrow,' I said. 'We had a good time in the end. What have you done with Nala?'

'Oh, he's down there in his basket,' Pete Frinton said. 'You've worn him out today. Listen. I found something that'll interest you. Though I expect you saw it at the time. It was from some long piece about my brother the *Observer* printed, about his whole story. It was about a year ago. My mum sometimes sends me things like that.'

He took a copy of a colour magazine from his apron pocket and handed it to me. The cover was completely occupied by his brother's face and the two words 'HISTORY CALLS'.

'I didn't see it,' I said. We're not great readers of the mainstream media, especially Sunday newspapers.

'It's a silly piece,' Pete Frinton said. 'But it's got some photographs with it you'll like.'

He disappeared, almost shyly. I turned the pages, Joaquin looking over my shoulder. Quite soon I came to the photograph that Pete Frinton must have meant. I had never seen it before. It must have been taken in the summer of 1983. I remembered it. We had all gone out for a day in the country – a bit of a hike over the hills. We were still at school. In the photograph, we were posing on top of a hill, next to some monolith. Kate had come, too. Mohammed must have been taking the photograph. It was not a very good photograph, but you could see all our faces. I would have predicted that we would look terribly young. But in fact we looked utterly middle-aged. It was the hairstyles we had, which our generation has carried into their forties and fifties, and which now seem suitable only to the ageing. The paper had identified most of us. For the sub-editors, this was clearly a remarkable document in its own way. The legend underneath read 'L to R: Kate Rothenberg (now a prize-winning poet), Eric Milne (now Lord Milne, QC), Percy Ogden (author and journalist), Tracy (Alexandra) Cartwright, unknown, James Frinton (now Home Secretary)'.

Joaquin craned over my shoulder. 'You are really in the luck,' he said. 'You are the guy nobody knows.' Of course it was me that had defeated the *Observer* journalists. I had sunk into oblivion, and merited the label 'unknown'. Joaquin, of course, was right. I wouldn't have wanted this ancient connection known about. But the photograph's label gave me a small stab. As I said, I have lived a quiet life. The fact that every other person I had known had gone on to *something* made me feel for a moment that my quiet life has been not just overlooked but wasted. Even Tracy, brackets, Alexandra. What she had gone on to was three days of gleeful coverage in the tabloids between her death and her funeral. Fame of some kind. Joaquin must have understood this. He took my hand; he squeezed it; he left his hand where it was.

'Come through, gentlemen,' Pete Frinton said.

We were eating in the large kitchen. The windows and door were open to the warm summer night. They gave onto a chaos of trees and high grass and, not far away, the little river that ran through the village. The table was set with six dishes: a chicken curry, three vegetable dishes, a pile of poppadoms and a tureen of rice.

'I don't know what Sybille's going to eat,' he said. 'Sometimes she pulls a face and goes straight to the fridge.'

He raised a hand in a karate chop, and brought it down on the poppadoms. We fell on them.

'You never get a good curry in this country,' Pete Frinton said. 'They don't understand it. I had to teach myself how to cook it. It's the only thing I can cook, to be honest.'

It was one of Sybille's good days. She was eating everything. Her eyes went round the table. Her inspection of us was very thorough.

'So what do you think?' Pete said.

'It's all very good,' Joaquin said. 'I like everything.'

'Actually, I meant – well, thank you – but I actually meant about the piece in the newspaper. About my brother. I mean all that about what he learnt growing up.'

'I didn't read it, I'm afraid,' I said. 'That photograph was interesting.'

'When I looked at it again today,' Pete Frinton said, 'I realized that you were in it too. I should have recognized you as soon as you came through the door.'

'I've changed a lot,' I said. 'It was a long time ago. What did the piece say?'

'Did you hear my brother's speech to Conference last year?' Pete Frinton said. 'It was the one that all the commentators said showed what he had in mind. I mean, they thought it was a fairly naked bid for the top job. Usually the Home Secretary gets to talk about prison and police and law and order – they love that stuff. But last year, in the middle, he started to talk about his *journey*, like a contestant on a talent show. It got my attention. He knew what it was like to grow up with a parent with mental-health issues. His father, the small-business owner. He knew what that was like, too. And then he had always had friends from different cultural backgrounds. Black friends and Muslim friends. That had been a help in knowing what it was like. There were friends who had been struggling to come to terms with their sexuality, too. He was happy that people in that situation had found life easier in the years since. When I heard that, I assumed he was talking about his friend Percy Ogden. But I don't know. He might have been talking about you. Did you struggle?'

I didn't think the Home Secretary had been speaking about me.

'And he knew what loss was like,' Pete Frinton went on. 'When his friend Tracy died. It was quite moving. He really understood what thousands of people in this country had gone through, watching loved ones succumb to the horror of drug addiction and alcohol misuse. And for these reasons he could assure Conference that he was determined to—

'Do you know what? I can't remember what he was determined to do. Was it to carry on opposing the legalization of something? Or to stamp out this menace from our inner cities? Or to take firm new measures to show young people that drugs and alcohol don't pay? It was something like that. I guess the *Observer* heard that speech and thought maybe they could write a profile about him that went into his whole story. The speech made me laugh, though, it really did. Only someone who had allowed love to die, long ago, could talk so fluently about his feelings in a hall in Wolverhampton. Reading it all out from an autocue, I mean, not talking. I don't want to be vile about my brother. He was doing his job, long after …'

'Long after what?' Joaquin said.

'I was going to say something poetic,' Pete Frinton said. 'I was going to say he was doing his job, long after he let love die in his heart. Sorry. That sounds over the top. But it's what I think happened. When did you last see him?'

'That's an easy one,' I said. 'It was when Tracy Cartwright died. He got on a train for two hours. He came back just to tell me.'

'He got praised by the judge,' Pete said. 'The boyfriend got prosecuted for supplying the stuff that killed her, didn't he? Got six months. My brother did all the right things, apparently. He took her back to the flat. He saw how drunk she was. At least, he thought she was drunk. He made sure she got back all right. He found her keys in her bag. He put her to bed. She was totally incapable all this time, he told the court. He even left an answerphone message for someone or other who had a spare key, saying he'd appreciate it if they could look in on her in the morning. The judge said that showed a sense of responsibility. He wanted to draw a contrast between my brother and the boyfriend, who handed over a bag of heroin, watched her get drunk and high and then wandered off, leaving her alone and incapable.'

'That's pretty much what he told me when he came round,' I said. 'I didn't know what to think when I opened the door to him. I hadn't seen him for years. I was back where we had grown up, living with Joaquin in the same flat. I asked him in. I gave him a cup of tea. He told me straight away that Tracy had died. He thought he should tell me before I read it in the papers. It was very good of him. He gave me the whole story.' Or what I had taken to be the whole story at the time. He'd been at home, reading. There was some talk in the office about the situation in Afghanistan. He thought he might take the opportunity to amass some deep background. There was a banging on the door. It was Tracy. She was celebrating: she'd been sacked. He should come out with her! she said. Someone was having a party in – where was it? – Clapham. No, Chiswick. It would be divine. One drink, no more than that. He told her she should probably go home. The landlord appeared: this sort of thing couldn't happen. He didn't care. James Frinton should just ask his friend to leave, please. In the end James Frinton just thought that the best thing was for him to go with her to the party in Chiswick. Hand her over to someone he could trust.

James said frankly that there wasn't anyone at the party he thought he could trust with her. She was drunk already. She carried on drinking. By nine she was passing out on a stranger's sofa. There was no sign of Blaise, her boyfriend. James was the only sober person in the room. He took responsibility. And then it was as he told the court. He managed to bring her round. He took her back to her rooms. He took the keys from her bag and got her in. There was no one else at home. He laid her out on her bed and hoped for the best.

'It's true,' I said. 'The whole story was very shocking. I don't think I thought there was anything else for your brother to tell. There was one curious thing about it, though. There was a bottle of gin only a third drunk on the table, and two glasses. She had probably had a drink with someone before she set out, but nobody could identify who that had been – it certainly wasn't Blaise. I wondered afterwards whether your brother had sat down and had a drink on his own, once he had got her into bed. But that makes no sense – there were two glasses. Your brother behaved in a very responsible way. Everyone said so. He wouldn't take someone as drunk as she was, and let her drink any more. It must have been obvious that she would pass into unconsciousness if she had any more.

'I heard your brother through to the end. I thought I was under control until I started to say something. My voice just dried up. Before I knew it I was crying. James Frinton sat and watched for a few minutes. He patted me on the shoulder. But quite soon, I guess, it would be time for him to go. I wouldn't be the only person he'd want to inform. "I know it's upsetting," he said. "This grief, though," James Frinton said, "this display of grief, I mean, you shouldn't bring it out in public. It's not commensurate, to coin a phrase. I've got to go now. I'm really sorry to be the one to tell you."'

'I liked Tracy,' Joaquin said simply. 'She was a good girl.'

There was one thing I never understood. Why did James Frinton come up to tell me the news? We hadn't spoken in years. Did he want to say goodbye to the person he could have become? I would never have expected him to come in person to break the news. I wouldn't even have expected that the duty ought to fall on him. For years afterwards I could never understand why he had done it. I think I know now, however. In my opinion, James Frinton had thought about his future. He could suddenly see a profile writer, a biographer even, wondering about our little group at school, and speaking to us, one after another. He wanted to leave me with a heart-warming anecdote to share. He wanted even me to be able to say to his biographer that the last time I had seen him was a demonstration of his humanity, his care, his thought for others. Those biographers were emerging now. Although they had not found their way to me, at last I got the point. Of course he couldn't tell that story himself. He wanted to perform an act of extraordinary goodness. His notion of extraordinary goodness was to waste an entire day travelling, and half an unnecessary hour with someone he despised.

We said goodbye the next morning. We were down in very good time for the bus. The weekend had not been the catastrophe we had at one point anticipated. The two big walks we had taken had been well worth it, apart from the extraordinary coincidence of finding a part of my youth in that silent corner of Germany. Pete Frinton took payment from my credit card. The dog Nala padded out of his private quarters and sniffed around me. Joaquin was pacing up and down outside, our rucksacks by the door. The bus back to Wernigerode was due in twenty minutes. It was with difficulty that I had resisted his suggestion that I phone the bus company to make quite sure of it.

'It was good to meet you,' I said. 'I hope business picks up, anyway.'

'You were the one who never changed his mind, weren't you?' Pete Frinton said, smiling. 'Coming from an old Trotskyite, that really means a lot. You don't mind being called an old Trotskyite? I thought the small-business owners like me were going to be the first up against the wall when the revolution came.'

'I don't know that we really think in those terms any more,' I said. 'But anyway. I hope you keep going. You've got a nice life here.'

'*Wo die Füchse und die Hasen sich gute Nacht sagen*,' Pete Frinton said. I knew the expression: *where the foxes and hares say good night to each other*. It is German for *the back of beyond*.

It suited the village of Sorge as well as anywhere else. 'Actually, we're thinking of packing it in. It's quite a lot of effort, to tell you the truth. Sybille's got her eye on a big house that's come up for sale in the middle of the forest, miles from anyone. She likes not being bothered.'

'I'm not an expert,' I said, 'but it might be even harder to make a living from somewhere any more remote than this. What did you have in mind?'

'I'm going to live on Sybille,' Pete Frinton said. 'Like an idle kept man. I might take to shooting and fishing. She wrote this – didn't I say?' He picked up the paperback novel that lay on the reception desk. The cover image was familiar, not just from German railway bookshops but from our local book-shop. I hadn't read it. I could only vaguely say that it was about two rich American teenagers, one of whom dies of cancer. 'It's going to be a movie, too, apparently. I'm never going to laugh at another word Sybille writes. She's just finish-ing the next one. She says it's about a country girl who falls in love with a much older Englishman. Fancy that. I'm not allowed to read it yet, though.'

'Crikey,' I said. 'I didn't make the connection.' I picked up the book. The author was announced as 'S. T. Grobel'. Now I looked at it, I could see that it aimed at a mysterious anonymity in this regard.

'She's not up yet,' Pete Frinton said. 'She liked having you here, too. Take it – there's boxes of copies out the back, in every language you can think of. You know, I was thinking about that photograph in the magazine of you and the others. They must have asked my brother if he could tell them who everyone was. I don't know who gave them the photograph.

Maybe that poet woman. He must have decided he didn't want to bring you into it. I'm sure he could remember your name. You mustn't be hurt.'

'I'm not hurt,' I said. 'It really isn't important.'

'What I mean is, I'm sure he was thinking of your best interest,' he said. 'The others are in the public eye, more or less, but my brother knows that most people – most private people – don't want to be bothered by journalists. I bet he thought that if he identified you, you'd always have investigative journalists phoning you up or turning up on the doorstep. Imagine what it's like to be known publicly as a good friend from childhood of the Home Secretary. Or the Prime Minister, I expect. Do you have your number in the phone directory? Your surname's quite unusual.'

It had never occurred to me not to have my phone number in the public directory.

'I'm sure that's it. It was a kindness, really. My brother thinks about other people more than you might imagine. He's quite a thoughtful person. That's your bus. You don't want to miss it, I'm sure.'

We said goodbye. I went outside. I'm sure Pete Frinton was right. There was some residual consideration there. The magazine would have asked the Home Secretary's office to ask him if he could identify the last person in the photograph of the teenagers clowning around. He would have said that he could not, untruthfully. That would spare me. But there was another reason there. The magazine article had said nothing about anything we had all done together. We were, apparently, to be regarded as a bunch of civic-minded kids who liked to hang around together. You might have thought we had met on a

Duke of Edinburgh Award Scheme, orienteering. He was quite safe in this belief, or almost so. I had long ago come to the firm conclusion that on the last night of Tracy Cartwright's life, he had taken her back to her room and, finding that the brisk walk was sobering her up, he had given her a final couple of glasses of gin to put her under once more. Then he had done what needed to be done. It wouldn't have been hard to find the letters. I wouldn't have been surprised if he'd bought the necessary bottle of gin himself. The letters he had written to Tracy, full of everything the Spartacists had got up to, were gone. Nobody afterwards knew they even existed.

Apart from me. In the photograph the magazine used, everyone else could be identified. Lord Milne QC, and the liberal poet, and the Blairite newspaper columnist – they would not be tempted to reveal that, when they were young, they had smashed windows, and painted 'ARM THE POO' on walls, and broken up the meetings of pacifists, and punched the wives of mayors in the face, even if it was in the course of explaining that they had the Rt Hon. James Frinton MP by their side at the time. I have done nothing much in life. My life has been devoted to a cause that has sometimes seemed impossibly remote and retreating from its realization. The political purity of my beliefs has been untainted by any deals with what may be achieved now, today, this minute. I would always leave a negotiation rather than accept something that inadequately contained my ideals. And so would Joaquin. And, as a result, we have lived lives of quiet satisfaction; lives of the utmost insignificance, you may think. It appeared to me that the Home Secretary had thought about this. He had realized that, in fact, his coming up to break the news in a blind panic would not be enough to demonstrate his extraordinary goodness. I had other things to tell. Apart from Mohammed, who had taken the photograph and was not in it, I was the only person there who had nothing to lose. I had been there at the time. I knew that James Frinton had written many letters to Tracy. I had seen some of them. I also knew that those letters were not to be found among her things after she died, and what romantic teenager does not keep letters? Of course, none of this is proof. I am a witness who had a partial glimpse of events, no more than that. Good lawyers could discredit me in a moment. And yet James Frinton had thought last year about whether it was a good idea to identify Spike, the friend of his youth, to journalists. When they had told him, perhaps, that Kate was unable to remember my name, he had said, untruthfully, that he could not remember it, either. I was the one who had said to him, in front of his mother, that he shouldn't come back late 'because you'll wake Eartha Kitt'. Of course he could remember my name. I had hurt him, when he was sixteen years old, as badly as anyone could be hurt. He had thought about it last year. He had come to the conclusion that I had no reason not to hurt him again. The magazine had been obliged to write *Unknown* under my face.

The lives we have lived have been devoted to the political principles we found when we were young. At sixteen, we were already wearing the comic hairstyles of people in late middle age. Our lives have been lived under the direction of those principles, or they have been lived in reaction to them. At the moment I am writing about, those processes of reaction and renunciation had taken many people into a debate about whether my country should leave the community of Europe or not. The principles that I and Joaquin had remained true to had left us in a place where this debate seemed of the utmost triviality. Either course could change nothing fundamental. We waited for the upheaval that would transform everything beyond the ordinary imagination. It had not come yet, but it would. Some of the friends of my youth would live to see it. Others would not. James Frinton would become Prime Minister, or he would not. Another man or woman would take his place, and sustain the crumbling structures of this society for a year or two longer. It hardly mattered.

'Do you think we did the right thing?' I said. We were sitting in the front seat of the empty bus to Wernigerode.

'Oh, yes,' Joaquin said. Then he understood that I was asking a bigger question from the emphases of my tone. 'Of course. You have done the right thing and I have done the right thing. There was never any alternative.'

'Do you think anyone else will understand that, ever?'

'Oh, no,' Joaquin said. He grinned. I think I can say he grinned – *boyishly*. 'There is never any reward of understanding. This is not the Oscars. There is no prize to be had. What are you talking about? We should pretend we were wrong? You know how this story ends. They are kidding themselves.'

'Pete Frinton and that girl. They're saying they're going to go and live on their own in a house in the forest, miles from anyone. He's going to buy a shotgun. Take to shooting things.'

'He's going to use that gun for bigger things than little birds in the forest. When things start to change.'

'I don't know that things are ever going to change,' I said. 'I mean in our lifetime. I've seen too many moments when things could have changed. And then they didn't.'

'We've done what we could have done.'

'And it wasn't enough. It hasn't been enough.'

'That I don't believe.'

We fell into silence. The dead had spoken once more. And the dead are worse than the aged, as I have been told. Once they begin to speak, they will not be silenced. The bus stopped every two minutes at a different town or village, or sometimes at a crumbling concrete bus shelter surrounded by woodland. No one got on. The bus driver paused, consulted his watch. He started to drive again. At one point he must have realized he had gained more than a few seconds. At a woodland halt he turned off the engine to wait. He opened the doors of the bus. There was a breeze. The forest was rustling like a sibilant crowd. It must have rained in the night. The smell of pine was everywhere. It was extraordinary to me that these woods had been there for decades, perhaps centuries, before either of us had been born. We had been driving through them for half an hour. Until two days ago, I had not had the slightest suspicion that they even existed. I still had no idea about anything that had ever happened in them. The world, it seems to me, is full of things we know nothing about. Mystery and obscurity are the most banal things in our existence. The narrow tarmacked road of our lives is a thin ribbon, laid out in front of us, that most people follow without question, the forests to either side catching only the edges of our vision.

I raised my head. I looked out of the open bus door, beyond the bus shelter. I looked into the layers of light and darkness, of tree and shadow. I looked into the forest as far as I could see. Deep within it, it appeared to me that something had changed. It was a steady movement in the deepest shade. It might have been an animal of some sort, or something inanimate falling, or the movements of a man cutting a tree. Something that had had its back to me had turned, as if preparing to howl in rage or despair. But from here it was no more than a movement in the forest dark, and perhaps I might have been mistaken altogether in what I thought I had seen.

Champel-Battersea, October 2018